Praise for bestselling author Lora Leigh's
Elite Ops series

"Has everything a good book should have: suspense, murder, betrayal, mystery, and lots of sensuality. So rarely do you come across a book that you can lose yourself in and *Midnight Sins* is definitely one of them. Lora Leigh is a talented author with the ability to create magnificent characters and captivating plots." —*Romance Junkies*

RENEGADE

"Leigh delivers . . . erotic passion. This is a hot one for the bookshelf!" —*Romantic Times BOOKreviews*

"Smoldering romance, suspense, and mystery. Add to that the cast of interesting characters—and their pasts—and you have the perfect recipe for one amazing novel."
—*Night Owl Romance* (4.5 stars)

"Will have you breathless . . . gets your blood running hot with the physical attraction." —*Romance Reviews Today*

BLACK JACK

"Overflowing with escalating danger, while pent-up sexual cravings practically burst into flames." —*Sensual Reads*

DEADLY SINS

LORA LEIGH

St. Martin's Paperbacks

This is a work of fiction. All of the characters, organizations, and events portrayed in this novel are either products of the author's imagination or are used fictitiously.

DEADLY SINS

Copyright © 2012 by Lora Leigh.

All rights reserved.

For information address St. Martin's Press, 175 Fifth Avenue, New York, NY 10010.

ISBN: 978-0-312-38909-3

Printed in the United States of America

St. Martin's Paperbacks edition / March 2012

St. Martin's Paperbacks are published by St. Martin's Press, 175 Fifth Avenue, New York, NY 10010.

10 9 8 7 6 5 4 3 2 1

PROLOGUE

For Immediate Consideration.
Corbin County, Colorado.
One Million in US Funds.
All expenses reimbursed.
Three Marks, plus Collateral at one hundred thousand per hit.
Deposit one third. One third at first hit.
Remainder upon Completion.
Immediate Reply Requested.

Ryan Calvert stared at the message for a long time, lips tight, jaw clenched in fury.

Son of a bitch.

He had to admit he had expected this sooner. Hell, years sooner.

His cover as an assassin worked perfectly.

He'd put out feelers twelve years before that he

wanted any jobs going through Corbin County. He hadn't expected them to take this long though.

What had tipped the scales?

Was it the Callahans' return, or was it, as he suspected, one of the Callahans' imminent marriage?

Nuptials would open a whole can of worms that he was sure someone in Corbin County didn't want opened. After all, if one of the three Callahan cousins married, then that could mean possible heirs, and he was certain the barons wouldn't allow that to happen.

That is, *if* it was the barons behind this.

He'd been investigating the situation since he'd first learned of his birth parents' deaths and the situation behind his adoption.

He had arrived in Corbin County twelve years before, to find three young men—all orphans—who had been newly accepted into the Marines . . . and recently framed for the murders of twelve young women with whom they had been associated. They had barely gotten off.

"Is this what you've been waiting for, boss?" His second-in-command leaned back in his chair and stared at the message on the screen thoughtfully.

Ryan nodded, murmuring, "That's it."

The plans were already in place. Each year he'd had to refine them, tweak them a bit, but everything was good to go.

"Head back to the office," he told the other man. "I'll contact Stokesberry and send him the intel file we've put together."

"You know Skye O'Brien is there, right?"

Ryan leveled his gaze on the other man. "Douglas O'Brien's girl? The one Ferguson took in after her parents' death?"

"Yep. She rented a place about four months ago. The one right beside Logan Callahan."

Ryan breathed out heavily. He knew why she was there. She was investigating the person or persons who had targeted the Callahan cousins. Her foster sister had done the same and had ended up dead and the same fate might be in store for Skye O'Brien.

It has to end here, Ryan thought. *Now.*

The Callahans had stayed away as long as they could, they had done their best to sever their ties to Corbin County, probably telling themselves that their inheritances meant nothing to them.

In the end, it had mattered though. Their roots, and the inheritances their parents had lost their lives preserving.

"So much blood shed," Ryan said. "If the barons were behind this, we would have found evidence linking it to them by now."

"They're puppets," John said, shaking his head. "The ears we have in their homes are certain of it. Whoever's behind it is in Corbin County, and they're controlling those three."

Ryan sat up straighter in his chair, tapped his fingers on the surface of the dark walnut desk, and pursed his lips thoughtfully.

"Make a list," he ordered. "Give me suspects. I'll contact the Bureau and tell them we're a go. And make damned sure if O'Brien's boss finds out she's there,

that she's not moved. It's time to shut this down and
we're going to need her."

"Got it." John nodded quickly, moving to the bank
of computers and pulling up the required information.
"The team is in place and ready. You've planned well,
boss. We'll find whoever is behind this now."

All they had needed was the right time, and the right
offer and here it was. He'd make sure that everyone involved burned because he had a debt to repay.

It was time to rain hell down on Corbin County, and
he was just the man to do it.

With a little help when the time came.

CHAPTER ONE

He was just as handsome now as he had been in his picture twelve years before. Just as hard, just as tough, and giving just the same impression of a man a woman could depend upon.

A man a woman could find pleasure with.

For Skye O'Brien, the past six months had been an adventure in getting to know the man her foster sister Amy Jefferson had thought so highly of.

The man who had been the cause of Amy's death.

Logan Callahan hadn't wielded the knife that had slashed her throat. He had simply danced with a friend, maybe flirted a little.

The Sweetrock Slasher had taken care of the rest when he had raped, tortured, and murdered the laughing, caring young woman Skye had called "sister."

But she could clearly understand now why Amy had risked so much for him and why, as a newly inducted FBI agent, she had begun investigating the deaths that had occurred around him twelve years ago. She had died before she could ever report what she had learned.

Logan wasn't handsome in a pretty sense. He had that rough, tough, cowboy way about him that drove women crazy and no doubt had his ego stroked on a daily basis.

Broad shoulders, long, powerful legs. Big feet. Which made her wonder if what they said about big feet was true. And there wasn't an ounce of spare flesh on that hard, corded body either.

Men, her mother had always laughed, *were like fine, fine wine. They only got better with age.*

In Logan Callahan's case, it was true enough. At thirty-three, the small crow's feet at the corners of his sexy, velvet green eyes added to his appeal. The few fine lines at his forehead and at the corners of his lips spoke of a man who hadn't had an easy life, though she knew he'd made the most of the life he'd been given.

The gleam in those unusual eyes as he watched the women who stopped to chat, to smile, to entice, assured each and every one of them if he was of a mind to take them to his bed, then it would be an experience they would never forget.

They might not survive long afterwards, but while they were breathing, they would never forget it.

No doubt that knowledge was the reason he rebuffed each overture and flirtatious suggestion he dance with them.

After all, what man wanted to suffer the knowledge that his lovers would die simply because they were *his* lovers?

Instead, Logan went out of town for his amusements and he made a point to never choose a lover, resident or not, from the beauties that attended the weekend Socials hosted by Corbin County every year, much to their disappointment.

"Now, Mr. Callahan, you just know I can teach you how to move in perfect rhythm," Skye said as she moved behind him, mocking the last hussy's advances as she matched his sway. "Darlin', you just have to let me."

His lips almost quirked into a grin as he stared down at her ruefully. "I've seen you dancing in your living room," he drawled. "Sweetheart, you're so tune deaf you can't even stay in rhythm with that damn eighties music you like so well. I rather doubt you can teach me anything."

He could teach her though. In some very interesting ways.

"Oh my, be still my heart." She poured all her non-existent Southern charm into the mocking response as her fingers fluttered against the flesh above her breasts left bare by the tank top she wore. "I think I may expire of pure excitement. Dare you even deign to speak to me?" She batted her eyelashes at him as she gazed up at him from the corner of her eyes.

It wasn't far from the truth. There weren't many people Logan Callahan bothered to give more than monosyllabic response to.

He snorted at her mockery. "Sweetheart, I love a good comedy, and watching you dance has become the highlight of my evenings."

She narrowed her eyes at him. "Peeping Tom."

"Exhibitionist," he countered. "You knew I was watching."

"Of course I did." The lie came easily. "I thought you needed a little amusement. Don't expect a repeat performance."

She had had *no* idea he watched her. She could barely keep her cheeks from flushing in embarrassment.

"Now, you're breaking my heart," he said, pretending to bemoan the loss. "Tell me you wouldn't be so cruel."

Setting her beer to the table beside her and tucking her hands in the back pockets of her jeans, Skye had to laugh at the retort. Her gaze swept out over the courtyard of the small town square called City Park.

The central courtyard was a lush summer haven of rich blooms, flowering trees, and small grottos. The gazebo held the band; around it, concrete stamped in the form of bricks served as a dance floor.

She loved it.

"I still can't believe they have a crowd like this every weekend," she commented as she watched dancers sway to the sensual beat.

"Next year will make sixty years of the Weekend Socials," Logan agreed. "I've been coming to them most of my life, along with my cousins."

His youngest cousin, Rafer Callahan, was dancing with his fiancée, Cami Flannigan. Holding her close, her head against his chest, they swayed to the music with a sensuality that was enviable.

Damn, they needed to find a bed, not a dance floor.

"So why aren't you out there dancing?" he asked her.

"Not drunk enough yet," Skye grumbled, knowing he was laughing at her.

Logan grinned. "I've been watching you come here since the first Social of the season, Miss O'Brien. You never dance and you never get drunk."

"I know better than to humiliate myself in public." He made her want to laugh.

How long had it been since she had *wanted* to laugh?

Was it her imagination or did he drift just a little bit closer? Could she really feel his body heat just a little bit more?

"Don't know how to follow a lead either?" he asked.

"Whose lead?" she quipped, holding back a smile as she glanced over at him again. "Come on, Callahan, I think the only one out there that hasn't yet stepped on his partner's toes is your cousin. I like my toes unsquished if you don't mind too much. Besides," she drawled. "I hear the only nice Callahan is the one that's taken."

She gave him a wink and blew him a quick kiss before picking up the beer she had set beside her and moving off.

Logan watched silently from the corner of his eye as his friendly little neighbor stopped here and there, flirted a little, rejected every offer to dance, then slowly headed to the square's more public entrance.

He frowned. She was leaving and this was not the time for a woman to walk home alone.

The party didn't start breaking up before midnight. There were still the drawings for the homemade pies and gift baskets contributed by local bakers and businesses.

She would be on her own, and he knew, perhaps better than anyone, that there were monsters in the dark.

Setting his beer to the table beside him, Logan walked over to his cousin, Crowe, and clasped him on the shoulder. "I'm heading home."

"Go, man," Crowe murmured quietly. "I think I'm going to hang around and watch a while longer. See if I won that pie I bought chances on."

Logan stared back at his cousin askance. "Which pie?"

"That apple cobbler, a' course." Crowe grinned, though the curve of his lips belied the ice in his eyes. "You know I like me some cobbler, cuz."

It wasn't pie his cousin was fond of, but perhaps he was a little too fond of the baker of that pie.

"Good luck on that one," Logan snorted. "How much did you spend last week trying to win that cobbler?"

"Between the three of us?" Crowe growled. "Probably close to three hundred bucks."

"And this weekend?" Logan asked.

Crowe grinned to that one and leaned closer. "I had Jeannie Thompson, the sheriff, and that new deputy, John Caine, buy my tickets. I'll get it this time."

He was pissing in the wind and leaning on luck. Because only a blind man reading braille would actually call out the correct numbers drawn. That one was rigged from the start.

But hell, it was Crowe's money and his right to spend it wherever he wanted to spend it.

Moving off, Logan followed his own temptation, knowing he was making a mistake, but being too dumb to stop himself.

Was it safe? It was a question that raged through his mind day and night. Supposedly, the copycat Sweet-rock Slasher who had struck out several months ago against his cousin Rafer was dead.

His name had been Lowry Berry. He had tried to kill Rafer's fiancée, Cami, and had nearly succeeded, too. He'd killed one of Rafer's ex-lovers and thought he would take Cami out as well. Instead, he had ended up dead himself.

But was it really over? Lowry's final words had been a warning that he hadn't been working alone. Had he been telling the truth, or trying to ensure, as the sheriff believed he was, that the Callahans never had any peace? No evidence of a partner had ever been found.

Moving quickly along the sidewalk and crossing to the next, he came up on Skye as she walked along the well-lit streets.

Damn, she had an ass.

He had to grit his teeth, had to restrain the urge to reach down and shift his erection just a little to the side.

That cute little rounded butt made a man's hands itch to cup it, to clench his fingers in the rounded curves and drag her closer to him.

Or to have her legs wrapped around his hips, his hands filled with those lush curves as he buried—

Hell no. He wasn't going there.

But he could still watch her ass shift and sway, and

he would have kept his eyes there if he hadn't noticed her lower back suddenly tense.

She might appear as though she was walking unhurriedly to the casual observer, but Logan could now see the slight tension in her shoulders.

"You're not supposed to walk home alone, Miss O'Brien. The square has a good two dozen posted warnings about leaving the square on your own," he said when he was close enough that she would hear him easily.

Pausing, she turned back to him, her dark eyes suspicious as she waited for him to catch up to her.

"Now, Callahan, I'm sure axe murderers have better things to do tonight than pick on me," she quipped.

Any amusement he might have felt instantly evaporated. "And you should have better sense than that." Monsters existed and she should know it.

Monsters sometimes carried knives and drugs. They incapacitated their victims, raped them mercilessly, then tortured them by slicing a little here, a little there, before finally cutting an innocent woman's throat.

Long dark hair dipped across her face as she inclined her head, suddenly somber. "You're right; I didn't mean to sound so flippant. And I would appreciate some company." She rubbed her arms briskly. "The back of my neck was starting to itch the minute I crossed the street on the other side of the square. I was about to turn around and come back for one of those carriage rides home when you spoke up. The comment was more contempt for my own nervousness than an attempt to make light of it."

There was an edge to the night, he'd felt it himself

and couldn't seem to shake it. But hell, his neck had been itching for well over a week now. He let his gaze carefully sweep the area. "Did you see anyone?"

His hand settled at the small of her back as they began walking again.

"Not really." He felt her shoulders shift in a light shrug. "Your normal culprits. A raccoon in Mrs. Jakes's yard and Mr. Jakes peeping from his window."

"There's not much crime on Social weekends," he told her quietly. "Those not attending keep a careful eye out. The cameras installed on the corners help to ensure culprits are identified. If anything happens, it's usually in the more rural areas. And the courts are damned hard on anyone caught attempting to take advantage of the families attending. But those from outside of town don't always attend on a regular basis, so it's never easy to predict who's going to be where."

"The Socials are more a 'town' party then?" She looked up at him, seeing the dark, almost forbidding cast on his face as he watched the night.

"Pretty much." He nodded slowly. "Though 'most everyone is welcome."

'Most everyone. She knew from the investigation Amy had made into the Callahans' history a dozen years before that the Callahans hadn't exactly been welcome.

It had been during one of those Socials that Amy had died just outside town, her body left at the base of Crowe Mountain, the highest peak in the county and owned by Crowe Callahan himself.

Skye crossed her arms over her breasts. That chill was racing over her again.

"Here, you're cold."

Logan stopped, drew the long-sleeved over-shirt he wore off and helped her ease her arms into it.

Chivalry wasn't dead after all.

"Sure you don't need it?"

He snorted at her question. "I wear it just in case some little girl is too forgetful to wear her own."

She had to laugh at that. He was gruff and rarely talkative, surprising her with the fact that he was actually doing more than saying "yes" or "no" to her questions.

"What are you doing in this county, Skye?"

The serious, quiet question almost managed to throw her off guard. She'd expected it long before now to be honest. She was surprised he'd managed to hold off through the months she'd all but ruined the solitude he seemed to seek while he was home.

"It's as good a place to work as any," she told the partial truth. "And I needed someplace to hide for a while, I guess."

And she wasn't going to talk about it. She had her reasons for being here, and one of them really was to hide for a bit. She was on a forced leave of absence, paid thankfully, while she dealt with a few nightmares from her last case. A case that had touched too close to her sister's death and the unresolved injustice of it.

But tell Logan Callahan that and he would withdraw so fast it would make her head spin.

"Hiding from choices or a person?" he asked as she pulled the shirt more firmly around her.

"Choices, I guess." She glanced up at him again with

a slight smile. "Sometimes we don't make the right choices, do we?"

"So why come to Corbin County to hide?" There was still that edge of suspicion.

"I could go wherever I wanted. Besides I have a friend here from school. My last year of private school I was a mentor to a first-year student, Anna Corbin. She suggested I check Sweetrock out and I loved it."

He tensed, as she had expected him to. "Know Anna well, then?" The question was voiced carefully as though he were now doubting his choice to speak with her, let alone walk with her.

"As well as possible considering her granddaddy hates me." She gave a light, unconcerned laugh. "An orphan with no connections and few prospects isn't exactly the type of contacts the Corbins want for their children or grandchildren." He should know that well enough.

"Ah, yes, the life of privilege," he drawled. "The princess must have the right sort of friends."

"Or so her family believes." She gave another light laugh. She had to be careful here.

She didn't want to trip any alarms with this man. Logan Callahan had the ability to dig deep into a person's background, uncover all their secrets. If he managed to uncover even the slightest deception, he would completely distance himself. She couldn't afford that. Not if she wanted to learn the identity of a killer.

"You mentioned you're an orphan . . . ?" he finally asked as she felt him glance down at her.

"My parents are dead." She shrugged. "They were

killed when I was young." She didn't want to discuss it.
Not here and now.

His hand tightened at her back, slid to her hip and
drew her closer.

"Yeah, you're right, John Corbin would strenuously
protest your friendship with his granddaughter," he said,
mercifully changing the subject. They crossed another
street and stepped onto the street they both lived on.

"Corbin, his son, his daughter-in-law, his cowboys,
their wives, their children, their business associates."
She couldn't help but laugh.

"Sounds like the Corbins," he agreed. "Hell, it
sounds like the barons, period. Not one of those families has much worth where decency is concerned."

And he should know. He was the grandson of one of
those barons. His grandfather, Saul Rafferty, along with
John Corbin and Marshal Roberts, Rafer and Crowe's
grandfathers had disowned the three of them. They had
nearly destroyed them and it had only been in the past
year that they had won the twenty-year-old battle for the
inheritance that each of their mothers had left them.

"Yeah, well, I don't have to deal with them, thankfully. And Anna's different. At least, so far. She's still a
good kid."

But she worried, Skye admitted. Anna was still
young, still impressionable, and possibly so very easy
to turn into the puppet John Corbin wanted, under the
right circumstances. Or with the right betrayal.

"Looks like we're home."

She walked beside him as he led the way to the
thick, tall evergreens that all but created an impenetra-

ble curtain across the large side yard the two houses shared.

The bricks of the patios were less than thirty feet apart on the other end of the house where another heavy line of the thick evergreens grew. It created a hidden oasis between the houses. The one point that couldn't be spied upon unless the spy were in one of the rooms facing it.

"Thank you for walking me home." She slid his shirt from her arms, though she didn't comment on the friends.

She didn't want to appear the least bit curious about him or his family, let alone the friends of his parents. The curiosity ate her alive sometimes, but she had to be careful or she could destroy six months of dedicated work to get close to this man, to get close enough to make herself a target. If the Sweetrock Slasher had a partner who was still at large, Skye intended to draw him out.

She had never believed that Lowry Berry had been working alone, and from what the new deputy, John Caine, had learned, she was right.

Logan took his shirt slowly, his expression still, his gaze considering as he watched her.

Skye pulled her keys from her pocket and unlocked her door. She hesitated for a moment, then gave him a quick smile and a wink.

"Sleep well, cutie," she drawled before turning to go inside.

"Skye, stop this game you're playing."

Before she could evade him, his fingers curled around her arm and he pulled her back to him.

Skye found herself suddenly flush against him, staring up at him in shock as the hard imprint of his erection pressed into her lower stomach.

Swallowing tightly, the feel of the heavy shaft beneath his jeans sent a spike of trepidation racing through her. She now had proof that he wasn't exactly small in that department.

"What game?" Oh God, who knew that finding the strength to sound innocent would be so hard?

Then he was pushing the fingers of his free hand into the back of her hair, clenching, sending sharp spikes of sensation racing across her scalp, he tugged until she was staring up at him, eyes wide.

"Logan, you're acting strange." The accusation was nearly laughable. He was almost, just almost, doing what she wanted him to do.

Kissing her.

His lips were just a breath from hers. The scent of him, the taste of him, so close.

But she was not making that first move.

He had to want her bad enough.

He had to be unable to resist her.

But he hadn't reached that point yet. But he was so close.

Then he released her—slowly. His fingers loosened in her hair reluctantly as if he had to force them to do so. Soon he was stepping away from her.

"You're playing with fire," he growled.

She had to resist the urge to smile. "I never play with fire, Logan. Getting burned sucks."

And that was no more than the truth. She had no desire to fall in love with him, but she wouldn't mind sharing a bed with him for a while. Besides the fact he was hotter than hell, and the fact that he drew her as no other man ever had, there was no way she could accomplish her goal if she didn't get into his bed.

She was setting herself up as bait. To do that, she needed to be Logan's lover.

CHAPTER TWO

He was making a mistake and he knew it.

Each time Logan made his way to the patio door and looked out toward the soft light glowing from Skye's living room window, he knew it was a mistake.

A week had gone by since the Social. She hadn't shown up at the town's weekly get-together, and Logan had returned early because he was sick of waiting on her.

What a hell of a mess.

He was thirty-three years old and he'd managed to never let a woman get past his guard.

Definitely in the past twelve years he'd made damned certain no woman pierced the shield he kept around his heart.

It was a requirement, keeping his heart solitary, yet, here he was, watching her. And that was just one of his problems.

His dick was spike hard, throbbing with a hunger

that was damned hard to deny, and he was standing there like a fucking teenager staring into his best girl's window.

Son of a bitch, he was coming to a pitiful end and he knew it.

He'd told her to stop playing games, and she'd done just that, if she had been playing one at all. He wasn't so sure anymore.

Had he become so suspicious over the years, so hard and certain that everyone had ulterior motives that he couldn't accept someone for who and what they were? Was it impossible for him to accept that a woman could just want him?

Swiping his fingers through his hair, Logan admitted it was damned hard to believe that anyone in Corbin County did not have an ulterior motive.

He'd spent a week on the computer and on the phone with damned near every contact he possessed in the information business. The background check he'd done on Skye O'Brien had come up as clean.

Well, with the exception of a few too many speeding tickets. And there was that time in college she'd gotten a little too drunk and had propositioned a cop outside a bar.

Normal, everyday, run-of-the-mill, girl-next-door adventures.

And he didn't want to believe it. Suspicion was a vicious, sharp-toothed demon that gnawed at his mind.

Suspicion turned to hunger as she came into view.

Long, dark waves spilled down her back, and she was

wearing another one of those damned, vintage night-gowns that made the animal hunger that already tore at his balls rise to a howl of pure lust.

The black filmy lace looked so damned soft, he ached to touch it. To touch her.

The material molded over her breasts, all the way down to her delicate waist before falling to the floor in a long sweep that trailed majestically behind her.

He wanted to strip it from her body. To peel it slow and easy from her shoulders to her hips and watch it pool at her feet.

Naw, once he got it to her hips, he wasn't watching anything but those incredible breasts.

Suddenly the soft strains of a sensual R&B instrumental began to fill the night rather than the raucous dance tunes she usually played.

She wasn't the best dancer he'd ever seen, but damned if he didn't love watching her move.

She had a natural sensuality to every step she made, to every twist of her hips and every pleasure-loving step she made.

Even now, as she peeked curiously in the direction of his patio, he could see the urge to move to the music eating at her. And he had to grin.

He'd deliberately left the lights out, so she would believe that he was gone. For the past week, she hadn't danced for him once.

She closed the curtains on the sliding doors and kept the lights down low, and he'd known, fucking known, she was dancing and denying him the chance to watch. But now she thought she was alone.

Scratching at the raspy short beard that covered his lower face, Logan tipped his head to the side and watched as she began to sway.

Slow and easy, her arms lifting above her head, her hips began to move in langorous, sensual circles. Fuck him. He'd never been so hard, so tormented with the need to fuck one woman in his life.

The pulsating, let's-fuck music drifted like a heated breeze through the night as her movements, maybe not in rhythm to the music exactly, but definitely in rhythm to the hunger raging through him, tormented him.

She was dancing for a lover.

Enticing. Sensual. Pleading for a touch.

Her hands lowered, one crossing over her stomach as the fingers of the other slid down her neck, her head tilting back. The hand crossed over her stomach, gripped her own hip before her fingers curled just enough to allow her nails to rake over her hips.

His abs tightened, flexed, as he felt the ghostly sensation of those nails raking over his own hip, rasping over his flesh and sending bolts of sensation to strike at the taut sac of his balls.

Hell, he could jack off to the sight of that and probably come hard enough to lose the strength in his legs. A sight like that begged for sex. Pleaded for a man's touch. Made him ache to bury his cock between her thighs and demand that her hips sway and roll with just that rhythm.

He was a second from striding across the distance that separated them when a new sound intruded on the night.

At first, Logan was certain he had to be hearing things. A soft, distressed little whine.

Stepping into the house on silent feet, he grabbed the weapon he kept on the shelf next to the patio doors before moving to the edge of the doors he'd slid open earlier.

There it was again.

"Ease up, little bastard." The hiss of the demand had his muscles tensing, denial surging hot and furious through his body.

Stepping from the house, careful to stay within the shadows, Logan waited.

He didn't have to wait long.

Saul Rafferty had aged in the months since Logan had last seen him. He had been with his wife, Tandy, at the time.

He'd stared at the old couple, and told himself he hadn't seen the sheen of tears in Tandy's eyes, or the desperation on her face.

Saul had been just as cold and hard-edged as always. He had led his wife past their only grandchild, continuing on their way as though Logan hadn't existed.

"Come here, you crying little shit." Despite the harsh words, Saul's tone lacked the gruff disgust Logan normally heard in it.

Saul sure as hell couldn't be doing what Logan thought he was doing.

But he was.

Logan waited silently as the old man made his way around the edge of the house.

In one arm he carried a whining little bundle, in the other, his hand gripped a small Igloo pet house.

"What the fuck are you doing, old man?" Logan shoved the gun in back of his jeans, propped his hands on his hips, and glared at his grandfather.

Saul didn't even appear surprised.

"I should have known you wouldn't have the decency to actually be gone." Anger filled his rasping tone. "Can't just be up-front can you, boy? Have to keep the damned lights out and pretend you're not even here."

The response didn't even make sense, but the bundle in his arms gave an excited little yip and all but jumped from Saul's grip.

"You're not fucking doing this to me again," Logan snarled as Saul set the pup in the grass. It bounded ecstatically over to him.

Chomping down on the strings of Logan's sneakers, it gave little baby growls, tugging and begging to play.

The Chinese pug was damned small and cute as fucking shit and he didn't want a damned thing to do with it.

He didn't want to remember the one other pup he'd had as a kid, or its death. He sure as hell didn't want the responsibility of keeping this one alive.

The lights on Skye's patio flared on, the music shutting down as she became aware of the presence of Logan and his grandfather outside.

"Logan?" she called out to him, the concern in her tone making his chest clench.

Only his two cousins had ever cared what the hell happened to him. What was he supposed to do with a sexy neighbor who now seemed to feel the same?

"Everything's fine, Miss O'Brien," he called out, refusing to glance over at her. "Mr. Rafferty is just taking himself and his damned dog and leaving."

"Keep your voice down," Saul suddenly snarled. "You're stupid, boy, do you know that? Ain't got an ounce of the sense your daddy had."

"Don't." Logan was in Saul's face faster than he would have thought possible, definitely before he could consider his actions. He was almost nose to nose with the old man, staring down at him as fury pounded in his blood. "Don't mention my father. Don't mention either of my parents. Don't say their names. You've pretended they didn't exist for over twenty years, and now, as far as I'm concerned, they don't exist for you."

"Sucks don't it, boy?" Saul responded, refusing to back down. "Knowing we share blood."

"We don't share a damned thing, Mr. Rafferty," Logan sneered.

Saul didn't even have the good grace to flinch. "Keep hating me, boy. It's the best thing for both of us."

"Then stay the hell off my property and keep your damned animals away from me."

"Your grandmother's dying, Logan."

Saul's comment, so out of character, so outside of the conversation, caused Logan to still, to stare back at him, confused.

"What the hell did you say?"

"She's dying." Saul's voice thickened as he lowered his gaze and stared the pup that suddenly sat next to Logan's foot, its wrinkled face filled with happiness as it panted up at him. "That one's from the last litter of her favorite little bitch. The runt. She wanted you to have her. She begged me to bring her to you."

Begged him?

She'd wanted him to have it for what reason? She hadn't cared if he lived or died for over twenty years and now all of a sudden, she gave a fuck?

He highly doubted it.

He should tell Saul that he didn't give a damn, Logan told himself, but he couldn't get the words past his lips. There had been a time, long ago and far away, when he had idolized this old man and his wife. He had spent hours playing with their puppies and had sat on his grandfather's knee as Saul read to him.

He'd convinced himself he only imagined those years. They couldn't have happened.

But they had.

"Take her back," he ordered. "You're not doing this to me again."

Again. He'd been ten when Saul and Tandy had given him his first pup. Three months after Saul's daughter—Logan's mother—and his son-in-law had died in a blazing crash on a mountain road, that pup had been poisoned.

It had died in Logan's arms, the vet refusing to answer his door, to help the boy who stood outside screaming for help. Begging the son of a bitch to save that dog.

"I didn't do it to you." Saul met his gaze. "I had no reason to try to kill you, Logan."

"You killed the dog."

Saul shook his gray head. "The pup ate your food at that damned Social, in the community center. Your

food. I wasn't there and I sure as hell didn't hire someone to kill a kid. If I wanted you dead, I wouldn't a'
killed an innocent animal just to get to you. It broke
your grandmother's heart—"

"Nothing about me ever broke either of your hearts."
It wasn't possible. They would have had to care first.

"Boy, you don't know shit." Contempt filled the
words, then Saul glanced to his side.

Skye was still standing in the doorway. She couldn't
hear what was being said, but she seemed to be keeping watch.

Her arms crossed over her breasts, a glare on her
face. She didn't look the least bit happy to see Saul Rafferty there.

"That girl's worried about you." Saul lifted his lip as
though to sneer before giving up the effort and shaking
head wearily. "Tandy wanted you to have her. I brought
her to you. It's that damned simple."

"Take it back. She didn't want me and now I don't
want either of you or your fucking dogs."

"No, all you want is your be-damned pride and your
certainty that you have all the answers," Saul bit out
furiously, his aged body seeming to tremble. "That's
why I say your daddy was a damned sight smarter, Logan. He knew better than to just listen to his own fucking pride."

"And whatever he listened to got him killed," Logan
snapped. "Didn't it, Saul?"

It was their suspicion. Logan, Rafe, Crowe. They
knew their parents' deaths hadn't been an accident.
Their fathers had grown up on that damned mountain,

had learned to drive on that road. They would have never headed across it during a blizzard.

Unless they'd had no other choice.

"You're a fool." Saul lost the anger in his tone. "A fool, boy, and you're too damned blind and filled with pride to see it."

"Oh, I see it." Hatred burned inside him and clashed with the memories of the boy he'd once been and had hung on to for so long. "I've seen it for a long time, Mr. Rafferty. Seen you for the monster you, Marshal Roberts, and John Corbin always have been. Tell me, did you kill my father's parents like you killed your own daughter?"

The old man flinched then. Agony filled his gaze, and though Logan wanted to deny it, wanted to convince himself that Saul Rafferty didn't have enough feelings to know grief, still, he couldn't deny it was there.

It twisted his lined face and tightened his lips and caused the other man to shake his head slowly.

"No," he finally whispered, his voice so rough Logan could barely understand the words. "No, Logan. I didn't kill them like I killed my own child."

Stunned, not by the non-admission so much as by the single tear that slipped from Saul's eye, Logan could only stand in shock and watch as, head down, shoulders weighed low, Saul turned and walked quickly out of the yard.

The sound of a vehicle starting up at the side of the street pierced the darkness long moments later and reminded Logan that the old bastard had forgotten something.

"Son of a bitch," he cursed as he stared down at the pup. It had curled against the side of his shoe and was now asleep.

"Logan?"

Turning his head he watched as Skye made her way across the short distance between their patios, her expression worried as she watched him.

"Want a dog?" Keeping his tone cool and unconcerned was suddenly the hardest thing he had ever done in his life.

"She looks like she knows where she wants to be." Bending to her knees, unconcerned of the grass beneath the delicacy of her gown, she ran the backs of her fingers gently down its tiny head.

She was rebuffed quickly.

A tiny growl and the pup moved from her, curling at Logan's heel before he bent, picked it up by the scruff, and deposited it in the little doghouse Saul had brought.

He stalked into the house then, slamming the door closed against the sad little whines it sent up at being barred from the house.

"Logan?"

She had to follow him, didn't she?

"Go home, Skye," he told her wearily. "This really isn't a good time."

"Is any time a good time for you?" Her tone wasn't confrontational, but neither was it kind and caring.

What the hell did he expect? He'd known months ago tact wasn't her strong suit.

"No. No time is."

He turned back to her as she shifted, moonlight

spilled through the glass doors, washing over the gown and robe, making them no more than a shadow around her body, outlining her in an aura of dark magic.

"Fine, I can leave." She shrugged. "Stay here and enjoy your own miserable company, Logan, since no one seems to be good enough to share it with you."

Before he could stop her, she turned and stalked away from him, leaving the house quickly, careful to keep from slamming the door on the wiggling little pup attempting to get in.

He waited.

He made himself wait.

He waited at least a nanosecond before he followed her, catching her at the big oak tree that sat between the two houses and pulling her quickly into his arms.

CHAPTER THREE

It was the kiss that destroyed him. That brought home the realization that ignoring the attraction simply wasn't going to work. He couldn't ignore her. Not when she tempted him with a siren's gaze and lips so lush he hungered to taste them.

Not when she drew him, challenged him, and with every look assured him that teasing him, touching him, was her ultimate goal.

Not when he held her like this and felt the perfect fit of her body.

He'd fought it for six months. Now, too damned late at night for common sense, the darkness wrapped around them and the sultry summer heat sizzled outside the doors and inside them at the same time.

He gave in to hunger and knew that moment when the loner inside him realized just how lonely he'd been.

Logan stared into her dark eyes, realized his fingers were wrapped, tangled in long, dark, silky tresses, and he couldn't let go. His cock tried to push past his jeans, her shorts, and straight into the heart of her feminine core. His entire body throbbed with the need to possess her until nothing else mattered, until no other hunger dared to intrude.

He hadn't even known he was going to kiss her. Hell, he didn't even remember what she was saying as she laughed up at him, chiding him the way she did over whatever she was chiding him over. He couldn't even remember what he'd done this time. All he remembered was that destructive thought that he knew the perfect way to shut her up.

By kissing her.

And now he had no idea how to stop.

He wanted to pull back.

He told himself he was going to pull back.

He told himself he wasn't going to let this go any further. She was his neighbor. She was off-limits. He didn't mess with any women within a hundred miles of Sweetrock because they ended up dead.

"What are you waiting on?" Her voice trembled along with her lips as sensually drowsy lashes brushed against her cheeks, then lifted as though weighted.

That siren's gaze, sensual and seductive, and filled with an innocent hunger that, frankly, amazed him.

Amazed him that she could feel such hunger for him. That any woman who knew his history, knew the deaths that followed him, could possibly want him.

His fingers tightened in her hair, slowly pulling her head back, tugging at the strands and her obviously sensitive scalp as a moan whispered past her lips.

Oh yeah, she liked that.

"I think I'm waiting for my common sense to return."

Sensual, sexual hunger tore at him, raced through his veins, tightened his gut, and left him all but shaking in the face of the knowledge that he couldn't let her go.

Surviving meant holding on to her just a little longer.

"Should we be showing common sense at this moment?" The question almost brought a smile to his lips.

He hadn't had reason to smile in a very long time.

Why wasn't he surprised that the smile was tempted with this woman? A woman he couldn't seem to take his hands off?

Hell, he'd never had a problem letting a woman go before. He'd never had a problem stepping back or walking away. Sex didn't control him; he controlled it.

Until this woman. Now he had a very bad feeling she might end up controlling him.

"I'm sure we should be." But his lips were still lowering to hers, settling against them, rubbing over the softest silk in the world as he parted them.

Sensation sliced through him again. The instant his lips touched hers a sizzle of heated electricity seemed to sweep through him, bringing his senses to heightened alert.

Damn. It was like sinking into pure sensation.

Her lips parted beneath his as his tongue swept over them, licking at the soft flesh, tasting the inner sweetness, and becoming drunk on the ambrosia.

Each cell of his flesh was drinking her in and becoming intoxicated with her.

He'd never felt this with a kiss in his life. He'd never

felt his entire body come alive in quite this way. And it was definitely coming alive. Every nerve ending was suddenly tingling with heat. His flesh was drinking in her touch at every point of contact.

Pressing her tighter against the trunk of the tree he'd braced her against, he suddenly wanted more than he'd ever believed he would want from a woman.

He wanted her against him. Naked. Just this willing. Just this hot, with nothing between them. No clothes. No gowns. No second thoughts. No regrets.

No knowledge of where it could end.

In her bed or in his.

He wanted her lush, naked body spread beneath him, her thighs parted for him, her cries filling his ears as he sank inside her.

His lips lifted from hers just enough to move to the side and place a delicate kiss at the corner of hers. "Skye, you're killing me here."

Her head turned, following him, brushing against his lips.

And all thought evaporated.

It could have been the first time he'd kissed a woman for all the finesse he could grasp. There was no finesse. There was no sense of time or place as he kissed her like a man dying for touch, for sensual pleasure.

And he couldn't understand how such pleasure could exist in such a simple touch as two lips melded together.

His tongue swept over hers, then tangled with it in an exotic dance. His hands slid down her back, gripped her hips, then slid to her thighs and lifted them.

Ah hell yes. He wasn't about to break the kiss again to groan in pure undiluted fervor.

He wouldnt do it.

He wouldn't remember the past, the present, or the nightmares he often walked the night to forget.

Tugged at the strands of hair he held, his entire body tightened at the throttled little moan that fell from her lips. He ground his hips against hers. He swore he could feel the heat and dampness of her sweet little pussy through their clothes.

Against his chest her breasts pressed like firm, hot weights, her nipples hard enough he could feel them through his shirt.

He wanted to do more than to feel them through cloth. He wanted his hands on them, his fingers playing with them. He wanted to take them into his mouth and taste the sweetness of them.

Pushing his hand beneath the hem of her shirt, he stroked up her stomach until he was cupping one of the full globes with desperate fingers as she arched against him.

He'd never believed pleasure like this could exist in just a kiss. Hell, not for a man. A woman maybe; they were softer, sweeter. They thrived on the romance and the soft words and gentle touches. A man was just fucking hungry.

And he was damned hungry, but he was also experiencing the pleasure. The pleasure of touching her, the pleasure of her touch.

But even in that hunger he felt something more. A something that had his self-preservation instincts scream-

ing out in alarm. A something he knew could very well
end up destroying them both.

Skye wasn't expecting the sensations that assailed
her.

She hadn't expected it when she had realized there
was a confrontation going on between him and someone else.

She'd had no idea it was his grandfather.

She'd had no idea it would end here.

Skye tightened her hold on the man leading her
through an abyss of sensation and didn't know whether
to cry out in fear or scream in pleasure.

She was crying in pleasure.

Shards of pure, unadulterated excitement sang through
her body as his hand cupped her breast, his thumb and
forefinger gripping her nipple and applying just the right
amount of pressure. As she gasped, arching to him, a
shudder raced through her body and seemed to explode
between her thighs. The detonation was an explosion of
hunger. Her senses were flooded with a need that didn't
make sense, as her sex grew impossibly wetter, preparing, begging for possession.

A startled moan of protest escaped her throat as his
lips suddenly pulled back for her. A tingling rush of
heated sensation attacked her scalp as he pulled her
head back and blazed a path of erotic pleasure down her
neck.

Highly sensitive, soaking in his touch and begging for
more, her skin heated, and another moan escaped her
throat as his teeth rasped against her flesh.

"Logan." She needed more. More of the pleasure and the heat that came from each touch, each stroke of his lips against her flesh, each exciting touch.

She felt like a virgin again, experiencing her first sexual touch. No, she couldn't say that. Because even then it hadn't been this exciting or this sexually dark.

She could feel him holding back, holding on to his control, and the knowledge of it sent a rush of bravado racing through her.

She didn't want his control.

She wanted him out of control. She wanted all that dark, intent hunger she could feel threatening to escape.

"You don't know what you're doing," he growled, his voice rasping, as dangerously sexual as the knowledge of the hunger he was holding back.

"Bet me." Oh, she knew what she was doing, and she knew now exactly what she wanted.

This was why she couldn't stay away from him. Why she had taken one look at him and all she could think about was his touch, his kiss.

Not just the reason she was here, or the sister she needed vengeance for. God no, she needed him for her as well.

A stinging little nip of his teeth against her neck was her reward for her challenge.

But if that was her reward, what was the slow lowering of the straps of her grown until they cleared her breasts?

Skye held her breath, waiting, watching, as his gaze dropped to her breasts, despite the fact that it had to be too dark for him to actually see much.

His thumb raked over a nipple again, drawing a quick, muted moan from her lips.

"How pretty." He cupped the mound, lifting it further. "I've been dying to taste those hard little nipples. Every time I've seen you I've watched your nipples harden, press against your clothing as though begging for my lips."

Oh yeah, that was exactly what they were doing.

She could beg him verbally if that was what he wanted.

She would probably end up doing it anyway.

His head lowered.

The warmth of his breath was the first warning of what was to come. When his tongue raked over the excited little tip, though, nothing could have prepared her for the sharp burst of radiant heat that exploded against it.

His tongue licked, rubbed against her nipple as though to soothe it, but it only grew tighter, harder.

Needier.

"You taste like candy, Skye." His voice was a dark rasp of hunger. "I have a helluva sweet tooth."

The almost-playful quality in the sexually roughened male tone had a flood of weakness racing through her. A lassitude edged with hunger and need.

His hard, corded body tightened beneath her touch as her hand slid from his shoulders to his neck, then buried itself in the overly long strands of dark blond hair.

The thick strands were just slightly coarse against her fingers, caressing her palms as she filled her hands with them and tried to bring him closer. She just wanted to bring him closer. To make him assuage the need his playful tongue was building as he bent his head to the hard peak of first one nipple, then the other.

His tongue was a velvet rasp of exquisite pleasure as it rubbed over the sensitive tip. His tongue hardening to probe at the bundle of nerve endings as she arched to get closer, to feel more.

It wasn't enough. *Oh God. Just a little more pressure. Just a little more sensation.*

His teeth suddenly gripped the taut point, tugging at it, sending a furious rush of nearing rapture to tighten through her womb, to clench at her clitoris and spill a rush of dampness between her thighs.

It was like being thrown into a wild vortex of increasing sensual eroticism. A pleasure she had no idea how to counter and absolutely no desire to fight.

"Yes." She couldn't hold back the little moan as he sucked the tip into his mouth, the suction of his mouth sending pulse after pulse of heat surging from her nipple to the tight, furiously throbbing bud of her clit.

Each draw of his mouth pulled at the tip with demanding pressure, increasing each sensation until she felt a swirl of overriding, overwhelming ecstasy building in her womb.

She wanted him. Every touch. Every fierce stroke she could get.

Rolling her hips and stroking the hardened bud of her clitoris against his jeans-covered thigh only increased the pleasure. It hurled her down a brilliant white-hot path to the complete sensual destruction that was only a touch away.

Just the right touch.

Just the right pressure and the climactic explosion would destroy any peace she thought she had in her life.

It was the most pleasure she had known in her life. But she knew there was more. She could sense it; she could almost feel it.

"I'm going to end up taking you here against this tree if we don't stop this." His voice was ragged, a gravelly sound of hunger that clenched her womb and amped the power of each sensation charging through her.

"Okay." Yeah, like she was going to object.

A serrated chuckle inflamed her already overly aroused senses.

"It might not be a good idea." His lips stroked over the curve of her breast as she arched again, trying to get closer, to push her nipple back into his mouth.

"Stop thinking," she demanded. "I don't want to think."

But they had to think.

Logan laid his head against the curve of her breast as he fought to draw in a breath that wasn't filled with her scent.

This close to her, it was impossible. There was no way to breathe without pulling in the sweet scent of her, or tasting the silk of her flesh.

And he had to think. He had to protect her, protect this. This pleasure he had never imagined could actually exist for him. In his wildest imaginings he had never believed there was a woman he would actually want more than he wanted his own sanity.

Or that there was a woman he would place above his own or his family's protection.

Before he could allow himself to be drawn further into the heat and the wild promise she represented, Logan forced himself back.

"What are you doing?" Disappointment filled her voice as he set her on her feet, filled her gaze as her lashes lifted so she could stare up at him.

"If we keep this up, I won't stop with a few kisses beneath this tree," he warned her as he stared down at her intently, fighting himself more than he was anything else.

"I said okay," she reminded him fiercely.

"And I don't want a lover, Skye." He forced the words past his lips, forced himself to stare into her eyes as he said what had to be said. "This won't begin a relationship for us; you have to understand that."

She frowned up at him then. "I'm not asking for a wedding ring, Logan," she said impatiently.

"Are you asking for just one night of hot, nasty sex?" he asked her then. "Because that's all I have to offer. One night and then never again. No matter how much both of us might want more. Because when morning comes, that's it. No more."

She stared back at him in disbelief. "You limit the amount of time you spend with a lover?"

"One night," he repeated, hating himself, hating the hunger eating at him, assuring him he was a class A bastard.

"One night, huh?" She stepped away from the tree, facing him.

They were still enveloped by the darkness beneath the tree, sheltered from prying eyes and the possibility of an enemy learning more of his actions than was safe for either him or Skye.

He had to clench his hands to keep from jerking her back to him, to keep from throwing them both back into that whirlwind of pleasure and the race to ecstasy.

A siren's smile tipped her lips again and aroused every self-preservation instinct he possessed that wasn't already busy keeping his ass alive.

"And you think one night with me would be enough?"

His brow arched as he longed to join in the play, the teasing, sensual challenge.

"I'd make it enough."

Her laughter was as soft and sensual as the sultry summer night surrounding them.

"One night with me would never be enough, Logan," she promised him, surprised him. "Because whatever just exploded between us would rock both our worlds to the point that staying away from each other would be like sawing off a limb."

God, no woman should be so fucking intuitive.

He already knew that. Knew it, and feared it to the depths of his soul.

Adjusting the top of her gown to cover the full, firm globes of her breasts and smoothing her hands down her sides, she looked at him again from the corners of her eyes. "You started this, and you've opened a door I don't think you can close. But you keep lying to yourself if you want to. Because I don't think it's something you can deny yourself now. We both want it until we're ready to beg. But I'm willing to wait until you've gotten a clue and figured out how little you actually want a one-night stand."

He already knew. That was the problem.

Watching her step from beneath the branches of the tree, Logan slowly followed, careful to keep her slight, delicate body sheltered from any prying eyes that might be watching.

"Let me know when you've come to your senses." Turning back to him, her gaze met his, and Logan only barely controlled the flinch.

Now, in the sparse light that fell from the patio, he could see the living, breathing evidence of pure hunger.

It raged in her eyes, at odds with the calm tone of her voice and careful restraint in her body. "And if you wait too long, you may lose far more than you even imagine."

And he had a damned good imagination.

"Conceited, Skye?" he asked, forcing the mockery into his tone, because he knew it wasn't conceit. It was pure confidence based on the explosive power of the pleasure that had surged between them.

"Confident," she echoed his thoughts. "Because I know I've never felt pleasure like I just felt in your arms. And I know for a fact you haven't either."

His lips quirked knowingly, though that impression of knowing was the biggest lie of his life. "Sure of that, are you?"

A light laugh drifted through the night. "As sure as I've ever been of anything."

Turning on her heel, she moved quickly through the side yard from his patio to her own.

"And take care of that damned puppy," she called

from the door. "I don't want to have to listen to her cry like that every night. It's pitiful, Logan."

His gaze swung to the animal.

Barely more than a handful of fluff and bones, the tiny pup huddled at the patio door, a soft whine filling the night. And breaking Logan's heart.

Turning away from her tore a piece of his soul out, just as another piece had been ripped from him when he'd been forced to let her go.

The pup was too tiny, too delicate, to defend herself. The little scrap would be too friendly and too eager to please to ever realize the danger she could be in if hell came calling.

He would give her food and water. He'd have his cousin Crowe put a small shelter at the corner of the patio for her and Logan promised himself he would attempt to get the neighbors to take her.

He'd find her a home, because keeping her meant possibly watching her die.

Just as he had before.

Corbin County was his curse, Logan decided. Because it wasn't just a damned pup he was risking, he was risking the most vital, passionate woman he had ever met.

He never, ever took a lover from Corbin County, not even for one night. And he'd nearly broken that rule with Skye.

And he knew, knew to the soles of his feet, that the killer that stalked them twelve years before was still out there, waiting, watching, and still, he'd touched her. Still he'd let the hunger for her rage inside him.

A monster waited to strike, to torture and kill any woman Logan and his cousins gave so much as an appearance of caring for. He raped and maimed them, found pleasure in watching them die, and now Logan was risking the only woman who had ever made his heart race out of control.

The only woman who had touched him, and made him ready for just one more caress.

Because of that woman, Logan was standing in the darkness, staring around him, and wondering how he could have her and keep her safe from the monster determined to find and kill any woman he could care for. To keep her from attracting the attention of the demon that haunted them.

The demon he and his cousins were determined to find and destroy first.

CHAPTER FOUR

Like Sleeping Beauty she lay in the middle of her bed, her shoulder-length blond hair tangled around her head and fanned out over the pillow she slept on.

The pillow beside her was empty but for the wide red silk ribbon tied in a perfectly neat little bow.

Learning how to tie that bow hadn't been easy.

Just finding the girl hadn't been, he had to admit. He'd only glimpsed her that night he and his boss had followed Logan to Boulder and kept tabs on his movements. Watching, waiting for him to choose a lover.

She had been just a one-night stand, sadly. This one would only warn the Callahans that the game was on once again and, this time, there were no rules.

Convincing his boss of this hadn't been easy.

Unfortunately, he hadn't been able to convince his boss to allow him to handle this himself either.

The bastard liked the game, he decided. He liked experiencing his victims' fear. He liked the tension and

the arousal. He couldn't figure out why his boss refused to participate in the abduction though. He hadn't
yet figured out why he held himself so aloof.

Pulling a Ziploc bag from his light jacket pocket, he
pulled a drug-soaked cloth from it silently before bending and placing it over her mouth and nose.

Her eyes flared open.

He had to smile. She had pretty, pretty hazel eyes.
Now he saw what had drawn one of the three men
known for his love of exotic beauties.

It was her eyes that were a little odd, that drew attention and made her stand out in a crowd. Eyes that were
a mix of amber and brown. They were slightly tilted
and had a sexy cast.

Holding the cloth in place, forcing her to breathe in
the potent drug, he could feel arousal beginning to bur-
geon in his jeans.

Well, in Callahan's jeans. He wanted to chuckle, but
he was too busy watching, waiting, then giving a little
satisfied sigh as the little beauty went slack beneath his
hands.

Excellent. Not a single mistake had been made thus
far, just as he had promised.

He was well aware of his employer standing in the
shadows behind him, watching, his gaze shuttered and as
icy cold as always. He was frozen inside, his employee
decided as he pulled the blankets back from Marietta's
body and gazed down at her nakedness with anticipation.

His fingers went to the zipper of his jeans.

"Not yet." Harsh and unyielding, the sound of his

boss's voice had his jaw clenching in irritation. "Dress her. We have to stay on schedule."

He nodded rather than speaking, and hid the sneer and anger that burned inside him.

Taking the clothing he had laid out when they had first invaded her bedroom, he took his time dressing her. She had to look as she always did when she went out late. Marietta Tyme took care with her appearance.

She wore her jeans carefully pressed, her shirts in colors that would emphasize the odd swirl of gold and brown in her eyes. It was really a shame that she had to die just because she had been with a Callahan.

But it was the course he'd been hired to take, and he had to admit, he did enjoy inflicting the pain, hearing them cry and beg for mercy. He loved it. But this timid little mouse hadn't seemed his type. There was very little fight in her. And he'd have thought Logan would enjoy that spark of fire.

He couldn't rape her here, but Corbin County wasn't too far away. He could have her soon.

No mistakes, he reminded himself as he bent and pushed her sneakers onto her feet before carefully tying them.

The neighbor across the street stayed awake until dawn watching the late-night skin flicks to be found. The neighbor next to her had a surveillance camera that would only glimpse what he and his boss had planned for it to glimpse.

"Sleeping Beauty," he whispered again. "Sleep just a little longer for us."

He ran his palm up her leg to her thigh, then the warmth of her inner folds, shielded by her jeans.

He had made no mistakes, and he wouldn't make any.

Replacing the drugged cloth in the Baggie, then sliding it back into his pocket, he lifted her to her feet and roused her enough to convince her to attempt a shuffling walk as he kept her tucked to his side.

Moving her to the front door, he glanced back before opening it, checking that the other man had already disappeared as planned.

The boss was gone, out the back door that had been unlocked just as he had known from an earlier visit that it would be.

He'd planned everything to the last detail.

Moving from the house to the large black 250 King Ranch crew cab pickup parked on the street in front of her home, he congratulated himself on a job very well done.

Unlike Thomas Jones twelve years before and Lowry Berry last month, he wouldn't screw up.

He wouldn't allow anyone to interfere in what he had been promised once the Callahan cousins were imprisoned or out of Corbin County.

He would have preferred dead, but his boss wasn't willing to go that route. Yet.

He knew people, he thought as he helped Marietta from the porch to the sidewalk, then down the flight of cement steps to the passenger side of the truck. He knew people well, and he knew the thought of killing his enemies was constantly in his boss' mind.

He hoped his boss let him help.

He wanted to help.

He would make certain it hurt them really bad.

Until then, he had Marietta. And before long, he would have another; he knew he would. He had the three picked out. The lovers Logan had taken, the whores who had been willing to settle for a one-night stand rather than holding out for a commitment.

Strapping the nearly unconscious woman into the passenger seat, he touched her cheek gently before closing the door and loping around the vehicle to the driver's seat.

Ah yes, he was being watched.

Clete Olen was standing in his window across the street, obviously watching closely.

He ignored him.

Witnesses. There were several neighbors watching from their shadowed porches. After all, it was a nice summer night and this was one of the safer neighborhoods.

Pulling into the street, he chuckled at the thought of it.

The Neighborhood Watch hadn't helped Marietta much. This was the last time they would see her, and they didn't even know it.

He wondered if Logan Callahan even had a clue that the lovers he had tried so hard over the past six months to slip out with weren't hidden after all.

He knew each one of them, where to find them, and exactly how to strike.

Now he just had to be patient.

Hours later

Her screams echoed through the dreamscape of a forested night, filled with agony and rage as they penetrated his senses. Logan could feel the terror as it tore through him, the knowledge of what he was hearing and whose screams it was.

It was a dream. The same dream. And he couldn't escape it.

The knowledge that he would never be able to save her was replayed through his soul, nearly breaking it now as it had then.

Because he couldn't save her.

No one could save her.

Jaymi.

His cousin's lover.

His friend.

Logan could feel his feet pounding across the uneven terrain as he, Rafer, and Crowe fought to reach her, though a part of him knew they would never get there in time. Fate had already delivered the deadly stroke of destruction and now all that was left of it was the memories and the nightmares.

Blood raced through his veins, pounded through his heart, and adrenaline poured into his system as rage began to eat at his senses.

The sound of her agony penetrated the darkness. He could hear Rafer curse ahead of him, the sound of his voice broken, enraged. Logan couldn't hear Crowe, but then he and Rafer never heard Crowe. Their cousin was as silent as the night itself, bearing down and promising death.

Twelve-year-old memories surged through Logan's sleeping mind, bathing the night in a bloody hue. Time seemed to be locked in slow motion as blood spilled from the deep, gashing wound the monster had sliced into Jaymi's side.

She wasn't crying, though. Instead, she was looking over Rafer's shoulder, whispering, "Tye's come for me, Rafe. He's here. Tye's here."

Her deceased husband.

In her pain and fear it was the man she had cherished above all others whom she had conjured up to take her from the reality she was suffering.

Rafer was screaming as he fought to hold the wound closed, to push her blood back inside her body, begging her to hold on.

Begging her not to leave him.

After all, who else would ever accept him as she had? Who else would look beyond the ravages of the cousins' past and see more than three cursed young men?

As Logan crashed through the night after Crowe and the serial killer who had made Jaymi his sixth victim, he could feel the sorrow, the grief, and the horrifying knowledge of what this night could bring creeping through him.

Each of the six women who had been killed through-out the summer had been tied to the cousins. Each of them had either slept with one of them or was sleeping with one of them at the time of her death.

Logan had lost two past lovers, Crowe had lost three, and now Rafer had lost the woman who had helped him find a measure of peace in the past year.

As Logan reached Crowe, crouched in the dirt next to a mountain trail, his cousin's hands and face stained with blood, he drew to a stop. Chest heaving for breath, failure thick in his senses, he watched the tears that welled in Crowe's eyes as he lifted them to him.

"Damn. Damn. He got away." Crowe's breaths heaved as harshly as Logan's now while his voice filled with pain. "Fuck him. Damn him, he got away."

Logan stared at his cousin's hands as he turned them up. They both stared at the blood before Crowe lifted his face to Logan, a tight, savage smile contorting his expression. "He's carrying my fucking knife buried in his gut," Crowe snarled. "He won't live much longer."

Jagged blade, sharp and deadly, Crowe's knife was meant to kill, and he had ensured that it had served its purpose.

They were too young for this, was a hazy thought. Yet here they were, and there was no escaping.

"Jaymi's dead." Logan helped him to his feet as Crowe staggered, his gaze bleak as he leaned heavily against Logan for precious minutes.

Grief tore at Crowe's voice as well. "Fuck. Logan, we're all screwed tonight."

They hadn't been fast enough. They hadn't saved Jaymi, and now they would be lucky if they could save themselves.

As they entered the clearing to see their youngest cousin, Rafer, rocking Jaymi in his arms, his tears falling into her hair, Logan knew that night could well end up being the last night of their freedom. If not of their lives.

Logan watched solemnly as Rafer leaned his head further against Jaymi's and continued to rock her.

Tall, broad, Rafer dwarfed the much smaller woman. She looked far too petite, too delicate, in his arms. And much too still.

Too still because the cousins had failed to protect her.

Rafer had sworn to his best friend, Jaymi's deceased husband, that if anything ever happened, then he would protect Jaymi with his own life. That he would watch out for her. That he would care for her.

Yet the cousins hadn't been able to save her from a madman.

Logan stared at Rafer's blood-soaked clothes and hands and turned his gaze to the flames of the fire that seemed to build. Laughter began to echo, and as Logan jumped to save Rafer from the knife that suddenly sank into his side he felt the cold bite of steel as it penetrated his own back.

Logan jerked awake with a suddenness he had become used to over the years.

As he lay there, though, his senses on high alert, a sound so out of place with the night as to cause him to stiffen penetrated the silence of the room.

Irritation strained his patience as he clenched his teeth against the need to curse. Son of a bitch, was sleep a frickin' sin in this damned county?

For the fourth night in a row he'd awakened to the

knowledge that something or someone was prowling the night outside his home.

Usually, it was the sound of the little squatter Saul Rafferty had dumped in his backyard. The one he still hadn't been able to find yet another home for.

Tonight there was more, though. Something larger, something quieter, no, some*one*, moving with deliberate stealthiness.

Logan was a cranky bastard when someone messed with his sleep. He could feel his fingers tingling, the need for the fight he could sense brewing around him beginning to irritate his knuckles, to make them ache for the hard, powerful force that only came with a good fistfight.

It was a mood that had followed him since the night he'd forced himself to send his delectable little neighbor back to her empty bed.

Hell, since he'd returned to his own empty bed, only to find the couch more bearable.

Hell, it was more bearable, but he heard every fucking sound outside. He was too well trained not to.

Each night he awoke to the knowledge, not so much a sound, that someone was sneaking outside his house, that they were moving around it as though probing at Logan's security.

Between his late-night awareness that someone was outside and the pup whining and scratching pitifully at the patio door, aware he was only feet away, Logan hadn't managed much at all in the way of sleep.

Day or night.

Tilting his head to catch the sound again, he found himself hearing only the pup's whines. Logan finally gave up all thoughts of lying there undisturbed to stare at the ceiling another night.

Hell, if that awareness of something invading his space hadn't awakened him then his nightmare would have.

That was no good.

He was damned if he wanted to relive that night again.

Instead, he listened to the sound of the puppy whining as she scratched against the door again. A second later, it wasn't so much a sound he heard. His senses were just so well-honed that the knowledge of the familiar sounds of the night to the side of his house weren't there. The owl wasn't whooing, crickets weren't calling. Something or someone was disturbing them.

There was a sense of danger, a sense of intrusion. The trespasser hadn't yet caused harm, but Logan could feel the intent that was there.

Fuck. The little scrap that refused to be owned by anyone else was too small, too delicate, for where she was currently camped, especially with the enemies the Callahans had. And now, with something or someone stalking the night, there would only be increased danger.

She was still far better off there, though. With the impression of being ignored, than with the certainty that there was something Logan Callahan cared about, it would only save the pup's life in the long run. His reputation for having no friends, no lovers, no ties, was so well known that so far no one had suffered for having being associated with him.

The sound of the pup's questioning little whimper had him staring at the ceiling in irritation.

Did people on this street forget the rumor that the Callahans were lazy, shiftless bastards? That they needed their damned sleep?

No doubt it had to be a neighbor looking to find a way to irritate him. To find a weakness. To add to the tension that everyone hoped would run him from his home and cause him to default on the trust.

Fuck. They could give him a break. His intruder could give a single night a break and the nightmares could surely evaporate for one night and allow him to enjoy the fantasies of the luscious little neighbor whose kiss still burned through his body.

Moving his hand silently from where it rested against his abdomen, he slid it to where he had tucked the handgun at his side earlier that night. Logan forced himself from the comfortable position he'd fought to find over the past hours, blowing out a silent breath as he did so.

He should shoot the trespasser just for irritating him. Or maybe just beat the shit out of him.

If he could catch him this time. So far, he'd just been shit out of luck. Whoever it was had been slick enough to run before Logan could get to him.

Holding the weapon securely, Logan sat up before sliding his feet, still shod in leather sneakers, to the smooth hardwood floor of the dining room.

His cousins Rafer and Crowe had laughed when Logan had begun sleeping on the old couch. He didn't explain why, and he wasn't about to. His eldest cousin, Crowe, was already concerned about the neighbor.

As though he knew Logan well enough to know exactly where his fantasies lay.

There were no fewer than four large bedrooms with attached bathrooms upstairs, all with large beds, Crowe had commented. When he had, his expression had stilled and a single memory seemed to haunt all three of them.

At one time, three Callahan couples had lived in this house, along with their children. Three boys, Crowe, Logan, and Rafer, and one infant daughter. The first daughter born to the Callahans since before they'd immigrated from Ireland.

They had come together for the sake of their children's safety. For their own safety as they planned to set in motion their final vengeance against the three powerful men trying to destroy them.

There wasn't always safety in numbers, though, and the innocent didn't always persevere. The Callahan men and their wives had learned that one snowy, miserable night on a mountain road as they made their way back from Aspen. With them had been an infant daughter. Bright-eyed, dark-haired, and just beginning to smile. She too had been taken from life far too soon.

Placing his feet silently on the floor, Logan rose slowly from the couch. The memory of the infant's baby sounds drifted through his mind as he held the weapon at his thigh and moved through the dining room, keeping close to the shadows.

Pushing back those long-ago memories, Logan concentrated on the lack of sound that processed along the side of the house. He was listed as a medic with the special forces, inducted from the marines, but he'd been far more than that. Just as his cousins had been.

Logan had been expecting problems since he'd returned to the house nearly six months earlier.

Another sound drifted into the house. The sound of tiny growls, immature and fierce. The sound had a silent snarl of fury curling at Logan's lips.

The little squatter camped on Logan's patio outside the living area was already fiercely territorial, even for her small size. The pup was an innocent bystander in the war beginning to heat up between the Callahans and the patriarchs of the three ruling families of the county. The Barons, as they were called. Logan's, Crowe's, and Rafer's grandfathers had set out to destroy the sons of their only daughters the moment those daughters had died.

Logan could see that particular little ball of fluff being harmed just for the hell of it. He knew Saul Rafferty had brought it simply to torment him. He'd done it to give Logan something to care about so she could be taken in the cruelest way possible.

Just because she was small enough, innocent enough, and because enemies would assume it belonged to Logan.

If only someone could convince her to actually come to them or take a treat from them, then they could harm it. Thankfully, the little female pup refused to associate with anyone but Logan.

Hell, trying to get the little squatter to come out from the sheltering evergreens that bordered each side of the yard as well as the side of the house had proved difficult even for Logan's neighbor each time he caught her attempting it. Hopefully, the little invader would stay out of the way while Logan took care of the intruder slipping through the night. Because every time Logan walked out to the yard, the first thing the pup did was try to sleep on his sneaker.

The pup was silent now, hidden in the evergreen and mass of plants bordering the side of the house. The knowledge of that assured Logan that the intruder was coming much closer.

Fuck. Logan didn't need this. Not another death on his conscience. Not an innocent pup, an innocent woman or friend.

Please, God. How much more guilt was he supposed to carry?

A second later there was another fierce little growl and puppy yap.

As though someone was trying to entice the tiny invader from her hiding spot in the bushes next to the door.

For what reason? To make her pay perhaps for the perceived sins of the home's owner?

He wasn't even going to consider it. He sure as hell wasn't going to allow it.

Hell no! If anyone was daring enough to even try to harm her, then Logan promised himself he was going to get the fight Logan been brewing since moving back into the house earlier in the year.

A tight, hard curve curled his lips. He hoped whoever was out there *was* brave, daring. Or just plain stupid enough to let Logan catch them, because he had years of pent-up fury that had brewed inside him.

Sneaking along the wall to the glass doors, silent, his senses open and alert. Logan watched the shadows outside the glass carefully.

Then, surprisingly, a shadow moved into view.

The moonless night didn't help to identify who crouched at the side of the house, or their intent.

Their position, movements, and the darkness that filled the inner yard aided the intruder, and they were reaching for the pup.

Before they could slide beneath the sheltering evergreen, Logan jerked the door open before gripping the back of their neck and jerking them inside.

Who was more surprised, herself or the intruder, he wasn't certain.

He couldn't have expected it, and he sure as hell couldn't explain the anger that rose inside him at the sight that met his eyes.

"What the hell are you doing?" he growled.

Shoving the weapon into the waistband of his jeans, he reached down, gripped the young woman trying to rise from the floor under her arms, and dragged her to her feet.

"Hey, bully!" Surprised and not the least bit happy, his trespassing little neighbor stumbled back before staring up at him with a glare on the pert features of her gamine little face. "What's your problem, Logan?"

Rising to her full height wasn't much of a stretch. At five feet, four inches, she wasn't exactly the tallest woman around.

That short, delicate little body had fit him to a T when he had braced her against the side of a tree and kissed her senseless, though. Not that he'd had many of his senses left himself that night.

Standing on her bare feet, hands propped angrily on her hips, she confronted him with an expression of outrage.

Dressed in another of those filmy, lacy gowns, she looked like pure temptation. It wasn't black; instead, it was the softest spring green he'd ever seen. The robe brushed the floor, shielding the filmy gown beneath that only just showed the shadowed hint of feminine flesh between her thighs, and pert nipples topping her breasts.

"Manhandling women went out in the Dark Ages, Callahan," she informed him tartly when he didn't respond.

He ignored her sidekick completely. It had expertly wiggled in just before he slammed the glass door closed.

Son of a bitch, this woman was more than just the reason for his hard-on. She was the star of every sexual fantasy that could spark in his too-sexual brain. The terrifying fact was, she was beginning to play in fantasies that, surprisingly enough, weren't all sexual.

He couldn't allow that.

"What's my problem?" he snapped as hunger, emotion, and a need clenched his guts as his resentment, his fury against the circumstances he could chance, flooded his system. "It's three in the morning and you nearly got your head blown off sneaking around to play on my patio like a nine-year-old. Why the fuck didn't you just cross the yard rather than sneaking around?"

His door was right across from hers. What the fuck was her problem?

Folding his arms across his chest as he glared down at her, watching as the dog sat on her haunches and stared up at Logan as well, panting happily now. The squashed-in dark little face was creased in bliss, as though just the sight of him pleased the little scrap. And he couldn't understand why.

He was the bastard trying to give the dog away, not a savior.

Skye snorted at his statement, her gaze as confrontational as her smart-assed mouth. "I'm a vampire. I prefer the night," she replied drolly. "There now, you have your explanation. Can I go back to visiting with the only sociable member of your little family or do I have to deal with you too?"

He wanted to wipe his hand over his face in an attempt to convince himself he was still asleep, but there was no way in his wildest fantasies that he could conjure up such a farcical dream.

Especially the part where he swore he could glimpse her nipples through the lace and soft-as-silk chiffon covering them.

"I didn't ask for infantile bullshit," he said slowly, clearly, desperate to ignore the warmth now penetrating his sneaker as the pup crossed between them and flopped over his sneaker to sleep. "I asked what you were doing on my back porch irritating the hell out of me. I thought we agreed you were going to stay away from me?"

Her eyes widened before her gaze slid down his body, though not in appreciation of it, but rather to glance at the now drowsy little bag of fur on his feet as though the answer to his question were self-evident.

Son of a bitch. He hadn't asked for this. He distinctly remembered not asking for these kinds of problems.

"The sociable part of your family," she stated again. "I was visiting. I was not bothering you."

"Then take it home," he ground out between clenched teeth as the puppy shifted for a better position on his foot. "It's not and never has been a part of my family."

A slender brow arched mockingly. "I think she's under the impression she's already home."

Logan didn't stop to think or to consider his actions. The feel of the warm little body draped over his sneaker, her little heart pounding against the leather, brought back memories he rarely allowed himself to revisit. Reaching down, he gripped the scruff of the puppy's neck as he opened the door and with the utmost gentleness deposited the puppy back onto the patio before closing the door in the scrap's disappointed little face.

"Take it home with you," he told Skye coldly. "It has no business here."

And neither did she.

And his heart was breaking.

The pup's cries threatened his determination and the look of disappointment and pity on Skye's face threatened his control.

CHAPTER FIVE

Logan had known, even as a child watching the hell his parents had gone through in their battle against his grandparents, that unless it ended, his wouldn't be a life that could be shared with a woman and a pup. And when you had the woman and the pup it wasn't long before the kids or, in his parents' case, the kid followed.

And it was that kid who was left to suffer when the parents were no longer there to protect him.

He almost shuddered in pure, gut-wrenching male horror because he could actually imagine the kids. A girl with Skye's dark hair and delicate features. Or a boy with his dark hair and her dark eyes.

"Do you have to be an ass all the time, Callahan?" Slender arms crossed over pert breasts he knew intimately as a frown creased her brow and the image of kids, thankfully, disappeared. "What's your deal anyway?"

"My deal, as you put it, is being disturbed in the middle of the night because of your dog fetish," he grumped as he forced himself to turn and stomped back to the kitchen.

He would have preferred a stiff shot of whisky, but his cousins had been bitching about the amount he'd been drinking lately. He'd promised to cut back, so he'd just cut it out instead.

"I don't have a dog fetish. What I have is a cold-hearted, selfish neighbor who refuses to take care of the animal parked on his patio," she informed him as she followed, bare feet and all. He was trying to ignore the fact that all she wore was a damned long shirt.

Making his way to the kitchen as she followed, Logan made the coffee in the dark. He didn't want to turn the lights on and risk seeing through the soft, soft material to silken flesh and dark, hard little nipples.

Definitely no panties.

His cock was like steel wedged beneath his jeans, and it would probably be prudent to ensure she wasn't aware of it. All it would take was the slightest spark to set fire to the arousal he could feel threatening to burn out of control between them.

"I'm going to assume you dislike puppies," she said as though it were a crime as he remained silent and measured grounds into the basket of the coffeemaker. "How can a man that kisses like a pirate dislike puppies?"

Bemusement filled her expression as the last part of her comment made his lips actually ache to kiss her again. "That should be illegal or something."

The fact that she was staring at him accusingly did nothing to deter the want-to surging through his senses.

He ignored her, just as he pretended to ignore the whine coming from the patio and the hunger raging between them.

"You're not answering me, Callahan," she reminded him with an edge of anger now.

"You didn't ask a question; you made a comment," he reminded her. "You said you were going to assume I didn't like puppies, and said I kissed like a pirate. Thanks by the way." He shot her a mocking smile, hoping it would piss her off enough to make her leave, because he couldn't seem to do it himself. "Why argue the assumption when all it's going to do is delay your departure before we both make a helluva mistake."

He ignored that fist-sized lump of regret that seemed to grow in his gut.

And in his balls.

"Wow, that just sliced to the bone," she said mockingly as he watched from the corner of his eye. "I don't think I've ever been called a mistake before."

It didn't seem to bother her overmuch.

She propped herself against the counter and his dick nearly pushed past his zipper.

Son of a bitch, that confection of lace and, according to his research, chiffon, a chiffon so soft, so silky, it almost vied with her flesh in softness.

"Evidently it didn't slice deep enough, because you're still here tempting me to make that fucking mistake."

Her lips tugged upward in a smile at his comment as she glanced at the counter. "You set out two coffee cups. My mother would be appalled if I were to be so rude as to leave now."

He dropped his gaze to the counter. There were indeed two coffee cups set out. Matching cups. He was unaware he owned matching coffee cups.

It hadn't been intentional.

"Why would you want me to share my coffee if that cut went so deep?" he asked even as he poured the coffee before picking up both cups and turning to her.

"Thanks, though it's no wonder you never sleep if you drink coffee this early in the morning," she pointed out knowingly as he handed her the drink. "And I rarely refuse coffee. If I did, I'd never get to drink it."

She was obviously ignoring his question.

"I sleep fine."

"You're terse enough, so I highly doubt it," she said with obvious patience.

Terse.

His cousin's fiancée, Cami, had a tendency to call him that on occasion as well.

Lifting the cup to his lips, he sipped at his coffee rather than making a comment. He contented himself with the fact that he was trying to glare at Skye.

Unfortunately, it wasn't fazing her. She was merely laughing at him as she sipped at the heated liquid herself.

And he still wasn't certain how he felt about that. He knew standing in his kitchen arguing was only going to push him faster into taking her straight to his bed. And only God knew when Logan would allow either of them to come up for air after that.

Maybe weeks.

He could bet on months.

The problem was, he was pretty certain that he would keep this woman around indefinitely.

Big mistake there.

"Good coffee." She shrugged as she lowered the cup, still watching him with gleaming emerald eyes. Tempting him. As though she knew his dick was fighting to take control and just waiting for the moment he would break.

Logan frowned. "Of course it's good coffee. How can it be bad coffee?"

"I make bad coffee. Horrible stuff." Her nose twitched as though in distaste.

She was lying to him. She had to be.

"You measure it into a filter, slide it in a pot, add water, and flip 'ON,'" he said. "How do you mess that up?"

"Easy." She shrugged as though it didn't matter.

"I would have thought editors of boring tech manuals would have to know how to make coffee," he pointed out.

Which might well be true, since she really wasn't an editor, but telling him that was a great big no-no at the moment.

"And I would have thought a man of your intelligence and determination would be doing more than lazing around his house, ignoring his puppy, and waiting on an inheritance rather than proving his innocence," she retorted sarcastically.

He only laughed at her.

"You think I have anything to prove to the bastards around here?" he questioned, though she was beginning to doubt the amusement in his gaze. "Come on,

Skye, you should know better by now if you've listened to any of the gossip at all."

She did listen to gossip, which was why she highly doubted it.

"Why do you do it, Logan?" She didn't mean for the question to come out with such somber intensity. "Why do you let this county try to rip you apart without striking back?"

For a moment, she wasn't certain he would answer her.

"Our mothers were the county's sweethearts," he said softly, surprising her. "Our fathers were the county black sheep, even before their parents' deaths. Wild as hell and completely unconcerned about tact. When they married the daughters of the barons, everyone said David, Samuel, and Benjamin would bring them to a bad end. Thirteen years later, they did just that, as far as everyone was concerned."

"That's not a good enough reason."

He laughed. "This place is like a fucking little fiefdom for the barons and their families, Skye. They are the reason for employment here. The reason why the county is sustained. And our mothers," his voice softened, "they clothed the poor, fed the hungry, played Santa's elves at Christmas, volunteered every weekend at the Socials to watch the children. They were everyone's sweethearts. Everyone's little sisters. And the fact that each of them was pregnant when they married our fathers only fueled the belief that they were somehow forced into marriage."

"Incredible," Skye murmured, shaking her head as

she watched him closely. She could feel the regret and sadness that filled him.

She risked the question. "And twelve years ago? What happened then?"

Knowing sarcasm filled his expression. "I wondered how long it would take you to ask about that."

She lifted her shoulders, her expression, she knew, was filled with the sympathy and regret she felt.

Logan sighed. "They were all wonderful, beautiful women. That's what I keep trying to tell you, Skye. We didn't kill them, but they definitely died because of us. Do you really want to join them by continuing to tempt me?"

Thankfully, the puppy saved her on that as it cried out as though in agony once again.

She started to say something anyway; then clamped her lips shut before she glanced toward the door leading to the living area, her expression turning accusing.

The pup was scratching at the glass. Whining. Again.

Logan pretended he was ignoring the dog even though she was slicing through his senses.

Again.

"You can't let her just sit out there alone," Skye finally said. "She cries every night, Logan. She's breaking my heart."

Logan sipped at the coffee again before replying. "I didn't tell the little squatter to take up residence, now did I? Or to howl like it was dying every time someone else took it home, until they brought it back? If it bothers you so much, then take it home with you."

The laughter was gone now. Just that fast, it erased quickly from her face and she was glaring at *him*.

Her eyes sparkled with nothing less than disapproval. Could have been more than disapproval, but tonight he was in an optimistic kind of mood. He was going to go for disapproval rather than the optional dislike.

"You really don't like dogs?" She blinked back at him and the dislike—no, *disapproval*—was completely overshadowed by shock.

"Never met anyone who disliked dogs before?" He sipped at his coffee again, preferring not to answer the question directly.

"I have never in my life met anyone who didn't like puppies. Kittens. Babies." She shook her head as though it were completely inconceivable.

"Babies?" He paused in the act of lifting his coffee cup to his lips again.

As though he needed the caffeine after *that* statement.

"A very broad term." She lifted her shoulders again, that graceful little shrug that lifted her breasts and rounded them just a little bit more. Just delightfully.

And made his hands itch to cup them, plump them, possess them.

"Ah, a broad term." He nodded sharply. "Whatever the term, if you want the puppy, take it home with you."

"My lease doesn't allow puppies." She glared back at him.

"Neither does mine," he snapped back, almost in triumph. Hell, he should have thought of that excuse before.

Maybe not. Her expression became entirely too skeptical. "You own your home, Callahan." There was just the cutest little snap to her voice.

He almost laughed at her. He would have, but that little mutt scratched at the door again, reminding Logan— He didn't need puppies, kittens, or babies. Things happened. Bad things happened, and they could get taken away. They could be taken away permanently.

"I know your landlord," he stated coolly. "I'll have a talk with him."

And he would. The little mutt was killing him, but he didn't dare allow himself to get attached to the dog. No more than he dared to allow himself to get attached to his neighbor.

For the briefest second, he glimpsed sympathy in her gaze before it turned curious. "Why do you have to be a grump all the time? I know for a fact that the man who warned me away from him last week isn't an asshole. Why do you have to pretend to be one?"

He finished his coffee.

"I *am* an asshole," he assured her. "It's just easier to warn prospective lovers that it's only one night. I like my privacy and I don't like ties."

Her eyes narrowed. Pretty, dark eyes that seemed to mesmerize him, ensnare him. And almost made him choke on the lie he just let spill from his lips.

Hell, maybe he was hitting his midlife crisis or something, because it was all he could do to keep his hands off her or his heart from wishing. Hoping.

He was too fucking old for this shit.

"You're lying," she said softly. "Do you think everyone I meet in town isn't real quick to warn me of the dangers of living next to you?"

Fuckers!

Logan sipped his coffee before replying. "You're not listening."

"I rarely do, "she agreed. "But it's been twelve years. Surely you can afford to have a life now.

"And just four weeks ago some nutcase decided to copycat the Sweetrock Slasher and nearly killed my cousin's lover." His tone was intentionally harsh. "And that was after he'd already killed another woman. No, Skye, I don't think it's safe yet to have a life. And it's sure as hell not safe to have a dog."

It probably never would be.

"She's an orphan, Callahan," Skye finally sighed softly. "Like you. Like me." She gave a small sad smile. "For some reason, she seems to want you, not me, and not anyone else. That's a gift you rarely get. Can't you just take her in for a few days?"

Logan set his cup back on the counter, careful not to allow himself to feel anger or to show any emotion where that unneeded information was concerned.

"I can take it to the shelter." He lifted his shoulders as though it didn't matter. "I'm sure it can find a family there."

The recrimination in Skye's gaze was, frankly, pissing him off. Because she had no idea how much he wished—

She breathed in slowly, as though forcing herself to maintain patience, before she set her coffee cup on the counter carefully.

"You don't need anyone, do you? Did you even check on your grandmother?"

"I don't have a grandmother." He kept his tone even, but the anger and the hunger for things he knew weren't his still burned inside him.

"I saw her at the pharmacy the other day," she said then, her tone too soft, too filled with sympathy. "She asked about you."

"And why would she do that?" It was almost a sneer, but he couldn't seem to get it just right.

Her shoulder lifted negligently. "I don't know, but she seemed very worried."

"Stop." It was time to put his foot down and get her the hell out of his life and out of his head. "If you've heard the gossip, then you know everything. Stop being so fucking nosy."

"And stop caring about you?" That couldn't be an edge of regret in the question. "The big, bad, tough Logan can't have anyone care about him, or care for anyone, can he?"

"They end up dead."

And he couldn't forget that.

"And you just sit back and accept it?"

"Hell, baby, it's millions in cash, bonds, and property." He laughed mockingly. "Wouldn't I be stupid to turn my back on that?"

He would in a heartbeat if he thought it would change a damned thing.

But it wouldn't. Just as leaving before hadn't changed anything.

"You're stupid if you think I believe a word of what

you just said," she said, her voice low now. "I listen to everything I'm told and I know how to put two and two together. Three big tough military heroes aren't going to take this lying down. You're here. You're investigating it, aren't you?"

Logan stared back at her narrowly. "I don't give a fuck, Ms. O'Brien. All I intend to do is live here until those bastards die in order to prove to them they aren't stealing a fucking thing from my parents or from me. After that, Corbin County can kiss my fucking ass."

Silence stretched between them. Disappointment finally filled her gaze and the sight of it tightened in his chest, far too close to his heart.

"Do whatever," she said coolly. "It's time I head home. I have better things to do than try to charm Scrooge tonight. Have a nice, lonely life, Callahan." She turned as though to leave.

He was damned if he wanted her to leave.

"Take the dog home with you," he finally snapped as anger got the best of him. "If I wanted it, I would have brought it in. And I don't have time for a trip to the shelter. Remember they put down unadopted dogs there. There's no way that mutt is going to get a home the way it howls and cries twenty-four seven."

And the puppy needed out of the mountain air. Pugs could sicken easily. They needed care. Just like women and babies did.

"If she wanted me, she would have come into my house the first two times I sweet-talked her across the yard instead of turning and hightailing it back to a door that stays locked against the poor little baby," she informed Logan with that hint of anger. "What is your deal where this puppy is concerned? You can't keep her and you don't want to take her to the shelter. What do you want to do? See her starve in your backyard?"

"I don't have a deal," he said between clenched teeth, trying to ignore that deeper spark raging at him to end this now. "And I feed it."

That spark that had his dick hard and his hands itching to touch Skye. It was the same spark he'd felt the first time he'd met her, strangely enough, in his own backyard just after moving into the house.

"You have something," she informed him as she slowly straightened. "But nothing that relies on you, depends on you, or could survive without you. Right?"

And she just had to point that out, didn't she?

"Deliberately," he assured her as he watched her expression, her expressive eyes, and what he saw there had his chest tightening in both anger and regret.

Because he saw pity there. Pity and sorrow.

And he didn't like it. He didn't like it at all.

"You think all that responsibility is something to sneer about then?" she asked him accusingly, anger sparking in her own eyes then. "That it doesn't matter, because there's nothing or no one you can survive without?"

That wasn't exactly true.

"I have my family," he stated.

He heard that rasp in his voice that assured him he was losing control of that tight rein he had on his emotions, on his angers. On the fucking hunger to have her.

She had no idea—

No idea the hell he and his cousins had suffered through over the years and the losses they'd had no choice but to survive. Losses that had forced them out of Corbin County, only to once again force them back.

"Your grandfather?" she asked archly. "Or just your cousins? The cousins who own everything you have ever worked for or deserved in your life? One of whom has his own fiancée now? The other who has just invested in his *own* business? Possibly two of them? Everyone in this county is gossiping about the fact that you signed over everything you own, everything, Logan, to two cousins who are evidently determined to at least try to have a life."

"And what the fuck is your point?" he snarled, feeling the loss of that precious, careful control now.

Damn her to hell, she had no idea how much it hurt to sign over everything he had ever dreamed of having in his life. To watch Crowe and Rafer fighting against the hell he could see was coming with every shred of lost dreams that still existed inside them to have a life.

He had no choice. Someone had to watch out for the other two. Someone had to be seen as the Callahan monster to, he hoped, make the monster haunting them back off.

"What do you have for yourself, Callahan?"

"One too-nosy neighbor who doesn't seem to know how to call me by my first name rather than my last and a too damned delicate pup that refuses to let me find it a home?" he questioned harshly as his arms dropped from his chest and he advanced on her, his head lowering as he glared down at her. "What business is it of yours, Ms. O'Brien?"

The anger and needs surging through him had him moving then. Had him making what he knew, even as he did it, was the biggest mistake of his life.

He touched her.

Before he could think or stop himself, he had his hands on her upper arms, pulling her to him, bringing her flush against his body as though he needed her.

"I have a hunger eating my guts out for a woman that I know has happily-ever-afters shining in her eyes." He held her like a desperate man. As though he needed her touch. "That won't happen with me, and you're determined to hurt both of us by pushing it."

As though he needed something or someone to claim.

And Logan knew he didn't. He didn't dare.

"You would never make one night with me enough," she repeated her warning, her eyes spitting back at him furiously. "What kind of game are you playing? You warn me off, then jerk me in your house as though you have no other choice but to fight with me over a dog we both know you want. You want that damned dog almost as bad as you want me in your bed. Why, Logan? Why can't you have either of us?"

"Because I don't dare."

As he stared into her wide, surprised gaze Logan realized he'd wanted her since that first glimpse he'd had of her. And he shouldn't. That small taste he'd had of her last week as he held her beneath that tree hadn't been nearly enough.

He shouldn't want her, but he craved her. Craved her with a need that made no sense and a sudden, over-whelming hunger that he couldn't seem to control.

And maybe she was right. One night would never be enough. But they would both pay for it.

"Are you waiting on your common sense to return again?" she whispered, her fingers gripping the tops of his biceps, kneading them.

She wasn't protesting or pushing him away. She wasn't fighting it. But he was, with every ounce of control he was fighting it, and he was losing.

Her fingers were kneading the tensed muscles of his biceps. Straight little nails nipping into the hard flesh covering them and sending sparks of fiery sensation straight to his balls.

"Hell if I know." He was trying to stop himself. "I didn't show any last time. Why should I do it now?"

There was no way to stop what he knew he was about to do.

Holding her gaze, drawn by her, feeling as though he was held to her by chains as invisible and yet as tight as any made by man, Logan knew he was doomed.

His head lowered, his lips touching hers, feeling them part, feeling the silk and heat, the tremble of hunger. As he watched the darkening of her gaze and the flutter of her lashes as they drifted closed, he knew he was a goner.

He'd fantasized about fucking her for months. Hell, he had so many scenarios in his head that sometimes he thought he could fuck her for a decade and never experience all of them.

But this one he'd never envisioned.

This one he'd never allowed himself to have because he'd known what it would do to him. The very thought of having her, here in his home, where he would never eradicate her memory, did things to him he couldn't consider.

A flood of sensation seemed to wrack his body as every muscle tightened furiously. Slowly, exquisitely slowly, her lips parted further, accepting the intimacy of his tongue with tentative excitement as he licked against hers.

Her hands stroked over his shoulders, her breathing becoming hitched as her heart pounded as furiously as his. Tightening his grip on her hips, he dragged her closer, lifting her. Pulling her against his body. Running his hands to the luscious curves of her ass, he had to hold back a groan of sheer male hunger. Gripping, lifting her before he could stop himself, Logan had her on the center island and her legs curled around his hips as he pushed the hardened ridge of his cock against the heated, wet warmth between her thighs.

She was short, curvy, delicate as hell, and he fit between her thighs perfectly. Pushing the thin, incredibly soft fluff of her gown and robe over her hips, he groaned in need, and realization.

She wore no panties.

His hands slid beneath the material to her back.

God, she was killing him with this need for her.

His dick was throbbing in a little happy dance that was driving him insane as she pressed more firmly against him.

The rasp of denim against the sensitive engorged head of his cock became an erotic agony. He wanted to slide his hardened flesh into her soft, liquid heat. And it was liquid. That sweet syrup was flowing from her, preparing her, and dampening his jeans.

The need to fuck her was a hunger he was afraid he wouldn't be able to walk away from. And there couldn't be anything in his life that he couldn't walk away from. He couldn't allow it.

But he couldn't walk away from her either.

Her thighs tightened at his hips, her legs curling around the backs of his thighs.

Her lips rubbed against his, parted and accepting, her tongue stroking against his, tasting him as he tasted her.

A rush of pure sensual adrenaline flooded his system, intoxicating him faster than liquor.

The need to have her became a furious, driving impulse he could no longer restrain.

Never, not in his entire sexual life, had he known a need such as the one he felt at this moment.

Dawn was just hours away. Darkness wrapped around them, the night spiced with summer's heat. It met with the surging, blistering heat of their desire, flaming so bright inside them that Logan felt a moment of sharp male trepidation.

Just enough to throw the thinnest shred of reason into the mix. Enough to assure him he was getting so fucking deep over his head that drowning was an imminent possibility.

It was becoming a certainty.

Such a certainty that he found himself giving up.

Giving in.

He didn't even have the will to fight.

The only thing left inside him was the hunger for this woman.

Releasing the tie of the robe between her breasts, he pushed the thin material over her arms. Releasing her from it, he then pushed the straps over her shoulders, lowering them slowly as she lifted her arms free as the material pooled at her hips. Within a heartbeat his hands were beneath her breasts. He had the warm, addicting weight of them filling his palms as he caught the hardened nipples between thumb and forefinger.

Pushing her back, leaning over her, he kissed her with all the driving, destructive hunger raging inside him.

He couldn't take her.

He wouldn't.

God as his witness, he knew one night would never be enough. But he could have part of her.

Her pleasure.

Her cries filling his ears.

The response that filled his senses.

Before he let her go he'd have her release spilling to his lips.

"I can't sleep for wanting you!" she cried out as his lips moved from hers to take stinging little kisses along her jaw.

Skye couldn't restrain herself. She didn't want to restrain herself. "I toss and turn and tell myself there was no way it was that good."

She was tortured by the memory of it, by the hunger to have it again.

Lifting his head, he stared down at her, and the torment in his gaze sliced through her soul.

"It was really that good, wasn't it, Logan?"

She knew it was. The taste of it was on her lips again, the flaming need for it rushing through her body again.

"It was just that and fucking better," he growled, and for some reason the thought that the words were all but forced from him struck her mind. It filled her with a feminine fear that he would leave her aching again. Leave her desperate for a release she couldn't reach on her own.

He couldn't leave her aching.

Logan watched her eyes, felt her hands as she pulled at his T-shirt and clawed at the material until he was jerking it from his body.

He could see the sensual pain raging through her.

As he disposed of his shirt then eased the gown from her hips to drop to the floor, he knew he would ensure she never forgot this night, or the pleasure he was going to give her.

She would never forget him or how much he needed her touch.

His lips lowered to the hard, pointed tip of a nipple and sucked it into his mouth.

Soft, feminine growls of demand left her lips as her hands moved to his head, speared through his hair, and held on tight. Held him closer to her.

As he sucked at the sweet flesh, tasted her, burned for her, he felt himself falling into that pit of uncontrolled need.

His.

The thought raged through him as he fought to reject it.

His.

The demand tore at him.

Ah God, giving her up, letting her go, would kill him.

If nothing else, tonight, he would have her pleasure.

Skye gasped, fighting to throttle the cries welling in her throat as Logan gripped her hips and dragged them to the edge of the center work counter. Gripping her thighs, he pulled back as his tongue stroking, working over her nipple demandingly. His hand slid up her thigh, moving slowly, so damned slowly, to the core of torturous need.

Her clit was so swollen she could barely stand the pain of need. She'd never in her life known a hunger for a man that had her body so sensitive, her pussy so wet.

She was so slick and heated that when his fingers met the highest part of her thigh it was awaiting him.

She couldn't contain her moan or the shift of her hips as she arched to get closer, to feel his touch there, on the most sensitive part of her body. To feel his fingers caressing her—penetrating her.

She needed it. Needed it like she had never needed anything in her life.

"Please!" The word, a hoarse, desperate cry, fell from her lips before she could stop it as she felt his fingers brush against the soft, bare flesh of the inner lips.

Strong male teeth gripped her nipple erotically before his head turned to find its mate, sucking it into his mouth with the same hungry force that he had used on the first.

Emerald-green eyes glittered from behind the ridiculously long dark blond lashes, gleaming with lust as he raked the tip of her nipple with his tongue.

Skye arched again, knowing he would die if he stopped, knowing that the almost-teasing brush of his fingers against the saturated flesh between her thighs was driving her insane.

"Logan, please!" she cried out as she felt those diabolic fingers part her, the tips of two caressing a slow, agonizing circle of flames around her clit.

The little bud clenched, throbbed, the need for release building in it with painful intensity.

"Please!" she cried out again.

"Please what, Skye?" Dark, rough, the question was whispered against the slope of her breast as he rubbed the short growth of his beard against it. "Tell me what you want, baby. Give me that at least."

"Please stop teasing me, Logan." Her fingers kneaded against his scalp as he caressed the flesh between her breasts with his beard.

"How am I teasing you, Skye?" he demanded, his voice a gravelly sound of increasing lust. "Tell me where I'm teasing you."

"Damn you, Logan!" she cried out.

"No, give it to me," he suddenly snarled, his head rising, his expression tight, flushed with sexual heat. "Tell me what you fucking want. What you feel. Give me the words, Skye. Give me that pleasure."

He needed it, she realized.

For some reason, he needed to hear the words.

"I need your fingers," she gasped as those wicked fingers stroked down the slick slit of her pussy.

"How do you need them?" he demanded. "Tell me how you need them."

She'd sworn if he ever had her, once would never be enough. She was going to keep that promise.

"Fuck me, Logan," she whispered, excitement beginning to build with a rush of sexually charged adrenaline. "Fuck me with your fingers. Use your lips and tongue on my clit. I've dreamed of your lips and tongue between my thighs—" She arched with a strangled cry as he began kissing slowly, teasingly, down her body. "I dream of it while I try to find my own pleasure. But my fingers aren't good enough. And your mouth and tongue aren't there to complete it."

The rumbling, desperate male growl against the sensitive flesh of her belly as her womb clenched in desperate response.

"I'm going to eat you like my favorite treat." There was the slightest hint of male tease in his tone mixed with the gravelly sound of increasing lust. "Slow and easy, baby. I'm going to lick all that sweet cream, suck at that pretty clit, and fuck your pussy until you're clawing at me to come."

Her hips arched, a cry raking from her throat at the sensual threat.

"Oh God, please, yes." She couldn't hold back the plea. "Just like that, Logan. That's what I need. I dare you to make me beg."

His lips brushed at the top of her thigh, kissed lower, until she felt his heated breath ruffling the short, well-trimmed curls just above her clit.

A second later she swore she was going to die. Her

orgasm nearly exploded through her as he delivered a stinging, blissfully heated kiss to her clit.

He sucked it between his lips only to release it just as quickly while sensation raked through her senses with blazing promise.

Then his tongue came out to play and nothing else existed; nothing else could penetrate the cloud of a pleasure so extreme that Skye knew she would never be the same again.

CHAPTER SIX

Sensations crowded, one on top of the other, and rushed through Skye's body as she felt Logan's lips, his tongue, and the heated confines of his mouth torturing the swollen bud of her clit. Lower, his fingers parted the silken smooth flesh of her pussy and with slow, incremental thrusts began to push their way into the clenched, snug entrance of her vagina.

It was like being tortured with pleasure.

Lifting her legs as he bent to her, her knees bending, he placed her feet on his shoulders with a rough order to keep them there as he dragged one of the nearby stools into position for him to sit comfortably as he did as he had promised.

Eat her like his favorite treat.

As two fingers worked slowly to stretch the unused muscles of her vagina, his tongue licked, stroked, caressed, and rubbed through her slit before doing the same to her tortured clitoris.

It had been years since she'd had the time or even the inclination to search for a lover. One-night stands really weren't something she felt she could deal with, so she had never gone after them.

She wasn't about to go after one now.

Before the night was over, once he was finished driving her insane with his mouth, then she would do what she had been fantasizing about doing to him for months.

Driving him insane with her mouth. Tasting him as he tasted her. Filling her mouth with his cock and feeling him come as undone as she was coming herself.

"Logan!" she all but screamed his name as his tongue pressed more firmly against her clit and rubbed against it erotically. His fingers were creating an exciting, exquisite pleasure-pain inside her vagina.

He stroked inside her pussy with little more than the tips of his fingers before parting them and aiding the tight entrance in relaxing.

She'd never known she'd become so snug that just the width of his finger would feel as thick as the first lover she'd taken almost ten years before. That or the need to draw Logan farther inside her had tightened the muscles further.

She wasn't sure which. She found she didn't care.

She could feel her juices flowing, aiding the penetration and the heat his touch was arousing.

His lips and tongue were wicked instruments of torture, never quite allowing her to climax but keeping her poised at the precipice and begging to fall into the maelstrom.

Clenching her fingers in his hair, she fought to draw in

a ragged breath as his tongue nudged at her clit again. With just the tip stiffened, his tongue then slid lower as his fingers released her.

"Oh God, Logan." Her hips arched as his tongue speared inside her. "Please. Please more."

She was already begging and didn't even give a damn.

He delved deep, causing her juices to flow faster as he licked and stroked, using his tongue to fuck her with slow, deliberate thrusts as he tasted her with erotic intent.

She'd never known pleasure like this could exist outside a book. And she'd read plenty of those books. She'd always seen the descriptions as the fantasy women wanted rather than the reality that could actually be out there.

It was reality. Right here in Logan's arms was the fantasy she'd only read about, fantasized about.

He was taking his slow, sweet time as he tasted her, as he fucked her with his tongue and refused to hurry no matter how much she begged.

It was his hands holding her legs in place as she strained beneath his touch, and when his tongue licked through the parted folds once more it was his fingers pushing deeper inside her.

Her hips were rolling, twisting, forcing each shallow thrust to go deeper as Skye fought to reach the climax that remained just out of reach.

She was certain she would die if he kept teasing her. She would die if he stopped. And if he would just give her a moment to find her release, then maybe she could live the fantasy she had played in her head for so many months and drive him just as crazy.

Logan heard the shattered cries that fell from Skye's lips and nearly lost his control to the point that he swore he was going to come in his jeans.

Hell, he'd never done that, even as a randy teenager with his first lover.

But Skye did things to him that didn't make sense. She made him break his own rules, made him hunger when he knew he shouldn't, and made him desperate to have what he knew he couldn't have.

Easing farther inside her, he had to remind himself that taking her wouldn't be rushed. If the feel of her tight inner muscles was any indication, it had been years since she had had a lover. Far too many years for the size and hardness of his cock if he weren't careful.

Being careful of his lovers was his uppermost thought, but Skye had a way of making him so fucking hungry he feared hurting her. A part of him wanted to raid the hot, clenched little pussy wrapped around his fingers. Made him want to feel every sharp sensation of it bearing down on his cock, sucking him inside as it stretched to accommodate his width.

God, she made him crazy.

Sucking at her hard little clit, he felt the little bud pulse harder beneath his tongue and he knew she was close.

Too close.

He didn't want it to end yet. Once she climaxed, this interlude would be over and he would have to send her back to her own house. To her own bed.

He couldn't keep her, no matter how badly he wanted to.

Pushing his fingers farther inside her and feeling each

contraction that attacked the heated channel, Logan could feel his balls tightening in response.

She was slick and wet; she was soaking his finger. The taste of her against his tongue was like summer itself. Hot as hell and filled with life. And he wanted nothing more than to release his tortured cock and—

Hell, it was already released.

When had he managed to undo his jeans and release the pulsing, straining flesh?

Holding the thick shaft with one hand, his fingers massaging the sensitive head, he fought, tried, prayed to hold back and hold on to the control he could feel slipping through his fingers.

He wanted the feel of that hot flesh wrapped around his dick so bad it was about to kill him.

If he didn't let her come, if he didn't finish this now, then he was going to end up finishing it with his cock buried, unsheathed, so deep inside her that neither of them would know where one began and the other ended.

Capping his lips over the throbbing bud of her clit as he worked his fingers inside her, stretching her further, easing the tender tissue as her slick fluids gathered further, Logan knew he was riding an edge that was fast approaching meltdown.

Pulling his fingers back, he used his lips and tongue and the suckling of his mouth on the hard bundle of nerves as he thrust both fingers inside her and began working her flesh with quick, hard little strokes that had her exploding in seconds.

Rapture surged through her.

Skye's eyes flared open as the shift of his fingers and the movements of his lips and tongue changed. Between one breath and the next he was sucking her clit with a force that had it sensitizing to the point of exquisite pain just before his tongue tucked against it and began rubbing in quick, rhythmic motions.

His fingers pulled back, then surged inside her in a series of hard, rasping strokes inside the clenched tissue, then tilting upward and stroking against a spot so sensitive she immediately lost her senses with the explosion that detonated inside her.

He didn't stop with the initial release. Just because she had tightened and cried out, he didn't ease in the demanding, dominant strokes of his fingers or the rasp of his tongue against her clit.

He increased it. Kept it going and rumbled a moan of pure male hunger against her flesh to send her racing higher.

It seemed never ending.

Her thighs clenched as they fell to his shoulders, her hips arched and trembling as shudder after shudder tore through her body. The waves of sensation jerked up her spine and crashed into her senses with a violence born of desperation and tore another ragged cry from her lips.

Wave after wave of blissful rapture tore through her, exploding inside her pussy with a power that left her crying out breathlessly, weak and still riding an edge that only he controlled.

And he controlled it ruthlessly. Drawing every sensation out to its highest peak before allowing it to peak.

Pushing her higher, further than she'd ever known a release could be pushed.

With his lips, tongue, and heated mouth, his thrusting fingers, and the deep, internal stroking of hidden nerve endings buried against the walls of her pussy he took her to a realm of pleasure she was loathe to leave.

He pushed her to an edge of complete ecstasy, held her there, kept it vibrating inside her, then gently allowed her to begin to descend.

It was a descent she fought with everything inside her. Because it wasn't enough. It was violent, encompassing, so sensually destructive that she knew for a fact she'd never been even close to such pleasure. Still, there was a pulse of need, a completeness that she knew was missing. One she knew her body was greedy to experience.

Still, he eased her back to reality until he finished her with a last, gentle lick to her violently sensitive clit as he held his fingers still inside her.

Her muscles were shuddering as they continued to grip and suck at his fingers. Her juices didn't ease from her; each inner convulsion had copious amounts of fluid spilling in rapid succession to his fingers and her thighs.

When that last ecstatic shudder rippled from her pussy, it was to the feel of him easing his fingers free and the knowledge that there was still so much to come.

There was still more to experience, because she wasn't quite satisfied yet.

Far from it.

"It's not enough," she whispered as she felt him moving away, and she tried to sit up, tried to touch him, to caress him and fulfill all those pent-up fantasies racing through her veins.

Some sense, some hidden intuition, warned her that it was over. Her chest tightened with it as her eyes opened and she glimpsed the tightness of his expression, the regret in his gaze.

As he helped her sit up he caught her hands, holding them between their bodies as she stared back at him in surprise.

"Logan?" She could feel her chest tightening, a realization that even though it wasn't enough, in his eyes she could still see it was finished.

"It's enough, baby." With his free hand he stroked back the hair that had fallen over her face, his gaze tortured, the hardened length of his cock free of his jeans and throbbing fiercely against her thigh.

She looked down at the thick, heavy shaft before lifting her gaze again.

"Is it?" she asked then, feeling a vein of pain-filled anger beginning to unfurl inside her.

"It has to be." Stone-hard, his emerald eyes like green ice despite the ragged sound of his voice, he denied what they both knew for a certain fact.

They were both still desperate, aching for the completion.

He stepped away from her, fixed his jeans, then bent and picked his shirt and her nightgown from the floor.

Skye didn't say a word as he pulled the nightgown over her head and helped her arms into their places. Once he pulled the material over her breasts she realized it was all she could do to keep from crying.

Her lips were actually on the verge of trembling.

How long had it been since she had cried?

Surely not since she was an adolescent. She'd always fought not to cry, because her father had always told her that big girls didn't cry.

Well, she was a big girl now, and all she wanted to do was sob as Logan turned away from her and pulled his own shirt over his head.

His back flexed, the muscles clenching with hard ripples as he jerked the shirt on, then pushed the strands of hair falling over his rugged face.

Turning back to her, he stood silent and still, watching her, his breathing as harsh and uneven as hers.

Drawing in a hard breath, Skye slid from the counter slowly before he crossed the distance to help her down. She didn't want him to touch her again. She was terrified if he did, then she might weaken from the force of the emotions racing through her.

Who could have known that he would have superhuman self-control? For damned sure he had more than she. Because there was no way in hell she could have denied him after experiencing the power of the need racing through both of them.

Her stomach clenched as emotion and ragged regret swelled inside her. And anger.

Damn him. He might be a glutton for self-punishment, but she sure as hell wasn't.

And she'd just fucking had enough.

She was here for a reason, and it wasn't to torment herself over a man who wanted nothing as his own. Not a truck, a house, a puppy, or a lover. He sure as hell obviously didn't want a future with anyone or anything and had no dreams of sharing his life outside whatever fucking bond he had with his cousins.

Fuck him.

Fuck him and fuck destroying herself over something, someone, she should have known from the beginning— hell, she *had* known from the beginning—could never be hers.

Bending, she snatched the robe from the floor, pulled it on and tied it quickly, clumsily as she held back her tears.

Turning on her heel, she moved quickly from the darkened kitchen and all but raced to the patio doors.

"Skye, goddamn it, wait!" he snarled behind her, his voice barely loud enough to hear despite the fury she could feel throttled inside it.

She didn't wait. She couldn't.

She would end up either sobbing on the floor in front of him or begging him to fuck her and finish it.

Sliding open the patio doors before he could reach her, she bent, scooped up the little Chinese pug puppy, and all but ran across the short distance to her own patio, then into the house.

Skye was tired of listening to the baby cry alone. At least she would have someone to cry with now, she thought as the puppy's whines became more pitiful as Skye closed and locked the patio doors behind her.

She flipped the curtains closed without turning around.

She was too frightened that if she turned, then she would see Logan. If she did, she would definitely end up begging. And if she didn't, then the pain might actually bring her to her knees.

Holding the little scrap of fur to her chest, she moved through the house to the other side and the small in-law suite she had taken for her bedroom.

Closing the door behind her, she breathed in roughly and stared down at the sad, damp eyes of the puppy as she stared up at her. The pug's expression was puzzled and hurt, as though she, too, simply couldn't understand why Logan couldn't love her.

Why Logan refused to love her.

"It's okay, little baby," Skye said roughly as the puppy whined sadly once again. "It's okay; I'll just cry with you."

Because for some reason, for one insane moment last week beneath the sheltering branches of the old oak tree, she'd actually believed Logan Callahan might want, just a little bit, to consider a lover, a puppy, a future.

And she had never imagined just how wrong she was.

She'd never realized just how serious he'd been when he'd told her it couldn't happen, that he wouldn't let it happen.

She would be no more than a one-night stand. And that was something she knew her heart wouldn't survive.

It was something her reason for being here couldn't accept.

For the first time since her parents' deaths, the first tear fell, and the puppy whined against Skye's chest again.

For such a small, young animal she was unnaturally attached to a man who didn't want him. She didn't want to leave Logan's property. As though leaving might steal a chance of her seeing the man she had already decided was her owner.

"It's okay, little girl," Skye murmured as the puppy whined again.

Skye put the puppy on her feet before picking up a newspaper on the bedside table and spreading the pages across the floors.

"I'll get you a blanket," she told the puppy as she bent and ran her fingers down the soft apricot fur as the pug lay down slowly on the floor next to the door.

Dark brown eyes stared up at Skye despondently.

"You're not the only one he didn't want," she told the puppy softly. "Evidently, he didn't want me either."

Unfortunately, it seemed she wanted him far too much.

"Get some sleep." She sighed deeply before moving to the bed and sitting down.

Reaching out, she opened the drawer on the small bedside table and drew out the photo she kept there.

Amy was leaning, her head against Skye's, her brown eyes filled with laughter.

God, what would she have done without her foster family, her foster sister, in those first years after witnessing her parents' deaths?

After seeing her nanny and her father's bodyguard shoot her mother and father in the head before searching the house for her.

Amy had kept her sane.

She had made Skye laugh.

She had made her want to get up in the mornings.

And she had held the younger Skye when brutal nightmares had brought her awake screaming and crying.

A tear landed on the picture.

Wiping it away, Skye bent over with the pain that struck at her stomach, her chest. The agony of the loss had never broken her. She hadn't had Amy nearly long enough to heal before a killer had taken her away.

"Logan Callahan is a baby doll, Skye," her sister had sighed. "He's cute as hell, and so sad. Something's going on there, and I have to find out what. He and his cousins are good men. They don't deserve this."

Amy hadn't told her what was going on. She hadn't told Skye she was chasing a killer. But Skye had known, whatever it was, it had darkened Amy's eyes and left her filled with worry for Logan.

"One day, maybe I can find a good man like Logan," Skye had said somberly. "Someone who won't get killed like my daddy and mommy did."

Amy had smiled and brushed her hair back from her face. "I'm much too old for Logan, Skye. Maybe, when you're a little bit older, we'll find him again so he can fall all kinds of in love with you. I want you to have someone who will protect you, little sister. Someone who will love you with all his heart and soul."

That had been their last conversation.

Days later, Amy had gone missing. Two days after that, a hiker had found her body, beaten, broken, horribly molested, and bled out.

"Oh, God!" She hadn't realized sobs were tearing at her chest as she clenched the picture, or that tears were falling from her eyes.

She'd only been fifteen. Her parents had died five

years before and still the nightmares had tormented her, terrified her.

Finding her way in life after witnessing their brutal murder wouldn't have been possible without Amy. Then, she had been taken from her, too.

A soft whine had her staring down.

The pup sat at her feet, head tilted for a second before moving to lick her ankle as though in consolation. A second later she jumped up, placing her front paws against Skye's legs, obviously wanting up.

And Skye needed the comfort, she admitted.

She needed Logan. Needed his touch, and needed that something she had seen in the pictures Amy had shown her twelve years before. That spark of laughter that hadn't been extinguished then. That hint of a smile that had stolen her fifteen-year-old heart.

She needed the man she had claimed when she had been no more than a teenager. And she needed vengeance for the sister stolen from her.

And Skye promised herself, she might not be able to hold on to the man, but she would have the vengeance.

Daylight was beginning to edge through the curtains now. She'd conquered another night. If she didn't sleep in darkness, then she found the nightmares didn't visit.

Skye walked through the house to the back bedroom she'd taken.

The house was far too large for one person, just as the one Logan Callahan owned was.

Four large upstairs bedrooms, plus what was more

commonly called an in-law suite at the back of the first floor.

That room worked perfectly for Skye.

The small sitting room, bedroom, and roomy bathroom with its garden tub, full-sized shower, and wide vanity cabinet was the size of her apartment in D.C.

The upstairs rooms were nicer but, still, upstairs, and she'd found herself feeling isolated and too damned alone there.

Moving to the bed, she picked up her gown and robe before heading to the shower. Dawn was already edging across the mountains. It was her bedtime. She hadn't been able to sleep at night for far too many years. She was too aware that often evil used the cover of night to strike.

By the time she had showered and moved back to the bedroom, the sun was peeking through the opened windows and spreading its warming rays across the bed.

The little bundle of fluff was sitting at Skye's bedroom door, her low, almost-imperceptible whines breaking her heart.

For over a week she'd watched that baby scratch at Logan's door and sat on her patio and listened to the dog whine.

Closing the curtains securely, Skye left the bedroom to check the house one last time.

The puppy followed her curiously. She whimpered at the front door as Skye checked it, then followed her up the stairs until she picked her up on the fifth step and just carried her with her. The puppy was too small to try to climb those stairs. Holding the pug close to her chest,

Skye checked the windows and the balcony door that led to the balcony straight across from Logan Callahan's.

There was no sign of him in the bedroom. No sign of him outside.

The puppy whined again.

Shaking her head, Skye moved back downstairs. Giving the puppy a drink of water, she set her on the paper and praised her when she did her business. Giving in to a moment of weakness Skye hoped she wouldn't regret, she placed the pup in the bed next to her. The pug moved to the middle of the bed, the pillow, then to Skye's side, and finally found a spot she seemed to be able to live with, if not comfortably, at least quietly.

"What is your story, little girl?" Skye asked as she ran her fingers down the apricot fur of the puppy's back. "What makes you think you belong over there rather than here?"

Skye had never had a puppy before. It hadn't been allowed after she'd gone to live with her foster parents, because her foster father had been allergic to both cats and dogs.

Before her foster family . . .

She stared up at the ceiling for long moments before turning her gaze back to the puppy as she whined once again.

"At least you're welcome here." Poor little baby. Skye knew how it felt to be an orphan, to beg to be one place while being forced to live in another.

The puppy gave a low, saddened little sigh before laying her wrinkled little face against her paws to stare back at Skye with the same confusion and sadness Skye felt herself.

Sliding her hand to the pug's back, Skye petted her gently before staring up at that ceiling and wondering if sleep would come this morning or if, as she had the last week, she would simply toss, turn, and awaken herself time and again as her fingers found the aroused flesh between her thighs.

This time, she at least had something warm next to her that wouldn't ask questions. That wouldn't probe or curse when she didn't get answers, if the nightmares did by chance invade the daylight.

At least this time, Skye might feel lonelier than ever, but she had company.

That thought had another tear sliding from her closed eyes. She still felt unwanted, though.

Logan couldn't hear the pitiful whines coming from the patio anymore. The scratching against the glass was silenced; and the knowledge that while sleeping on the couch Logan could at least hear if she was in distress was no longer uppermost in his mind.

The little bit of fluff was a replica to one Logan had owned twenty years before, the last gift he'd received from his grandfather before his parents' deaths.

Logan's grandparents had given him the pup, a male that time, because he was about to drive them insane.

According to his grandmother, who bred the animals, the pup had cried since the first breath he took. He had been crying when Logan's grandparents stepped into the house, glared at his father, then turned and looked at Logan with expressions that to this day he couldn't decipher.

A mix between pain and rage in his grandfather's gaze and the agony filling Logan's grandmother's.

His grandmother, Tandy Rafferty, had stepped slowly to him, the whimpering puppy in her extended hands. Large, wet brown eyes, creamy coat, and a black face. The minute Logan had accepted the tiny bundle he had stopped whining. His wrinkled face had stared up at him as though he was finally where he belonged.

Tandy had turned and left the house immediately without saying a word.

Saul had stared at Logan silently for long moments.

Crouching down, Saul had looked Logan in the eye and said, "Sometimes, there's a gift waiting for you that you didn't even know existed. That little baby has cried since the day he was born. Keeping it alive has been a pain in your gram's rear. He's yours now. He was meant for you. Take care of him, son."

A year later he had died in Logan's arms from a poisoned hamburger he'd found while Logan was at one of the socials the county threw through the summer.

He'd died as Logan and his cousins had stood outside the vet's door banging and screaming at the man to help.

He'd been home.

He'd opened the door seconds after Jack, as Logan had called him, had taken his last, agonized breath.

Now there was another pup whose whimpering

sounds of misery and distress hadn't stopped since the day Logan had returned home to find her.

She couldn't be more than ten weeks old. The same age as the pup Tandy Rafferty had brought Logan.

Grimacing, he stalked to the living room, jerked up his cell phone, and made a call.

"What do you want?" Ill-tempered, filled with anger, Saul Rafferty answered the phone on the first ring.

Logan paced back to the kitchen. "Why did you do this, you old bastard," he snarled. "Come get it."

Saul grunted. "That little bitch has squalled since it was born. Your grandmother wouldn't rest until I gave it to you. Now you have it. Shut the fuck up and take care of it."

"So you can kill another one?"

Silence filled the line for long moments before Saul Rafferty sighed with what seemed like weariness.

"Never turn your back on your food." His voice dropped, and Logan was certain he only heard that hint of grief in Saul's tone because he wanted to hear it.

"Fuck you!" Logan snapped.

"That's the last litter out of My Gal, your gram's favorite." Saul ignored the curse. "She was diagnosed with canine cancer last week, only weeks after your gram was. I won't take it back. She made me give it to you; now you have it."

"I gave it away," Logan said with distinct pleasure. "I don't want a damned thing from either of you."

Saul snorted. "You've given it away six times since I dropped it off and every time it's been brought back. Stop being so fucking hardheaded. It's from your gram."

"And I don't want a fucking thing from her, either. I'll drop it off if it comes back here again."

"Return the little bitch and I'll slit her throat before your gram sees it. I won't see her upset."

"As though anything about me could upset either of you. Other than the fact that I live. That and your inability to steal every fucking thing my mother wanted me to have. I gave every goddamned bit of it away too, Saul. All of it."

Saul was silent for long moments before he said, "That's what I would have done, boy. It's exactly what I would have done."

The call disconnected.

Standing alone in the kitchen, Logan stared around the darkness, wishing the anger and the grief raging inside him were just because of Rafferty.

Logan just wished he could say it was because a grandmother he'd never known, one who had never wanted him, was dying.

He just wished the rage eating at him could be placed somewhere but where he knew it lay.

In his own aloneness. In the fact that there was something he wanted right now, more than any kid could possibly want a pup.

Because he couldn't have the pup, or the woman.

As Logan stood in the darkened kitchen, his hands braced on the counter where Skye had just lain, her body spread out for him, willing and heated was the image that played behind his closed lids.

What the fuck was he doing? What the fuck was he doing to her as well as himself?

He'd stared into her eyes and seen something he'd never believed he would see, something he sure as hell hadn't expected.

He'd seen a woman he finally wished he could share the future with.

A woman who wanted him more than anything at that moment.

Until he'd tasted the burning response of her need and turned her away, not fully satisfied. Aching. Dreams in her eyes.

Before he could stop himself he turned, his fist flying out and cracking into the wall behind him.

"Goddamn it!" The words burst from his lips as he punched through the drywall, fury mixed with a hunger he knew was going to destroy him erupting inside him.

His hands buried in his hair then, pushing the strands back from his face as he grimaced at the feel of slick warmth against his knuckles where he'd busted them open.

This had to be over soon. It had to be finished before he made himself crazy, because with God as his witness, he knew his self-control where she was concerned was eroding fast.

He was going to have her. And like she said, once would never be enough.

She'd been a fighter after all.

Pulling the black truck into the shelter of trees that bordered a shallow creek, he slid it into park before taking a deep breath.

He was sated, for the moment.

Physically, sexually sated.

The need to inflict pain, to feel the fear that raced through a delicate, weaker body, to see the blood flowing and feel the clench of rejection as he raped and tortured was now fulfilled.

For the moment.

Sliding his gloved hands from the steering wheel, he opened the door before stepping slowly from the truck.

His boss hadn't made this trick with him.

He'd helped though, at first.

He grinned as he walked to the back of the truck.

Finally, after only a few hours, even his boss hadn't had the stomach for the pain he could inflict.

Even that old bastard hadn't been able to hold up against her screams, her agony, and her pleas. He'd had to walk away.

Strange, how men such as that couldn't stomach the actions they condoned, even requested.

But after the son of a bitch had left, she'd screamed harder, begged until her voice broke and only croaks of agony were emitted.

It was over then.

Once they broke their voices, the only satisfaction left was to watch the blood flow. To run his tongue over each slice as he fucked the lust out of his system.

Finally, he just slit her throat.

She might have been breathing through the last few hours, but she hadn't been there.

She'd stared sightlessly up at the ceiling of the

basement, her gaze distant and even the terrified, pain-filled croaks hadn't been there.

She'd lasted two days and it had been damned good. Better than he'd ever imagined she would be.

Sighing deeply at the thought, he lowered the tail-gate, grabbled the end of the tarp, then pulled the body slowly from the bed.

He'd bleached her from head to toe, inside and out, under her fingernails, her toenails, and everything in-between.

There wasn't even a speck of dust on her body. She was as clean as a surgical table with nothing to link her to anyone.

Carrying the broken body to the edge of the creek, he laid it down before gripping the tarp and quickly flipping her body from it.

She'd be found here quick enough.

Rolling the slick material up, he moved several yards from it, pulled one of the gloves from his latex-covered hand, and dropped it behind a tree.

Moving against a thorny bush, he laid a torn piece of denim on one of the thorns, careful to make it look as though the material had ripped from the jeans against the bush.

The pants were Logan Callahan's, as was the glove. Both had his sweat on them, and nothing more.

He'd been careful to make certain he'd shaved his legs clean and wore specially coated long underwear beneath the pants to ensure no other DNA or material was left behind.

One down.

This would incriminate Callahan as nothing else could. Prison was in that boy's future, he'd just made sure of it.

CHAPTER SEVEN

The tension between Logan and Skye was growing thicker by the day, Logan admitted five days later, and they weren't even coming in contact as often as they had before. They'd watched each other across the expanse of the side yard. From the upstairs master bedroom as she too checked the windows each night.

He almost grinned. He saw her more now, he thought, than at any other time since she had moved into the house. And he was growing hornier by the day, which he hadn't thought possible. If he didn't lose the hard-on torturing the hell out of him, then he was going to have a permanent indent from his zipper pressed into the thick shaft.

The night before, he'd walked naked into the living room and pretended she wasn't staring from the living room across from him.

Then, before she went to bed this morning? The little wench. If she'd been naked it wouldn't have aroused him more. Dressed in a black floor-length, flowing gown and a see-through black chiffon robe with just the slightest little train behind it, she'd blown his fucking mind.

That was the romance in her.

Fuck him six ways from Sunday but that romance had never been the turn-on that it was now. With this woman.

He'd known it was there. He'd seen it in the softness of her eyes every time he looked into them. He'd felt it in her kiss and in the innocence of her response when she'd come in his arms.

But son of a bitch! God have mercy on his black soul!

She'd looked like a damned fairy princess or something and his dick had responded with an iron hardness that had been damned uncomfortable. All he wanted to do in that moment was replace the innocence with pure sensual, sexual knowledge.

With a temptress's heat.

A lush, sexual goddess who knew how to make him insane and used it ruthlessly.

But even in her innocence she was already doing that.

At times, he found himself actually having fun with the teasing games they were playing.

Then, he would glance across the yard, wouldn't see her, and the disappointment, the loneliness, would grip him again.

Son of a bitch, he wished Rafer and Crowe would track down whoever had hired the bastard who had attacked Rafer's fiancée, Cami, last month.

As Rafer and Crowe worked their end, Logan had

been attempting to work his during the day, but his excursions into town weren't too successful.

It didn't matter where he went or who he tried to talk to, he was still watched with wariness, suspicion, and even fear. He wondered if threatening a few would work.

Sighing, he leaned against the door frame again, his gaze narrowing on the shadowed house across the side yard before a frustrated curse slipped past his lips.

This was it.

The minute he saw her moving around, he was going over there. He would explain what he could. Attempt to make her understand the threat, the danger, she could face if she dropped his guard and let her into his bed.

He'd have to make her understand what losing the sight of her, the knowledge of the life that glowed in her eyes, would do to him.

It would destroy him.

The teasing, the sense of waiting, it was going to have to stop. His attention was becoming too divided by the woman he couldn't keep his hands off.

So much for all those years of training the government had paid so much money for.

It could work if injected with truth serum or if any number of other agents designed to compromise him or his strength. But he'd be damned if he could work past the thought of the pain he'd put in her eyes that last night.

It was after two in the afternoon, and still he hadn't seen Skye or the pup venture through the house. But then, he hadn't really expected Skye to.

He never saw her in the morning. Once the sun rose,

the house became still and quiet until late in the afternoon. She slept through the day in the small in-law suite that had been built onto the house by a previous renter.

Logan hadn't been so sure about the addition when he'd agreed to it; now he almost wished he hadn't allowed it, despite the additional rent he was able to charge for the place. Because he couldn't stare into the windows of that suite. It was on the other side of the house, away from his own.

Where he couldn't see Skye, where he couldn't watch her, get to know her at least through her habits.

He knew from her rental application that her employer was listed as a major software firm, her job title that of editor for instruction and design manuals.

It sounded damned boring to him and not really a job he could imagine she would have subjected herself to.

Pushing away from the patio doors at the sound of the doorbell ringing, Logan grimaced and made his way from the room, despite his reluctance to answer the door.

He should ignore it.

He didn't want company, and he sure as hell had no intentions of putting up with it. For twenty years the good citizens of Sweetrock, and of Rafferty Lane in particular, had ignored the injustices against the Callahan cousins and watched as they were disowned, participated in snubbing them, and refused to testify to the fact that Mina Rafferty Callahan had cherished her only child as well as her husband.

Moving down the stairs, Logan raked his fingers through his hair and grimaced at the memories of the past. Memories he simply didn't want to revisit yet had no choice now that he was back in the house where he'd spent the first eleven years of his life.

Pulling the door open, he stared at his visitors coolly despite the small tingle of warning that came to life just beneath the skin at the back of his neck.

"Archer, can I help you?" Logan leaned against the door frame and crossed his arms over his chest as he noticed the neighbors gathered on the porches and in their yards along the street.

Another day in Sweetrock, he thought furiously as he turned his gaze back to the sheriff and the stranger standing still, watchful, and armed behind him.

Archer pulled the dun-colored hat from his head before raking his fingers through his dark hair in a gesture of frustration.

"Logan, this is Detective Ian Staton from Boulder. We need to talk to you."

Dark-haired, his craggy features set and stone-hard, the detective watched Logan from icy, hard blue eyes. Jeans and a cotton shirt, a casual sports jacket that hid the shoulder holster Logan detected beneath it, and well-worn leather boots on his feet.

"Now, Logan."

There was something about the demand that grated on his senses and had the small hairs at the back of his neck tingling in warning.

Logan stared back at them coolly. "So talk."

"Privately, if you don't mind," the sheriff sighed. "You don't want this here in front of your neighbors."

Logan narrowed his gaze warningly at the sheriff. "Crowe and Rafer okay? Cami?" His gaze shifted to the detective.

"As far as I know." Archer nodded. "This isn't about them."

Logan stared at the family standing on their porch across the street.

Mr. Williams, his wife, Nila, and their four children were staring back at Logan as though he had killed their dog. Williams had his brawny arms crossed over his chest, his rounded belly curving out beneath them.

"Fuck it." Stepping back, Logan let the two men into the house. "Want some coffee?"

"If you don't mind." There was an edge of relief in the sheriff's voice.

"We really need to get this taken care of, Sheriff," the detective demanded, his tone harsh. "Coffee wasn't part of the agenda."

"Then pencil it in, dammit," Archer ordered, his tone harsh. "I told you, you'll handle this my way."

Judging by the look on Archer's face, he was pretty damned sure he didn't want to know.

Logan led the way to the kitchen, put the coffee on, then as the dark liquid ran into the pot turned back to the two men.

Archer was keeping a careful distance between them and him, assuring Logan that his cousins might be fine, but someone wasn't.

Or something wasn't, and Logan was damned sure he didn't want to know what it was.

Weariness, guilt, sorrow. The emotions flashed through him as he fought the knowledge he could see in the sheriff's gaze.

A knowledge that hell was about to revisit.

"What's happened?" Logan asked as he turned and poured the coffee, more to give himself something than out of any need for the caffeine. Setting the two cups on the center counter, Skye's counter as he now thought of it, Logan crossed his arms over his chest and waited.

"We've talked to your neighbors," Archer sighed. "No one will say one way or the other if you were here Saturday night/early morning or not, if you left or if they saw you at all." There was a growl in his voice, an edge of anger as Logan felt himself tensing.

Archer needed an alibi for him.

No one was going to stand up for him here, though, in other words, and it was obvious he was going to need it.

He found it strange, though, that they weren't swearing whatever the hell they thought would get him in the most trouble.

"And I haven't finished installing the security system either," Logan stated.

That was a lie, but he had no intentions of revealing the extent to which the inside of the house had been wired. It was the outside he hadn't yet gotten around to. He'd only reveal the fact that the inside was done though, if he had no other choice.

"Do you have an alibi for Saturday after midnight, Logan? Specifically, between three thirty and five?"

Logan paused as he lifted the coffee to his lips. His gaze locked on Archer's before he completed the motion, brought the cup to his lips, sipped, then lowered it.

"Does it matter?" he finally asked.

Skye O'Brien hadn't been happy when she'd left the other night, so he wasn't certain she would attest for his whereabouts that night.

"It fucking matters, Logan," he snapped as the detective beside him shifted, his hand lying on the butt of his weapon, a secondary at his hip. Logan set his coffee on the counter and recrossed his arms over his chest.

"Do you have anyone who will go on record as having seen you between three thirty and five that morning?" Archer's tone was sharp now.

Logan gave a mocking laugh. "What do you think? Why don't you just tell me what the hell is going on?"

"This is bullshit, Sheriff," the detective growled then. "Why are you wasting your time? You have the DNA evidence and it matches. Stop fucking around."

Logan felt something in his stomach clench as the words "DNA evidence" filled the room.

"Archer, what the hell is this?"

The sheriff slapped his hat against his thigh as his jaw clenched, fury raging in his gaze.

"A rancher found Marietta Tyme out by Wiley's Creek early yesterday morning," the detective stated coldly before Archer could speak. "She'd been raped, tortured, sliced in so many areas she looked like a cutting board, and her throat sliced. A witness places you at her home at three Saturday morning, putting her in that black pickup parked in your garage. You tore your jeans on a thorn bush, Callahan, and forgot a glove. We have your fingerprints and we have your DNA, on scene. I want you to lower your arms and turn around, we're taking you in for the murder of Marietta Tyme."

Logan wanted to sit down.

He needed to sit down.

He wanted to give in to the need to ram his fist down that arrogant detective's throat, then find a way to accept what he was being told.

Instead, he stood silent and still and just stared back at both men.

He wanted to convince himself this was just another nightmare, that somehow he'd manage to slip back into sleep and find himself once again enmeshed in the tortured dreams he found there.

"The Slasher?" His voice was even but now harsh with fury. He could hear it, and he knew the two men watching him warily now heard it as well. "There's no way my DNA was there, Archer." But mistakes like that weren't made. If Archer was there, and he wasn't denying it, then there was no mistake.

"You're going to have to come in with us, Mr. Callahan," the detective repeated. "Let's not make this difficult."

"Was it the fucking Slasher, Archer?" he snarled back at the man he liked to call "friend."

"Same MO, same type blade." Archer nodded. "We found your fingerprints at her apartment as well as a leather jacket you're known to wear, also with your prints." Archer swallowed, glanced away for a second before his gaze returned. "Several feet from her body we found a piece of torn denim, there was enough perspiration to run DNA. It was unmistakable, Logan. It was yours. As were the prints on the glove we found."

Logan's teeth were going to crack, he was clenching them so hard.

"I left the jacket there last month." He breathed out roughly as he met Archer's gaze. "It was the last time I saw her. It was the only time I was at her house."

But she had called a few times. Laughing, flirty, inviting.

He'd ignored the invitation and hadn't returned for his jacket.

And now she was gone.

"I need an alibi, Logan," Archer said again.

"He doesn't have an alibi, Sheriff," the detective bit out with icy rage.

Logan let a harsh, mocking sneer curve his lips as he watched the sheriff. "Because myself and my cousins haven't been targeted to be framed again, right?"

Archer sighed wearily. "One of her neighbors became worried when they hadn't seen her in the past four days. He called her employer, found out she hadn't been to work, then reported it to Missing Persons. The report came in to Detective Staton yesterday morning. He was on his way down here to question you when Tim Robbins called. He owns that little place on Wiley Creek? He reported a naked female who appeared dead at the creek's bank about a mile from the main entrance to his place. I sent my deputy, John Caine, out to check on it."

Logan nodded slowly, fighting the truth of what he

was hearing as Archer continued. "Staton and I drove straight out there as soon as he contacted me, and the detective confirmed her identity. But Caine had already found her ID. We came straight here from the crime lab, Logan." Archer shook his head. "It was bad. The coroner puts her death between three thirty and five Sunday morning, and her killer put her through hell first."

Between three thirty and five Sunday morning. Yeah, Logan had an alibi, but he doubted very seriously Ms. O'Brien would stick her neck out for him. No one else on the fucking street was willing to do it.

"Logan, you have to give me something," Archer demanded. "Something to at least give me some room to maneuver. If I don't arrest you on this, then the Barons, the mayor, and the city council will have my ass. Give me a fucking alibi, man."

The Barons. John Corbin, Marshal Roberts, and Logan's grandfather Saul Rafferty. The city hall was made up of their puppets, and no doubt the mayor may not have given in to the pressure to target the Callahans yet, but Logan had faith he wouldn't hold out much longer.

"Who is your alibi, Logan?" Archer was clearly running out of patience.

"He obviously doesn't have shit, Sheriff," the detective sneered. "Or he would have given it. And any alibi he could have would only be a suspect in the crime." He pulled the cuffs free from the back of his jeans. "Now, how are we going to do this?"

Logan had parted his lips to order the sheriff to go straight to hell when a determined, clearly imperious knock sounded at the back door.

He knew who it was. He would know the attitude behind that summons anywhere in the world.

His guts tightened in the knowledge that she was going to be drawn into this.

That the one person in his life whom he'd managed to protect from his own personal hell, would now be thrown smack in the middle of it.

It didn't matter if she lied or if she told the truth, she would be drawn into it.

She would become a part of his nightmare, and there was no way he could keep her out of it.

The knock came again.

Logan stared back at the sheriff coldly. He wasn't about to open that door and invite Skye into the confrontation beginning to heat up between him and a detective Logan couldn't even blame for his arrogance.

Unfortunately, Archer wasn't nearly as stubborn. Before Logan could stop him the sheriff stepped to the door and jerked it open.

The first thing Logan heard was a hard, furious puppy snarl.

What started it, Skye's surprise or the puppy's sense of the tension, Logan wasn't certain.

A second later the puppy had nearly managed to jump from Skye's arms. Archer jumped to catch the puppy, dragged her against his chest, then gave a surprised yelp as two tiny canine teeth raked his neck before he could shove the bundle of fur back to Skye.

The dog didn't want Skye. A puppyish, furious bark emitted from her immature throat, a furious part wiggle, mostly jump, and she was out of Archer's arms.

A tiny little bundle of apricot fur and too-delicate bones was heading for the floor.

Logan jumped to catch her, reaching out for her and managing to catch the still-snarling little heathen before she managed to bounce to the floor.

And did she wiggle around wanting to be petted? As Logan set her on the floor, hoping Skye would just leave, he found out fast that being petted or helped, unless by him, wasn't on the pup's agenda.

Logan stared down at his shoe as the pup plopped next to him, laid her little snout on the toe of his sneaker, and stared back at the world, utterly content, if a bit drowsy.

The first pup he'd owned had been calm and laid-back. This one was anything but.

"You are going to have to do something about her." An imperious feminine finger pointed to the dog as Skye stood at the doorway, clearly displeased.

"Really?" Logan's brow arched mockingly. "I'll get right on that. You can run on home now."

He wanted her out of here; he did not want her involved in this.

"Oh, can I?" Delicate fingers spread out on her hips as one cocked and a tiny fragile foot pointed out confrontationally. "Well, that just sucks for you, Callahan, because you owe me. That little monster has made my life hell."

"I didn't tell you to take her out of here." For the briefest second, Logan almost forgot about the detective determined to take him out in handcuffs.

"The hell you didn't," she argued fiercely. "That's exactly what you told me."

"So I'm an asshole," he reminded her, keeping his voice cold. "Now, can you come back later, I'm a little busy here."

"She has not allowed me to sleep since I took her Saturday night. She destroyed a new pair of designer jeans, a silk blouse, and nearly gnawed the leg of my antique coffee table in half. I must have been insane. She has tried to destroy everything in my home in her attempt to get to you. What do you do? Bewitch females? I will never, ever make such a decision again at three in the morning unless there's a gun to my head."

Skye was incensed. Until Logan looked into her eyes and saw, rather than anger, a cool, determined purpose.

As though somehow, she knew exactly what was going on.

Logan bent, picked the puppy up by her scruff, and, holding her back from him, stared into the dark brown eyes as the apricot pup hung from his grip.

Who would have figured? He'd ignored the animal for a week, other than providing food and water. Now she was the key to proving that once again, he hadn't killed anyone. Because Skye had just informed both of them that she had been with him, the night, the hour, he needed an alibi for.

Wiggling in his grasp, the little mutt stared back at him with eyes he could have sworn were almost wise and a canine smile of bliss.

Shaking his head at the irony of it, Logan set the animal back on the floor, unsurprised when she flopped on her belly at his feet and laid her wrinkled little face on the toe of his sneaker.

"Sheriff Tobias, Detective Staton, meet Skye O'Brien," Logan introduced them as he met Archer's gaze intently before glancing back at Skye.

"Nice to meet you." She blew away the introduction before turning back to Logan, an expression of frustrated feminine fury creasing her brow, but it sure as hell wasn't filling her eyes. "Look, she wants you; not me. Now, you can take her and love her or you can watch her die of a broken heart on your back porch. Your choice. Five days of this is more than enough for me."

"Five days ago at three in the morning?" Archer's tone was harder now. "Was this Saturday night, Ms. O'Brien?"

"Drop it—"

"Yes, it was; why?"

Skye crossed her arms over her breasts and glared back at Logan.

Her gaze flicked back to the puppy as she lay at his feet, the cute little face relaxed in bliss as she watched everyone with drowsy unconcern now that she lay where she wanted to be.

"Ms. O'Brien, could you and Mr. Callahan possibly discuss the pup later?" Impatience could be heard in the detective's voice as he glanced at her, his gaze definitely irritated.

Irritation seemed to be the normal attitude when dealing with Logan Callahan.

She could definitely understand it.

"Or you could tell me what you meant by being here at three in the morning five days ago," the sheriff ordered.

He expected her to lie; she could see it in his face. If she were going to lie, then she shouldn't have run here the second her contact had informed her of what was going on.

Skye cleared her throat, as though comfortable, looking between the two men. "What did you do, turn me in for trespassing?" She doubted it. "Hell, Callahan, you didn't seem the vindictive type to me."

"Go home, Skye," Logan snapped, and she could see the anger beginning to burn in his gaze.

Now wasn't it just too bad that he was getting all angry with her?

Archer's lips quirked. "I promise I'll stop him short of vindictiveness. Now, if you would just tell us where Logan was about three o'clock Saturday morning, then we could just leave the two of you alone."

"Like hell," the other man murmured.

She pressed her lips together in irritation.

"Specific times, if you don't mind," the detective stated then, causing Logan to shoot him a warning look.

One the detective ignored.

Skye wanted to roll her eyes, but the look on the sheriff's face wasn't exactly inviting.

"Times." Cocking a hip, she glared back at Logan before turning to the sheriff again. "I left my house at two o'clock Saturday morning and slipped around Mr. Callahan's, then into his side yard, hoping the puppy wouldn't bark at me like she usually did when I *trespassed*." She pretended to glare at Logan. "I don't know what time I made it to the back porch, but I was there, playing with the puppy, when He-Man here jerked me into the house about three thirty. We had coffee, sniped at each other a few minutes, long enough to learn he doesn't like puppies or babies. He does kiss like a pirate though, I was able to re-affirm that." Archer seemed to almost choke. "Daylight was just coming over the mountains when I left for my house." She glared at the puppy then. "With the Tasmanian Devil there."

The puppy yawned before blinking back at Skye innocently from the toe of Logan's sneaker.

The sheriff let out a sigh that sounded amazingly relieved as Logan, arrogant male that he was, simply glared at her as though she had just committed a crime.

"I so can't believe you turned me in to the sheriff," she muttered, shooting him another one of those mocking glares. "That was such a sissy move, Callahan."

His brow arched instantly as his eyes gleamed with a moment's amusement. "Sissy?"

"A man does not call the sheriff over piddling trespassing episodes," she accused Logan in irritation. "Besides." She turned to the sheriff. "It was a humanitarian act. He was letting his puppy lie under the patio and cry all night." She pointed to the little hellion. "If he continues to be a crybaby over a little trespassing, then I may press charges for animal cruelty."

Logan's eyes narrowed warningly as the sheriff seemed to have a scratch in his throat that caused him to cover his mouth to cough. The detective just looked even more pissed than he did when she arrived.

And she had no doubt he was. She knew exactly what was going on. Her own contact, the only person in the county who was aware of her background, had just gotten off the phone with her as Archer and the detective showed up.

"This has nothing to do with trespassing," Logan finally assured her with icy disdain. "I needed an alibi."

She saw it then. That glimmer of some emotion in his gaze that she hadn't been able to truly decipher until now.

And it was sorrow.

"An alibi?" She frowned among the three men as though completely in the dark. But she knew his sorrow. "What sort of an alibi?"

"A friend was killed this morning," Logan stated, his expression tightening as the grief in his gaze darkened the green further. "She was murdered."

Skye blinked back at him. "And they believe you did it after this town's history of attempting to frame you?" she asked incredulously before turning to the sheriff, then the detective. "Are you insane? Have you heard of lawsuits? Do you know he could sue the entire county for such harassment after the past he and his cousins have with this place? Archer, I'm completely disappointed in you."

"She's lived here six months and already knows our entire history," Logan growled to the sheriff then. "This town is like a fucking information sieve. They can't keep shit to themselves."

"That's any town, small or otherwise, in any part of the world," she informed him as she turned back to the sheriff confrontationally. "Rumor has it you're his friend, Sheriff. Shame on you for coming here accusing him."

"I wasn't accusing him, ma'am. I was the one trying to save his ass." Archer frowned at her before glancing at Logan once again. "I just needed to know where he was. That's all."

There was obviously more to it.

She knew there was.

The tension in the room was enough that even the puppy lifted her head with a bemused expression.

"Well, now you know," Skye informed Archer with blatant hostility.

"I'm taking the word of a woman who obviously has a sexual interest in the suspect," the detective stated coldly.

"Oh, but I assure you, you will take my word for it." Skye dropped any pretense whatsoever of being the innocent, offended neighbor.

She was about to completely blow her cover, and likely piss Logan off for the next decade.

But she was tired of this particular little game.

She'd spent nine years training and serving as a highly regarded undercover agent for the Federal Bureau of Investigation. These three men might be completely unaware of her background, but that didn't mean she didn't know how to use it.

Detective Staton sneered back at her. "I don't know who the hell you think you are, Ms. O'Brien, but I don't have to take your word for jack shit." He gripped the butt of his weapon at his side as he turned to Logan. "Let's go, Callahan."

"Now hold on, Staton," the sheriff injected.

"No, Sheriff, you hold on," the detective snapped furiously. "This has been a comedy of errors since we walked through this damned door. A woman is dead, her body found in your county, naked, tortured, raped, and her goddamned throat sliced. I'd be a fool to take her word for anything." His finger stabbed in Skye's direction insultingly.

Her brow arched. "I suggest you contact your local FBI office, Detective Staton. While you're doing that, I'll make a call to the Director of the FBI in DC, then I'll contact his wife, Lena, who considers me more or less a part of the family. I'll even shed a few tears when I tell her how rude you're being to me. Tell me, how do you think that's going to go over?"

Logan stared at her, careful to keep his expression completely blank, to show no outward emotion. Not anger, not suspicion, and certainly not the betrayal crawling up his back like invisible fingers of savage fury.

He could feel it burning in his gut, racing through his senses, and for one insanely violent moment he was ready to put his fist through the wall.

He should have just told Archer about the phone call to Saul Rafferty. Hell, he wished he had just told Archer and that bastard detective about the inside video footage, time-stamped and including audio.

He could have gotten rid of the half-hour portion that showed him with his head and his fingers buried between the little betrayer's legs. He could have told Archer why it was deleted and then refused to open the back door when she came knocking.

"You need to leave now." He opened the door politely. "Good-bye, Ms. O'Brien. And don't worry about the pup; I'll take care of it myself from now on."

Skye stared back at him silently now, all too aware of what she had just revealed and exactly how quickly the knowledge would spread through town once each authority had filled out his paperwork.

She was smart enough to know, though, that very, very soon she was going to have to tell Logan anyway. Tell him that as a matter of fact she had been with the Federal Bureau of Investigation since she was twenty-two years old.

But she didn't have to tell him the whole story right now. Not yet. Her heart might not survive the rejection from the man who was slowly stealing her heart. ·

"Leave now." His voice lowered, throbbing with warning, with danger.

"I'm sorry." She finally found her voice as she fought the sudden realization of what her silence may have cost her. "I was going to tell you—"

"Now."

She had to forcibly still the trembling of her lips and fight back the sudden fear.

The fear that she might have lost him before she ever had him.

CHAPTER EIGHT

Slamming back into the house, Skye jerked the cell phone from the case at her hip and quickly hit a secured number.

"Damn. I think Detective Staton taught me some new cuss words," her contact commented, his tone so low she could barely hear him.

"No doubt," she murmured. "Meet me somewhere. I want to see the crime scene."

Silence met the demand.

"Don't even bother coming up with excuses. I don't have a lot of time before Staton has the director on my ass and I need to get this done."

"You don't want this," he denied quietly. "Let it go, Skye. You have enough nightmares."

Unfortunately, they'd covered each other's asses enough that he would be well aware of her past, her loss, and her nightmares.

"I know where it is. I'll go alone."

She was gathering up her weapons, latex gloves, paper covers for her boots, and the bag she carried her evidence kit in.

"There's nothing there, dammit," he hissed. "Don't you think I would have fucking found it? Just like I found the denim and the glove."

"And did you tell anyone it was planted?" she snorted.

"Why do you think Archer was able to bargain for a chance to question Logan rather than being ordered to arrest him outright?" she was questioned fiercely. "For God's sake, Skye, you can't do this. You're not ready for it."

The sharp, hard facsimile of a laugh she emitted held a bitter vein of pain and anger. "Don't bet on it. I have my gear and I'm rolling. You can meet me out there and give me validation if needed, or I can keep doing this myself. I've been on my own before. Haven't I?"

It was a reminder.

Yes, she had been on her own, and she'd nearly paid dearly for it because the partner she'd had at the time had refused to listen to her.

Thankfully, this agent hadn't been her partner at the time.

"Fuck," he cursed brutally.

"I'll meet you at the exit to the property. I want all the crime scene photos and the evidence log. And I know you can get it for me," she informed him. "I've always covered your back when you've needed me, John. Even when neither of us knew you needed me. Are you going to leave me out in the cold?"

He wouldn't.

She disconnected the call before grabbing the laptop case she'd packed everything into and moving quickly from the house.

She rarely drove the older model sedan she'd requisitioned on her last assignment. The agency had given her the use of it as long as she kept the cover, and until the final appeal was made in that conviction, she'd be able to use the cover. She hadn't had to testify, which ensured the background created for her remained unsullied.

Driving from town, she resisted the urge to allow free the pain tightening her stomach. It wouldn't be the first time someone she cared for had walked away from her. In her line of work, either she walked away, or they did.

She'd never cried before. The drive gave her a chance to think. A chance to figure out what she was going to do where Logan, the Callahans, and her reason for being in Corbin County were concerned.

At the moment, Corbin County was an interesting little place, not just to Skye but to the FBI in general.

Twelve years before, the bureau had been called to the county to profile and investigate the deaths by the Sweetrock Slasher—a rapist that kidnapped his victims, tied a perfect red bow around their would-be lovers' pillows, and several days later left his victims' naked bodies in areas the Callahan cousins were known to frequent.

It had been evident, even at the time, to the profiler that someone was trying to frame the Callahan cousins.

The profiler guessed there were two or more killers

from small differences in a few of the ribbons tied around the pillows and the angles of the knives into the bodies. But, and this had never been told to local authorities, the profilers had never believed the Slasher was one or all of the Callahans. The bureau had kept that information as "eyes only." Just as they had kept the reasons for their profile under the same directive.

The fact that there was a conspiracy to frame three young men had concerned the FBI, just as the evidence they'd uncovered of a political conspiracy had concerned them.

Evidence they had never been able to substantiate until the past year.

The fact that the killings had stopped in Corbin County after the Callahans went to the military had only strengthened that profile.

Now the Slasher had struck again. Skye was expecting a call anytime. Once the agents assigned to the investigation in Corbin County on other matters learned she had given Logan his alibi, hell, that she was in town, period, they would call the director and have her pulled from the area immediately

Thankfully, "medical leave" would go a long way to getting her a little leeway, but not much. The director could, and she knew he would, pull her out, though. That leeway would only give her a few days if she were very lucky.

And God help her when her foster father, the governor of Colorado, learned what she was doing. He would hit the roof and probably come to Corbin County to pull her out himself.

The drive to the turn-off to the area Marietta Tyme's body had been dumped was perhaps thirty minutes from town, and only a matter of miles from Crowe Mountain.

Whoever was committing these crimes definitely had a hard-on for the Callahans.

John was waiting for her.

Leaning against the deputy SUV, a glare on his face, the dunn-colored cowboy hat pulled low over his eyes, giving him a dark, dangerous look.

"I don't like this," he told her as she slid into the passenger seat of the SUV after parking and locking her own car. "Fucking Archer will have my head for this. You know that, right?"

"I know you're going to piss me off if you keep protesting," she told him in exasperation. "Give it up, John. I'm here. This is the first solid lead we've had in years. The girl who went missing last year was never found, even though proof that Lowry had her was found in his basement. Come on, John. There has to be something, somewhere, that was missed."

"Nothing was missed." His fist suddenly slammed into the dash of the SUV he drove with violent precision.

Skye didn't bother to flinch, though she rocked with the force of the SUV slamming to a stop as he turned in his seat to glare at her.

"I processed the motherfucking scene myself," he snarled, his expression twisting in lines of fury. "The son of a bitch disinfected her, Skye. Inside and fucking out. Do you get that? Everything was disinfected but that damned glove and piece of denim we found."

"And that didn't trip anyone's radar but yours?" she asked, shocked.

"Archer's." Grabbing his hat from his head, he tossed it to the dash before raking his fingers through his hair viciously. "Definitely the agent in charge. But Staton was chomping at the bit. I've never seen a man so determined to crucify a man with such a history of attempted framings behind him. He was a madman."

"Did anyone check into his background?" she asked as he slammed the vehicle back into drive and threw gravel and dirt as he hit the gas.

"We have a background report on him due in by the end of the day," he growled, glancing at her as he drove along the bank of the swift-running creek. "But if we were going on evidence alone, without your alibi, he'd be in handcuffs and behind bars."

Skye breathed in roughly.

"Everything is clean. The tarp, the sand around the body. There were no tire tracks, no prints, no blood. The scene was so damned clean it sent a chill up my spine. The body was so clean—"

He didn't go on.

"Everything but the denim and the glove," she finished.

"Yeah, that was about it." He brought the SUV to a smoother stop several yards from the crime-scene tape that stretched from tree to tree in a half-acre radius.

He didn't say another word as he handed her the file he'd brought along. It would hold pictures, a complete computer-generated 3D layout of the scene, as well as satellite images if possible.

Moving from the SUV, she quickly covered her shoes, pulled on gloves, but didn't bother to pull the evidence kit from the case.

She knew John. If there was any evidence out there, then it was left after he'd vacated the scene.

She was aware of him hanging back as she stepped behind the tape and moved to the marker still labeled as the location of the body.

Pulling the picture free as she bent her knees and rested on her haunches, Skye stared at the faint outline of a body in the sand.

Then she laid the picture over it and dropped her head. To hide her tears. To hide the sudden jerk of a sob that tore through her and sliced through her soul.

It wasn't Marietta Tyme she saw. It was the pictures she'd managed to pull of Amy's death. The sight of her foster sister sprawled out on the forest floor, her eyes wide and unfocused, the evidence of her pain forever frozen in the mask of death she'd carried.

"I'm sorry," she suddenly whispered as she covered her lips with her hand. "I'm so sorry."

Whether she was talking to Marietta or Amy, she still wasn't certain.

What she knew was that this crime scene, other than the location, had been nearly identical to the details of her sisters.

"How long did she lay out here?" she asked the other agent.

"Not long, Skye," he promised her. "Overnight, I imagine. No one saw anything though, so I can't say for sure. There are too many variables we won't know until her killer is found."

He moved away again and Skye realized her face was damp once again with her tears.

God, this made twice. Her emotions were so ragged right now she had no idea how to repair them once again.

"Six dead twelve years before. One missing and presumed dead six weeks ago. Cami Flannigan attacked twice and nearly killed both times," she murmured.

"Multiple murderers controlled by one puppet master," John finished.

"All bows tied within acceptable parameters of the one before it. All bodies disinfected before being dumped. Twelve years ago, the rapes were committed in the forest, the missing girl and now Marietta, each without a primary crime scene. All fourteen, linked to the Callahan men because they slept with them or were presumed to have slept with them."

"To drive them out of town?" John mused. "The men, that is."

She shook her head. "That's how it appears, isn't it?"

"Making it immediately suspect," he grunted.

"There's something deeper going on here," she murmured.

"Sheriff Tobias has been investigating it since Logan Callahan and his cousins returned to town," John told her. "I'd just been hired as deputy when they showed up. Days before their arrival, their uncle was killed in the weirdest damned tractor accident that a country boy could imagine. It's been downhill for them from there."

She spread out several more of the pictures, each taken from various directions around the victim's body.

"He enjoyed what he was doing," she said softly as she noted the slicing marks in Marietta's pale flesh. "He cut her throat last."

"Coroner believes she was brain dead at that point," John stated. "The report came in just before you called me."

Turning her head, she glanced back at him before returning her gaze to the pictures once again.

This woman had shared the same fate as Amy. She demanded justice in the same way.

"Suspects besides Logan?" she asked.

"You're kidding, right?" he grunted.

Yeah. Right. No one wanted to look past Logan.

"Who knows I'm here now?" She glanced back at him and saw the mockery on his face. "Everyone. Staton was calling the director in DC as I left. I think I even heard the director scream in rage. Sounded like your name, too."

No doubt it was.

Flipping through the file, Skye couldn't help but grin as she reached the back copy. A full copy of all the information inside.

Yeah, John knew she would take it. That didn't mean she could let him see her do it.

Sliding the file beneath her t-shirt, she picked the pictures from the sand, ensured no grains remained, then returned them to the folder.

She had to quickly wipe the tears from her face.

Men in the Bureau, as well as other agencies, still had problems with their feminine counterparts shedding tears for the dead or dying.

They saw it as weakness rather than the pain of the knowledge of what the victims had suffered.

Few female agents allowed themselves to cry. Few male agents acknowledged their need to do it occasionally.

The tears would come again, though, Skye was running on borrowed time there and she knew it.

She'd just lost a man she hadn't meant to care for. She'd seen it in his eyes. Seen it in his expression.

If he could, he'd ensure she never became a part of his life.

Or a part of his heart.

CHAPTER NINE

Crossing the street to the town square, on foot, after parking the car back at the house more than an hour earlier, Skye headed to the tavern at the far end of the street.

Thankfully, "medical leave" would go a long way. The director couldn't force her into the operation. At least, not yet.

The Sweetrock Tavern was the only bar in town—or in Corbin County for that matter—with a liquor license. To say that the Barons, the three largest ranch owners, ran the county and the town was an understatement.

The owner of the Sweetrock Tavern, Amos "Chando" Wright, was John Corbin's half brother's son. When Chando's mother had died in childbirth with his father working as the ranch manager, Regina Corbin had taken the infant in and raised him herself. As Chando had matured, a rift had seemed to grow between them, though no one seemed to know why.

Corbin, along with Saul Rafferty and Marshal Roberts, retained a loyalty to Chando, though, that their grandsons had never known. Using one loophole after another, they kept any other applications for a liquor license from being approved.

Skye knew it was a situation that was currently being looked into by the FBI under their white-collar crime division.

Not that Chando seemed to be involved in the conspiracy, but he might get caught in the cross fire if it was proven the Barons were indeed involved.

That wasn't her investigation, though. White-collar crime wasn't her forte.

Throwing a cheery wave to Chando where he was playing bartender for the afternoon shift, Skye made her way to the back of the bar, where she and her two friends met for lunch once a week.

"You're running late again, Skye." Anna Corbin's smile was as quiet as it had ever been. Skye, Anna, and Amy had attended Brighton Preparatory School, an exclusive boarding school in Mensa, California, together. Anna had been painfully shy, but the confidence Skye had helped to build inside the girl since then had only strengthened.

The other, Skye had only met after moving to Sweetrock. Several years older than Anna, Amelia Sorenson was the county attorney's daughter and personal assistant. She was also the former best friend of Cami Flannigan, Rafer Callahan's fiancée.

Amelia was even quieter than Anna, always watchful and wary, and always paying close attention to anything Anna said.

"I woke late," Skye apologized as she slid in beside Anna, giving her an unobstructed view of Amelia's face. The other girl didn't seem nearly as prone to shush Anna if she thought Skye was watching. Besides, that put Skye's back against the wall, where she much preferred it.

The tavern was fairly empty at two that afternoon, with the lunch crowd having just returned to work. There were a few of the Corbin cowboys at the bar, but they were far enough away and Anna and Amelia met with Skye often enough that the cowboys no longer felt the need to sit directly behind them.

"Now that you're here, you can tell us exactly what the hell you were doing at Logan Callahan's the night that poor girl was being kidnapped," Anna whispered, her voice barely carrying the distance between them.

"Anna, you agreed not to discuss him," Amelia reminded her as she dipped her head toward her menu.

"So I lied." Anna rolled her eyes expressively as she shot the other girl a grin, causing Skye to turn her head to Amelia with a smile.

"She worries worse than Granddad," Anna said quietly as Amelia shook her head slowly. "He tried to make me stay home today. So did Amelia." She nodded to the other girl.

Skye lifted her gaze to watch Amelia under the cover of her lashes. She looked distinctly uncomfortable with the conversation.

"I don't want you hurt, Anna," Amelia told her, her

voice as low as the other girl's. "And whoever killed Marietta Tyme won't stop there. It never has."

Skye watched Amelia closely. "You're talking about the Slasher? This is a copycat, right?" Skye highly doubted it, but if Amelia had information, then she would never give it to Skye if she appeared to know too much.

"Who knows who the hell or what the hell it is." Amelia wiped her hands over her face wearily. "I just prefer, if possible, that should he decide to pick on nosy women, then he doesn't start with her." She frowned over at Anna.

"You never did answer the question," Anna reminded Skye as she ignored Amelia's concerns. "Why were you at that sexy Callahan's house at three in the morning?"

"Logan's grandfather dropped a puppy off at his house several weeks ago and he can't get rid of her." Skye sighed. "He's given the dog away to anyone who would take her, only to have them bring the wailing little baby back to him. He keeps her on the side patio. We were fighting over the fact that I can't sleep because of the crying." Skye was careful to make certain there wasn't even a hint of a friendship between her and Logan. "When he refused to take care of her, I took her home with me, only to learn why he gets her back every time." Skye pretended to shudder in horror before relating the destruction the baby had caused.

"That sounds like Uncle Saul," Anna said.

She glanced at Amelia before playing with the edge of the menu uncomfortably. "Aunt Tandy hasn't been herself lately," she sighed. "She has periods where she's really ill, lately. I heard Granddad talking to him about the pup. He said Logan caught him?"

Skye grimaced. "Yeah, that one was a battle. Those two acted like snarling lions that night."

"They're too much alike," Anna sighed. "Gran'pa always says that."

"Funny, he says a lot, Anna, yet he refuses to have anything to do with his own grandson," Skye pointed out.

"It doesn't confuse you any more than it does me, Skye." Anna sat back and ran her finger along the edge of the menu as she frowned down at it for long seconds. "I've never understood why." She finally lifted her gaze, staring back at Skye sadly. "There's such a sense of pain and anger when they discuss the Callahans. But none of them will even try to fix what they broke."

"You need to let this go, Anna," Amelia said with an expression that suggested it wasn't the first time she'd given the warning.

"Like you've let things with Cami go?" The sympathy and understanding in Anna's tone went far beyond her years.

"Let it go, Anna." Weariness seemed to fill Amelia's tone. "I don't want to argue with you here."

What the hell was going on?

Skye sat back in her seat and watched the two, rather like she'd watched Saul Rafferty and Logan fighting the week before.

Anna almost glared at her before a frown snapped between her brows. "Speaking of Cami, where is she anyway?" she questioned Amelia.

"She and Rafer left." Amelia shrugged as the waitress brought their drinks and sandwiches. "I've not seen her since the night Lowry Berry was killed trying to rape her."

Amelia lowered her gaze to the sandwich, the look on her face making Skye wonder if perhaps she had tried to contact the friend she had once been so close to.

She was preparing to question Amelia about the rumored friendship when she felt a distinct little vibration against her hip from her cell phone.

"Just a second," she told her friends with an apologetic smile. "I need to go to the ladies room."

Escaping quickly, she pushed into the restroom, pulled the phone free, and activated the app her foster brother had made for the security system they had installed in the rental. Her lips thinned, eyes narrowing at the sight that appeared on the screen of her phone. She had expected it, but she would be damned if she had been expecting who it was.

Smothering a curse, she peeked out of the stall and made certain no one else was in the bathroom before moving to the wide window on the other side of the room. Looking out carefully, she gave her head a little shake before leaving the ladies room, turning in the opposite direction of the dining area and heading to the back office.

She'd shared drinks with Chondo there one night after the bar closed. She knew there was a door in his office that wasn't easily seen from the alley, or the road.

Considering who was currently going through her

home, she knew for a fact someone would be watching for her.

Slipping out the door and into the narrow, enclosed patio of sorts, Skye moved quickly to the door of the small supply building next to it.

The door was unlocked. Chondo used it often through the day and didn't bother locking it until closing time. It was filled with boxes of liquor, restaurant supplies, and old equipment, making it easy to slip through without anyone outside catching sight of her.

It was the perfect escape buffer. The loading bay in the back opened to a narrow alley and from there she was able to use the back alleys to sneak home.

One of the first things she'd done when scoping out the town was to make note of any and all possible escape routes from each building that she knew she would be entering. She had used them several times, just to become familiar with them and ensure she had the best chance possible of escaping if she had to.

If she had to. There was always a small chance she would have to considering the plan she had come up with after meeting Logan Callahan. She just hadn't imagined it would take her six months to convince him to kiss her.

And after he had—

She wasn't going to think about that, not now. Her chances of ending up in his bed were about nil at the moment.

She just might end up shooting him first.

That was, after she convinced him to allow her to help catch a killer.

And considering her talents, she knew he could use the help she could provide. She could do what he or his cousins couldn't.

Get information.

Skye worked better at gathering intel. She could draw people to her, make them trust her, and manage to draw details and gossip around her like a magnet.

Just as she had while in boarding school.

The benefits of being raised by a state representative whose hunger for the governorship and the death of one daughter ensured his foster daughter attended those private schools.

Not just one, but three. And surviving there had meant learning how to gain information and where and when to use it.

She hadn't attended just one private school, but three altogether. At the last one, she'd been a mentor for a new student, Anna Corbin.

One of the benefits of attending public school? It was like pre-training for any job requiring covert specialties. Skye had learned how to sneak out of a room on the fifth floor, bypass securely locked doors and security cameras, only to slip back just as stealthily as dawn was making its way over the horizon.

Her foster sister, Amy, had taught her all the tricks she could teach the young Skye as well. Then, after joining the FBI, she'd taught Skye a few more in the guise of teaching her how to escape, how to fight, and how to defend herself against every eventuality Amy could think of.

In turn, Skye had taught the too-quiet, too-shy Anna Corbin the same tricks.

Their friendship had been cemented through that year. Enough so that the information Skye had targeted the Corbin County native for, at the time, had been readily given. As well as information Skye had never imagined.

Anna had no idea Skye's foster family was then-Representative Carter Jefferson, just as no one at the schools had known.

"Daddy Carter," as Skye called him, had always been very careful about keeping their relationship hidden. To protect her, he'd always told her. To ensure she was never targeted or hurt because of him.

A part of her had always wondered if he was ashamed of her, though.

He and Momma Marla loved her, she had no doubt of it. They had doted on her even before Amy's death. But Amy had never attended private school under any name but her own. She'd never had to pretend her parents were anyone but who they were, and she'd never had to visit her family at vacations only.

Before Amy's death, vacations had always been spent on the family estate and vacations to the beach were only during Christmas break.

Using the back streets to slip home gave her plenty of time to think. Time she probably didn't need, because Skye didn't enjoy the suspicions she raised within herself whenever she remembered that past.

Because thinking of the careful secretiveness that

Carter had used in "keeping her safe" always made her think of her parents.

Their deaths.

The fact that they had died in the middle of a drug deal gone bad, and that their deaths had caused a brief investigation to focus on the Jeffersons.

And the past wasn't what she needed to focus on right now.

Right now, she needed to focus on the fact that Logan Callahan had finally gotten suspicious of her. Suspicious enough to break into her house and begin searching for things he didn't need to know existed.

Now Logan completely understood why her job description didn't mesh with the woman he had been getting to know. Editor for instruction and design manuals, his ass.

How could he have missed that she was FBI? It meant that as good as he was, Skye O'Brien might be better, which just burned him. But the woman was too smart, too intuitive, and, if he was guessing right, too damned good with electronic surveillance systems. Covert surveillance, to be exact.

So covert that Logan couldn't track down the system he knew was installed in the house she was renting from him. A system that he wouldn't have known about if he hadn't started his search of the house, and her secrets, in the basement. If he hadn't seen the door to the box unlatched and pulled it open just to make certain everything was okay.

Slipping through the house after she left for lunch

with Anna Corbin and Amelia Sorenson, Logan had learned things about Skye that all his interactions with her in the past six months hadn't even hinted at.

She loved pictures. Family pictures. Pictures of friends and who he assumed were her parents as well as her foster parents were carefully packed in boxes in the basement.

Several of the pictures had been taken out and looked at often, if the wrinkled state of the paper they were wrapped in was any indication.

There were pictures of her as a gawky teenager with Carter Jefferson and his daughter, then a new FBI recruit, Amy Jefferson.

The small album lying on the bed was filled with pictures of Amy from when she was a teenager to the year she died. All of them with Skye included, most of them showing just Amy and Skye.

The album contained cards sent to her from Amy. Letters. Enough that Logan put it away with a mental note to return the next time Skye was away to go through it. He had a feeling that album would contain more information about Skye than she was ever likely to tell him.

The pictures though—they were more than just years of Skye's life. Part of them were years of his life as well.

Not pictures of him, but pictures of a young woman he'd only known as a friend. One who had shared coffee with him, who had laughed with him. One who had died because of him.

The anger that rose inside him was slow-burning,

but once it reached critical mass, the searing pain of it tore through his heart.

She had been lying to him all along.

The secrets he'd suspected she was harboring and the ones he knew she was determined to hold back from him.

She was Carter Jefferson's foster daughter. The papers of guardianship he'd found in the album proved it.

And she was the much loved younger foster sister Amy Jefferson had once mentioned.

When Logan had first met Amy, who was three years older than he, she was like a damned goddess. Tall, her hair a sun-streaked caramel, straight and silky soft. She'd always laughed at him. She'd had nice legs, though. Toned, as soft as satin, with a pleasant strength to them that had enabled her to keep up with him when they went hiking.

She'd actually danced with him at the weekend county social she'd attended when they first met. She'd thought it was amusing how everyone watched them.

If only he'd known then why she had danced with him and why she had sought out his friendship. If he had known he would have stayed as far away from her as possible.

Realizing who he was and hearing about the Stalker, Amy hadn't told him what she was doing or who she was, and he hadn't known until after her death.

She'd lied to him just as Amy had and she hadn't given a damn how he would feel if she managed to get her ass killed.

Keeping his calm, keeping his head was nearly impossible now.

Damn her. What the fuck was he supposed to do now? How was he supposed to deal with the fact that she was evidently determined to get into his bed for one reason only?

To draw a killer to her.

Just as Amy had become his friend to do.

At the time, he'd been shocked that Carter Jefferson hadn't blamed him for Amy's death, though Logan had definitely blamed himself. Carter had even flown into Sweetrock to meet with Logan, his cousins, and their lawyer when the Barons had pushed to have the cousins jailed for Jaymi's murder.

With him, Carter had brought the file Amy had put together while investigating the murders. She'd taken what the profilers had put together and attempted to find a monster on her own.

He'd found her instead.

Logan had spent several hours, after learning about Marietta's death, on the phone contacting the other two women he had been with since returning to Colorado.

He had warned them of the danger, told them what had happened to Marietta.

They were pissed, to say the least. That and terrified. Because the news stations were already carrying the story of the rebirth of the Sweetrock Slasher.

Thankfully, for some reason, and Logan wasn't certain why, neither his nor his cousins' connection had yet been mentioned.

Remaining silent rather than discussing the problem with Crowe on the other end of the communications earbud he wore, Logan continued to follow a white heavy electrical line from the electric box where he had found it in the basement through the house.

He would lose it in one room, find it in another, tucked beneath a piece of carpet, the only sign being a frayed edge of carpet against the wall, a hint of wood shavings, no more than a speck that the sweeper had missed against another wall.

He tracked the line through every damned room of the house until he came to the small suite Skye used to sleep in.

The additional electrical line hadn't been installed by a legitimate electrician, because Logan hadn't received notice of it.

Even with his knowledge of covert surveillance and electronics, he'd been unable to pinpoint any specific area that the electrical line had powered.

But it was the memory of Amy, a friend he hadn't intended to have, a part of his past he'd believed could never return to haunt him, that was twisting maliciously through his mind.

He should have found the information while doing the background check on her. It should have been there somewhere.

Unfortunately, Rafer hadn't been able to escape Corbin County with Cami. Hell, Cami hadn't been able to escape far, because Rafer had damned near gone crazy that first week when they had sent her to the Caribbean for fun and sun.

She'd returned as white as she left, crying tears as Rafer gathered her into his arms at the private airport he'd had her flown into.

Kneeling on the floor, Logan lifted the edge of the carpet where the slightest hint of upraised threads indicated it had only been loosened from the metal strip it was attached to.

Skye was fucking good. If he hadn't helped install the new electric box himself during one of the brief furloughs he'd had, then he would have never known there had been an additional wire run to it. The job was that damned good and that well hidden.

What the hell had she been up to? And had it been her or someone else?

This job hadn't required not only time but also experience and patience. Did Skye actually possess enough of each to install this electric line? And what the fuck did it go to?

Evidently the background check Crowe had done on her hadn't gone nearly deep enough. That had been proven when her connection to Governor Jefferson hadn't been revealed.

"We have a problem here," Logan reported as he stood and moved into the spacious bathroom to see if he could track the cable farther.

There was no carpet there, he thought as he heard a puppy's excited growls at the sound of his voice on the other side of the communications device. The open receiver was the only way to keep that little mutt from howling for him.

Frowning, he scanned the floor carefully.

The ceramic tile was a bronze and sunset hue. The dark, blended colors would make it damned hard to find the cable if it ran through this room.

Bending to his hands and knees, he began running his fingers over the grout, checking it carefully. It was all well maintained, and the color matched from line to line.

Probing at the wall and the tile, he narrowed his eyes before pulling the high-powered magnifier from the back pocket of his jeans and moving to the baseboards.

"Bathroom tile has been replaced in at least one spot," he murmured to Crowe. "I can't find where it goes, where it ends, or what it's for."

"Sucks, bro," Crowe drawled. "But I'd be moving out if I were you. One of her lunch partners just got a call and now both of them are paying their bill and getting ready to leave. She's flown."

"Not possible," Logan argued quietly as he probed at the baseboard again. "No way she could have known."

Sitting back and preparing to rise to his feet, Logan suddenly came to a stop, his body stiffening in surprise.

Against the back of his head cold steel pressed into his scalp, assuring him that it was indeed possible.

"Never mind," he murmured, "I think I just found her."

Or, more to the point, she had found him.

CHAPTER TEN

With the cold barrel of the gun pressed against his head, Logan rose slowly to his feet, careful to keep his hands slightly out from his body.

"I'd take that damned thing from you, but I have a feeling you'd use it," he stated, trying to hide a smile and wondering why in hell he found this so funny.

When the weapon eased from the firm pressure against his scalp eased and Skye stepped back, he turned slowly.

Yep, she'd probably shoot him.

But he still wanted to grin.

Her expression never wavered, though. However, there was no amusement on her face, no affection in her gaze. As a matter of fact, her eyes were as flat and hard as any soldier's.

"Give me the earbud," she ordered. "Crowe and Rafer have no business in this conversation."

"Just Crowe," he murmured, wondering if she was

simply guessing where Rafer was concerned. "And I
don't know if I want to turn over my only link to help.
If you shoot me, who would know?"

An imitation of a smile that didn't even come close
to reaching her eyes curved her lips, making him a bit
wary.

"I can sincerely make you regret being here without
killing you. And how did you slip in without tripping the
house alarm?"

His brows arched. "Evidently I did trip it; you're here,
aren't you?"

She gave a quick shake of her head. "That wasn't the
house alarm. I have a separate alarm on my bedroom.
You tripped that one."

Logan removed the earbud slowly. He had a feeling
he didn't want to know the many and varied ways she
could make him regret anything.

"You might want to turn that off; it has good range,"
he offered as she held the earbud loosely. He could practically hear Crowe laughing his ass off now.

"I know."

Flipping the hidden little button at the side of the earbud, she pocketed the device, then without a word turned
and stalked from the bedroom.

Logan followed her curiously, especially when she
jerked open the double doors on the walk-in closet and
moved inside.

Standing at the entrance to the closet that could have
arguably doubled as a good-sized bedroom, he watched
as she began pulling clothes off the rod in the back of

the closet and placing them on the rods on each side of the wall.

It took a minute, but the clothes were moved out of the way and she was stepping back once again.

Turning to him, she stared at him, her gaze still flat, her expression remote, as she indicated the wall.

Moving to it, Logan surveyed it closely. Seeing nothing out of the ordinary, he then peeked into several areas that would have indicated if the wall was solid or part of it was hollowed or had something built behind it.

Checking the corner joints and telltale indents of nails in the drywall, he finally stepped back and turned to her. Clearly, she was trying to show him something. He just couldn't figure out what.

Logan stepped back, looked at her, then arched his brow in question.

Her demeanor bothered him.

The silence, the air of complete emotional distance and hardened, icy anger, assured him that the woman who had sought him out, who had been willing to tease him, had given way to another side of her. This side he didn't like much, not when it was directed at him.

It reminded him too much of fellow soldiers, of the look he sometimes saw in his own eyes—that of someone who had seen too much blood and death. Just what kind of life had Skye O'Brien lived, he wondered.

Pulling what appeared to be a television remote from her back pocket Skye pointed the device at the wall and pressed several buttons. Detecting the order used was damned impossible, but when she pressed the "SELECT" button he frowned. A slight pop and the wall that should have been, had appeared to be, nailed into the joint there separated about an inch.

Logan turned back to her, glaring. "Your rental agreement demands permission, in writing, for any construction made inside or outside the house."

The irritation surging through him didn't have a damned thing to do with her knocking down some walls. It was the fact that her secret room was a hell of a lot bigger and better than his room was.

It should have been insulting.

Instead, it was rather arousing.

His dick was hard.

She'd lied to him. Well, perhaps not lied, but she'd deceived him.

Again. Another part of her that wasn't as she'd led him to believe. Another part that she'd hidden from him and kept him in the dark with.

Damn her, his dick shouldn't be hard, not while his stomach was clenched with the fury burning through him.

He'd trusted her.

He'd let her into his life when he'd known better.

When he'd sensed the deceptions but couldn't prove them, he'd convinced himself it was the situation. It was the danger swirling around him. It was a defense mechanism to protect a heart already opening up to her.

And now she was there and all he wanted was to rip her the fuck out.

Her arms crossed over her chest as her hip cocked

with such feminine arrogance his balls tightened and the anger seemed to burn higher.

Why hadn't he acknowledged the fact that he knew, knew his instincts were so finely honed for a fucking reason?

Her brow arched mockingly then. "And as you're the silent owner and received no such request, then you of course had no idea it was here. Neither did the rental agent, the agent, or the assumed owner."

In other words, it was a complete secret to everyone, with the exceptions of her and whoever had helped her.

Turning back to the wall, Logan opened the wide panel to inspect the narrow room. About three feet of the closet, as well as perhaps three feet of the large kitchen pantry behind it, had been taken.

The wall of the six-foot-wide room held six monitors, each screen split with a different camera view.

There were twelve cameras total.

Two of those views covered the entire perimeter of the side yard that separated his house from her rental.

He turned to her slowly. "You had proof all along that I never left the house the night Marietta was taken or killed. Yet you revealed your ties to the governor instead and put yourself smack in the middle in the sights of a killer?"

The anger was like a beast, gnawing at his soul. It was doing nothing to soften the hard-on filling his jeans, though and for a moment, he almost hated her for that.

There was nothing arousing about the fact that she had deliberately placed herself in danger. There was nothing that should have cooled his desperation to have her faster.

"The detective pissed me off," she told Logan with a shrug, her tone icy cold.

That tone, the lack of emotion on her face and in her eyes, the emotional and physical distance between them, was beginning to do more than irritate him.

"You're lying to me."

She laughed then, a sound devoid of humor.

"I wouldn't bother lying to you, Logan. I had no reason to. You never suspected I was anyone other than a renter, and an irritating one at that."

That wasn't necessarily true. At least not the irritating part.

"Why?" he asked, turning to her fully as anger surged as hot, as furious, as the arousal tearing through him. "Why are you here, Skye? A governor's daughter, real or fostered, doesn't just up and move to some two-bit county in the mountains of Colorado."

"Medical leave." Her brow arched, her lips thinning as a spark of anger began to gleam in her eyes then.

"Medical leave?" He turned to the room, then back to her. "Don't fucking play with me. Trust me, I won't tolerate it."

"Let's say I'm here because of a hobby then." The curve of her lips was strained, tight. "And I'm paranoid."

He shook his head slowly. "No, this is no hobby. You're here because of me. To prove I killed those girls. To prove I killed Amy."

"Wrong." The anger wasn't just a glimmer in her eyes

anymore. It was burning bright and strong between one heartbeat and the next.

It flushed her face, made those damn dark eyes of hers spark.

"Don't you fucking lie to me!" he yelled at her.

He was the laidback cousin.

He was the one who never became pissed off to the point that he raised his voice.

But this was Skye. And she was lying to him.

He wouldn't have it from her.

Not now.

Not after the deliberate challenge she had thrown out to a killer.

Not after deceiving him with the clear intent of, one way or the other, putting more blood on his hands.

"I never believed you were guilty of anything but being a prick and an asshole when the mood suited you," she snapped back.

Moving to her, his gaze holding hers, the challenge gleaming in them only intensifying, he backed her into the bare wall next to the hidden room. He placed both hands on either side of her head, and leaned in close, until he was nearly nose to nose with her.

"You're here because of Amy," he bit out, his body so tight he wondered if, for the first time in his life, he was going to snap. "You're here to find her killer. You thought *I* was her killer."

She, like everyone else, believed he had killed Amy Jefferson and the other girls who had died that summer.

"Wrong." Straight, pretty teeth snapped together furiously. "Yes, I'm here to find a killer. But I never, for even a second, believed you were that killer. I didn't believe it any more than Amy did."

Tearing himself away from her, he turned, and cracked his fist into the wall.

Son of a bitch. At this rate, he was going to end up breaking his hand. However, a broken hand would be preferable to what he was feeling now.

Emotions that made no sense.

Feelings that were tearing through him, tightening his stomach and ripping through his guts with enough force to lay his soul bare.

Fists clenched, he turned back to her slowly and just stared at her.

Wariness filled her gaze, but there was no fear.

She had no reason to fear him. She had no reason to be wary of him either.

He wondered if she knew he would give his life for her? That he would die to ensure she never suffered so much as a day in her life?

Because he loved her.

He stiffened. That knowledge was like a spike of agony tearing through his guts.

It ripped through his system and jerked aside the veil of deception he'd been practicing on himself as well as her.

"She said once that you were going to be her best friend," Skye whispered now, and Logan hated the words falling from her lips. "The night before she disappeared, she was crying, Logan, because she was certain whoever was trying to frame you was going to succeed."

"Shut it up!" His hand sliced through the air. "Pack

your shit. You voided your rental agreement and you're being evicted. I won't have you here." His voice rose again, though not as loud this time. "Do you fucking hear me, Skye? Listen to me well or I'll have you tied, gagged, and locked in a room so fucking secure I never have to worry about so much as a motherfucking scratch marring your flesh, let alone a rapist's knife tearing into your goddamned flesh."

Rage, powered by a fear for her life that nearly weakened his knees, and for one, impossible moment, stole all hope of control.

Before he knew it, he had crossed to her again.

Logan's hands moved, his fingers wrapping around her upper arms, tightening just enough to ensure she didn't escape, before pulling her to him.

The hunger was impossible to deny.

He'd want her on his deathbed. He'd ache for her, crave her touch, and crave touching her no matter where they were or what was going on between them.

He would ache for her, hunger for her, he would die for her no matter the lies she told, or what she might or might not suspect him of.

"Don't lie to me, Skye," he snarled.

He wouldn't have it from her. Not now. Not after the deliberate challenge she had also thrown out to a killer.

"I never believed you were guilty of anything but being a prick and an asshole when the mood suited you," she snapped back.

As he moved slowly to her, his gaze held hers, the challenge gleaming in it only intensifying as he backed her into the bare wall next to the hidden room and placed both hands on each side of her head, flat against the dry-wall, and leaned in close, nearly nose to nose with her.

"You're here because of Amy," he bit out. "You're here to find her killer."

Him. Skye, like everyone else, believed he had killed Amy Jefferson and the other girls who had died that summer.

"Yes." Straight, pretty teeth snapped together furiously as he and Skye leaned closer, now, definitely nose to nose. "I'm here to definitely find her killer. But I never, for even a second, believed you were that killer. I didn't believe it any more than Amy did."

Logan's hands moved, his fingers wrapping around her upper arms, tightening just enough to ensure she didn't escape, before jerking her to him.

As her body came flush against his, the hardened length of his cock pressing into her lower stomach, a startled cry fell from her lips and heat washed through her.

A shudder tore up her spine.

Her pussy clenched, her juices spilling in a wave of pure, erotic sensation.

God, she loved it when he went all dominant and fiercely male on her. She'd sensed the need inside him to loosen the reins on his sexuality, but she hadn't expected the effect on her.

His hands were just that extra bit firmer, his lips plundering. His tongue thrust and surged past her lips to conquer her kiss as her body began to sensitize.

Pleasure whipped through her body, need firing inside her with a suddenness that left her gasping.

Skye had intended to fight if he dared to touch her.

She had meant to deny him if he even thought to have the nerve to suggest he touch her.

He'd been an ass from day one when all she'd wanted to do was get to know the man her foster sister had thought so much of, while trying to find a killer.

Skye was trained in a hundred ways in how to get out of a man's arms.

A kidnapper's grip.

A killer's hold.

But she had never been trained to break free of the hold of the owner of her heart.

She should have used that training to kick his ass.

If possible.

Instead she moaned as his lips covered hers forcefully, taking them, mastering her, and overwhelming any objections she might have had. Any objections she might have had flew out the window the second he touched her, though. Just as they always had.

It was like being caught in a whirlwind. Jerked into a realm where sensations were living, breathing, and possessing her with a strength she had no hope of fighting.

It was a pleasure she had no desire to fight. All she wanted to do was sink into it, enjoy every second of it, because for the first time in her life there was something worth fighting for, for herself.

He did this to her.

Pleasure like this wasn't usual, she thought hazily as her hands smoothed over his broad shoulders. Finding pleasure like this was a once-in-a-lifetime event.

It was something neither of them would ever have
again with anyone else.

Something that would tear their souls apart if they
decided to walk away from it.

Pulling back to nip at her lips, Logan ran his tongue
over the little sting before sipping at her lips again. Deep,
drugging kisses that had her moaning into them and
desperate to get closer to him.

Logan's hands moved over her back and hips, stroking, first through the light cotton blouse she wore, then
beneath it. A second later the feel of her top being pulled
up her body had her lifting her arms languorously and
opening her eyes as he pulled back and slowly, so slowly,
lifted her blouse over her head.

Her hands gripped his shirt and with a quick, hard
yank, she sent buttons scattering as she stared back at
him in challenge.

Logan's gaze narrowed, and if she didn't know better,
he had just accepted that challenge.

"Be careful how you tempt me, Skye." Guttural, the
hunger in his voice matched the lust gleaming in his
gaze as he stared back at her. "Be real fucking careful
how far you tempt me right now."

With his fingertips only he stroked up her right arm,
causing her flesh to tingle as the rasp of the calloused
tip sent pleasure skating over it. Moving his fingers upward, his gaze locked with hers, he hooked his finger in
the strap of her lacy demi-bra and slid it over her shoulder seductively.

"Evidently, I wasn't as deceptive as I thought I'd be,
because you were checking my home. And perhaps I'm

not tempting you enough because you're standing here talking to me, Logan, instead of fucking me." She breathed out, her voice shaky and breathless as she ran her palms from the warm, curl-sprinkled hardness of his chest to the waist of his jeans.

There couldn't be so much as an ounce of fat on his lean abdomen. It was all muscle, hard and warm, rippling in response to her touch as she moved to his belt.

She wanted him naked.

As his lips lowered to her shoulder, his teeth raking against the rounded curve and bringing a gasp of response to her lips, she found herself jerking at the leather. She wanted the heavy length of his cock released and taking her before he could change his mind again and pull away.

As she moved her hands to the metal buttons of his jeans—not a zipper, heaven forbid that it should be made easy for her—her fingers fumbled.

The denim stretched over the straining length of his cock, making the buttons harder to undo.

And Logan wasn't helping, she thought hazily. He was too busy slowly releasing the front catch of her bra and slipping the straps over each shoulder.

Excitement and anticipation surged through her. Arching against him in reaction, she found her hands moving, her nails scouring against his abdomen in retaliation before returning to the next metal button.

She wanted him. The need was building inside her to the point that she wondered if she would survive it if he did manage to take her.

As his teeth nipped the curve of her shoulder lightly, Skye lifted herself closer to him.

His lips moved from her shoulder to the curve of her neck, where he took hard, suckling kisses of her flesh.

He was marking her.

She knew beyond a shadow of a doubt that Logan Callahan would have never marked a woman before.

As she tilted her head to the side to give him better access, her lips and tongue licked over the hard flesh above a flat male nipple with hungry intent. Kissing, nipping at his skin, and tasting as much as possible, she was aware of nothing but Logan's lips at her neck and the pleasure burning through her, electrifying her.

A shattered cry tore from her lips as one hard male hand cupped her breast while the other moved to her hip. Tightening there, she felt the harsh, heavy movements of his chest and heard a rumbled groan as his lips moved lower.

He would have never marked her if he wasn't serious about a hell of a lot more than a one-night stand.

"Please," she whispered. "Please, Logan."

She needed more, so much more.

"Please what?" Fierce and commanding, his voice echoed with the same hunger. "Tell me what you want, Skye."

He wanted the words. She'd never had a lover ask for the words. Hell, she'd never considered begging for anything either.

"My breasts," she whispered. "My nipples. Logan, my

nipples ache. Please suck them. Suck them hard like before."

The need to feel his lips surrounding them again was making her crazy.

A hungry groan passed his lips as he bent farther to her, his lips moving over the curve of her left breast, his tongue stroking until both lips reached the nerve-laden, pebble-hard tip of her breast.

His tongue stroking over the tight peak had her fingers working harder, tearing at the denim until the last button slipped free.

Strangled, rough with the sensations that filled her senses, overwhelming her and bordering on pain, she fought to smother a cry only to have it escape despite her attempts.

All but writhing in pleasure, unable to function past the needs tearing through them both, Skye slid her hand beneath the opened denim of his jeans. As she did, Logan pulled her nipple into his mouth, sucking it deeply, hungrily, as his palm cupped it, lifting the hardened peak closer as he sucked it deeper. Each draw of his mouth had her clitoris pulsing with agonizing pleasure as the muscles of her pussy clenched in desperation.

Release was only seconds away, only a few more draws of his mouth from ripping through her, blinding and intense. She was poised on a razor's edge of orgasm. Sharp and fiery, each pulse of sensation clenched every muscle of her body and had her straining to race into the abyss.

Finally managing to part the fabric of his jeans, her fingers slid inside, immediately stroking over the thick, straining length of his cock. The parted fabric allowed the broad length to slip free of the material, pulsing and too thick for her to wrap her fingers around it, so hard and heavy she wanted nothing more than to have it impaling her.

Stroking over it, her fingers pumped it once, twice, before she stroked it again and allowed her thumb to rake over the thick, mushroomed crest as pre-come slickened it. The silky essence was warm against the pad of her thumb, the hot flesh below it clenching tight with the caress.

Tipping her head back, she felt the brush of her hair against her bare back as Logan quickly unfastened her jeans, his hands sliding in, cupping her ass and lifting her closer, trapping her hand between their bodies.

She couldn't move. She couldn't stroke the fiery flesh or caress it as she wanted.

His lips lifted from her nipple, his hands releasing her ass to grip the band of her jeans as he moved back.

She couldn't wait. She wasn't going to wait. She'd waited too long for this, needed the taste of him too desperately.

She'd hungered for it.

Ached for it.

Pushing back at his chest, Skye locked her gaze with his as she backed him against the opposite wall now.

Logan's smile was tight, his gaze warning, as she ran her hands down his chest. "Oh, baby, you don't know what you're doing."

"Bet me," she breathed out, finally feeling that edge

of complete emotionlessness that had gripped her before he touched her washing away entirely.

There was no way to remain unemotional in his arms. There was no way to close her heart and soul to the pleasure or the needs he sent crashing through her.

Kissing her way down his chest, licking, tasting his skin as she went slowly to her knees, Skye stared up at him, seeing the burn in his gaze that flooded her body.

As she gripped the hard, throbbing flesh, her lips moving down his chest, over his abdomen, then to the hard, clenched power of his thighs, her lashes drifted, her eyes closing.

Needs that had built for far too long attacked her.

Needs she hadn't imagined she would ever know coursed through her. She wanted him as she had never wanted anyone or anything.

She wanted to make this last as he had made her pleasure last in the kitchen that night. She wanted him to feel the same desperation, the same loss of control, as she had felt.

She wanted him to feel, needed him to feel, the same blazing emotions that she couldn't control within herself. The same realization that this hunger was stronger, brighter, than any he had ever known before or would know with any other woman.

Her tongue circled the broad head, flattened and licked around the engorged, heavy crest. The heavy throb of blood in the thick veins beneath the flesh assured her of his pleasure, The taut, corded strength only barely controlled as he remained still in front of her thrilled her.

Taking the tip of the thick crest into her lips, she teased it with her tongue, licking and tasting before teasing the narrow slit centered there.

"Oh, hell no, baby," a dark, rasping growl left his throat as she began teasing him. "We're not risking you like that. We're not risking your pleasure by tempting my control to go fucking haywire."

Burying his fingers in her hair and gripping the long, loose curls as he gripped the base of his cock, Logan held her head still.

His fingers tightened on the base, a grimace pulling at his face as his balls flexed in imminent release. Holding tight to forestall his climax, Logan rubbed the crest of his cock against her lush, kiss-swollen lips.

Silk whispered over the straining flesh. Warm, damp, her lips were the gates to paradise, and only God knew how bad Logan wanted to take them fully.

Watching her lips part for him wasn't enough. Feeling the stroke of that soft satin, as fucking good as it felt, wasn't all he wanted. He wanted that hot, sweet mouth surrounding the aching crest. He wanted to feel her licking, sucking, taking him as deep as she could take him as he fucked the hot confines.

"Open more," he ordered roughly, knowing time was limited, his control shaky as hell. "Take my cock, baby. Show me how much you want it."

Watching as she ran her tongue over her lips in anticipation, dampening them further, slickening them for him, had his body tightening impossibly further.

Her eyes gleamed with pleasure and with arousal. Her parting her lips as he ordered, softening them as he slid slowly, slowly inside, nearly broke him. As her tongue played at the tip, then beneath the engorged head, her stroking over that one violently sensitive area had his hands tightening in her hair.

He was only seconds from filling her mouth. Only seconds before completely losing control and perhaps doing something they would both regret. At the very least, something that could affect the rest of their lives.

His abdomen clenched furiously at the implication of the pleasure to come, her intent clear in the long, slow lick of her tongue as he eased inside her mouth, then pulled back fully.

Her eyes snapped open, her gaze meeting his as he palmed his cock and considered— God no, he couldn't pull back. He didn't want to pull back. He wanted her, wanted this like he'd never wanted it before.

Tucking the crest against her lips, Logan held her head firmly, pressing, easing inside again, watching as the engorged, agonized flesh stretched her lips. Reddened and as soft as silk, those lips were a satiny stroke of incredible bliss as they stroked over the tight, hungry flesh of his dick. Pushing the engorged crest deeper, he watched her face, felt her tongue as it rippled against the thick head thrusting over it. Logan fought, clenched his teeth tight, to keep rein on the hungers threatening to slip free.

All he could hope to do was keep control of her, as well as his own, desperation. The need clawing at him. And the emotions he was determined not to acknowledge.

She had intended to tease. She was going to tempt the dominant power she'd felt racing through him each time he touched her. She had every intention of making him beg as he'd made her beg. Oh God, she needed it.

She needed him so much.

Watching his eyes, she watched the shift of color, the darkening of the emerald color, gem bright and filled with a hint of pain. So deep and dark it was like staring into the farthest depths of the ocean and marveling at the secrets contained there.

Parting her lips further, Skye let the broad, hot crest slip farther into her mouth as she sucked it inside.

Male heat attacked her senses. The hard, steady throb of blood within the thick veins assured her of his pleasure and had a cry slipping past her lips.

She was going to enjoy every minute of this. Every second. Every taste and every hard groan that escaped his lips. She was going to take her time and love every memory she gained from it.

Just in case.

She'd waited so long for him. So many years. Far longer than he could know.

Swirling her tongue around the engorged head, she then probed beneath the crest, stroking beneath it and tasting a small spurt of pre-come that seared her senses.

He tasted of a mountain storm as it rolled across the mountains. Wild and untamed.

Sucking him deeper, working her tongue over the heated flesh filling her mouth, she found that roughened, extra-sensitive spot just beneath the crest and heard his growl of pleasure.

Both hands were clenched in her hair now, holding her still as he began to move, to thrust slowly and shallowly past her swollen lips.

Logan stared at the woman he couldn't seem to get enough of. Knew he would never get enough of.

Reddened, swollen lips were parted and stretched around his flesh as she sucked him deeper. Her eyes were glittering, her cheeks flushed, her nails kneading his thighs, rasping his flesh, and creating a pleasure he'd never known before.

"God, Skye, baby." Groaning her name, he fought against the pleasure that threatened to have him losing the tight hold he had over his release. The pleasure was like a white-hot surge of ecstasy building in his cock and tightening his balls.

Skye had never been so close to orgasm with no more to stimulate her than her lover's pleasure. Each building sensation whipping through her body had a moan tearing from her body. Each time he tightened, her womb clenched and a surge of moisture raced from her pussy.

Swirling her tongue around the head of his cock, Skye once again probed beneath the under-crest, stroked it, and tasted a small spurt of pre-come.

Logan's hands clenched tight in her hair now, holding her head still as he began to move. Thrusting slow and shallow, he pushed past her swollen, sensitive lips as she gripped his thighs.

The sound of her name was a rough groan falling from his lips as reality seemed to turn to shadow and only this erotic, sensual act existed.

Pleasure was like a white-hot blaze of sensation surging through her as she whimpered around his cock. The pleasure was building through her. Each time his body tightened, her womb clenched and a surge of moisture raced from her pussy.

Her nipples throbbed. They were swollen and aching, needing his touch even as she needed to touch him.

Wrapping the fingers of one hand just above his, Skye tightened her mouth around the head of his cock as it shuttled between her lips. The heated taste and sensual emotions wrapping around her making every cell in her body ache for the touch of him.

For the taste of him.

She wanted to feel his release, wanted to taste it.

"Sweet, hot, fucking mouth. Ah God, baby. Suck my dick with that hot mouth." His hands tightened further in her hair.

Skye clenched her thighs together, desperate for the pressure against her clit, never needing to orgasm as badly as she needed to now.

She was loving his cock. Loving the heat and hardness, the taste and the throb of power. Loving it until nothing mattered but the rapidly nearing release she could feel as her free hand stroked over his balls.

His cock flexed warningly, suddenly spilling a heavier spurt of pre-come. His balls clenched and Skye moaned, knowing he was close.

She could sense his release. It was one stroke, one heated draw of her mouth, away when he suddenly pulled back and his cock exited her mouth with a suddenness that left her grasping for what had happened.

"No. Logan, please." Shocked, she stared up at him, wondering what the hell had happened.

"Hey, Logan. Did she kill you or what?"

Skye jerked back quickly, scrambling for her blouse at the sound of Crowe's voice at the bedroom door.

"I'll be there in a minute," Logan called out, his voice tight and rough as Skye jerked her blouse on, then turned to watch as he quickly fixed his jeans.

There was no hope for his shirt. She smirked a bit at the thought.

"Minute's up, bro," Crowe called back, dark amusement and warning echoing through the room. "I hope you're dressed, because I'm tired of waiting."

CHAPTER ELEVEN

Fastening his jeans, Logan had no choice but to leave his shirt unbuttoned. The buttons were scattered over the dark hardwood floor.

Not that his cousin would have given Logan time to button his shirt.

Crowe had never really been the patient sort unless a situation demanded it. Logan assumed Crowe didn't believe that was the case in this situation.

As the other man stepped into the entrance and came to a hard stop, Logan's gaze was drawn by a flicker of movement on one of the monitors at his side.

Rumbles had found the corner of the heavy, fringed bedspread at the corner of Skye's bed and was playing with one of the hanging cashmere strings.

Crossing his arms over his chest, Logan watched, silently noting the crisp, high-quality HD and near-perfect resolution. There was no graininess, fuzziness, or blurred areas. The quality bespoke excellent equipment as well as some serious know-how in the electronics department.

As Crowe stepped up behind him, Logan realized he never did ask where the cameras were actually located, nor could he figure it out himself. They were never still enough to pinpoint. Each flash of movement had the designated camera for that area moving. He noticed a complete 360-degree turn of one camera, making it impossible to locate.

Three he knew had to be on the roof, but where on the roof?

He frowned, moved in closer, and focused on one particular camera. The image that played back from the mountain behind the house had a perfect angle into one of the areas Rafer had pinpointed as a possible place where the house was being watched.

"How well does it zoom?" Logan asked Skye.

"Well enough, to a point." She shrugged. "About halfway up the mountain the picture starts to degrade."

He nodded slowly. That sounded normal, even for the best of cameras outside military or federal use.

"This is what you need to see," she said, picking up the remote that had fallen to the floor.

Pointing the device to the remote DVR, she once again programmed a series of commands.

"I found this last night." The time stamp showed the night he had pulled Skye from the patio into the living room.

There were two different views of the yard, each with night vision and optional thermal imaging.

"Watch cameras three and four." The picture began to zoom in on the images.

Camera three showed Skye slipping across the yard at the far end of the house, toward the front. Camera four showed a shadow moving along the edge of the house, closest to the patio.

"Camera five," she said quietly.

The camera switched to thermal imaging, showing only a glimpse at certain points of the reddened outline of a male moving toward the patio. The figure stayed close to the house, ensuring that even with the excellent view the cameras could pick up that he was still unidentifiable.

As Skye neared the house, audio suddenly kicked in. The sound of the pup's whimpers as Skye moved closer to the evergreens she hid in at the edge of the patio became more distressed.

"Your owner's just an asshole, isn't he, baby?" Crisp, clear, Skye's voice would have been easy for the trespasser to hear. And there was no doubt that he had.

Pausing, the figure waited at the edge of the house, his identity hidden even as the camera focused on him.

"I would steal you away, sweetie, if you would go with me. All that crying at night is just breaking my heart."

Frightened, the pup turned her head to the corner of the house even as she edged out of the shrubbery toward Skye.

Belly flat to the ground, her wrinkled face pitiful, the big brown eyes appeared larger in her fear.

"There you are, little baby," Skye crooned. "Who-

ever was mean enough to give you to Logan should be
kicked for not leaving you at my door instead."

The pup suddenly growled ominously, despite her
size. At the same time, the figure at the side of the house
had begun to take another step forward.

The shadow paused at the sound of the growls.

"Don't feel bad; I can't get along with that mean ole
Callahan either," she said regretfully. "When I can't get
along with them, there's just no hope for them. Your
previous owner should be arrested for thinking such a
little thing like you could have managed it."

Slowly the shadow backed off and eased away.

"That wasn't you." Logan heard his own icy warning
in his voice as he turned on her.

She had told him she had come around the front and
sides of the house.

Why?

Skye shook her head quickly. "I slipped along the
other side of the house, which is what I thought you
meant, until I remembered exactly what you said that
night. That's why I pulled it up and ran the video back."
She waved at the monitor as the thermal image ran
across the backyard to the stream that ran through it.

Jumping the stream, the intruder moved into the trees,
weaving his way through them expertly.

"He was wearing night-vision goggles," she informed
them. "There's no other way he could have traversed the
woods that easily without them. It was too dark and he
was moving too quickly to be doing so on his own."

Logan had to agree with her.

Propping his elbow on the arm still crossed over his

chest, Logan stroked the short growth of beard next to his lips with his fingers as he nodded thoughtfully.

Still following the figure as he made his way up the mountain, Logan noticed the thermal image didn't fade out, it simply disappeared.

He jerked back and turned to stare at Skye.

"Noticed that, did you?" Her gaze flickered with anger now. "Yeah, he just disappears. There's no thermal indication of a vehicle, and to my knowledge the only way he could have simply disappeared like that is—"

Logan finished the sentence, "Some sort of natural barrier between him and the cameras." He turned to Crowe.

Logan's cousin knew the government land in and around Corbin County better than anyone else Logan knew.

"I'd have to map the exact location, but the natural barrier is possible." Crowe nodded thoughtfully. "So is a cave system. There's always been talk of several of them around here that possibly connect to those on Crowe Mountain, but so far I haven't seen them."

"You were just going to keep this from me?" Logan asked Skye. "You found this last night and didn't even think to inform me of it?"

That brow snapped again. The arrogance of the action was something he rarely saw in a woman. In Skye, he was damned if he didn't like it.

"I would have contacted you either tonight or tomorrow." She lifted her shoulders carelessly. "If you recall, you rather rudely demanded I get out of your home the last time I was there. I wasn't about to venture back until you had time to get over your little snit."

"My little snit?" he growled.

"Your snit." She gave a sharp nod. "And I didn't inform the sheriff of the cameras for the same reason I didn't ask permission to put them in."

"The element of surprise," Crowe murmured as he stepped closer to the cameras and began to study the ones recording real time.

"Which raised the question, why did you feel you needed them if you weren't watching us as potential suspects in the Slasher's crimes? And what the hell makes you think you can play the bad assed FBI agent and risk your life without so much as a partner for backup?"

Skye's expression was anything but emotionless now. Her eyes grew damp for a moment before she blinked back the sorrow he glimpsed there, as well as the need and the hunger, for him.

"Because the moment I met you, Logan, I knew I wanted you. And I want more than one night. Amy didn't protect herself when she began the investigation. She didn't notify anyone in the agency that she was on the investigation to ensure she had backup if it was needed, and if she kept operation notes then none of us found them. I didn't want to make the same mistakes."

Logan could feel his guts clenching in dread. Just as he'd suspected, she was there to investigate Amy's and the other victims' deaths. Skye was looking for a killer, and like Amy, once she found him, she wouldn't live to regret it.

"At least she was trained for it. You're nothing but a paper pusher in the agency. Do you think I don't have my own contacts?" Logan snarled, unable to hold back the fury that the thought of her death sent racing through him. "It's a great setup." He waved his hand to the monitors. "They won't fucking keep you alive any more than the training Amy got at that fucking academy kept her alive. Go home, Skye!" His voice didn't rise this time, but Skye flinched at the rage building in it anyway. "For both our sakes get the hell out of Corbin County."

Her lips had parted to argue, to present her case, when he suddenly turned and stomped out of the closet.

The puppy's excited bark at seeing him was followed by a small whimper and, seconds later, the hard slam of her bedroom door.

Once again, she flinched.

She'd never known nerves while on assignment. She'd played prey to stalkers since her first assignment, and she'd never had her stomach jerking with any sort of fear.

It was jerking now.

Turning to Crowe, she stared back at his somber expression for long moments before whispering, "He won't even listen, will he?"

He didn't want her to deceive him, but he didn't want the truth either.

She was no paper pusher.

Crowe shook his head. "This isn't a job for you, Skye," he breathed out roughly. "You're too soft. Too easily broken." He followed Logan then, though Crowe's exit from the bedroom was done more quietly.

Clenching her teeth, she moved quickly and followed

them, catching them in the kitchen as they neared the back door.

"The Slasher found Marietta in Boulder." They both stopped. "My own search has turned up two other lovers Logan's had since returning to Corbin County. Ellen Mason in Grand Junction and Jenny Perew in Mount Sterling." Logan's eyes narrowed as he became so dangerously still Skye felt her mouth drying. "If I found them, Logan, then the Slasher already has."

"And how did you find them?" Even the puppy stilled now at the sound of Logan's voice.

"Research," she admitted. "Phone calls to the bars and restaurants you're known to frequent and asking the right question that indicated I knew what I was talking about." That and some help from the same friend who had helped her set up the security room. "I finally got their names last week. If anyone had followed you—"

"No one followed me," he snarled.

"I did once," she admitted. "You didn't lose me until you actually got into Laramie city limits. I stayed as far as possible behind you and risked losing you several times. But you didn't lose me. If I leave tonight, it's not going to change anything. I've alibied you. Gossip is already swirling. If you couldn't hide Marietta, Ellen, and Jenny, then there's not a chance in hell I can hide when I return to Denver!"

Logan stared back at her, so still and silent that the only sign of life was the enraged gleam of his emerald eyes.

She knew what he must be feeling, or at least understood it. He'd lost lovers, friends. He'd been the reason they'd died and he'd been unable to save them. Just as he was unable to protect his cousins now. To stand between them and a killer.

"She's right, Logan." There was a gleam of rueful acknowledgment in Crowe's gaze as it met hers. "She's in just as much danger if not more than Marietta was."

"God damn that bastard to hell!" Logan's voice was filled with fury, but his eyes, his eyes promised death. "Why the fuck did you involve yourself in this? Do you want to fucking die?"

Logan watched as Skye's fists clenched at her sides, a deep-seated pain and anger pouring into her expression as she stared back at him.

"He killed my sister!" she cried out hoarsely then, blinking back tears. "Amy saved my life when my parents died. She stood by me and she looked out for me. He's going to pay for taking her away from me."

"He'll kill you just like he killed your sister." Logan knew the words were cold, brutal, but he had a feeling gentleness wasn't going to work with Skye. He would be lucky, extremely lucky, if he could just convince her to show a little bit of fucking caution. "For God's sake, I can't believe you placed yourself in danger like this," he continued as he thought about it and Skye remained silent. "Why the fuck didn't you just stay out of it?"

"How can you ask me something so asinine?" she yelled back at him. "I knew why Sheriff Tobias showed up. The neighbors were talking about it before he even arrived. I knew they had found Marietta Tyme's body and I was damned if I would see an innocent man pay for a crime someone else committed."

"Why did you think I was staying the hell away from you?" Logan moved closer, forcing himself to stop at the small table with its heavy wood chairs surrounding it. Gripping the back of the nearest chair with fingers that paled at the force he used, he stared at her in recrimination. "Why, Skye, did you think I wouldn't take you when I had the chance? Why I never fool with women from Sweetrock?" His fingers went ruthlessly through his hair. "God, I never imagined he would learn about one night in Boulder. Do you really want to become his next victim?"

"Do you really want to remain celibate the rest of your life?" she argued heatedly then, moving closer to him as her nails bit indentations into the skin of her palms, she was clenching her hands so tight. "Or continually watch your lovers die? How about just leaving the fucking county and giving up everything Rafer's uncle helped you fight for until his death? What about Crowe?" She waved her hand toward him. "Or Rafer? If they're really all you care about how do you think it's going to affect you if that bastard finds Cami? What if he succeeds in actually killing her, Logan?" she cried out. "Could you live with it?"

"And what the fuck makes you think you can or will survive it?" He was almost yelling at her now. The rage at the situation, the fear that burned in his gut that the Slasher would target her, was eating Logan alive.

Skye smiled at the question. A smile of amused confidence and a challenge to fate.

"Because I'm no fucking paper pusher, Logan. I wasn't just trained to survive it," she informed him coolly then. "I'll forgive your lack of confidence in me because I'm sure you don't realize you have one highly trained, fully certified, class A, stalker-tracking Federal Bureau of Investigation agent right here in your corner." She held her arms out in invitation. "Now, why don't you do what any sane, reasonable man in your position would do? Use me?"

"Who said I was sane or reasonable?" He glared back at her. "You've lost your mind, Skye." He couldn't even find the will to yell at her now. A real man didn't yell at those who weren't exactly sane themselves, he told himself. "What the hell do you think you're doing, Skye?" he asked her again. He hadn't received a credible answer last time, so he wasn't really expecting one this time.

"Trying to help the three of you find the killer whose only intent is seeing you in prison for his crimes?" Her brow arched mockingly before continuing with facetious logic. "Why don't you stop playing the Lone Ranger all by yourself? Let Tonto have some fun."

"The Lone Ranger?" he questioned her in disbelief.

"Before your time?" She shrugged. "Sorry, darlin', I watched the old westerns with Daddy Carter when I was little. How about He-Man? She-Ra just wants to play a little too, you know?"

His dick was steel hard. Blood was thundering through his veins, and rather than walking out of the house as he should have, all Logan could do was stare back at her incredulously.

There was a glimmer of anticipation and adrenaline in her eyes that was making him crazy. Crazy to have her.

He'd always steered clear of women in law enforcement or the military because they made him hard. Dominant, they made him think they were strong enough to do exactly what she was trying to do. Exactly what Amy had tried to do twelve years before.

Skye made him want to believe she was strong enough to tempt a killer and survive.

That perhaps she might even be strong enough to love Logan forever and survive it.

But Logan knew nothing lasted forever. Nothing lived forever. There was no such thing as immortality, not in life, nor in love.

Staring back at her, seeing her gaze, cool and confident, seeing the experience in her eyes, he wanted nothing more than to know it was possible.

Arousal was a hard, furious throb in his blood, mixing with anger. The sheer confidence in her gaze was like throwing fuel on the erotic flames. For a second, for the briefest second, all that mattered was fucking her.

He took a step toward her, intent on picking her up and carrying her straight to her bed and fucking her into exhaustion.

But nothing lasts forever. He could have her. He could take her just one time. Then he would have to force her out of his life.

Out of his life and perhaps, if he did it right, out of a killer's sight.

And that was all that mattered. Keeping the woman who was becoming far too important to his heart alive.

CHAPTER TWELVE

"Damn, Logan, didn't we discuss staying out of the neighbor's bed?" Crowe chose that moment to speak up mockingly. "We did discuss this, right?"

Skye glanced at Logan, then at Crowe knowingly. Of course they had. They were cousins. As he was the oldest, Crowe felt the need to try to protect Logan, and Rafer. But they were all fiercely protective of each other.

And now Logan was desperately trying to figure out how to protect Skye as well.

"Yeah, that neighbor of his, Mrs. Reisner, is a real wildcat I hear," Skye said with a slight smile. "I don't think Logan goes for cougars, though." Of course, Mrs. Reisner would have been appalled at this whole conversation. Maybe.

Crowe snorted with something less than amusement.

Watching him closely, Skye caught a glimpse of raging grief as he glanced at Logan before he pulled the sunglasses from the collar of his T-shirt and slid them onto his face.

Crowe's grief was deep, dark. It pulled at the corners of his mouth and had created a shadowed, darkened bruise on the forest green of his eyes.

According to the psychologist she had discussed the cousins with, Crowe would be the one to just leave one day and go hunting the killer. And the good doctor had been certain. Once he found the Slasher, and the psychologist was certain Crowe would, then he would cause him to suffer in ways he'd never imagined hurting one of his victims.

With the killer's blood staining his body, Logan would simply drift away, the doctor surmised. He just wouldn't wake up. That or he'd become such a vigilante that making history would be the least law enforcement had to worry about where he was concerned.

"Yeah, it wasn't Mrs. Reisner I was worried about," Crowe assured Skye mockingly. "I believe it's the redhead with more bravado than good sense to tango with a Callahan."

"You tango?" Skye could play dumb all day if she wanted to and actually make it appear convincing. "Sorry, that wasn't a dance my instructor taught me. The Texas Two-Step was his favorite." Her smile was all teeth.

Logan shook his head. "I have things to do." Looking around, he frowned. "Where's that little monster? I just sat down!"

"The pup? You left her unattended in my house again? You were supposed to be watching her."

This was a disaster in the making. Turning around, Skye searched the room quickly. "If she destroys more of my clothes, Callahan, then you're getting me a whole new wardrobe."

"She was right here under the table," Logan growled as he began checking under end tables in the living room and in corners. "Little escape artist. She's been trying to get over here for the past five days."

All she'd tried to do as long as Skye had her was get to Logan.

Ignoring the other two men as they called for Rumbles, Skye thought it was no wonder the pug didn't answer to a name like that. She moved quickly to the bedroom.

She came to a hard stop at the end of her bed, remaining quiet and simply staring at the picture of innocence that Logan had called a little monster.

An impish, mischievous little bit of fluff was what she was. And once again, she'd destroyed one of Skye's favorite articles of clothing.

Where the hell she had found the pale green silk blouse Skye didn't have a clue. It had been missing for days. But there she was, lying on her back in the middle of the bed, the torn shirt covering the upper half of her body and part of her squished little face. One little eye peeped from the side of the material as she slept, and her little legs were sprawled out as far as such short little legs could sprawl.

It was her favorite sleeping position. And for some reason, the entire time she had been with Skye, each morning she'd found her way off the bed without waking her, done the impossible and found a piece of clothing before climbing back up, tearing it just enough to make it unusable, then falling asleep again.

She was going to have to move the makeshift steps at the end of the bed, she thought with a sigh. The stacked boxes that led to the trunk in front of the footboard made it very easy for the pup to find her favorite spot on the bed.

Skye missed her, she realized. The past days without the pup's warm weight against Skye's side as she slept had made the nightmares come harder, darker. She didn't want to dream. She didn't want to relive things she should be able to forget.

As Logan moved behind her, his chest brushed against her shoulder as he laid the side of his face against her head.

"I see her and all I want to do is wrap her up in cotton and find a steel vault to protect her in until all this is over," he said softly.

Skye knew where he was going with it.

"She would die," she said just as softly, aware that Crowe could be somewhere behind them. "She's little, but she thinks you need her. She needs you to need her. If you don't, then she's going to lose all that love, all that heart, she's given you."

And the puppy wasn't the only one Skye was talking about. She was talking about her own heart, the one she had given him when she was fifteen years old, at her sister's funeral, as Skye watched that single tear drift down his cheek and into the beard he had worn, even then.

"You named her?" Skye kept her voice so low it barely had sound.

She felt like crying herself, because she knew him, knew the type of man he was, just as she knew what the thought of losing another lover did to him.

"Rumbles," he said softly.

Skye shook her head. "She'll come to you if you call her Bella," she said quietly.

Logan sighed heavily behind her.

The anger, frustration, and tension still raged between them, but then so did the hunger. There was no getting away from it, and they both knew it.

His hands settled on her hips as his forehead pressed against her shoulder.

"I knew to stay away from you," he whispered. "The first morning I awoke and saw you sunbathing, all but nude on that damned patio, I knew you were trouble."

She leaned into him. She'd deliberately lain right there so he could see her. So she could see if the untemptable could be tempted.

"Logan," she whispered his name on a sigh, a plea. "You have to stop them now. You have to let me help you."

"I don't need help, Skye," he denied. "I don't need your help or anyone else's, because I'm not doing anything."

"Since you and your cousins have no idea the resources I can tap or the fact I've trained for this my entire adult life, then I forgive you this insult. Just this one." It was a shaky laugh, one that she couldn't keep the pain or the disillusionment out of.

"I feel honored." There was a breath of a sigh in his

voice. "But I think I'll definitely pass on your lovely of-fer, baby. Another death on my conscience might finish destroying me."

Especially if it was Skye.

Holding her to him, feeling her warmth, he couldn't imagine living if a monster took her away from him.

"That's what they want," she said then. "What all of them want."

His jaw tightened as he stepped away from her, re-gretting the loss of her warmth more than he wanted to admit. But stepping away from her was imperative. She was too confident, and she was making him think, mak-ing him wonder—

"Did you hear me, Logan? They want to destroy you." She faced him now, her expression imperative, her gaze filled with emotions he didn't want to see. Because they made him ache, made him hungry for what they repre-sented.

"There is no 'they,' Skye." He gave his head a hard shake. "If there was, then the other two are gone now. We just have the third to capture."

"Logan, the profiler hasn't revised his opinion."

His jaw tightened. "The other two are dead, Skye. Thomas Jones died the night he killed Jaymi. Lowry Berry was killed more than a month ago when he at-tacked Cami. There's only one left."

She shook her head. "I talked to them, Logan. They sent an agent to Marietta's crime scene, to her home, and to the autopsy. Their profile stands. I specifically ques-tioned that. It hasn't changed."

"And my mind hasn't changed," he assured her as he moved to the bed, scooped up the pup and the ruined shirt into his arms, and headed to the doorway.

Before leaving the bedroom, he turned back to Skye one last time.

She stood in the middle of the room staring back at him, that long, dark hair cascading around her, nearly to her hips, making her look even tinier, even more delicate, than she actually was.

Her blouse was still a little uneven, her hair finger mussed; at some point she'd kicked off her sandals. She was the most beautiful woman he'd ever seen and, to him, the most deadly.

A woman he could love.

"Go home, Skye," he ordered her again, wearily. "Move back in with your foster parents; hire a bodyguard. Hide until this is over. I'll come for you then."

She shook her head. "You won't. And I'm not leaving. I'm smart enough to know I can do this without your help. I'd prefer to work with you. Trust me, Logan, you really want to let me in on this."

The rejection in his gaze broke her heart. "Trust me, Skye," he answered then. "I really don't."

CHAPTER THIRTEEN

As he'd noticed with Marietta Tyme, Logan had excellent taste in women. And he was damned efficient, for a while, in keeping his lovers hidden.

He knew there had been more than the three he knew of.

Marietta in Denver.

Jenny Perew who lived in a little house on several acres of land in Mount Sterling.

Ellen Mason in Grand Junction. Unfortunately, she had several roommates. As a journalist for a local paper, she didn't have a nine-to-five job and she wasn't as predictable as Perew was. That meant sweet little Jenny got to die first.

His boss wasn't happy that he'd found no others, believing that Logan, the only blond Callahan, was perhaps sneakier than the others, because it was reputed he had an incredibly high sex drive.

It was laughable.

The old bastard he was working with had probably forgotten what a real sex drive was decades ago.

Getting it up without the taste and feel of his victims' blood was something his boss hadn't been able to do for a while.

It wasn't a problem he had, though.

To all appearances, his sex drive was normal, if a little vanilla. His life was predictable and he was trustworthy.

He almost chuckled at the thought as he cut the lights on the quiet little car he'd stolen to drive into Mount Sterling. He doubted Jenny would even hear it as she drove up the lane.

She had no dogs. She had no boyfriend or housemates. And tonight, she was home.

He checked his watch. It was two in the morning, there would be no witnesses, and Skye O'Brien, Logan's last alibi, was out of town for the night.

Something about an early doctor's appointment, he'd heard her tell another customer at the post office.

And his boss had a meeting that evening, keeping him busy and out of the way while preparations were being made.

What excellent timing.

It gave him a chance to choose his own victim, to take her, to complete the sexual, fear-filled, agonizing acts that he'd begun to crave.

And to do it in a way that would show his boss once and for all that he knew exactly what he was doing.

Still, each plan he'd come up with had been rejected

after Logan had managed to escape jail for the murder of Marietta.

As though it were his fault.

He'd warned his boss, warned him countless times not to dismiss Logan's winsome little neighbor, Skye.

He'd watched them at several of the Socials, their smiles just a little warmer than ones they gave others. Their gazes lingering just a second longer on each other than they should have.

But no, Skye knew better, he'd been told. Skye wasn't a trollop for the Callahans to take advantage of so easily.

The old fool. He would be amusing if he weren't threatening to become so damned dangerous.

And now, to tell him to halt any further plans until he had considered their options?

Their options?

Didn't he think they were just a little too deep here to pull out?

Stepping from the car, he latched the door quietly and moved around the house to the back door whose lock he'd sabotaged that morning.

It would feel locked from the inside. Jenny would be certain she was secure. But from the outside, it would be as simple as turning the knob to open the door. Stepping into the house, his head lowered, the Stetson he wore shielded his face just in case there were cameras.

Identical to Logan Callahan's.

Moving silently through the house, he made his way to the little downstairs bedroom and slipped into the open door.

It was dark.

He was early.

And Jenny was sleeping deeply.

Pulling the drug-soaked cloth from his jacket, he removed it from the protective baggie before stepping to her bed.

Moving quickly, he gripped her head, slapped the cloth over her mouth and nose, then held tight to her struggling form.

It only took seconds actually.

The fear in her eyes for those seconds, though, had the cum pumping from his engorged penis to fill the condom he'd already rolled over it.

Shit. He would have to be damned careful disposing of it.

He had all the time in the world to be careful now, though.

Dropping the small duffel bag from his shoulder next to the bed and drawing in a deep breath, he willed himself to patience.

Turning his hands palms-up, he flexed his fingers, still not quite certain of the feel of his new "hands." Latex of a sort, with the prints he'd managed to get on two fingers, none other than Logan Callahan's.

Just in case the son of a bitch couldn't come up with an alibi. That was the plan. He was just hoping it would work now.

He wasn't quite so cocky this time, though. Logan had escaped every attempt to frame him. There was no sense banking on this working, but at least he'd have fun for a few hours.

He'd planned this, just as he had Marietta's death,

down to the last detail. No mistakes. There was never so much as a hint of any evidence he didn't want found.

Why couldn't his boss see the genius he was working with?

He took all the risks, and his boss thought he could just hang him up to dry until he wanted to taste the blood himself again.

It wasn't going to happen that way and he would just make certain his boss realized that.

His dick was hard, blood pumping fierce and heavy through the hardened shaft as he moved then to cut away the pretty little woman's nightgown.

The cotton gown wasn't near as soft and pretty as Skye O'Brien's, but peeling the strips of it from her body sure as hell was fun.

Like an early Christmas present.

He was going to fuck her until she was gasping.

He was going to watch her bleed slow and easy.

He was going to leave her right here when he was finished. Naked, spread, her blood soaking the bed and nothing more.

He tied her to the bed, spread eagle, then unpacked his supplies.

Plenty of disinfectant.

He wouldn't leave anything this time.

No scrap of material.

No fingerprints.

There would be no hair.

No DNA but one very pretty little woman.

Pulling his hat from his head, he laid it upside down on the dresser.

He undressed slowly, his newly shaven body free of hair and scrubbed of dead skin cells. The mix of thin latex and aerosol he'd put together and sprayed over his body ensured nothing of him would be left behind. He just had to make certain he wore a condom and kept his balls in the baggie taped around them.

The precautions were necessary.

But the terror in her wide, wide brown eyes was so worth it—

Ahhh, and what a hell of a good time his boss was gonna be missin'.

The meeting wasn't set for midnight; it was set for four. It would have looked too unusual to see his vehicle leaving his house that late at night. Too many would have noticed.

To see him driving into the mountains after noon, though, wouldn't have seemed that unusual. He did it often enough that it wouldn't have been remarked upon. And this meeting was too important to allow others to witness.

Twenty-four years, two attempts, and still the job hadn't been completed. He'd allowed himself to be swayed by intricate plots and imaginative schemes designed to fail and to keep him from his ultimate goal. To ensure he never gained what should have been his all along.

So many years.

When it had begun, he had been a younger man. A man with optimism. A man who believed in all the careful details and plans he had made over the years.

Only to learn that too often there were so many others willing to destroy those carefully laid plans.

That final triumph had been denied him, despite the years and the hard work. No matter how hard he tried, no matter how many he killed or how often he conspired or with whom, he had been denied what he had worked so hard to attain.

He had bled for it.

He had shed blood for it.

More than two decades later and still he was denied all he had dreamed of.

He was taking the simpler route now. Time was running out. He was no longer a young man, nor was he in the prime of his life. And he had been fighting this battle far too long, just as his father and his grandfather had fought for what should have been theirs, only to see it taken from them. He should have done this sooner.

As he made the turn into the mountains and drew ever closer to the meeting he had planned, he acknowledged the error he had made from the beginning. This was the route he should have taken. Rather than forcing his partners to stain their hands with blood as well, he should have forced them to contribute the funds.

He should have allowed someone else to stain their hands with blood. Allowed someone else to simply kill those fucking Callahan brats or their fathers before they'd had the chance to breed. To steal what he had thought to claim as his own.

What had he done instead?

Instead, he had allowed himself to be convinced, to

feel that smallest iota of sympathy for those incompetent twits he had been working with.

To have mercy on the children.

His father had always told him that killers of children were given a very special place in hell. It had been the only rule his father had, never shed a child's blood, and neither his father nor he had done so.

And that had been his first mistake.

The second had been in believing the Callahan cousins had given up the fight for the land their parents held when they went off to the Marines.

Clyde Ramsey had somehow known the plot to frame the three young men for murder had only been a stay of execution. They would have died in prison, and Clyde had known it.

Wily, intuitive, that old bastard had ensured the cousins shipped off to the military instead. The one place their enemy had no influence. Then Clyde had fought the battle for them.

That son of a bitch. He was wilier than most and it had taken far too many years to kill him. Far too many years and too many resources. He'd been blocked at every turn, and in those years he'd learned his partners in crime were no more than enemies in disguise.

There had been a time when he had considered letting it all go. A time when he had convinced himself he could do without that dream that his father and his father before him had envisioned.

He'd been willing to accept life as it was.

Then David Callahan had returned to Corbin County.

Along with his brothers, he had returned with a hunger for vengeance and a refusal to relinquish the past. That refusal had ensured more blood would be shed.

Pulling the vehicle to the clearing in front of the rotting line shack he'd indicated, he sat for a moment and allowed memories he rarely visited to intrude upon him.

A woman, eyes so bright with life, her hair long and filled with a multitude of curls as she laughed up at him. Her lips were pert and bow shaped, and soft as the finest silk. Her kiss had made him forget about the plans his father had made him swear to complete.

He wanted nothing more than a life in her arms. Nothing had mattered but loving her. Seeing her smile when his eyes opened each morning. Seeing the love he knew would soon glow in her gaze.

Nothing else had mattered.

Nothing—

His hands tightened on the steering wheel as the remembered fury began to rage through his soul.

For years he had courted her, loved her, tried to seduce her. For so many years he had convinced himself that the way to her heart was his patience.

She had taken one look at that Callahan bastard and within weeks had eloped, her belly already filling with their first child.

He had to force back the agonized sound of overwhelming pain that escaped only when he slept. That ripped at his throat each time it raged through him.

She had been his soul and she had torn it out with such a lack of mercy that it had destroyed him. He had never imagined that woman, whose smile was so innocent, whose laughter had filled him with such joy, could rip him apart as she had.

His sweet, precious—

The door opened.

Dark, silent. No flames flickered, no demons emerged, but he knew it for what it was.

The entrance into hell, and he was going to walk into it willingly.

For vengeance.

Taking a deep breath, he stepped from the pickup and moved to the entrance of the old line shack. The one place he had known peace and happiness. Here where he had once met the only woman he loved.

" 'Bout time," a voice drawled, dark and as merciless as pure, blood-red hatred. "Stay in the doorway. I can't see your face; you can't see mine."

But he had no doubt the shadow across the room knew exactly who he was.

"I have no desire to see your face." He knew who he was dealing with; that was all that mattered.

"I received the down payment," he was told. "The half million looked nice in my account. Just as the next payments will as well."

A half million per target, a half million on deposit. Two million dollars. It had taken a lifetime to embezzle the money he had hidden around the world, and now a hefty chunk was missing from it.

"Are you certain this course is the one you want to take?"

He was stepping into hell—for fury and for hatred.

For a past he couldn't forget.

"I paid the deposit." He shrugged as though he had never had a moment's hesitation.

"I have to hear the words," he was told. "I won't take the job without them."

"I paid the deposit," he protested.

"Doesn't matter," the assassin assured him with a slow, amused denial. "I have to have the words. You won't cry later that you didn't know the consequences."

He knew well the consequences, and they would result in the dream that had driven his family for far too many years.

For the most deadly sin of all.

"Rafer Callahan's bitch Cambria Flannigan. Target one.

"Logan Callahan. Any whore who slept in his bed within the past three months. Crowe Callahan. Any lover he's had as well that could possibly be carrying his brat. I want no more Callahans to claim any part of Corbin County. And I want the Callahan cousins broke. Frame them for it if possible, but be warned, in twelve years I've not been able to frame them for breathing, even though everyone knows they have to do it."

Silence filled the darkness for but a moment. "Half million per Callahan lover. What if there's no chance of conception with the lover? Or extenuating circumstances but no conception?"

He stepped into hell for love. "No matter who whores for each of them, I want them dead if there's even the barest chance of procreation."

"Done." Silence stretched between them then. "You

can go now. If it's all the same to you, I'll ensure the woman isn't breeding before I go after the youngest of the bunch. I want the strongest targets first."

"Crowe," he murmured.

Laughter whispered through the room. "Ahh, how little you know your enemy. No, the strongest isn't the eldest, nor is it the youngest. The strongest is the one with the least to lose, and the least to love. The other two have other concerns, but this one lives only to see those he loves safe. And there's very little he loves."

"Logan." There was no inflection in his voice; he ensured it.

He was rather relieved actually. It was Logan whose eyes seemed to see the most, whose silence was always the most condemning.

He nodded to the assassin. "Once each target is disposed of, then payment will be made." Turning, he strode quickly, confidently, back to the truck, slid into it, and drove away.

The assassin moved to the window slowly, leaned against the frame, and stared out at the back of the truck as it drove around the bend of the rough track leading into the line shack.

He scratched the side of his cheek before feeling absently at the growth of beard that shadowed his unshaven cheek and jaw. A frown pulled at his brows and a sense of disappointment filled him.

Hell, sometimes a man just didn't know people the way he thought he did, because he would have never

guessed the Callahans' enemy was the man who had
arrived and reaffirmed the contract to kill.

He just would have never guessed—

The next day

He watched Skye leave, his nostrils flaring, fury burning sharp and bright through his senses.

Resentment was like a heavy, hot cloak, smothering
him, weighing him down, and causing paranoia to creep
inside.

It wasn't fair.

It wasn't right.

He had found the other two.

And now Jenny was dead. Her blood had tasted as
sweet as hell as he filled his condom. Her eyes had
been filled with agony as he slit her throat.

He'd done everything perfectly when they'd kidnapped and killed Marietta. He'd left her broken body
lying in her own blood. Her arms were left tied to the
bed. One leg had become disjointed at some point and
lay at an odd angle, but that was okay.

And still, still, his boss said he was considering another route because Cami Flannigan still hadn't been
found. Because he hadn't killed Skye O'Brien?

Lord love them. Not yet. That would be idiocy.

As he'd tried to point out, killing Skye O'Brien right
now simply wasn't a good idea.

Let him take care of Ellen Mason and Cami Flannigan first, then they could discuss killing another of Carter Jefferson's daughters. But if they killed her before they took care of the others, then the FBI was going to come down on them like a ton of bricks before they could ever finish.

The governor would make damned sure of it, and the assassin wasn't ready yet to have to attempt to kill three other women and try to do it around a federal investigation that would all but shut the fucking county down.

He hadn't had time to find Cami, but he'd been working on it. Rafer Callahan had her hidden. They were good at hiding. It wasn't his fault.

Hell, he wasn't even going to bother telling him about the contact he'd made, the bodyguard he might have in his pocket now. The one looking for her.

His boss was going to have to give him more time. But as he stared into the other man's cold, cold eyes night before last, he'd seen the refusal to do so, even though he'd said he would consider it.

He drew in a deep breath.

Jenny's body would be found in a few days, but it wouldn't take much longer than that. She might be a little nobody, even to most of the people she worked with, but she did have that brother in Arizona. He would check on her when he missed her calls after a day or so.

If he was lucky, sooner.

Maybe by then his boss would be done considering it.

Consider it? After all the work he'd done, it would be considered?

He would follow her at a sedate pace, joining the other individuals walking to the town square for the weekend social, a weekend of music, food, and socializing hosted by the county every weekend during the summer months.

His employer was making this job more difficult than it had to be. All his meticulous planning for what? So he could decide that actually watching the house the night they kidnapped Marietta wasn't as important as being a part of the kidnapping?

Then to decide that because in a matter of days, just fucking days, he hadn't found the Flannigan girl he was too slow and they needed help?

That because he'd allowed Logan an alibi, that perhaps he might not be effective?

Might not be effective?

Yeah, he could predict that little fucking whore would be screwing around with Logan Callahan at three in the morning, couldn't he?

What the fuck was his boss's problem?

Was he losing his mind?

Hell, he couldn't do it all.

He was one man.

He couldn't watch those Callahan bastards, find the women his boss liked to play with before he killed them, women the Callahans had had, and find a missing Callahan and his woman, and kill the girl.

It wasn't his fault that those stupid women who gave birth to the Callahans had written their trusts to try to ensure that no one killed their boys for their inheritances.

It wasn't his fault that the only way to steal everything

the Callahans had was to either see them in prison or force them to leave the county before this year was out.

What he knew was that this wasn't working and his boss was now trying to blame him.

Callahan had an alibi, but it was her word over the witness's. Unfortunately, Skye's word actually seemed to carry a little weight. Not just in Sweetrock but in the state itself because of her foster father.

Who would have figured?

Carter Jefferson had lost his daughter in Corbin County twelve years ago to the Sweetrock Slasher, and now the girl he'd all but adopted was here trying to pull the same shit his daughter had tried to pull.

She was trying to identify the Sweetrock Slasher. And he was willing to bet his life that good ole Logan Callahan had no idea little Miss O'Brien was using him just like good ole Amy Jefferson had been.

He didn't mind killing her. It would be a pleasure.

But it had to be done carefully. He had to take her without witnesses. Not even witnesses that thought he might be Callahan. Without anyone being the wiser. Especially his boss. She could just disappear.

Unfortunately, his boss had made a major mistake twelve years ago when he targeted the governor's daughter just because he didn't like the politician and because she was *friends* with Logan Callllahan.

She wasn't his lover. She had just been his friend.

Carter Jefferson held a grudge. If they dared to strike against his foster daughter, then all hell was going to break loose in Sweetrock.

He would follow her tonight as he was ordered.

He'd chitchat, mingle, be himself, and decide the next move to make.

The one move he hesitated to make, though, was the one his boss was demanding.

Kidnap Skye O'Brien and hold her for him.

He shook his head as he moved closer.

That wasn't a very good idea.

Carter Jefferson was a very, very bad enemy to have, whether he knew who you were or not.

He wasn't an enemy he wanted to make.

Not even the unlimited license to kill that he'd been given was payment enough.

CHAPTER FOURTEEN

She had a headache.

A headache, a strained muscle in her neck, and she was riding low on sleep.

That was what she got for watching the video cameras for most of the night. Now her ass was dragging as she walked to the town square the next night and her enthusiasm for her volunteer night at the community center was lagging.

Seven- to twelve-year-olds.

She loved children dearly, but tonight all she wanted to do was curl up in bed and sleep away the feeling that no matter what she did, what she said, no matter which way she turned, Logan still wasn't there, and he wasn't going to be there.

She couldn't give up. She was in too deep for that. The fact that there were already two different operations being run in Corbin County was a damned good sign that sooner or later this place was going to explode from the inside out.

Turning the corner and heading up the sidewalk, she smiled at the sound of the music rolling from the center of the square and the people milling around.

They could bitch all they wanted about the subtle blackmail the town placed on attendance, but once they arrived, they had a damned good time. It wasn't as though everyone was just sitting around morosely and putting in their time before leaving.

Hell no.

Small groups were forming, the food and drinks were flowing, and the sound of laughter was echoing from the square. Glancing up the street at the small group who had amassed on the corner, she couldn't help but grin.

She called them the Second Avenue and Main Street greeting party. Every week she could count on finding them on the corner of Second and Main. They sat on the knee-high stone wall that bordered the Baptist church, greeted everyone walking in from that direction, and kept a watch on parking along the three streets there.

Jack Townsend and his wife, Jeannie, had just reached the corner, while Sheriff Tobias was already there, to Skye's surprise, with Crowe, who was leaning against the streetlight. Tobias' new deputy, John Caine, was cutting across the churchyard, his hard face and narrowed gaze giving him a dark appearance. Amory Wyatt, the Social Services director, was moving across the opposite corner with a wave and smile toward Skye as he joined the group while County Attorney Wayne Sorenson crossed from the town square to the corner as his Amelia and Anna Corbin parked their car in one of the reserved slots on Second Street.

"There she is," Jeannie called out, a smile creasing her face as Skye neared them. "I didn't figure Logan would let you come out and play tonight."

She snorted at the thought and rolled her eyes. "I didn't ask permission to go out and play. Was I supposed to?" She blinked back at Crowe innocently.

"Probably," Crowe drawled as he leaned against the steel support to the streetlight. "You know how he gets when he's got a burr pricking his ass."

Her brow arched. "I'm not hard to find if he needs to see me."

She turned back to Jeannie to see her and Jack both watching in amusement.

"I kind of doubt Logan would venture out here to drag you back," Jack consoled Skye. "He hates these things, but he never tried to cause a scene."

"I think they're a wonderful idea." Perhaps some of her enthusiasm was returning.

Music was drifting around them as the band prepared for the night, and the town square was starting to fill up.

"A wonderful idea, yes, but one Logan doesn't necessarily subscribe to," Crowe stated, his brown eyes dark and quiet as he pulled two thin cigars from the pocket of his vest and handed one to Archer.

Accepting the tobacco, Archer brought it to his nose, inhaled, then let a little sigh of pleasure pass his lips.

Lighting it, then handing the lighter to the sheriff, Crowe continued to stare around, watching the crowd and the incoming attendees silently.

Was his neck tight and filled with the same tension as hers?

That tension that assured her she was being watched. Though admittedly, it had finally eased up several blocks before she turned up Second Street.

"Amelia, Anna, I have the toddlers to the twelve-year-olds tonight." Skye turned to the two girls. "Stop in and see me if you have time."

The two women volunteered often in the Community Center and always gravitated to the younger children and those difficult enough that most parents tended to ignore them.

"Definitely," Anna promised as she slid a look from her friend, Amelia, to the silent Crowe.

Watching her head turn and the look on her face, Skye almost frowned thoughtfully, then caught herself.

Amelia was watching him with a hint of anger, and though Skye would have loved to know why, still, this was the wrong place and time to question it.

She wasn't the only one who must have noticed something off about Amelia's mood, though. As Skye left, Crowe was watching as well.

Turning back to her before she could hide the fact she was observing him, Crowe narrowed his gaze on her. Evidently, Logan wasn't the only one pissed off at her.

"Time for me to go," Crowe finally stated quietly as he straightened from his slouched position. "It's time to head home and make sure that wolf bitch hasn't managed to get back into the house."

"I thought you fixed that dog door?" Jack asked in some surprise.

"I did," Crowe informed him. "Didn't help. She's heavy with pups and somehow found her way back in. If I don't watch her ass she's going to end up having those pups there in my living room, right in front of my fireplace."

The story had been told for weeks about the wolf Crowe had pictures of slipping into his house. There were even pictures of her circulating on the Internet now after someone had convinced Crowe to send the photos to them.

What Skye was certain very, very few people knew was that Crowe had raised the she-wolf from an orphan of only a few weeks of age.

"Look at it this way," Jack suggested. "A momma wolf is better than a guard dog."

"Yeah, but the guard dog would let me in my own house," Crowe drawled ruefully. "Sleep in my own bed. All that good stuff."

"I could send Animal Control, Crowe," Wayne Sorenson suggested in concern. "They'd get her out for you and take her to one of the wolf preserves."

The offer surprised Skye. It was the first time she'd heard of anyone outside the very small circle of Callahan friends offer to do a damned thing for them.

"Naw, I wouldn't like it much if she were locked up that way." He shook his head. "Let me see if I can't figure something else out first. But thanks for the offer."

Wayne nodded his graying head, his gaze thoughtful. "Let me know if you change your mind."

"I'm heading out of here too. Later." Throwing a friendly wave to the group, Skye moved quickly across the street, up the sidewalk on the other side, passed the gazebo where the band had set up, and moved quickly to Central Street on the opposite side of the small park and to the community center. The two-story brick and yellow building housed a large central kitchen with scattered eating and amusement areas on one side and the other side set up with dozens of cots and a few cribs. Upstairs were meeting rooms; in the back were offices, a cinema room, and a nursery.

There were dozens of kids between six and twelve years old whose parents had dropped them off for the weekend or were volunteering in other areas. The kids were divided up; those in the main room were those who weren't interested in watching the movies being played in the cinema room or being with their parents outside.

Skye had two hours' babysitting duty. Then rather than staying for the party, she was seriously considering heading back home and perhaps playing with the cameras some more until daylight.

She'd accidentally fallen asleep through the night as she watched the cameras the night before, and not just her neck was paying for it.

The nightmares that had visited her through the night had seemed stronger than ever, the memories always more graphic than the reality of the operation and always spiraling out of control until she became the victim and the pain and fear began overwhelming her.

Moving through the large room to acquaint herself with the kids, she noticed the teenagers there to keep the younger kids entertained. The high school's program for extra credit for the students volunteering had been a wonderful idea. But there were times when the teenagers were more involved with one another than the jobs they had taken on.

Moving through the large room to the kitchen prep area where two of the teenagers were currently standing next to the counter, more involved with themselves than their jobs, Skye resisted the urge to shake her head at them.

There were currently six young girls from the school's home economics group and three varsity basketball players looking for that extra credit.

Johnny Ridgemore, the captain of the basketball team, and Callie Brock, the president of the Future Homemakers of America, were more involved with their conversation than the kids whom they were assigned.

"Do you need that extra credit you get for performance this weekend, Johnny?" Skye asked the teenager as she moved up to them.

Just showing up wasn't enough to earn that credit; the teens had to actually have performance points to get that extra credit.

Johnny turned to her, though Callie's expression was frankly thankful, as though being there with Johnny wasn't her preference.

Johnny's pale blue eyes gleamed with irritation as he stared back at Skye, his expression turning insultingly mocking as he faced her with a bravado and youthful arrogance that she simply wouldn't deal well with.

"Yeah. So?"

"So, Callie's not six to twelve years old," Skye reminded him.

Sneering at Skye, he turned back to Callie. "You can call me Daddy anytime, babe."

Callie flushed in embarrassment and the look she shot Skye was faintly relieved, until she moved to leave.

It was then that Skye realized Johnny was holding on to Callie's wrist, and if the look of the grip was anything to go by, then her wrist was going to be bruised.

"Let her go, Johnny," Skye warned him.

Johnny let the girl go before swinging back to Skye, his head bending until he was almost nose to nose with her. "Look, bitch, do you know who I'm related to?" His lips twisted in snide disbelief.

"Johnny, I really don't give a damn who you're related to," Skye assured him coolly. "All I care about is that you do what're supposed to to earn that extra credit. Now, I can give you a nice report for my two hours on duty, or I can fill out a complaint against you instead. You choose."

"My uncle's the county attorney," Johnny snapped at her then. "No Callahan whore tells me what to do."

Skye could feel the boy preparing himself, gathering his courage to actually do to her as he'd done to Callie and attempt to intimidate her with strength.

Oh, she was just waiting.

"Do you hear me?" he snarled, his lips pulling back from his teeth.

"Let's see if the Callahans can't convince you then."

As Johnny was lifting his hand to push her away, Skye was tensing, preparing. He was eighteen. He was responsible for his own actions. But it was Logan who laid his hand on Johnny's shoulder, while the boy winced and paled.

Not that Skye could tell Logan was doing anything but laying his hand there as though in camaraderie as Logan lowered his head to the boy's ear.

"I think you want to apologize to the lady," Logan suggested, his voice low as he used his body to block anyone from seeing what was going on.

"Sorry, Ms. O'Brien," Johnny said in a voice strained but with only a hint of anger. The boy looked directly between her eyes rather than meeting her gaze in any semblance of respect.

"Thank you, Johnny," she said softly, as though she actually had some hope that he understood the lesson Logan was trying to teach him.

But she doubted it. She doubted it very seriously. She could see it in his eyes, and she could see it in his expression.

When Logan let Johnny go, he stepped far enough away that he believed Logan couldn't jerk him back before he turned back to them.

"I don't give a damn what you write on that report," he told her, and she could see the rage burning in his expression. "And I don't give a damn about this fucking place either."

As he glanced at Logan, a sudden spark of fear gleamed in Johnny's eyes for just a second before he turned and hurried to the exit, leaving so quickly that the door slammed closed behind him.

"He's nothing like his mother or his uncle," Skye said softly as she felt Logan move behind her.

"Oh, I don't know," Logan said behind her. "I remember when Wayne wasn't much different. When it comes to Callahans, you'll learn, Skye, any respect they show is only skin deep."

"I don't believe that." She couldn't let herself believe it. "I know a lot of people are still wary of pissing off the barons, but their ranches aren't the main source of income any longer. The county is growing, and it's growing with people who aren't as dependent on the Corbins, Raffertys, or Robertses any longer."

"Doesn't matter, Skye," Logan told her cynically. "But that kid is going to be a problem. A problem I'll take care of if he gets in your damn face again."

Logan couldn't believe the sudden, overwhelming rage that had nearly taken him over as he'd seen that kid in her face, heard him call her a Callahan whore.

Logan wasn't having it.

The fine citizens of Corbin County had treated the Callahans like trash since their parents had died, but before that they'd fucking known better.

"How much longer do you have here?" He nodded to the room, all the while ignoring the little girl tugging at the knee of his jeans.

"Hour and a half." Skye's lips twitched as she reached out and petted Bella's happy face as he stared down at the little girl. "Ignoring her isn't going to work any more than ignoring Bella did."

Logan frowned at her.

He was right.

When Skye and that damned pup had stood before him that first night looking so fucking hopeful, he'd known it.

First the dog, then a woman, and now a kid.

Kids didn't belong in a Callahan's life; their parents had proven that. The parents had died and then the kids were left with very little to protect them.

"We need to talk," he told Skye as Bella tried to jump out of his arms again to get to the kid.

"Yes, we do," Skye agreed, then glanced at the child again.

She was staring up at the puppy as though she were a very special gift just for her.

"My daddy is 'lergic," the little girl whispered up at Skye, her big brown eyes as bright as new pennies as she watched Bella. "Can I jus' look at him better?"

Skye lifted her gaze to Logan. "She just wants to see her better," she whispered.

He just wanted to run for cover. "It's a kid," he growled, then watched as Skye gave a little exasperated roll of her eyes.

"And Bella is just a puppy. Puppies and kids go together, Logan. Don't you know that?"

She was ready to laugh at him. He could see it in her eyes.

She was going to start laughing at him and then he was going to end up kissing her again.

Son of a bitch.

"Jus' for a minute?" the little girl asked in a whisper that would have melted stone.

Then he made the mistake of looking down at the child.

Just as he'd made the mistake of kissing Skye that first time.

Big brown eyes. Puppy dog eyes. They matched Bella's.

The kid was all but jumping up and down in excitement as he bent to her and let her pet the pup.

Her little hands were trembling like a leaf in a storm from excitement. Little chubby hands that petted the dog as though she were glass that could break at any minute.

Hell.

Hell because Logan could almost see Skye with such a precious, precocious little girl. She'd have Skye's dark hair and his shade of green—

Oh hell now.

He cleared his throat as he rose slowly. "Time for me to go."

He had to ignore the little girl's disappointed gaze, but he felt like the lowest bastard in the world when tears filled her eyes.

It was time to get the hell out of Dodge was what it was time for. Time to get away from the kids who could break a man's heart with their love for a puppy and a woman who stared at Logan with stars, puppy dogs, and kids in her eyes.

Skye's laughter was soft, knowing, as he rubbed at the back of his neck, then turned and left.

Yeah, they had to talk.

They had to straighten a hell of a lot out.

He had to get her the hell out of Corbin County, but he had a feeling that wasn't going to happen.

Moving from the community center, Logan made his way to a sheltered spot at the side of the building where he let Bella down in the grass and, keeping a firm hold on her leash, let her sniff and play for a few minutes.

And he watched. He watched the darkness and the fine people of Corbin County as they milled around the town square, chatted, and laughed.

He'd never really been a part of the socials. He'd rarely attended them once he was old enough to tell Rafe's uncle he wanted nothing to do with them.

First Logan had gone off by himself; then Crowe and Rafer had followed. They weren't accepted there, even as kids, not really. And other than the summer Rafer had been Jaymi Flannigan's lover, they hadn't attended the socials as adults either.

Logan had a feeling he would be attending more often now, though. Especially after that little punk had dared to call Skye a whore.

Oh, Logan knew Johnny Ridgemore, just as he knew Johnny's parents and his uncle. The Ridgemores had once been friends of Logan's parents, Sam and Mina. Chloe Ridgemore and Mina Rafferty had been so close that Chloe had slipped away and stood up for Mina when she eloped with Sam Callahan.

Within a year, Chloe had deserted her friend. Within two years, Chloe wouldn't even talk to Mina when she saw her on the street.

In the weeks before Logan's parents had been killed, he remembered Chloe slipping over to the house on Rafferty Lane, though. And he remembered his mother's tears after Chloe left.

There were pieces to the puzzle that he was only now remembering. Little things brought those hidden memories back.

Little things like Amelia Sorenson just before Cami was attacked leaving her a note that said they had to talk.

That note had caused Cami to leave the basement of her house unlocked so Amelia could slip in as she had done when they were children.

But it hadn't been Amelia who had slipped in. It had been a killer. The man they had believed was the Sweetrock Slasher.

But, just as with Thomas Jones, Lowry Berry was nothing more than a plant, Logan believed.

Rubbing at the back of his neck again, he stared around the shadowed night, his gaze narrow, his senses on red alert.

Crowe had felt the same sensation, that warning tingle that someone was watching and that someone was filled with pure malicious intent.

An intent Logan intended to do something about.

CHAPTER FIFTEEN

At least he didn't completely leave, Skye consoled herself nearly four hours later when the next volunteer finally arrived. As Skye stepped from the community center, it was to find Logan and Bella waiting for her.

He was leaning against the porch support, looking entirely too lickable and entirely too dominantly male.

There was something about him that was different as he stood there, staring out at the crowd with the tiny pug curled at his feet, her head on the foot of his sneaker as she slept.

He was definitely attracting some attention. More than a few of the attendees were watching him. Some with animosity; others, the feminine group, well, it wasn't animosity in their eyes, that was for sure.

That flare of jealousy snapping inside Skye had her lips tightening as he picked the sleeping pup up and began walking with her.

"Anything you wanted to do before we leave?" he asked as Skye paused beside him.

"Not tonight." She shook her head.

"Sounds good."

He didn't ask for a reason or an explanation, which surprised her. Most men she'd known in the past would have pouted like a ten-year-old because she refused to say what she was doing. The point would be that she wasn't doing what they expected, therefore, something was wrong.

Cradling Bella in the crook of one arm, he placed the palm of the other between Skye's shoulders.

"This way," he murmured, directing her away from the park to the next street rather than going straight through the square.

Crossing the street to the next, he then headed up the back alley.

For the moment, that tingle at the back of her neck eased away. Whoever was watching, following, had lost sight of them.

"You feel it too," she said softly. "The eyes watching."

"The sign of a natural soldier," he murmured. "You're accomplished as well. You're not the only one over the months who was tracking a neighbor. You lost me several times."

The times she had been en route to the doctor in Denver.

Her lips twitched. "That was you when I made the trips to Denver."

He cut through a private yard and used the cement walk that passed between homes.

"Wayne Sorenson came into the Center a while after you left," she told him as they kept mostly to the darker parts of the sidewalk. "He apologized for Johnny and promised something would be done to punish him."

"Yeah, that's what he told me, too." There wasn't a lot of belief in his tone.

She shoved her hands in her pockets as they crossed one of the deserted streets.

"You don't seem confident he will."

"Sorenson usually says what's on his mind and means what he says," he stated. "His sister is another matter, though, and she flat dotes on Johnny. She'd never allow him to be punished for striking out at a Callahan or a woman suspected to be tied to them."

"Don't you ever want more than this, Logan?" Her heart broke when she thought of the lives they'd lived, as well as the lonely, desolate lives they were trying to live now.

Their lovers were killed as soon as a monster could find them. And Marietta had proven, unlike in the past, one-night stands were no longer safe. "Who wouldn't want more, Skye? It's not like we woke up one day and decided we wanted to be targeted by the murdering bastard." Laying his hand on the small of her back, he led her quickly through a narrow street that led to the next block.

"I know," she said softly, easing a little closer to him as they cut into the next alley, then, rather than proceeding to the next block, turned instead into the back street and walked along the darker edge of the rough road.

Moving his hand to her hip, he pulled her closer against his side, causing tears to prick at her eyes.

She wanted to be closer to him. Wanted to feel as though the fury he'd directed at her when he'd learned who she was wouldn't permanently sever the fragile bonds she'd felt building between them.

As they reached the end of the back street, Logan turned again, led her to the corner, across the street, then up another alley.

She wasn't certain how she felt about all these shadowed, dark alleys, but the tingles and the roiling in her stomach she sometimes got when she headed for danger were absent.

"Why do you even stay here?" she finally asked. "Is the inheritance so important for you that you would die for it?"

At first, she thought he wouldn't answer her.

"While I was in the military, I tried to convince myself I didn't miss this place," Logan said as the darkness of yet another back street enclosed them. "We haven't had a moment's peace in this place, Skye, but for some reason, it's home."

"Even though both Callahan and your mothers' sides of the families have disowned you?" And it was the truth. For over twenty years they'd been ignored and persecuted by family members from all branches of their family trees.

"Hell, it's a small town," he sighed. "The barons control their livelihoods, the food they put on their tables, and the peace they gain in their lives. They haven't had a choice but to follow their examples."

That wasn't a good enough excuse for her.

"I saw several people coming up to speak to you while you were waiting for me outside. You should have spit in their faces."

That's what she would have loved to see, but a part of her knew she wouldn't have done it herself, and neither would he.

He did give a brief chuckle though there was little amusement in it.

"They're just being nosy and trying to figure out if we really are killers or innocent bastards. Though we were innocent orphans when our parents died, and they didn't give a shit then either."

How very sad, and how very true.

"I would have stood beside you, Logan," she said then, the pain of the knowledge of the life he had lived slicing at her heart. "I wouldn't have turned my back on you."

"Yeah, I know." His hand moved from her hip to wrap around her shoulders and tugged her even closer. "And that's what terrifies me, Skye. I know you would." Silence filled the night once again, until he led her through another back street. This one's street sign was missing where she'd noticed no others were.

"What's the name of this street?" she asked.

She'd meant to assuage that bit of curiosity months ago, but had forgotten.

"Callahan." A world of mockery filled his tone. "They took the sign down when our parents died."

"None of this makes sense." She shook her head. "Weren't the families all close once?"

"The four founding fathers of the county were raised together from birth. John Corbin the first, Jason Rafferty, Andrew Roberts and James Randal 'Jr' Callahan the first. They were the same as brothers. They had saved each other's lives, killed for each other. The story goes that the bond between them was unshakable. They should have been running the country." The low grunt of laughter was amused and yet bitter. "If only their sons, grandsons, and so forth could have known that bond. Or at least the decency the four of them showed."

"So all of this began six generations ago?" she probed.

"Pretty much." He nodded. "They transferred their families, their ranches, and in a matter of months Sweet-rock and Corbin County were begun. Very quietly, but very quickly."

"They had a dream then?"

"Yeah, I guess they did." Another alley, another yard, then he and Skye cut over until they were walking along the mountain's base behind Rafferty Lane and using the trees for cover. "That dream sustained them. Our fathers told us stories that their father told them, that his father told him. Callahans were horse breeders, but the need for quarter horses faded away, leaving the farm. By the fourth generation Callahans were on the verge of losing it all. Eileen and James Randal's boys were in the Army, unable to help them. That was when Eileen made a decision that changed all their lives. She and friends of hers created an elaborate plot to allow them to buy her blond-haired blue-eyed son for an exorbitant amount. It was enough to save the ranch from being taken and to pay the hospital bills for her husband.

Then they set about ensuring they could rub the noses of the other families in the fact that they were unable to destroy them. They'd refused to help, even while her husband was dying because she couldn't afford the medical costs. She hated them, and once they were forced to lose their newborn, her husband hated his side with the same ferocity."

"Then they died."

"Yeah, then they died," he sighed.

His and Skye's homes came into view. Porch lights blazing, looking serene in the darkness, and safe.

Just as Corbin County itself seemed serene and safe. Unless one was a Callahan.

"These trees at the edge of the yard were planted by my father," Logan told her as he led her to the line of pines that stretched from the base of the mountain to the far edge of his home. "He wanted cover. After the boys returned from the war, Rafer's uncle, Clyde said they were just different. Paranoid at times, and certain they were being watched."

"Perhaps they were," she said as they entered the shadows of those trees.

"Perhaps," he agreed. "Perhaps it's hereditary. Crowe, Logan, and I have installed heat conductors all along the lower edge of the mountain beginning about a block above where we came in and then along the side of the house. Anyone using the thermal image scanners or cameras is going to have a hell of a hard time seeing us."

She frowned at the knowledge. "I haven't seen that on my cameras."

"Because it wasn't turned on until I left tonight," he told her. "I want to catch the fucker, Skye. But I also wanted to be certain we could get back to the house and get to the vehicles in the garage as well if we needed them."

Yeah, maybe the paranoia was hereditary, she thought, but from what she'd seen herself, she was doubting it. And there was truth to the old saying. "Just because you're paranoid doesn't mean someone isn't out to get you," she murmured.

"Pretty much." The rueful acknowledgment in his tone made her feel slightly better until he continued. "We'll go through my house; then you can reach yours through the side yard."

So much for that arousal that had been inside her for most of the evening.

She wasn't begging, she told herself. She simply wasn't doing it.

Following him into the house, Skye moved through the house behind him until he unlocked the patio door, opened it, and stood back.

Without a word she moved quickly past him as she pulled her keys from the pocket of her jeans, at once thankful that she'd had each door keyed to the same key.

"Good night, Skye," he called as she reached her door.

"Yeah. Night, Logan." Unlocking it, she stepped inside the house, closed the door, then growled, "Asshole tease, fucking prick."

She hated a man who teased. Not that she or any of her friends over the years had had that problem. Hell no, the men they'd dated were right there, ready to go, condom equipped and fully prepared to finish the night in their beds whether it was the first date or the second month.

She had to pick a man with frickin' morals when it came to her life, though, and one who had decided, for her, that he wasn't risking her life by sleeping with her.

As though that would change anything if the Slasher decided to come after her.

Locking the door behind her, she stared around the dimly lit living room and breathed out in regret before pulling the small automatic handgun from her purse and checking each room carefully.

Starting upstairs, she went through each bedroom, each closet, and looked under each bed.

Nothing was there, and nothing had been disturbed. And if anyone had tried to get into the house, then the vibration alarm on her watch would have warned her, just as it had warned her when Logan had slipped in.

Laying the gun on the kitchen counter, she was pouring a glass of water when the unexpected, the unthinkable happened.

She'd never imagined anyone but Logan could get past her security, and he'd only managed it because when he'd slipped into the house, the security system hadn't been able to connect with the cell phone reception it used to warn her of an intrusion.

That had been a fluke.

This wasn't.

She hadn't turned the lights on. She couldn't see the shadow that had hidden in the corner of the cabinets at the darkest place. She rarely did when coming in late.

She had the alarm tied to her watch. She would know if there were intruders.

Tonight, someone had slipped past.

A foul-smelling, choking, damp cloth suddenly clamped over her face as a hard arm trapped hers at her side. The other hand, clamped over her mouth with the cloth beneath it, held her head brutally to a hard chest.

After that first, shocked intake of air and the scalding sensation of the fumes eating at her lungs, Skye fought to hold her breath.

The fumes from the cloth burned her eyes, causing them to tear as she rammed the heel of her boot down sharp and hard on the toe of her attacker's.

He only laughed.

Steel toe.

God, she had to move.

She had to break his hold before she was forced to breathe in or lose consciousness.

Her hands and arms were immobilized.

High, steel-toed boots protected his feet and lower legs.

He still had balls though.

Jerking forcefully, obviously catching him just a little off guard, she was able to get one hand to his thighs, and before he could stop her, her fingers were digging into the sensitive sack.

A grunt, then a sharp cry, and the hold against her head loosened.

Lunging forward, Skye came back with enough force that the back of her head cracked into his teeth and nose, gaining her immediate release.

The alarm on the watch began vibrating against her wrist as she found herself flying. She was thrown away from her attacker, catapulted over the bar where her shoulder hit the edge with enough force to cause her to cry out.

A roar of pure male rage seemed to fill the night before the sharp sound of her back door slamming into the wall assured her the bastard was getting away.

"No!" She struggled to get to her feet.

Her gun was on the counter.

"Skye! Ah God. Skye. Baby!"

Logan was there.

She couldn't see clearly.

Her vision was blurred, and the thick, foul taste of the cloth that had been clamped over her face seemed to permeate every inch of air she tried to suck into her starved lungs.

"Go," she wheezed, certain she could breathe in just a moment. "He's getting away. Go."

"Like hell."

She found herself suddenly jerked into his arms, picked up from the floor as the world seemed to spin around her in dizzying circles.

Logan was yelling something. Or was he screaming? She could hear his voice, but she couldn't make out the words. They just didn't seem to make enough sense as she felt herself floating.

"Don't you dare. Don't you dare fucking pass out on me," he was definitely screaming at her. "Pass out on me, Skye, and I swear I'm going to spank your ass."

Well. Hell.

She might like it.

That hazy, distant thought was followed by a wave of weakness causing her head to slump back on his shoulder.

"The fuck you'll pass out on me." He didn't sound right.

There was something harsh, scratched about his voice.

"Breathe, damn you!"

Hell, he was screaming at her again, and the darkness was so—

Piercing, agonizing, air rushed into her lungs so hard that she almost threw up. Quickly, Logan gathered her in his arms.

Skye managed to tear herself away, only to find her knees collapsing as she fought to stand up. She was pitching to the floor when strong, warm hands suddenly caught her and one moved quickly to press her head to his chest again.

"No more," she wheezed, tears pouring from her eyes as they burned painfully. "Please—" another choking fit and Logan was rubbing her back firmly with one hand and massaging her diaphragm with the other.

But she could breathe again.

She was able to draw in air without choking. She was no longer drifting in that place where there was no oxygen, no strength, nothing to hold her rooted in reality. But God, she could smell that scent. The one that had saturated the cloth her attacker had clamped over her mouth and nose.

"God! Oh God. Skye."

Logan was rocking her?

She couldn't open her eyes, not yet. She might be able to breathe now but she was still so incredibly weak.

"I don't give a fuck what he's doing!"

Logan was screaming again.

Why was he screaming?

"Put me through to Tobias, or the next time I see you I swear to God above I'll tear your fucking head off your shoulders, rip your guts through your neck, and shit down it, Caine!"

If she had the strength, Skye would have winced at the deadly promise in Logan's overly loud voice. "Now patch me through to him now, goddammit."

She would have to have words with him over that particular vulgarity.

Damn, what was wrong with her?

She felt as though she were drifting in clouds, just a little thick, heavy, light-on-the-oxygen clouds.

But at least that beast with the sharp claws wasn't ripping at her lungs anymore. Nope, his cousin, the body gremlin, was wracking her with smaller ones.

But it wasn't as bad.

She could stand it.

The agency had been very proud of the fact that she had a high tolerance for pain.

The air became thicker, slowly. At first, she tried to fight to breathe, but something was so weak inside her that drawing that breath—

There was the beast again.

Ah hell, she was going to puke if this didn't stop.

Fighting to breathe, suddenly sobbing with the pain tearing at her lungs and eyes, Skye tried to claw at her chest, certain something there was the reason for her lack of oxygen.

She had to get her flesh peeled away.

If she could just open her lungs.

That sharp, pain-heralding scent hit her senses again as Skye found the strength to fight.

Pitching, trying to roll, jerking against his hold, and sobbing out in agony, she fought to get free of the arms that locked her in place.

"Chest," she gasped. "Get it—off."

She really couldn't breathe.

The only breaths she could take were those of what she was distantly aware were accompanied by the first-aid astringent used to force consciousness back.

Logan was jerking her shirt off, though, that was all that mattered.

He was cursing. He was using four-letter words she was certain even she hadn't ever heard before.

A second later warmth suffused the cold flesh of her chest and washed over her breasts.

Was he washing her?

A slick, soap-slickened cloth was scrubbing at her flesh as she was suddenly lifted again.

"Come on, baby. Please. Skye, baby, please." The pleas were so harsh, so desperate, she had to heed them.

She could hear the terror clawing at Logan's voice. What had him so frightened?

Something was wrong. Was he in danger? Did he need her?

She had sworn to herself she would be there when he needed her.

Where she found the strength to force air into her lungs she wasn't certain.

"Hurts," she finally managed to gasp as she felt him laying her to the floor. "Please—"

Then his hands were beneath her breasts, pressing firmly, at first sending dull-toothed demons to rip at her lungs before they slowly, so very slowly, eased away.

Each gentle manipulation of her chest helped. Finally, her lungs began to work on their own.

It still hurt. It still hurt incredibly badly, but it was getting easier.

As the ability to breathe returned, she became aware of more sounds, more shouts and orders, demands and furious male accusations flying back and forth.

"Please." She reached out for Logan, fighting to open her eyes.

The noise was piercing her skull.

"Logan, please." Even the sound of her own voice was ripping at her brain.

"Easy. No more." It was a whisper, soft despite the roughness of his tone. "Everyone's quiet, baby."

His head touched the side of hers and Skye could have sworn she felt his body shaking against hers. "Everyone's quiet."

Breathing in slow and easy, she just wanted to sleep now.

She could feel Logan's hands still massaging her diaphragm, hear his whispers against her hair.

Then her face was being covered and oxygen began to simply infuse her being.

Precious, life-giving, sweet, pure oxygen.

Logan gently eased one of his big shirts over Skye's arm, and with Archer's help they lifted her gently and eased it behind her back before pushing the other arm through.

After buttoning the shirt, he lifted his arm and used the back of it to wipe the perspiration from his face.

At least he told himself it was perspiration that soaked his face.

"Here, Logan, let me get those buttons." Looking down to see the trembling of his hands as he tried to button the shirt over her lacy bra, Logan eased back.

Quickly, efficiently, Archer slid the buttons into their holes, but Logan noticed even his hands weren't quite steady.

The EMTs were trying to work around them.

A blood pressure cuff was tightening on her arm as Zach Kilgore glanced at Logan warily.

Zach was a third cousin. One of the decent ones, Logan had always thought. At the least, he spoke instead of pretending his Callahan cousins didn't exist.

"Logan, we really need you and the sheriff to move," Zach told him again. "We can't help her if you don't let us."

Logan looked down.

Her breasts were rising and falling rhythmically.

She wasn't gasping any longer and her lips were losing their bluish tint.

"Come on, Logan." Archer nudged his shoulder with his own as he crouched next to Logan. "You know you can trust Zach."

Immediately Logan shook his head. He couldn't trust anyone with her life.

No one.

"Trust me, Logan?" Archer asked then. "Do you think that together, we can't stop anyone from hurting her?"

He lifted his eyes from the proof she was breathing before dragging in a harsh breath.

Nodding abruptly, he unstraddled her, watching the EMTs without an ounce of trust as they quickly moved into place.

Reaching behind him, he dragged the cloth that must have fallen just inside her shirt earlier from his back pocket.

The killer had finally a mistake. A mistake that Logan intended to use to ensure he tracked him down. And when he did?

He glanced at Archer, eyes narrowed as the sheriff stood watching, his hands braced on his hips as he glared down at Skye in worry.

"I'm going to kill him, Archer," Logan said then.

The entire room seemed to still. Even the walls seemed to have a sense of waiting.

"Shut the fuck up, Logan," the other man snapped, his expression forbidding. "You're not thinking clearly right now. But you go any further and you'll force me to do something I damned sure don't want to do."

Logan turned and stared at Skye once again.

She was still pale, but comfortable.

Every few minutes her lashes would struggle to lift, then drift closed again as she continued to gather her strength.

Lifting his hand, he stared at the cloth in his hand and knew what it was. The drug used to incapacitate each of the victims of the Sweetrock Slasher from now to twelve years before.

"What is it?" Archer asked as Logan rose slowly to his feet.

He could finally feel his heart beating again, feel the sense of unreality receding.

God help him, he'd almost lost her.

The EMTs had her stabilized and were talking to the doctors at the clinic. An IV had been pushed into her arm, a bag of fluids suspended from a metal stand beside her.

As Archer spoke, he'd grabbed an evidence bag and opened it quickly. Logan dropped the rag into it.

"It was trapped beneath her blouse after the bastard escaped," he said, his voice still so rough he wondered if he could continue to hold back his screams of pure rage.

Archer stared at the evidence bag in shock, then back to Logan.

"My God, it really was him," Archer said softly, the shock impossible now to hide.

"Oh, it was him." Logan sat down in one of the chairs that surrounded the small kitchen table. "Trust me, Archer, it was the Slasher. I just want to know how he got past her security system, and I want to know who the hell he is."

He didn't have to say anything more.

Whoever he was, he was a dead man walking, because Logan had every intention of killing him.

CHAPTER SIXTEEN

Hours later, much too long to suit Logan, he watched as Skye walked from the bathroom, slowly drying her hair as yards of silken material whispered from her breasts to her feet as she moved.

She'd insisted on returning to her house rather than his. Demanded that Logan take her home until he'd finally given in. He'd carried her into the house after Archer and his deputy, John Caine, did a thorough search of the house. He'd helped secure every door and window as well while she showered.

The doors were secured with more than the security system and door locks. Until he could figure out how the Slasher had gotten into her home, Logan had had Archer, personally, place heavy bolt locks on them while he went to the hospital with Skye.

Each window was secured with heavy boards placed between the frame and bottom portion to keep the window from being raised.

The less technical security measures would ensure
no one got in without making enough noise to warn
him well ahead of time. And they wouldn't have been
necessary if Skye hadn't insisted. Just as she wouldn't
be in her own house if she would have just listened to
him and come back to his instead.

She was herself again, albeit with a few bruises. Sassy
as hell and more than pissed off.

But she was alive.

That was all that mattered.

She was alive, and as she dropped the towel and
moved to him, Logan couldn't help but pull her to him,
almost shaking with the need to touch her.

To feel her breathing.

To feel her belonging to him.

As he held her, Skye couldn't help but close her eyes,
the memory of her brush with death striking at her with
terrifying clarity.

The overdose of chemicals on the cloth should have
killed her. The doctors had actually been amazed Logan had kept her breathing until the EMTs had arrived.

Her heart was racing so fast now it felt as though it
would race straight from her body. There was a fine tremble quivering through her body, quivering through her
hands as the need to touch him became overwhelming.

"You're not going to listen to good sense, are you?"
he finally asked as she watched him silently.

"And leave?" she asked as he moved to her.

At his sharp nod she could only shake her head back
at him. "I owe Amy more than to just walk away now."

"Let me take care of it, Skye," he asked softly then,

staring down at her as he watched her intently. "Vengeance is my job and I have this covered."

"And I've dreamed of taking this bastard down nearly half my life. It's not a dream I'm willing to give up. And I'm not willing to give you up either, Logan. I won't let him win."

"This isn't a game, Skye." His expression was somber, his tone filled with warning.

"No, it's not a game," she agreed. "It's twelve years of your life stolen and eight women dead who didn't deserve to die in the attempt to frame you and your cousins and ensure you have no one to turn to. For God's sake, Logan, don't you think there are people who care for the three of you? Who need to see you safe?"

"Then they need to stay out of it," he growled down at her as he moved back from her and raked his fingers through his hair with an edge of frustration.

Skye shook her head, smiling back at him mockingly. "That's not going to happen."

"Don't you know anything but fucking defying me? Would you listen for a change?"

"Say something sensible and I might consider it," she suggested flippantly before gasping at the hold that was suddenly on her upper arms and the pressure of his chest against her breasts as he dragged her to him.

Gripping his forearms and staring back at him in defiance, she arched her brow back at him.

There was nothing left for him to say.

Hell, he couldn't think of anything to say past the hunger, the need, and the desperation to have her.

The hunger to touch her, to taste her.

To fuck them both into exhaustion.

Tangling his fingers in her hair, feeling the silken mass of curls against his flesh, he pulled her head back slowly. Dark lashes dropped slumberously; her eyes gleamed with sudden, unmistakable arousal.

He didn't think about it before he kissed her. He never thought about it first. The overwhelming urge to just do it was always there, and always impossible to fight.

Their lips fit together like two pieces of a whole. Conforming naturally, heatedly, as he took long, drugging tastes of the sensuality that was so much a part of her.

Dragging her closer, his arms surrounding her, Logan could feel the warm weight of her breasts against his chest, feel the need surging between them, amplifying a hunger already raging out of control.

Tearing his lips from hers was almost impossible. He wanted her kisses like a man dying of thirst wanted water. But he wanted her naked. Wanted her warm flesh against him and the sweet heat of her need burning through him.

Gripping the edge of her soft blouse, he pulled it up slowly, watching the graceful lift of her arms as he pulled it over her head, then tossed it carelessly to the floor.

Firm, lush breasts rose and fell quickly, tight, hard little nipples pressing against the pure white lace of her bra. Cupping the generous weight, he raked his fingers over the hardened tips and was rewarded by a throttled, hungry little moan.

It was a flick of his finger and thumb to release the

catch between her breasts; then he was peeling the cups back and pushing the straps over her shoulders and down her arms.

Lowering his head, the need to taste her nipples had his mouth watering. Slowly dragging the straps of her gown over her shoulders and breasts, Logan brushed over the stiff peaks of her nipples,

Pushing the material over her thighs, Logan gripped them and pulled her closer, sucking a nipple inside his mouth and laving it with his tongue.

Watching her eyes closely, Logan ran his hands down her legs, then moved both to the soft rise of her ass and clenched his fingers delicately. As he drew on the tender tip, her nimble fingers went to the buttons of his shirt. She released them slowly as she breathed out raggedly, little moans rising from her as she worked around the fact that he refused to release her nipple and give her better access.

As she pushed the material from her shoulders, Logan released her nipple, gripped her hips again, and then turned her to lower her to the bed.

How much longer he would be able to wait before taking her, Logan wasn't certain. He knew that having her was something that was going to have to happen.

He wouldn't be able to survive without it.

Catching one of the tight peaks between his lips as he moved over her once again, the arch of her body, the cry that fell from her lips, filling his senses, he sucked it into his mouth with hungry demand.

He couldn't get enough of her.

Each flick of his tongue over her nipples, each draw

of his mouth, had her hands tightening at his shoulders or her nails raking against them as he sucked at her nipples demandingly.

The feel of her fingers raking through his hair, her nails rasping his scalp, had shards of sensation attacking his balls, tightening and pouring wave after wave of pleasure through his body.

God, he needed her.

Gripping her thighs, he spread them farther before sliding his hands to the sides of her ass and pulling her closer to him. His lips moved between her breasts, his tongue swiping over her flesh to taste the sweet vanilla and sugar taste of her before kissing his way down.

"Logan," she whispered sensually as he eased her further back on the bed.

Propping herself on her elbows, she watched him, her gaze drowsy, hungry as he began kissing his way along the silky flesh of her stomach to her rounded thighs.

His tongue licked over silky skin as his lips took sipping, sometimes-suckling kisses. He brushed his beard against her thighs and his body tightened at the moan that left her lips. As he brushed it against the soft, nude flesh of her pussy, her hands found their way to his hair again and bunched in the strands at the top of his head.

Fighting the need to rush, to relieve that ache driving inside him, Logan throttled the lust tearing at him. It was a battle to give her all the exquisite pleasure possible, because he had to convince her she didn't have his heart.

A heart he knew already belonged to her.

* * *

Skye couldn't hold back her cries any longer. The feel of his lips brushing against the sensitive folds of flesh, his tongue licking at it erotically, was unbearably good. Lying back, her fingers buried in his hair, clenched in the coarse strands, she held on for the riotous, fiery ride of pleasure building through her.

Heat flushed through her body. Like a wave of liquid flames shooting through her veins it tore through her and burned straight to her pussy, to her clit.

Each brush of his beard sent pinpricks of pleasure rushing through the naked folds and driving into the clenched tissue of her vagina.

She wanted—

"Oh, God, I want—"

"What do you want, baby? Tell me?" he demanded, his voice rough. "All you have to do is tell me."

She had spoken aloud? She hadn't meant to.

His beard brushed over the wet lips of her pussy and a flood of juices caressed the sensitive flesh inside.

"Touch me more, Logan," she whispered. "Please, I need more."

"How?"

"God, I don't know how!" she all but wailed. "Just give me more."

His fingers eased up the slit, parted her, only to follow with the wet heat of his tongue in a long, slow lick.

"Oh, yes," she breathed out, unable to hold back the low, drawn-out moan. "Oh, yes, Logan. Do it again."

He did it again, but as he licked over her clit his tongue stiffened to tuck against the side of it and rub. He just rubbed against it, using the thin layer of skin between his tongue and the side of her clit for added friction.

Pleasure built to an agonizing need for release. Her clit swelled and throbbed, her juices easing from her, saturating the folds of her sex, the feel of them caressing that inner flesh almost more than she could bear.

"Again," she moaned.

His tongue probed at the little bud again, circled it, added to the friction, and rubbed harder against the side of the bundle of nerves before flicking over it.

Broad male fingers parted her lips, rimmed the entrance. Lifting her hips to facilitate his stroking fingers, she moaned at the need. Skye cried out breathlessly as he worked it slowly inside her pussy.

So slowly.

She could feel every rasp of his finger inside her as he caressed her, moving with slow, deliberate motions and small, stroking thrusts until he buried the digit full length inside her.

His tongue tortured her clit with nearing rapture, holding back just enough to keep her from her orgasm, pulling her from the edge each time the rasp of his tongue rotated against the side of her clit.

When he capped his lips over it and sucked at it with firm draws of his lips she nearly went through the roof. Pinpoints of sizzling sensation struck at her clit, at the tender depths of her pussy. His finger stroked and rubbed deep inside her, adding to the friction that burned around the tender bud of her clitoris.

Her hips writhed beneath his touch. Circling against his tongue, arching to him, desperate to make each caress deeper, firmer. Until his hands clamped on them, holding her still as his tongue became a wicked instrument of sensual torture.

"Logan," she said, breathless, locked in a pleasure she couldn't escape and had no desire to end, despite the fact that she was certain she couldn't survive it.

Her head tossed, rolling from side to side as the need for more sensation became so overwhelming her hands unlocked from his hair and cupped the mounds of her breasts.

Tight and hard, her nipples were painfully stiff, demanding touch, if only her own. Gripping the rigid peaks, she pulled at them, gasping at the lightning-swift strikes of furious sensation that raced to her womb from Logan's suckling mouth, and the flares of red-hot pleasure that struck her nipples.

Her thighs tightened as his finger pulled back, her muscles clenching desperately at the loss of fullness until his finger returned in an even, pulse-pounding stroke, calloused and feeling thicker than it should as Logan worked it inside, careful to stroke every nerve ending possible along the way.

Crooking his finger as it reached the farthest depth of her, he then found a new, violently sensitive area to torment and torture.

She nearly lifted from the grip he had her in with his free hand. As she bucked against him, her fingers pulling at her nipples, a strangled cry came from her lips.

She was there.

So close.

She could feel it racing through her, each incredible

sensation, like fingers all over her body, inside every erogenous zone, stroking and rasping over nerve endings so delicate her body could barely process the pleasure.

She tingled. Burned.

Her clit became impossibly tighter, harder, throbbing with exquisite agony until the tip of his tongue tightened again, tucked against the side of her clitoris, and did that thing again.

That thing where he rolled it against her clit, rasping against such an incredibly sensitive nerve ending that she wondered if she would survive it.

She couldn't survive it. She couldn't breathe for it. Waves of sensation tightened, coalesced, until—

"Damn you. No!"

He was gone.

"Don't. Please, Logan, no." She would kill him. "You can't—"

Stop?

His hands curved around her thighs and jerked her closer as he came between them, tucking the head of his cock between the slick, swollen folds of her pussy.

"Logan," she breathed out harshly, realizing her nails were biting into his forearms.

Iron hard. Thick.

She breathed in hard as the entrance to her pussy began to stretch.

Skye couldn't decide if it was pleasure or pain. It was such a mix of both, so intense and overwhelming, that she felt as though she were burning from the inside out.

"So fucking tight," he groaned as she stared back at him, the sensations so overwhelming it was all she could do to keep from screaming with the agony and the ecstasy of it. "Are you a damned virgin?"

He paused, a flare of something like panic filling his eyes.

Skye shook her head desperately.

"Don't stop," she begged as she felt a rush of her juices spilling to further lubricate the entrance he was pushing into.

His hips jerked as her muscles tightened further, stroking the broad head a fraction deeper as she cried out weakly.

As he slid one hand from her hip, the pad of his thumb tucked against the side of her clit, as he'd done with his tongue moments before.

His thumb rolled and pressed against the little bud. Her clit swelled further, her juices, slick and hot, spilled from her pussy as he pressed in farther. Stretching her, the heavy flesh opening her, revealing nerve endings more sensitive than those found before and stroking over them, caressing them.

"Logan, oh God, it's so good." Her knees lifted, tightening on his hips as the crest slipped in completely and the hard throb of his cock pulsed just inside her.

Struggling to open her eyes, to stare up at him, she watched a fine bead of perspiration as it ran in a thin rivulet down his face to disappear into his beard.

Dark, dark emerald eyes stared into hers, held her, mesmerized her, as her pussy clenched around the heavy, invasive width of his cock head.

It was like a burning conflagration tightening inside her, moving slowly forward, possessing her.

"Logan, more—" it was a whisper, a too-quiet cry, because she wasn't certain he could hear the plea for the pounding of her heart.

Easing back, he came forward again, a slow, firm press of his hips, a stroke of burning sensation, a delicate rasp against flesh so excited that each caress was fire and ice.

His expression tightened, his jaw bunching, as she felt his cock throb harder, a feeling as though it was expanding thicker inside her, pressing against tissue already overstretched and struggling to accept the width.

Each throb of his cock and the muscles of her vagina clenched, stroked his cock head, flexing around it and tightening, desperate to draw him deeper.

She needed him.

She needed him fully inside her.

She needed all those incredible sensations racing through her.

Arching to him, thighs tightening at his hips, her back bowed from the counter and he was inside her deeper. Just a little deeper.

"No. Fuck. Skye, baby, slow." Hoarse and strained, his voice sounded as broken as her control.

But not broken enough. Not far enough in the same vortex she was fighting to slip farther inside.

"More," she moaned again. "Fuck me, Logan. Please, please fuck me—"

The words were cut off for the simple reason that she had to inhale. Sharply. Her eyes widened, her body tensing as he buried inside her almost halfway. He pulled back, and she watched his face tighten further, his eyes drifting closed before he gave in to it, the incredible hunger swirling around them.

Moving, his hips thrusting his cock deeper, deeper inside her, working it past the tight, flexing tissue of her vagina and stroking nerve endings she hadn't known she had or could have known were so sensitive.

She was more aroused than she had ever been. Each stretch, each fierce throb and heated stroke, amplified the sensations already expanding out of control.

Short, fierce thrusts. Once. Twice.

The third stroke buried him inside her to the hilt.

And then there was no stopping either of them.

Skye's legs wrapped around his hips as Logan's hands clamped to her rear and added yet more sensation to the mix. Parting the tender curves of her rear and sending striking flares of heat through the rear entrance as his thrusts began in earnest, Skye gave herself completely to the power of his touch and the pleasure.

A pleasure she had only ever read of and had known she could never experience.

Yet here it was.

Locked in his gaze, held by the thrust and power of his cock filling her, throbbing inside her with each impalement. Bearing down on the shuttling, iron-hard shaft, her muscles tight and quivering, flames beginning to race, to sear, to strike at her clit, her vagina.

Nerve endings flared, expanded, and as she felt his cock expand, the heat of it intensifying, Skye felt herself exploding.

The pleasure ruptured inside her in a wave of such destructive rapture that she was certain she wouldn't, couldn't, come out of it the same.

She tried to scream, but there was no energy, no breath, no thought capable of any other function but the hard, clenching power overtaking her, stroking through her veins, over her nerve endings like a thousand tiny electrical currents of ecstasy.

Shaking in his grip, held suspected within the rapture as he continued to thrust harder, faster, driving inside her, fucking her past reason and restraint. Another brutal explosion before the first had even had a chance to ease, then the pleasure drove into her very core with the final thrust and the feel of his release, hot and silky smooth, spurting into the unprotected depths of her pussy, only threw her further into the ecstasy.

It should have thrown her back to reason, to reality. It should have left her in a state of panic and chaos and screaming in fear.

Instead, the feel of his release jetting to the sensitive tissue, searing it, adding to the sensations, only sent her reeling into a wave of such ecstasy that for a moment she felt blinded, held suspended in a world the color of emeralds, dark and mesmerizing and filled with wave after wave of pleasure that she knew she would never find again outside his arms.

CHAPTER SEVENTEEN

Skye was replete, sensually satisfied and feeling the effects of complete exhaustion as it dragged at her body.

And she was waiting for daylight.

Lying against Logan's shoulder, if she opened her eyes she would be staring into the squished little face of the pup who had demanded to sleep on his chest.

And with both of them lying on him, Skye against his shoulder and the pup sprawled, front paws spread out from her wrinkled face, sleeping on his chest, Logan was still breathing heavily and sleeping as deep as she imagined he could.

She imagined that, like her, he rarely slept very deeply.

Was it a part of the life, the realization of the dangers that could visit as they slept?

Skye knew well what could visit as she slept; she'd been up close and personal with it. Just as she'd learned, as fate would set it for her, most of those monsters had rarely visited when the sun rose. They came in the dark, while hidden, while shadowed and unable to see themselves the horrible destruction they wrought.

Daylight was less than an hour away, though. If she stayed awake until she could see the dawn beginning to brush against the curtains covering the windows, then when she slept it would be without nightmares.

Warm, so drowsy that it would be a struggle to remain awake this last hour, she found herself visiting areas of her life that she never had allowed herself to visit. Memories she hadn't realized she had, hadn't realized were there.

She'd always been scared of the dark, she knew. A fear she remembered her parents actually encouraging.

Nightmares, her father had told her gently, if firmly, were the mind's way to warn her to be wary, to sleep lightly.

She frowned as she felt Logan shift against her, his hand stroking over her hip before he stilled against her once again.

Whenever the nightmares woke her, screaming and in tears, her parents had been there at first, soothing her but always making her aware that the nightmares were warning her. But her parents had never told her what the nightmares were warning her of.

Over the years, though, the screaming had stopped. By the time she reached her teens she found herself waking silently but unable to go back to sleep, always watching the night. It had been hell when she'd begun private school. She'd had to learn how to hide the fact that she was only sleeping a few hours a night. For a while she'd actually found herself depending on medicinal aids to stay awake.

She was in the academy before she'd realized what her parents had been doing and who they were. Even after their deaths she hadn't suspected what they were or the fact that from a young age she had been trained specifically for one thing. To join the academy.

Staring into the darkness, she wished that she'd known what her parents were doing, that they had explained it to her before their deaths. Instead, they had left the explanations to Carter, and there were so many of her questions that he couldn't answer.

Some people had no business being parents, she thought. They had no business breeding, because even with the affection they might feel for their children, to some people their children were still possessions. They were extensions of their parents rather than beings in their own right. And that was what she was to her parents. She was an extension of what they were, of what they were doing, and, in their eyes, the future of their ultimate goals.

Just as Amy had been to Carter Jefferson. And after Amy's death, Carter had transferred his plans from his daughter to his foster daughter, knowing that she had already been prepared for the life her parents had expected her to live.

Was that why the nightmares had grown so difficult? So bloody and violent? Or was it really, as she'd told her director and Carter, a result of that final assignment and a killer's vindictive nature?

She suppressed a shudder, knowing beyond a shadow of a doubt it would awaken Logan.

Instead, she gave a hard jerk at the almost-silent vibration of the phone beside Logan on the bed.

Instantly he was reaching for it and bringing it to his ear as he murmured to Skye, "It's Crowe."

"Which house are you in?" Crowe demanded quietly before Logan had a chance to speak.

"Skye's." He was moving even as Crowe spoke, knowing he would have never called if it weren't an emergency.

Skye was rolling from the bed as Logan gently set the pup on the bed and rose quickly to his feet, reaching for the clothes he'd brought into the bedroom after carrying Skye to bed earlier.

"Check the security cameras for anyone around the house," Crowe ordered. "I have Rafer and Cami with me. She was attacked and two bodyguards nearly killed. She's been hurt."

"The cameras," Logan told Skye as she quickly tied a pair of sneakers on her feet. "Crowe's coming in with Rafer and Cami. She was attacked."

Following Skye as he pulled his weapon from the bed stand and checked the clip efficiently, Logan felt himself slipping into the cold, steely skin he had used while in the military.

The door to the camera room popped open as Logan and Skye approached it, the door sliding back easily as Skye began working the remote.

The six cameras' four sections popped up instantly,

the thermal imagining and digital status reports lighting the closet.

Pulling up the three rooftop views rather than the sectioned displays, she began rotating the cameras slowly to scan the entire area around the house.

"We have an all clear if they come in around the back as we did. We have several neighbors preparing to leave for work, as well as a deputy drive-by beginning at the end of the street," she told Logan as he flipped the phone to speaker.

"All clear for a back entrance," Logan told Crowe. "Keep to the thermal path and you'll come in without detection."

One camera focused automatically on the three images moving into the heated path the cousins had lain in months before. The path, heated to varying degrees, showed shadowed shifts and temperature variants that could be blamed on the thermal activity the area also possessed. The same activity they had tapped into for the pipes buried just beneath the ground.

Turning to move, Logan saw that Skye already had her weapon in one hand, the pup in the other. A dark jacket covered the dark T-shirt Skye had pulled on, and a hat covered her head.

Taking Bella in his free arm, he led the way through the house to the patio doors.

Unlocking the doors and sliding them open soundlessly, Skye crouched and stepped out, covering the area as Logan followed and moved quickly across the small yard.

Opening his patio doors to his own house, he set Bella on the floor, closed the doors enough to keep her inside, then turned and gave Skye the motion to follow.

Having already secured her own doors, she followed him quickly, slipping into the house as he opened the door once again, then pausing as he stepped in.

Bella was across the room in her heated puppy bed, slipping back into sleep as though nothing were wrong. The puppy's appearance of unconcern assured him the house was empty. He'd been working with her, him and Crowe, teaching her to alert him to any other presence in the house, even one she was familiar with.

Motioning to Skye, they did a quick sweep of the house anyway, Logan headed through first.

She worked well with him. The house was given a quick scan within minutes before they moved through the dining room to the patio doors just as Crowe and Rafer approached the entrance, Cami cradled in her lover's arms.

Leaving their entrance to Crowe after unlocking the doors, Logan dragged the fully stocked military medical kit from beneath a cabinet in the kitchen and returned to the dining room as Rafer laid the delicate form of his lover on the long couch Logan had placed in the room.

"What the fuck happened?" Logan snarled as he knelt next to the couch where Cami lay on her stomach, a makeshift bandage covering the back of her shoulder.

Pulling the gauze and tape aside, Rafer cursed as she jerked at the pain. Her smothered moan had each man grimacing in fury.

Logan had turned to order Rafe to gather clean

towels when Skye was suddenly at his side, a stack of clean dish towels in her hands.

"Two of the bodyguards watching her were taken by surprise by the third when he tried to kill her. If that weren't bad enough, a fucking sniper decide to come out to play at the same time." Tortured and filled with pain, Rafer's voice was like a dark vision of coming death. "I was coming in as it happened. Cami managed to get out of the house with the help of one of the guards as the other tried to distract the sniper. She was clipped as the bodyguard threw her out a fucking window when they couldn't disable the third."

"Clipped?" The flesh wound was a vicious slash across Cami's shoulder.

The bullet had dug in deep, tearing across flesh and muscle in a ragged gouge that Logan knew had to be agonizing.

Cami's face was buried in the couch, and now that her lover couldn't see what she would feel was a weakness, Logan could feel the slight tremble of her shoulders and knew she was crying.

"It's okay, little sister," he murmured, knowing if Rafer saw those tears, he would go ape-shit. None of them would be able to control him then. "I've got something for the pain."

She gave a jerking nod.

Glancing at Rafer as he crouched at the arm of the couch, his fingers buried in her hair to keep some connection to her, Logan knew his cousin was well aware that she was crying. His gaze was tortured, filled with the knowledge of her pain. And he hated it.

Hell, they all hated it.

Pulling a syringe and small bottle from the med kit, Logan quickly filled it with enough of the medication to not just fight infection but also take the pain away. Something that would help her rest.

"Here we go," he murmured as he quickly gave her the injection. "Just a minute, sweetheart. All the pain is going to go away."

Literally, no more than a few seconds.

Logan prepared the sutures as he waited, watched the tension in her small body slowly ease away until she was breathing more normally and the slight hitching of her breath from her tears eased away.

"God. Thank you, Logan," Rafer whispered, his voice hoarse as Cami finally relaxed and drifted into a medicated drowsiness.

"She's going to be fine," he promised his cousin. "We'll just close this up and I'll even try to do it pretty enough that, hopefully, she won't even know there's been a wound there. I promise she won't be afraid to wear that bikini for you again." Logan smirked, hoping to take Rafer's mind off his fury. Just a little.

"Bastard." Rafer gave a rough grunt. "You weren't supposed to see her in that bikini."

"I promise, I kept my eyes closed." Logan forced a chuckle as he lied.

"God, Logan, I didn't think I was going to get to her in time." His voice was a tortured rasp of pain.

"But you did. That's what counts, Rafe," Logan assured him. "That's all that counts."

"Are the bodyguards alive?" Skye asked Rafer as Logan motioned to her to hand him the next suture.

"All but one. The one trying to kill her." Rafe's voice was hard now. "He was the one I was heading up to talk to. I received a blocked text informing me that the bodyguard had contacted John Corbin and offered to give up Cami's location for payment."

"And you didn't call us?" Logan snarled, careful to ensure the stitch he was applying pulled the flesh together gently despite the rage pouring through him.

"There was no time," Rafe snapped back. "You were too far away to help, Logan, and what you were doing was just as important. I was only ten minutes from her location going through that damned lawyer's files. I just ran when the text came through. I thought there was still time. The information said Corbin had just received the information."

The lawyer their parents had seen regarding the details of the resort they were combining their finances to go into in partnership with a resort developer the day they were killed. According to the lawyer, the Callahan couples had not been in that afternoon, while Clyde had known for a fact that they had been there. Clyde had known because he had set the appointment up himself.

Now, twelve years later, the lawyer was claiming he had never met the three couples.

"And why would someone at the Corbin ranch try to warn us of anything?" Crowe asked broodingly.

Rafer smoothed Cami's hair back from her drowsy

face, his eyes never leaving her as he answered. "I don't think the caller was from the ranch."

"If the Barons are upping the ante like this, then we're going to have problems," Crowe stated, the ice forming in his voice sending a chill of warning up Skye's spine.

"That shooter was good, Crowe." Rafer sounded strangled by the emotion in his voice as Cami gave a small, unconscious moan. "Damned good. There shouldn't have been a soul left living. And the only reason Cami was shot, according to her, was because the bodyguard bargaining to reveal her location tried to take her out himself. She tried to run when he turned the gun on her. The other guy threw her out the window but not before his partner shot. She turned in time to see the bastard's fucking head explode." His eyes blazed with fury; his face was taut with it.

Logan wiped his hand over his face. "This isn't worth it," he whispered, sitting back on his heels when he finished the fifth and final stitch. "Hell, give them fucking trusts. It's not worth another life."

"If we could do it, legally, I'd be all for it," Crowe snarled. "They don't get the property or anything else unless we leave the area and stay gone for three years. Or unless we die of natural causes or suicide. Otherwise, it goes to our heirs, if there's even a chance of an heir. Do you want to leave Cami unprotected that long, Rafer?" He turned to Logan. "Would you leave Skye that long?"

Logan glanced at Skye and knew he wouldn't.

"Hell, our parents weren't even certain they wouldn't try to kill us for it," Rafer stated, his voice grim now.

"Our mothers were spoiled every day of their lives until they married our fathers. The hell the Barons must have put them through to make them distrust their own fathers to that extent."

Skye watched the three men then, their expressions, the savagery in their eyes, the way their jaws clenched tight, the disillusionment and bitterness on their faces.

"Suddenly the bastard stalking us is using a rifle instead of a knife?" Crowe sneered. "If he was that damned good with one, why wait until now to start using it?"

"None of this makes sense," Skye said then. "There's no way he could be in two places at once."

"What do you mean?" Crowe turned to her quickly when Logan spoke.

"He was waiting in Skye's house when she came from the Social." He stared back at Rafer. "I'm going to guess, not long before Cami was attacked."

"A new player? Or do you think his partner is coming out to play?"

"His partner wouldn't be trying to save Cami," Skye pointed out. "None of this is adding up. The Slasher is suddenly changing his habits? That's very rarely seen in a serial killer. They get off on keeping to their agenda and to their little rituals."

"What do we do now?" Rafer whispered, desperation filling his gaze as Logan bandaged the wound. "Cami's not trained for this, Crowe. Hell, I can't even hire bodyguards to protect her. How the fuck are we supposed to keep her and Skye safe? Hell, I don't know if we're trained for this."

"She's considered a weak link," Skye stated softly, almost wincing as their gazes jerked back to her. "But even more, kill her, take your reason for fighting, and you could simply give up."

"Why?" Rafer lashed out, his gaze livid. "Why go after her at all, let alone consider her a weak link?"

"As you said, she's not trained," Skye pointed out. "And because she has the potential to conceive another heir. That heir would acquire everything if the three of you were dead or if you left the county and decided to just give up. That option would be considered voided if there's an heir. I think that's the same reason your lovers have been killed. That's the only reason to kill the women you've slept with, or had relationships with."

It was the only thing that made sense.

Skye had considered it from every angle she could find, and it all led back to the fact that there was only one thing that could have tied all the women together.

They all had the potential to conceive heirs to the Callahan trusts.

"My sister was killed," Crowe retorted then. "She was only two weeks old."

"Perhaps they were unaware she was in the SUV with them," Skye mused. "If your parents were murdered, and I believe they were, then it's possible the murderer was unaware she was in the vehicle."

Crowe's gaze was filled with such ice, it was so hard and blank, that for a moment she wondered if he had even heard her.

"They've targeted our lovers to implicate us in their

deaths," Rafer said then. "And to torture us. There's no reason to believe we'd risk impregnating them."

"That doesn't gain them anything other than the possibility that you'd be easier to kill. Having you imprisoned would result in the same end. You'd be out of the county for at least a year, longer if you're imprisoned for murder. The only way to gain what it seems they want, is to force you to leave the county, have you imprisoned, or if you die in a way there's no possible suspicion of foul play. At this point, no matter how you die, it would be suspicious simply because of the psychological profile that would be done on each of you and the fact that it would prove suicide was not in your nature. And they only gain it then if there are no heirs conceived before you left or before your deaths." She glanced at Cami. "She won't be safe until you're out of the county for the required year. That's a full year that they have to kill her. You won't be able to keep her safe that long," she said gently. "The only answer is to place her in federal protection until you can resolve this."

"Hell no," Rafer snapped then. "Whoever's doing this obviously has political ties. It's too big a risk."

It was a slight risk, Skye admitted. A risk she knew the Callahans would find unacceptable.

But there were no other alternatives. Unless—

If she called in a single favor from a source she had promised herself she would never contact.

Staring at Logan, she realized that ultimately he would give up his life, die, for each of his cousins or any of the women he'd ever known in his life. Just as Crowe or Rafer would. And at the moment, Cami's life was in grave danger. The cousins would die, or they would kill whoever they had to kill, to save her.

She was a part of all three of them. A part of their pasts and, through Rafer, a part of their hearts.

Skye breathed in deeply.

"I know someone who can't be bought and his men can't be bought," she said, her voice low. "Someone with no political ties that count and all the resources needed to keep her not just safe and alive but close enough that you won't have to worry about her because you'll know she's safe."

Federal protection would take her completely out of Rafer's life. Skye's contact would delight in keeping Cami close enough, and safe enough, that it would drive whoever was attempting to kill her completely mad with rage. Such games were the spice of his life and he practiced them diligently.

Skye's contact had the ability to do that. To enrage even the most calm, mild-mannered people.

The three cousins watched her suspiciously now.

"Criminals?" Logan guessed. "I don't know about that—"

She shook her head. "He calls himself a legal misfit. But to my knowledge, he's no criminal."

She just suspected that he was.

"Go on." It was Crowe who encouraged her to reveal her contact's identity.

"He delights in driving deserving souls insane with rage. He'll keep her close, well-protected but in plain sight. His men aren't bound to him by money, but by blood loyalty and ties created in ways that ensure he would never be betrayed. And if anything happens to the three of you, he'll ensure her safety. And the safety of any child she's conceived. Trust me, Rafe. No one could touch her if she's under his care."

"And who could have that kind of power at his fingertips, owe you a favor, and be willing to put himself out to such an extent?" Rafer was still suspicious.

Skye licked her lips, nervous, uncertain not because she didn't trust her contact but perhaps because she didn't trust his ability not to deliberately antagonize these three men.

And she couldn't say they weren't already suspicious.

"So who is he?" Logan was the one to ask the question, his expression carefully bland. "And why would he do it?"

Because he owed her. Because for one horrible moment, something had been out of his control.

"Why?" She sat back on her heels where she had been kneeling next to him. "I'm the agent who saved Amara Resnova's life two years ago when she was targeted by the DC Vigilante because of her father's suspected activities. He gave me a onetime, unlimited IOU."

Crowe gave a soft whistle, his eyes widening as Logan's narrowed. "An unlimited IOU and a very serious marriage proposal is the rumor in the alleys. And that comes from some damned high-level sources. Son of a bitch, no wonder I couldn't gain any information on you. You're part of a new, elite group of undercover bureau agents who are targeting the rise in stalker activity."

She inclined her head in acknowledgment. "You know things you shouldn't."

"I was offered a position," he informed her gruffly. "I politely declined."

"Interesting," she murmured. "I heard the position was only offered to those agents in training whose parents were part of the bureau."

"Or whose parents or themselves were in select circles in the military," he reminded her. "I was."

Ah, that made more sense then. It also explained why the three cousins were treated with kid gloves when it came to the Corbin County Slasher. If Crowe had been offered a position in the same unit she was in, then his abilities far exceeded those that the Slasher possessed.

She nodded somberly then. "It makes more sense now why the bureau profilers placed a definite 'no way' on the suspicion that one or all of you were involved in the Slasher's killings."

"There's also the rumor that most of the agents, even those who turned the position down, were being groomed for it from the womb," Crowe stated. "Is that true?"

She stared back at him then. "Were you groomed, Crowe?" she asked him.

His smile was tight, hard. "We were definitely groomed to beware of our enemies."

She shrugged, careful to keep her tone even, her voice soft. "As was I. I was ten when my parents were killed. So who's to say if I was being groomed or not? The rumors that swirl around the inception of the new department are no different than any others. It's something I take with a grain of salt."

She turned to Rafer then. "It's your call. Ivan Resnova has the power, as well as the ability, to ensure nothing or no one touches her. I can provide his help. But not without your willingness to place her there."

"If he's so good, how did the DC Vigilante almost get to his daughter?" Logan growled.

"Because Amara was a teenage girl who wanted to see her boyfriend. A boy her father didn't approve of, and she was secretly seeing. She slipped away from him and gave the Vigilante a chance to get to her."

Rafer stared down at his sleeping lover, his face lined with pain, with the decision facing him. "He doesn't have to keep her close if it's a risk," he whispered then, his voice echoing with such love that for one aching moment Skye felt her own chest tighten in pain as well. "She wasn't close before; I was just, thankfully, in the area."

Skye nodded to that. "Rafer, Ivan could keep her in Logan's backyard and keep her safe," she stated ruefully, knowing beyond a shadow of a doubt that he could do just that. "I'll make the call in the morning."

She made the mistake of turning to Logan then, just in time to catch the look on his face.

A look that sent both trepidation and pure, fiery lust surging through her. A look she had never seen on a man's face in her life.

At least, not where she was concerned.

Pure possession and the pure male intent to enforce his claim.

That was the look on his face, and only one emotion could inspire that look.

Love.

CHAPTER EIGHTEEN

Saturday, June 19, 4:30 am

The day had fully begun before Skye and Logan returned to her house to attempt to sleep once again.

At least, sleep was what she was considering.

The attempt anyway.

With Rafer and Crowe camped out in the living room of Logan's house, the heavy curtains pulled securely shut, they were reasonably confident of providing the security Cami needed until Ivan could be contacted.

Once he had been contacted, it wouldn't take him long to arrive.

Cami was still sleeping under the effects of the injection Logan had given her, and for once Bella hadn't howled when Logan moved from the house without her.

She had instead climbed onto the heavy mattress that had been pulled from one of the upstairs beds and placed in the most secure corner of the room. She'd then curled up on the pillow at Cami's uninjured shoulder and laid her wrinkled face against it as she stared back at Logan sadly. She'd then turned and swiped Rafer's face with a puppy kiss as she lay on the pillow beside Cami's.

Bella was going to watch over the young woman she'd never met, and one she must have sensed Logan was deeply concerned about.

Swallowing tightly, Skye had followed Logan back to her house, sensing with a soul-deep knowledge that the coming confrontation was one she might not be ready to face.

"Ivan Resnova." Logan's tone was merciless, his expression so arctic, Skye actually had to suppress a shiver as they reentered the bedroom. "Russian military, I believe. Gained his millions from his French father and his unique ability to embezzle a country already fighting to feed its people."

She breathed in slowly. "That's what the world was led to believe." She shrugged. "His money came from his American father and his French grandmother. He didn't embezzle from his country, because he was never Russian to begin with."

He had always been American. The day he was born his citizenship papers had been filed with the bureau to ensure his citizenship when his CIA parents gave birth to him. Once he'd turned eighteen and his father learned he'd been funneling CIA handler information from the low-level military position Ivan had held at the time, he'd been given the truth of who and what his parents worked for.

"I really don't give a fuck how he lines his pockets," Logan told her, his tone dangerously soft. "Resnova does nothing for free, Skye. What makes you think he won't expect more from you than a simple thank-you once all this is finished?"

"Because he already feels he owes me. There is nothing or no one that means as much to Ivan as his daughter," she stated, fighting for patience. "It's an all-inclusive IOU. There are no strings attached."

The look Logan gave her was filled with derision. "Men like that only understand strings, Skye. And that proposal he made to you meant he is serious about adding those strings."

"Perhaps he was at the time, but only because he felt he owed me, Logan, and Ivan believes there's nothing a woman wants or needs more than a husband. In his mind, marriage was the greatest gift he could give me. That and because Ivan wants a mother for his daughter. One he knows he can trust. He felt he could trust me. That's all."

"And he had no intentions of sleeping with you?" Logan questioned disparagingly. "Is that what you believe?"

"No, I don't," she answered, keeping her tone low, pushing back that instinctive need to get as confrontational as he was and just as horny.

He was filling out the front of his jeans like nobody's business.

For a moment, she wondered if she would ever get enough of him.

Nervous anticipation began building within her, and

with it a sense of sexual excitement that she couldn't seem to tamp.

There was something so arrogantly male, so possessive, in his expression that it was as if a shield suddenly snapped over her senses, pulling her back with a force that left her almost staggering.

A sense of panic threatened to rise inside her, a dark, ugly shadow of fear building through her emotions. Not a fear of Logan. A sudden fear of the unexplained emotions that were tearing at her, that, despite the panic, were only building inside her.

"He's a friend, nothing more, Logan." She fought to keep her voice even and wondered why it was suddenly such a battle. What was that tremble that threatened to overtake it?

What was the hunger that had her hands trembling? That had her stomach tightening not in dread but with the sure knowledge that something was about to change between them. Something she wasn't certain she could handle.

When he said nothing more Skye turned and moved to the closet doors. Pulling them open and stepping inside, she drew in a deep breath as silently as possible as her lips parted and she licked her dry lips quickly.

The door to the monitor room opened smoothly as she keyed in the code on the remote. Checking each one carefully for any present movements, she then set the controls to view any past movement in the time between their departure and present return to the house.

She felt him follow her. Felt his presence as he

paused at the entrance to the closet, his silence weighing heavily between them.

"There he is," she murmured as the shadow waited until dark to move from the tree line to the back door.

Once there, he drew a small black box from inside his jacket, inserted a slender line into the first lock, waited, then repeated the procedure on the second.

"What the hell is that?" Skye looked closer, frowning.

"Hell if I know." Logan watched over her shoulder, his gaze narrowed as she glanced back at him. "Definitely military, though. There's nothing like this on the market or Rafer's source would have picked it up for him. Hell, anything like that in the regular military channels and my source would have apprised me of it."

"What about Crowe's source?"

Logan shook his head. "If it were available to his source, then Crowe would know about it. It would have to be damned new, likely CIA. Whoever it belongs to, we'll have a line on it soon. Can you print this?" He indicated the device as the attacker pulled back.

Giving a quick nod, Skye moved to the keyboard and, using the control monitor, typed in the commands. Seconds later a series of printouts slid from the small printer beneath it.

"Here you go." Handing the photos to him, Skye turned her gaze to the monitor showing the attacker's movements.

He punched the code into the device and waited a few more seconds.

A green light blinked on the device and a drawer popped from the side.

There was a key lying inside.

Removing it, he inserted what appeared to be a blank key and repeated the movements.

"The alarm wouldn't have gone off if the key was used and the code put into the control panel once he was inside. The device, or another he's using, must have decoded the security."

As he moved into the house, she turned to another camera and watched as he punched the code in, without the use of anything.

"Could the device he was using have found the code?"

Logan shook his head. "Trust me, when I find him, I'll find out."

She had no doubt he would, but Skye also knew there was no other way to get that code.

"I'm going to shower." Gathering her gown and robe together, she turned and left the closet, moving past him as he watched her broodingly now.

"Were you in love with him?" he asked as she passed him.

She paused, looking back at him somberly as she asked in turn, "Does it matter, Logan?"

The look on his face earlier had been one, she'd convinced herself, might have been love. Now, she wasn't so certain, just as she had no idea how she would handle the pain of loving him if he walked away from her.

She didn't know why it should matter. He'd let her know from the beginning that this wasn't a relationship. It was no more than a few one-night stands.

She had accepted that. She was dealing with it. It was the story of her life, and she'd finally decided that there was no reason it should be any different with Logan.

Everyone in her life had been a version of a one-night stand.

Including her parents.

She hadn't loved Ivan. She didn't love him now.

She liked him. She respected him, and personally, she trusted him with her life.

Sleeping with him hadn't been a desire she'd had, though. And it was one Ivan would have eventually pushed for if she'd continued her friendship with him or with his daughter, Amara.

Showering, Skye had to force herself to push back whatever emotions were building inside her at the show of possessiveness Logan had displayed.

She hadn't expected this. She'd expected that non-relationship thing. Just as she expected that once the Stalker was identified and taken into custody, Logan would gently cut things off.

That look on his face before they had come back to the house, the one that assured her he would make damned certain she knew whose bed she was sharing, had triggered something inside her, though. Something she had no idea how to identify.

Something that was pulling at her, tormenting her, tightening her chest, her stomach, and, strangely enough, creating an arousal unlike any he'd inspired yet.

Pulling on the long black vintage silk gown that cupped her breasts like a lover's hands and smoothed to her waist with elastic silk lace before flaring out in yards of silken fabric to the tips of her toes, Skye admitted she simply wasn't prepared for a man like Logan.

But she wondered if any woman could be.

The long sheer black chiffon robe with its gathered sleeves and small train at the back went on as soft and light as a breath of air.

The sheer romance of the creation had always made her feel intensely feminine, soft.

That thought stopped her.

She *was* feminine, but she realized in that moment she hadn't been raised as most girls were.

To be delicate and soft and sweetly charming, or even secretly bitchy.

She'd been raised to be an agent.

She'd been taught from the cradle to trust no one.

And she'd been made aware of the monsters that inhabited the dark from a very young age.

Rumors swirled that the new division to the bureau had been created for children like her, but that wasn't really true. The parents of the children who had joined that division were those who had protected their children by teaching them how to protect themselves at an early age.

They were children who hadn't been trained to be agents, but *were* trained to either step into the agency, or one like it. They'd been raised, as Skye had, to always know the monsters that invaded the dark.

Giving her head a hard shake, she refused to allow herself to delve further into those memories or into the implications of the effect her emotions were having on her now.

Emotions she'd never felt before.

Or was it emotions she'd never allowed herself to feel before?

Whichever, rather than allowing them into the serenity she found in the daylight, she forced herself to face Logan and whatever the hell it was he was making her feel.

Stepping from the shower to the bedroom, she watched Logan returning as well. He'd obviously showered himself. His long hair was lying in dark blond, damp strands nearly to his shoulders and a bead of water gleamed on his beard.

It was sexy as hell.

He wore a pair of soft cotton pants rather than jeans, and his feet were bare.

He looked as sexy as hell.

As arrogant as hell.

His arms crossed over his chest as he stared back at her, his gaze somber but the look on his face implacable.

She didn't have time to deal with him. Calling Ivan had always been stressful, and after she had spent more than six months away from D.C. he would of course be curious. Especially if he had questioned her absence and found out about her medical leave.

Moving to the dresser, she picked up her cell phone before she stepped into the sitting room on the other side of the hall rather than, as she fielded Ivan's flirting and curiosity, enduring Logan's too-perceptive gaze if he was in the mood to be irritating this morning.

"I don't think so." Logan stepped in front of her before she could reach the door. "You can make that call right here."

She stared back at him silently for long moments. "Don't try to order me around, Logan," she finally warned him. "I won't deal well with it."

"It's not an order, Skye; it's a warning. This isn't something you want to do. Not right now. Not while my survival instincts are mixing with my possessiveness," he promised her. "As long as I'm sharing that fucking bed with you"—his finger stabbed at the mussed bed—"you belong to me. That means any time you're dealing with a man like Ivan Resnova on something more than a purely business level, I will be there."

"Says who?" she demanded in disbelief now. "All you ever have are one-night stands. How do you know if you can be possessive or not, Logan?"

Her arms crossed over her breasts defensively as one hip cocked forward and she faced him with pure defiance.

"Do you really want to push me on this?" he asked her. "Go ahead, Skye; walk out of this room and make that call."

She was trembling in reaction. The coil of emotions she couldn't seem to unravel was tightening in her belly now and sending dark fingers of shadowed impulses, fears, and needs skating through her senses.

And she couldn't handle them. She couldn't deal with them.

Gripping the phone tightly, she moved deliberately

around him before turning her back on him and doing just that.

She walked out of the room to make the call.

She left the door open.

She moved only as far as the curtained window at the side of the smaller room before flipping open the phone and pulling up the address book and choosing Ivan's secured sat phone number. Only God knew where he was right now.

"Ah, sweetheart, I was wondering when you would deign to inform me that you were still living." Ivan answered the phone on the first ring, his dangerously dark voice filled with amusement. "Amara has missed her shopping friend greatly."

"Yeah, you don't have the same sense of style, Ivan," Skye pointed out, fully aware that Logan could hear her side of the conversation from where he was standing.

"Ah, but what I have is a sense of my daughter's reluctance to dress as she once did," Ivan sighed, his tone suddenly somber. "It is still extremely difficult to get her to act as other teenage girls do."

"It's going to take her time, Ivan," Skye told him, not for the first time. "Is she still seeing the psychologist?"

"Weekly," he promised her. "Now, tell me, how does someone as sweet and delicate as my little Skye manage to get herself into the mess that you have managed in that dreary little town you're currently living in?"

She should have expected it. She knew she should have. Still, the fact that he seemed to know exactly what was going on surprised her.

"How do you know?" she asked. What did he know?

"How do I know that you are currently sleeping with a man whose very presence in your life has placed you in the utmost danger at a time when you should be healing?" She could see the dark frown on Ivan's face and instantly realized just how much he was like Logan.

"Do I have to repeat my question?" she asked softly.

He sighed heavily. "No, you do not. As always, my dear, those I cherish most I keep an eye on. My helicopter is prepped and Alexi is currently coordinating our best men to arrive with us to ensure Miss Flannigan's protection. Tell me, am I taking the pup as well? Amara is quite enamored of the pictures that were sent to me."

Ivan's tone was darker now, more dangerous.

Fuck, and she couldn't even rail at him. Logan was listening much too closely.

Ivan chuckled. "Ahh, you're not calling me an arrogant prick and telling me to fuck off. Shall I guess he's listening closely?"

She lifted her hand and rubbed at the bridge of her nose wearily. "What time will you be here?"

"Ah well, as I am currently in Colorado Springs, I would guess no more than an hour; what do you think?"

"An hour," she agreed.

"Hmm," he murmured. "Very well. But I do not consider this your IOU, Skye. That chip is for you personally; it does not apply to friends."

"In this case, it will have to," she stated carefully.

"It is in my discretion to decide how the IOU is repaid,"

he informed her. "Your friend Logan Callahan will pay this debt at some future date, or his cousin Rafer. Each man has skills I'm certain I may need at some point."

"That won't work," she tried to warn Ivan carefully.

"Now, my dear, that just makes me more determined to prove you so very wrong. Be prepared and have your friend ready to fly. We will apprise you of her intended location when we arrive."

"Do you have my place bugged or something?" she muttered. "How the hell did you know, Ivan?"

"Would you believe that I know you, my dear?" he asked her then. "I have many contacts in many areas. When your name came up six months ago in that tiny little hole, I of course was curious why. At dawn this morning I was informed that Rafer Callahan's fiancée was nearly killed by one of her bodyguards, and taken out of the safe house she was in by her lover. But what upset me more," his tone became pure, dark violence, "was the fact you nearly died because some bastard believes you are unprotected by anyone but your lover. It is my intent to prove him very, very wrong."

"And do you have any information concerning this particular situation?" she asked him as he fell silent for a moment.

"We will discuss these things when I arrive," he promised her again. "You have not the time for a nap, dear heart. Be watching for me, as I wish to get your friend out of there as quickly as possible to allow my own doctor to examine the injuries my contacts informed me she had. He will of course be with me to check you over and assure me of your good health as well."

Skye had parted her lips to inform him that she didn't need his damn medical care when she suddenly found the phone lifted from her hand, flipped closed, then tossed carelessly to the floor.

Logan was tired of waiting.

CHAPTER NINETEEN

He'd heard enough.

Logan stalked into the sitting room, one hand grabbing her wrist as she held the phone, the other snagging the phone out of her hand, flipping it closed, and tossing it to the floor as he gripped her robe and tore it from her as he swung her to the wall.

All in one smooth move until he had her, breasts pressed to the wall, his hard body pressed behind her, before she could do more than give a startled cry.

Hooking one hand in the back of the gown, he ripped it, the slender straps at her shoulders snapping apart. The sound of rending material, the feel of the power and dominance swirling around her like a heavy cloak of lust, sent a surge of moisture easing from her sex.

Pushing from her hips, Logan allowed the gown to pool in a puddle of silk at her feet, leaving her completely naked.

"Oh my God, do you know how much that cost?" she

cried out, more in amazement than any actual fear. More in arousal than in actual anger.

"Do you know how bad I want you naked?" he asked, pressing her to the wall, his head bent to her ear, strong teeth nipping firmly before his tongue eased, then teased the little sting.

She was ready to explode. Her womb was clenching in spasms of incredible need while her clit throbbed with imperative demand.

"Independent little cat, aren't you?" he growled before his teeth raked her ear again.

"Are you crazy?" Disbelief filled her voice. "Logan, what are you doing?"

"Showing you who's boss, baby," he said, scraping his nails lightly down her back as he held her firmly, ignoring her struggles. "Showing you when the day is done I fucking own that pretty little soft body." His lips brushed over her shoulder as his free hand, palm flat, smoothed down her quivering belly to the swollen, saturated mound of her pussy.

"And this sweet, tight little pussy?" He was suddenly cupping his hand between her thighs, his fingers curving, one tucking at the entrance to her pussy. "Mine, Skye."

Skye shook her head desperately. "You can't own me!" she wailed hoarsely.

"I already own you." His teeth raked over her shoulder, sending a hard, desperate surge of sensation racing through her.

Skye could feel her heart racing out of control, her stomach tightening nervously as her pussy creamed in reaction.

Her juices flowed along her tense muscles, heating them, saturating them, and preparing her for his possession. Preparing her to be taken by the man threatening to steal her soul.

"Deny it all you want," he growled. "Sing it to the fucking wind, sweetheart, but you know who you belong to."

Curling her fingers into fists, she closed her hands into fists and fought back the need. The need to belong to him. Because she had never really belonged to anyone in her life.

His teeth scraped over her neck before he kissed it. Laying gentle suckling kisses along the sensitive column before licking over it with hungry demand.

Shudders of sensation were wracking her. It felt as though flames were shooting through her veins. Each touch of his lips awakened nerve endings previously hidden and sleeping. Each touch drew out a part of her sensuality, a part of the hunger and the emotions she had been fighting since the day she had seen him.

His hand smoothed along her thigh, then up to her rear, where he clenched it, palming her rear with obvious pleasure.

"What are you trying to do to me?"

"Trying?" His tone grated with rough hunger. "I'm not trying, baby; I'm doing."

"Would you force me, Logan?"

Logan stilled behind her and she was certain she had won. Certain that the dark, addictive emotions rising within her would be vanquished by an end to the dominance he was displaying.

"You can say 'no,'" he told her softly, sending relief

flowing through her, and regret as well. Regret because she was too frightened of the emotions, too frightened of the needs tearing at her now. Relief because she knew she was on the verge of giving in and admitting she did belong to him.

"When you say no, I walk right out of here. I'll call your precious Resnova myself and he can take both you and Cami." A tight, triumphant smile curved Logan's lips. "And I bet he will."

He would, Skye admitted silently, to herself. Before he arrived in Sweetrock he would have the information he hadn't already gathered. And if Logan dared to even suggest she was in danger herself, then Ivan wouldn't have a problem forcing her to leave.

"Is that what you want, Skye?"

"He'll never be able to hold me," she snapped, knowing Ivan couldn't hold her when Logan already owned a part of her. She would be drawn right back to him, unable to stay away while danger swirled so thick and heavy around him.

"Say no and he'll be your only option until the year is out. Because I won't be here," Logan promised her as he bent his head to her neck, the caress of his lips sending chills racing over her body.

"Why?" Her forehead pressed into the wall as she tried to convince herself he was lying. He would never give his inheritance, everything he was trying to give his cousins, so easily.

She breathed in roughly as his lips moved to the back of her neck and his strong teeth tightened on her nape.

The animalistic bite had her pussy clenching, her

womb spasming with a hard punch of sensation that sent shocks of pleasure racing around her swollen clit.

"Oh God, Logan, what are you doing to me?" Panic threatened to take hold of her; hunger already had her.

"Proving to you who this sweet, hot response belongs to, baby," he assured her. "Showing you, Resnova may want you, but as long as you sleep in my bed he will not have you. No part of you, without my ability to oversee or overhear every second of it."

Before she could protest, before she could even think to protest or consider if that was what she wanted, he had her turned, her breasts suddenly pressing into his chest as his lips covered hers.

Delving past her lips, licking at them with arrogant greed, he drew her into that vortex once again. The one that grabbed her up, flung her into pure pleasure, and sucked her straight into the pure, unqualified lust she couldn't fight.

Pulling back enough to allow her to draw a breath, he caught her lower lip between his teeth and worried it gently for one heated second.

"You're mine," he growled as he eased back. "And I'll show you tonight just how much."

As he held her arms over her head, his lips returned to her. Each deep, possessive kiss was drugging, addictive. The pleasure sank inside her, built, amassed, and struck at each erogenous zone with lightning-swift power.

With his free hand he played with her breasts, her nipples. As he cupped the curve of the firm flesh, his thumb raked over the tender, pebble-hard tip. Nerve endings came awake with furious hunger, throbbing and aching for his touch. Any touch. More touch.

His lips sipped at hers, nipped at them. He loved her lips, and she loved his back in turn. Licking at them, tasting him as he tasted her. When he pulled back, his lips burning over her jaw to her neck, she couldn't help but arch to him, straining to be closer.

One hand continued to hold her hands overhead, ensuring the deepening sensation of feminine weakness built inside her. That sense of feminine hunger to be sensually dominated, to lay aside the demand for strength, and, in this part of her life, to just belong to a man whose inner strength exceeded hers, whose physical strength overwhelmed hers.

"Damn you, Logan!" she cried out as his lips traveled closer to her breasts, to the hard, peaked nipples.

"You damned me from that first kiss," he informed her, his voice hoarse, grating with his own pleasure.

His free hand traveled to the curve of her ass once again, cupped it, then pulled back and, before she knew what to expect, delivered a light, heated tap to the dip of the firm curve.

His hand flattened again, then cupped the curve and petted it with sensual strokes as the rasp of his calloused palm sent the rasping sensations to mix with the others and build the heat burning inside her.

Caressing the cheek gently, he then tapped at the curve again. Flares of heat attacked her pussy, her clit. As she rose to her tiptoes, he suddenly covered her lips with a hungry groan, his tongue slipping past her lips to lick at hers, to taste it. Lifting her from her feet, he picked her up and carried her to the bed they had shared earlier. Rather than putting her on her back, he rolled her to her stomach.

Trying to roll back, she was stopped by the simple measure of his hand flattened against her lower back.

"Stay right there, little cat," he ordered her, his tone harsh and commanding as his hand landed lightly on her rear once again.

"Oh God." Her hands clenched in the sheets beneath her, she was uncertain and confused at the feelings suddenly rising inside her to mix with the chaos that already existed.

Skye gasped as his lips brushed her lower back a second later. Then the dip above her buttocks, finally brushing over the heat lingering just beneath the flesh of the curve of her rear on which he had bestowed the firm little pat.

His hands smoothed down her thighs before gripping them firmly and pushing them apart as his larger body came between.

He'd shed the cotton pants he had worn. Bare male legs brushed hers as she tried once again to roll to her back.

"Don't." Gripping her thighs, Logan held her in place before allowing one of his fingers, knowing and determined, to slide between her thighs to find the sensitive, swollen folds of her pussy.

"So fucking hot and wet."

He parted the saturated folds, allowing two fingertips to slip farther inside to rim the clenched opening.

Skye couldn't resist parting her thighs further, allowing him greater access to the tormented depths of her body.

He tucked two fingers together at the entrance and pressed inside, working slow and easy as he began to part the tightened depths.

"So fucking tight," he groaned as he pushed his fingers in, burying the tips, pulling back, then pushing in more as she felt her inner muscles gripping him desperately.

"Let me turn—"

"Hell no." His voice was a low, sensually ravenous rumble. "You want to pretend you don't belong to me? Is that your plan, Skye? Is that how you want it?"

Was that what she wanted? She had no idea what she wanted anymore.

"Logan, please!" she cried out, wishing she knew what she wanted, wishing she knew how to understand what she felt.

His fingers worked deeper inside her, stretching her, easing her open. They stroked, rasped, against tender flesh as her juices flowed to them, saturating her pussy and his fingers.

As they slid back, releasing her, Skye arched, her rear lifting, a hungry moan slipping past her lips as the need for more sensation became overriding.

Needing him, fighting the waves of pleasure amplified by his refusal to allow her to turn to him, Skye arched again, her hips rolling, bearing down on his fingers as they lingered just inside the opening of her sex.

"No ties, is that how you want it, Skye?" he asked again. "No bonds? Just the same as a one-night stand, over and over again?"

His fingers slid back entirely as he moved fully between her thighs, his knees pushing her thighs farther

apart as he gripped her hips and lifted her. One hand
slid up her back, bearing down on her shoulders to keep
them to the mattress as she ground her teeth on a frustrated cry.

She tried to struggle again, to lift herself and force
him to allow her to turn. Instead, she suddenly stilled
as she felt the hot, broad head of his cock press against
her entrance.

Bent in front of him, her rear lifted to him, completely open, completely vulnerable to him, Skye closed
her eyes, whimpering at the pleasure of his touch, at the
emotional pain building inside her.

She had no idea how to vanquish it, how to stop whatever emotions were tormenting her, tightening through
her, because she had no idea what they were.

How could she accept them when she couldn't identify them? How could she fight what he did to her when
she had no idea what he was doing?

She needed to hold him, though, needed him holding her, needed to see his eyes, his expression, the dark
hunger in his gaze. She needed him to hold her. Needed
his kiss and the proof that she wasn't trapped in the
endless chaos of the exquisite rapture alone.

"Logan, please—" Even she could hear the pain
building in her voice as he began taking her.

It wasn't from the pleasure-pain of his entrance. It
had nothing to do with each inch of the hardened,
heated flesh taking her, possessing the snug depths of
her core.

"But this is what you want." Coming over her, his

tone savage at her ear, his hips pushed against her harder, driving him deeper, then deeper, each inch he forged inside her throwing her deeper into the realm of ecstasy dragging her in as her pussy sucked at his cock. "No emotions, Skye. No belonging."

"I didn't say that!" she cried out painfully, realizing how much emotion, how much pleasure and belonging, had gone into his kiss while he was buried inside her earlier.

"You walked away from me." As he pulled his hips back, his cock eased from her despite her attempts to hold him in, until it was poised at the entrance, throbbing and thick. "You walked away to another man."

"No." She shook her head desperately now. "You ordered me, Logan."

"I warned you. You're mine or this ends now. Make your choice." His voice was hard, unyielding, only to soften as he whispered in her ear, "Do you think it's any easier for me, baby? Do you think you would have reacted any different?"

She shuddered, shook with the incredible gentleness in his tone, at the knowledge that she would have hit the roof to have known about another woman what he knew about Ivan. To know Logan had walked away from her to talk to another woman he might have considered sleeping with or marrying.

"Let me turn around."

"Make your choice." His voice was savage. "I won't take you as a lover unless you intend to be one."

This wasn't a one-night stand to him any longer.

She hadn't realized that. The knowledge hadn't formed within her mind because so much had been happening. She also realized he wasn't going to relent.

He sank inside her again, his cock burying to the hilt, taking her, marking not just her flesh but also the burgeoning emotions she had no idea how to handle.

"Please, Logan," she whispered desperately.

The thrusts began to gain in speed, moving inside her with powerful strokes and throwing her closer with each thrust toward release.

A hard, detached release. He was working her body. Working her pussy, her clit. He wasn't stroking her, soothing her, as he took her; he wasn't building that release that would satiate every part of her.

"I take it back!" she cried out desperately, suddenly, realizing she would never be able to accept that. "I take it back, Logan; I swear."

"You're mine," he snarled when she said nothing. "As long as I'm the one fucking your sweet body, as long I'm the one sharing your bed, Skye, you belong to me."

As long as. She could handle "as long as." It wasn't forever. It wasn't the taboo she had understood since she was a little girl.

"Yes," she answered him brokenly now. "As long as you're sleeping in my bed, I'm yours."

He pulled back instantly. One second he was possessing her; the next she was empty, crying out at the loss even as he flipped her over to her back and moved to come between her thighs once again.

She moved first.

Before he could stop her she was on her knees, pushing him back and straddling his hips, very well aware that he only went down because he wanted to.

His hand moved to his hard cock, gripping the base as she knelt over it, her lashes fluttering in pleasure at the feel of the mushroomed crest parting the dripping folds of her pussy.

And that was where his gaze was centered.

As he grimaced hard, teeth clenched as he ran the thick crest between the swollen flesh of her pussy, his gaze jerked to her face as she gazed at the feel of the silk over iron circling her clit.

"Take me." Her fingers, so much smaller than his, pressed over his fingers, trying to guide him to the entrance once again.

"You take me." Unwrapping his fingers, he moved his hands to her knees, then slowly smoothed them up, over her thighs, to the swell of her hips.

Gripping the base now, aligning it with the frantic ache throbbing in her sex.

She was desperate for him now.

Pressing down, a wild cry falling from her lips at the first stretching heat as she began to press down on him, Skye gave herself to the needs tearing through her.

Moving both palms to his chest, her fingers curling, nails raking against the hair-spattered flesh of his chest, she let her hips fall on the stiff column of flesh rising to her.

Stretching her, burning her, his hips moving against her, shifting and lifting, aiding her possession of him.

Feeling the burning length as it pressed inside her, taking him, controlling each thrust her body took, only built the hunger overtaking her.

Skye became immersed in sensation, in the feel of him moving beneath her, the feel of him taking her, her taking him.

Each downward thrust of her body buried him deeper inside her, stretched her, sent a flurry of sensations amassing and shooting through her nerve endings.

Muscles tensed and shuddering, thighs straining and gasps of pleasure falling from her lips, Skye tilted her head back, feeling her hair caress her back, falling to his thighs.

His groan, hard and barely controlled, joined her cry. Hard male hands clenched on her hips as he moved with her, taking her as she took him.

His cock throbbed inside her, thickening, pulsing imperatively, as Skye gave in to the mindless search for pleasure.

She would consider the implications of the fact that he had taken her, twice now, without the benefit of a condom.

The feel of flesh caressing wet, slick flesh was a friction that only drove her higher, closer to rapture. Each stroke of his cock, each stretching thrust, pushed her, razed her senses, until she felt the impact of the next stroke of his cock inside her trigger a release that sent her hurtling through a vortex of pure, undiluted rapture.

As she shook, shuddering, her pussy clenched and tightened around his cock as she cried out with the sensations rocking every part of her soul. Stealing her emotions, racing through an overwhelming, brutal matrix of complete unimaginable release.

As she gave herself to the pleasure he built inside her, she felt him releasing himself to it as well. His cock swelling impossibly further, throbbing, then the fiery spurts of his release gushing inside her. Heating her further, extending her release, tearing at her until the final cataclysm raced through her and left her breathless. Left her sinking against him, his arms wrapping around her, his breathing harsh beneath her ear, his heart thundering.

"Remember it!" Logan growled. "Mine, Skye. You are mine."

CHAPTER TWENTY

Ivan Resnova arrived in a glistening, newly waxed black SUV. Traveling behind and in front of the vehicle he rode in were two exactly like it.

Skye knew those SUVs were customized, stylized, and as individualized as Ivan himself.

Moving in behind the three vehicles were the sheriff, his deputy, and behind him in the mayor's King Ranch crew cab pickup the mayor and county attorney pulled in as well.

The convoy of vehicles drew the neighbors from their houses and had them watching in surprise and suspicion as Ivan's bodyguards moved from the vehicles converged on the middle SUV and one opened the door quickly.

Ivan stepped out as only Ivan could.

Dressed in a charcoal-gray silk suit, his thick black hair brushed back from the strong, intently arrogant features, and his blue eyes as bright as sapphires. From one corner of that lean, savagely hewn face to the jaw on the other side, a thin, wicked scar bisected his face, but rather than detracting from the wickedly sensual looks, it only added to the air of danger that surrounded him.

Standing taller than Logan at six-four, his body all lean, powerful muscle, he moved like a jungle cat, stalking and always on the alert for his prey.

Whoever that might be.

Logan stepped to the front porch, his arms going over his broad chest as Skye came out behind him. He was scowling at the fanfare Resnova drew whether he wanted it or not. This wasn't what Cami needed. But Resnova had called before his arrival and had provided something they had needed. Logan just wasn't certain why.

Resnova's comment: "As your cousin Rafer has been injured as well, I suggest he accompany us and be given time to heal alongside his fiancée. The wound he received will only slow you down should more trouble arrive."

A clear message that Rafer was to pretend to be wounded as well. What the man's plan was Logan didn't have a clue. And he wasn't so certain how he felt about the suspected criminal taking over so casually.

As Logan moved behind Skye, they met Resnova and his bodyguards at the middle of the walk, and Logan's scowl only deepened as the bastard wrapped his arms around Skye and pulled her close.

Skye swore she could feel Logan's glare smack in the middle of her back. She had known he wouldn't get along with Ivan; they were much too alike. But this was the only way she knew to keep Cami safe long enough to deal with the problem.

"Ah, the most precious flower in this dreary little garden," Ivan sighed with an air of relief. "How you must brighten this place each day, my little Skye."

The snort behind her assured Skye that Logan had heard every word.

Ivan's blue eyes twinkled with something akin to merriment as he refused to glance behind her.

"Do I detect a bit of the creature known as jealousy?" he pondered in a bit of a stage whisper.

"Or the creature known as drama," Logan drawled.

Ivan chuckled before his gaze turned somber. "Come; we will go inside. There are things we must discuss."

He moved to grip Skye's arm, only to have Logan quickly step between them, his arm curving around Skye's back as he drew her into the house.

"I'm not a bone," she muttered.

"Ruff ruff," Logan all but growled. "This was your idea, and remember, you must have known what was coming, because you were damned hesitant to mention it."

"Because he's difficult to work with," she sighed.

"And shall I remind you, he is also listening?" Ivan asked behind her as his bodyguards surrounded him and led him to the door.

Inside the house, Skye and Logan stepped aside as Ivan motioned his bodyguards to remain on the porch.

Ivan stood for a moment, gazing around the large foyer, the marble floor, the sweeping staircase that led to the second floor, and nodded with a sharp, approving motion of his head.

Glancing to Logan, a small smile quirked Ivan's lips.

"You have hidden your ownership of this house quite well. It was only by chance I found it."

Logan frowned. "Then I didn't hide it well enough."

"Ah well, it would be hard to hide what I wish to find," he stated. "Are your cousins here?"

"This way." Skye stepped between the two men at that point and led the way to the kitchen, where she had put coffee on.

Cami was sitting in the large recliner Rafer had pulled into the room, while Rafer stood behind it. Crowe had taken position against the wall, next to the back door, but he'd placed coffee cups, saucers, and spoons in front of the coffeepot on the counter.

Pouring the coffee, Skye set each cup close to the Callahans, Cami, and then Ivan before getting her own.

"You have an interesting problem." He let his gaze run over the occupants of the room. "I've been quite intrigued with it since Skye moved here and I learned who her neighbor and landlord was."

"And it was your business?" Logan asked broodingly.

Ivan smiled. "I have no designs on your lovely Skye as long as you take proper care of her," he assured Logan before his expression turned dark, dangerous. "Harm her, make her unhappy, and I would change my mind quickly. Otherwise, there is no reason for this animosity."

"Other than the fact that she was here, smack in the middle of the danger without my knowledge, but evidently with yours," Logan pointed out. "You neglected to care for her when, according to your claims, you protect her."

Ivan tilted his head to the side in acknowledgment of

the point as Skye just sat back and drank her coffee. She'd dealt with men enough to know that they were going to do their posturing and engage in their pissing contests whether she liked it or not.

"Very well." Ivan still nodded. "We have the problem of Ms. Flannigan." He looked to each Callahan. "There has indeed been a professional assassin hired. One whose only job is to kill Ms. Flannigan, as well as any other woman sleeping in a Callahan's bed, before they can conceive."

"Fuck!" Crowe's muttered curse was barely heard.

"Ah yes, quite a problem I agree," Ivan sighed as he sat back in his chair. "The identity of the assassin has so far eluded me." He frowned in consternation at that fact, as though that in itself was a problem that needed to be dealt with. "What I did manage to learn was the code name he uses, though. King Arthur. Does this sound familiar?" He looked at the three men.

"He's struck three times in the past year," Crowe stated. "All political figures, mostly in third-world countries and in Russia."

"Bastard," Ivan muttered. "The Russian ambassador to America was a fine man. He was considering entering the election campaign for prime minister when he was murdered."

"Rumor is that's why he was murdered," Crowe pointed out.

"I have my men working on this," Ivan sighed. "Strangely, the normal chatter about this assassin is not there. And it is extremely rare for him to take such jobs as the murdering of women. Actually, I have never heard of it. King Arthur generally chooses his jobs based on the targets' sins. Not their sex or their lovers." The fact that this had Ivan confused was clear in the darkening of his gaze.

"He's good," Crowe said then. "How good are you?"

Ivan's smile was confident. "I am better, my friend," he assured Crowe. "My estate in Colorado Springs is highly secured, and will protect her like a cub in the middle of the lion's den. Her safety is assured." He glanced at Skye. "I've come to collect you as well."

Skye had to laugh at the statement. "Not happening, Ivan." She gave her head a hard shake. "You're not into kidnapping and I don't run and hide. I came here looking for this problem."

"As your foster sister came here looking for this problem?" He glowered back at her, then at Logan. "It is your place to change her mind."

"I'm not touching that one," Logan stated as he shot Skye a rueful look. "Besides, she would just be in the position of escaping you and being alone until one of us found her. I don't want to give that bastard a chance to set his sights on her."

Ivan's gaze was clearly concerned as he stared back at her.

"I'm working on the root of the problem," he told them then. "I have several men in the area keeping an eye on other concerns I've had. I've had them begin looking into this. Once I learn what is going on, I will of course ensure that you get that report."

"And what makes you think you can learn more than we have so far?" Logan asked, his gaze narrowing.

"Because I have sources you do not, as well as favors owed in circles I am certain you are even unaware exist," Ivan informed him.

Logan's lips quirked. "Point taken."

Skye, like Cami, simply sipped her coffee and watched the byplay.

"Very well then." Ivan turned to Rafer. "I have refused to accept Skye's IOU for this," he informed him. "I instead will require one from you."

"That wasn't the deal." Logan came out of his seat then. "Rafe has nothing you want, Resnova. If you want an IOU, then I'll give it to you."

"It is not your woman I am protecting," Ivan informed him as Skye glared at him now. "This will come from your cousin, and your cousin alone."

"No." Cami attempted to rise, winced, and sat back down. "No, I won't let him."

"Then you will die," Ivan said gently.

"Stop this, Ivan." Skye spoke softly, firmly. "Don't turn this into a pissing match. Don't make an enemy of me."

Ivan turned back to her slowly, clearly more than a little shocked. "You would do this?" he asked her. "When our history is much greater than that here? You would disavow it because I refuse to trade your life for hers?"

"That's not the case. You said you owe me. You're doing this for me, not Rafer and not Cami. For me."

"For him." He nodded his dark head to Rafer. "It is his responsibility."

"And one I'll accept," Rafer snapped.

"Like hell." Skye marched toward Ivan furiously.

"These men owe you nothing. You owe me. So let's not play games here. If anything happens to Cami because of your arrogance and determination to draw the Callahan men into one of your future schemes, I would hate you," she promised him. "But even more, I'd ensure Amara knew exactly what you had done. You've raised her much different than you were raised. Her illusions of you would be shattered."

He stared back at Skye silently for long seconds. "You would use Amara in such a way?" He seemed sincerely disappointed in her.

"I love him, Ivan." She spoke clearly, her tone even and firm, without a hint of the fear suddenly surging through her. "I would use any weapon I could find. And if anything happened to him because you refused to protect Cami, then yes, I would use Amara against you."

"I made the offer to allow you to accompany her," he pointed out, his tone dark, his gaze icy. "To protect you as well. Should you come along, then I would honor the IOU I gave you in exchange."

She shook her head again. "I'm not wounded. I'm trained for this, as you well know. And I won't let you manipulate me that easily to get Amara to come home."

His eyes became impossibly colder.

"His daughter refuses to come home because of the marriage he's attempting to arrange between her and his head of security," Skye informed the others as she crossed her arms over her breasts and stared back at Ivan mockingly. "Amara's currently in college, studying to be a lawyer."

"A prosecutor." He spat the word out as though it left

a bitter taste in his mouth. "And she threatens me often with it."

"I won't be the tool you use to get her home. And it wouldn't work anyway."

"It would." The sulk that suddenly shaped his lips was worthy of any two-year-old boy. "She loves you."

"She loves the career she wants more," Skye informed Ivan. "Now stop acting like a damned spoiled brat. You can take the IOU you owe me and stop trying to piss Logan and his cousins off just to see how hard they hit. Trust me. I've read their dossiers. They hit damned hard."

"I too have read them," Ivan snarled back at her.

"But I read the ones you don't have the contacts to acquire yet," she told him smugly. "Doesn't that suck? I might, *might,* be kind and feel extremely generous to you at a later date though, should you need to see a file in that particular 'eyes only' department."

That gleam in his eye was the same any kid would get at the thought of Christmas.

"Very well." He rubbed his hands together, leaned forward, and, using his utmost charm and engaging smile, began to outline the plan he'd already had formed.

Skye kept the triumph from her expression, knowing it would incite Ivan to be bad again. But God, she wished he were her brother. Or her father.

Somewhere in her life she wished she'd had a protector like him as she grew up.

"Are we all in agreement then?" he asked an hour later as the four men were huddled over the file Ivan had brought in with him that outlined not just his plans but also the security on his Colorado ranch and the two contacts whose identities he'd revealed.

"Agreed." Logan, Crowe, and Rafer all nodded before turning to shake Ivan's hand.

The air of male camaraderie was enough to turn a woman's stomach. Glancing at Cami, Skye watched her grimace and roll her eyes and knew she was thinking the same thing.

"Well then, Ms. Flannigan, shall we escort you to your carriage?" Ivan's grin was wicked as he glanced at Rafer. "As your fiancée has been wounded as well, I of course get the supreme pleasure of bearing your weight."

Cami's expression as she glanced between Ivan and Rafer was, frankly, close to fear.

As they'd talked, Rafer had torn his jeans, removed his boot, and wrapped his leg as Ivan had instructed him. The bandages had been stained with food coloring to imitate blood, and the appearance that he was now out of commission and unable to help his cousins, would be solid.

"Skye, you should have been my sister." Ivan turned to her suddenly, his expression somber. "Though, had you been my sister, I would have of course done more to protect you than those who were charged with the job. And you would have not had reason to run and hide in such a place to escape a job your heart was never truly a part of."

And how had he seen that when she herself hadn't known it until this moment?

"I would have liked you for a brother, Ivan," she told him as she accepted his hug, this time without Logan glaring at Ivan as though he were ready to cut his head off.

Minutes later, his bodyguards were called in. Two supported Logan's weight as another carried Cami to the middle SUV.

At the sight of Cami, her shirt ripped and the bandage showing behind her shoulder, and Rafer being supported by the two mountainous men and helped to the SUV, both Sheriff Tobias and his deputy, John Caine, along with the mayor and Wayne Sorenson, started toward him in concern.

Three of Ivan's men intercepted them, arms crossed.

"Get the fuck out of my way before I arrest you," Sheriff Tobias snarled, and he was more than serious.

When Ivan walked to the bodyguard, Rafer and Cami were safely in the vehicle and Rafer's "wounded" leg hidden by the closed door.

"What the fuck happened, Rafe?" Archer snarled.

"Someone came after Cami," Rafer told him quietly. "I had her stashed in Boulder with three bodyguards from a security firm I hired. One sold me out, Archer. He called John Corbin and within two hours an assassin hit the safe house she was in."

Archer seemed to pale. "Are you sure of that? Do you have proof?"

"Mr. Resnova here has the guard's cell phone and the text as proof. He'll be turning it over to the FBI as soon as we have it duplicated."

Archer looked as though he had been hit by a brick. Passing his hand over his face, he shook his head and swallowed tightly. "Damn, I was hoping—"

Hoping Crowe's grandfather, or any of their grandfathers for that matter, wasn't involved.

"Yeah, so were we," Rafer admitted.

"If you are finished threatening us, Sheriff, my jet is waiting at the Carstanza airfield in Aspen. We must be going," Ivan said.

Aspen wasn't exactly where the plane had been left. Actually, it was in the opposite direction.

Archer nodded before moving back. "You take care. Of both of you." He nodded to Rafer and Cami before turning and stalking back to the car.

Watching Archer, Skye was careful not to glance at the deputy leaning casually against his official car, the frown on his face as he watched the vehicles pull out a sure sign that no one from the bureau would have wanted Resnova involved.

She'd have to figure out exactly how to cover that one, she thought. Considering the bureau was well aware of her past with him, there really wasn't much she could do.

Making certain she avoided Caine's gaze, feeling it on her, knowing, just as she had known for days now, that he and his partner wanted to talk to her, Skye turned back to Logan.

He was watching her carefully, his gaze narrowed on her.

"Everything okay?" she asked as she moved close to him and felt his arm curl around her waist.

"Everything's fine," he promised. "Let's get back into the house; we have our own plans to make."

Plans that didn't include Archer or Deputy Caine.

Logan didn't glance back, but he wasn't a stupid man.

He'd seen Caine attempt to get her attention, and his suspicion that Caine was likely to be an agent was too strong to ignore.

The escalation of violence against them also seemed to be drawing in more hands to help than Logan had ever expected.

No, it wasn't the escalating violence, he admitted. It was his Skye.

She had drawn the townspeople to her first, then drew him to her. Now, it seemed, she was determined to draw them all together.

"I'm ready to sleep," she sighed as they entered the house.

"Crowe will keep the world out, baby," Logan promised as he led her to her bedroom suite. "You can sleep all you like now."

Because he had no doubt, once she awoke, the battle would only heat up more than ever.

CHAPTER TWENTY-ONE

"There are monsters in the dark, baby girl. Always remember that monsters love the dark. Don't sleep. Don't drop your guard. Don't ever let another know where you close your eyes. The monsters will always search for you. The monsters will always watch for you. Monsters are beautiful and their nice eyes are caring and their smiles are bright. Their teeth are jagged and their souls are black and they want nothing more than to destroy my bright and wonderful little girl.

Her mother's voice was a whisper in her ear, penetrating the serenity Skye had found in the darkness of sleep. Penetrating the warmth of Logan's embrace and bringing a frightened whimper to her lips.

Because she knew what came with the warning. She knew what lived in the darkness, what would seek her out if she dared to sleep—

But it hadn't been dark when she had gone to sleep.

"The monsters will love you, Skye. They will feed

you and they will warm you. They will care for you and they will clothe you. They will hold you when you cry, and laugh when you laugh. And when you close your eyes, they'll rip your heart from your chest. You can't love anyone, Skye. Because the monsters are everyone. Only Mommy and Daddy love you. Only Mommy and Daddy are not monsters. You can only love Mommy and Daddy—"

She hadn't remembered the order. She'd forgotten how her mother used to have the doctor put her to sleep and in that cold, white, sterile little room. And while she slept, her mother had whispered the words to her, and showed her with words and the horrific images that filled her young, sleeping mind, what the monsters were like.

But she remembered now—

Moving through the darkness, she wasn't a little girl any longer, though. She wasn't a child desperate to please her parents or to ensure that the monsters never found any of them.

"The monsters will kill Mommy and Daddy if you trust them, baby girl—"

And they had.

The monsters had come for them while Skye had slept, too young, her body too immature to keep up with the demands of remaining awake as darkness covered the ocean-front home they had lived in that summer.

Skye had lived in a lot of homes in her young life.

In a lot of countries.

And she was no longer a little girl to be scared of the dark, she told herself.

Yet it wasn't the darkness of reality she feared. It

was the darkness that wrapped around her as she slept, that weighed heavily on her mind, and once again danger visited in the form of monsters.

Because her mother was right. Monsters loved to hide in the darkness. That way people never saw their true faces, never saw the evil that was so much a part of them.

She moved through the darkness, pushing aside barely discernible shrubs, pushing past shadowed bodies and moving toward the light she could see growing ahead.

She had to reach the light—

As she moved around something lying in front of her, Skye came to stop, a broken, muffled cry passing the hand that covered her lips.

Looking down at her feet, she saw what she had stepped in, what she had stopped her. Her bare feet were immersed in the sticky, wet, scarlet-red puddle of warm blood.

Crouching on her heels, she pulled a pair of latex gloves from her pocket and drew them on slowly before pushing the body to its back and staring into the dark, recriminating eyes of the first victim she had tried to save.

Blond hair was red from the blood that soaked it. Blue eyes stared back at her in painful blame.

"Why didn't you help me?" The look seemed to scream. *"Why didn't you save me?"*

"I was too late," she whispered.

"You were too slow," the victim cried out in frustration. *"You forgot about the monsters."*

She had concentrated on the suspects she'd been given by her team commander rather than remembering her mother's words and focusing on the shy, scholarly old man who lived beside the girl. The one who swore he hadn't heard her screams.

"Hearing's not what it used to be." He would tug at his ear and gaze back in apology.

"You can't trust the monsters, Skye, you can only trust Mommy and Daddy," her mother whispered at her ear again.

Turning, Skye looked desperately for her mother, wondering why she refused to allow Skye to see her in her nightmares.

"Just love Mommy and Daddy, baby girl. Just Mommy and Daddy," her mother's voice became a hard, brutal snap.

"Trust me, Skye." Standing before her was her daddy's brother, Uncle Liam. With his bright, bright green eyes, his card tricks, and his laughter.

He winked at her and blew her a kiss.

Skye felt the smile that trembled on her lips though she knew what was coming.

"You can trust me, baby girl." Uncle Liam held out his hand to her as he turned to her father. "Tell her, Douglas, she can trust Uncle Liam."

Her father smiled gently and said the code words. "Skye baby, you can trust Uncle Liam with Daddy's life. Yes?"

That yes had to be in there. It was there. And it was her daddy with his smile and his warm arms holding her close.

But suddenly, he wasn't holding her close any longer. And Uncle Liam was a monster as he stood beside her parents' broken bodies, bathing in their blood.

"No. No," she whimpered, her arms wrapping around her stomach. Had it been her fault? Had she been the reason her parents had died?

"Love no one, Skye," her mother was screaming at her, though her lips didn't move. Her corpse only bled. "Love no one. I warned you not to trust the monsters, Skye. Never. If you love, then you love a monster. Or you love an innocent that a monster will kill. Because monsters will always follow you."

And suddenly, it wasn't her parents' blood dripping on the floor. It wasn't a victim's broken body lying in the dirt.

It wasn't Skye dying as she had always dreamed before.

It was Logan.

Suspended above the ground, his emerald-green eyes sightless, his arms hanging toward the ground as Skye began screaming.

Someone had to hear her screaming.

She went to her knees, only to feel his blood, warm and wet. She covered her face with her hands, but his blood was there, too.

She was screaming, screaming, begging him to wake up, begging him to live—

"I said fucking wake up!"

Her eyes jerked open as her body was suddenly hauled upright, a grip on her upper arms shaking her ruthlessly, forcing her from the nightmare.

Logan's face was white, his expression savage with whatever fury was building inside him as Skye stared up at him.

Her face was wet. Her hands were shaking.

She could feel the perspiration dripping down her body and the panic that still thundered through her senses.

"I'm sorry." her voice was hoarse, a sure sign that the nightmare had been a bad one.

"What the fuck was that, baby?" Smoothing her hair back from her face, his hands shaking, Logan stared down at her, his face still retaining a bit of a pale cast.

"Nightmare." A nervous laugh was all she could force past the tightness in her throat. "Just a really bad nightmare."

She wanted out of the bed. She wanted to get away from the sweat-dampened sheets and the reminder that sometimes she wasn't even safe to sleep in the daylight.

It was a sure sign that her senses were picking up something that her brain hadn't yet processed. Something that it would return to in a much more deadly, dangerous form if she didn't figure it out.

"Just a nightmare? Baby, that was nothing so simple as a nightmare."

She shook her head. "I need to shower."

She needed to get the feel of blood, thick and wet, sliding down her body, out of her senses.

Logan released her as she moved to the edge of the bed, forcing herself to stand up and not reveal the unsteadiness of her legs.

"How often do they happen?"

"The nightmares?" She breathed in roughly and headed to the closet for clothes.

"Yes, Skye, the nightmares." He followed behind her. "How often?"

"Not too often."

"Just if you go to sleep in the dark? Or if your senses are on such high alert that you know whatever's going on could strike soon?"

She stopped at the section that held her more casual tops and turned back to him slowly. "How do you know?"

"I've had them," he admitted. "When Jaymi died. I still have nightmares."

Rafer's lover from twelve years past, the one the Slasher had tried to have them framed with.

Jaymi and her husband Tye Kramer, before Tye's death, had been close to the Callahan cousins. After Tye had died in the military, Jaymi and Rafer had become lovers until her death.

She nodded slowly. "I couldn't save the last victim that the D.C. Vigilante kidnapped and tortured," she admitted as she pushed her fingers through her hair. "He didn't strike out at the criminals." Her voice became hoarse again. "He struck out at their wives, their nieces—" She swallowed tightly. "Their daughters."

Ivan's daughter had been luck. Skye and her partner had been close, they had already identified Martin Trinson as a suspect and were watching him closely for an attempt to take another victim.

They had been only seconds late.

Only seconds.

He'd managed to lose them just long enough to snatch

the twenty-one-year-old daughter of a major crime lord and what he did to her—

She gave her head a hard shake, a shudder racing through her as she swallowed back the bile rising in her throat.

Grabbing jeans, a cotton knit shirt, and underclothes, she turned and hurried to the shower.

Logan watched her go. Watched the fall of riotous curls as they flowed down her back, and despite his concern for her, felt his dick twitching in renewed interest at the memory of those curls caressing his thighs hours before.

Raking his fingers through his hair, he followed her, almost terrified to leave her alone with those memories, despite the fact that the case had ended and the D.C. Vigilante was dead.

Martin Trinson had been particularly brutal. Taking his crazed rage for his father's death and the rape of his mother by a drug lord, he had begun by first striking out at known and convicted drug dealers. Then, he had begun striking out at suspected criminals of varying crimes by targeting their families. Their mothers, sisters, nieces. All female. All maimed in ways that if they survived, the proof of their relations' crimes would always show on their bodies, not to mention their minds.

Waiting until he heard the shower running, Logan stepped into the large bathroom, stripped the cotton pants he wore, and then stepped into the large, multi-head shower with her.

She turned away from him quickly, but not before he could see the tears running from her eyes.

She had been screaming his name when he brought her awake. Screaming it as though her soul were being ripped from her body. As though she were standing in his blood.

"Hey, hiding doesn't make it go away," he said softly as he wrapped his arms around her and drew her against his chest. "When I have one of mine and wake up screaming as though the hounds of hell were after me, I send Bella squalling and hiding under the couch while it takes hours for me to stop seeing blood staining my hands." She shuddered at the words. "Will you let me run then?"

She shook her head.

"I won't let you run now."

Her breathing hitched. "My parents always taught me about the monsters in the dark," she whispered. "To only trust them. To only love them. When my father hired his brother, Liam, as his head bodyguard. Liam was unaware my parents were agents. Dad's cover was that of a diamond broker, his illegal activities involved moving drugs, weapons, and people as well. My father trusted Liam with his life. One night, after a large delivery of diamonds, Liam and his lover, my nanny, forced Father to give him the diamonds, then he killed them both as I watched on the monitors in the safe room. There were monsters in the dark, and my parents let one in."

She turned and buried her head in his chest.

Logan's eyes closed, his throat tightening at the thought of a child so young, so delicate enduring such a horrendous betrayal as well as witnessing it. "I wasn't to trust anyone," she whispered. "I wasn't to love anyone.

But my parents' trust and love in my uncle destroyed us all."

"And then you lost Amy amid blood as well," he said.

"Amy saved me." She sniffed tearfully. "When I went to stay with her and her parents, it was Amy who held me through the nightmares, who made me want to get out of bed in the morning. I couldn't let this go." She lifted her head and stared up at him. "I couldn't let you go. When she showed me your picture, talked about you, told me stories about you, I think I fell in love with you then."

Cupping her cheek with his hand, his lips lowered to hers in a kiss so gentle, so filled with warmth that Skye was forced to blink back tears at the knowledge that he could do so much in such a simple touch.

When his head lifted, Logan reached for the shampoo bottle, filled his hands with her shampoo, and began lathering her hair rather than speaking.

The long, long silken strands rolled through his fingers in ringlets that clung to them and held the suds with greedy curves.

Like Skye held him when he took her. Like her arms, legs, the sweet gripping muscles of her pussy hugged and loved his dick.

Directing her beneath the spray of water, he rinsed the curls slowly before applying the conditioner, then pulling the long mass to the top of her head and clipping it with the two large comb clips he assumed were for that.

Soaping her sponge, he began to wash her then, letting her talk, listening, his chest heavy, his heart aching for the little girl who had no friends, no family, no one but two parents who had ensured she would never endanger them, and would always be an asset to them and to the bureau.

The medical leave made sense now, as did the trips to the doctor each month.

She'd become burned out when she couldn't save the last victim of the DC Vigilante. Skye hadn't ever been meant to face such horror, such death, on a daily basis.

As he finished cleaning her, then rinsing her from head to toe, he stood back for a second, ensuring there were no suds left and that the fear in her eyes was now replaced by desire.

He didn't have to look to see that. Before he knew what she was about to do, she went to her knees, gripped the base of his cock, then surrounded the head with the heat and tight silken grip of her wet mouth.

"Fuck!" he breathed out, his hands burying in her newly washed hair as he leaned back against the shower stall. "Ah hell, Skye. Baby. There you go, suck my dick."

His balls were tight, the shaft of his cock pounding with such immediate lust, such instant hunger that he knew he wouldn't dare deny her, even if he could.

He was crazy for her. He'd realized one night was never going to work with her, that he would keep going back for more and more. He couldn't get enough of her.

Her sweet, hot mouth tightened on the head of his cock, sucked it deep into her mouth, swallowed against the tip and sent a clash of sensations to demolish his control.

The fingers of one hand wrapped around the base, stroked the shaft. She weighed his balls in the palm of her hand, then rasped the sac with the prick of her nails.

Fuck. Ah hell. He'd intended to make slow, sweet love to her in the shower. He had intended to show her how good he could make it. How fucking good it could be.

Instead, a second, no more than a heartbeat before he was spilling into her mouth, he forced her to her feet. Gripping the cheeks of her ass, Logan lifted her to him, turned, braced her against the shower wall and in the next second had the head of his dick buried inside her.

It was always slow going at first. He thanked God for that because it was the only thing that helped him keep his head long enough to make sure she had the chance to come for him before he spilled inside her.

They were going to have to talk about the fact that he hadn't used a condom so much as once since he'd first buried himself inside her.

The thought of putting anything between them, anything that would affect the pure, sweet pleasure that burned between them, seemed impossible to do.

She hadn't mentioned it, and he knew she was aware of it. She seemed just as reluctant to dim the sensations they shared when he took her.

It was like being immersed in a well of swirling, twisting rapture. An abyss of never-ending heat and pleasure that dug tiny fingers of pulsating energy straight through his balls and from there, through the rest of his body.

Thrusting upward, burying himself in the heat as the slick, milking muscles wrapped around his shaft like a tightening fist, he had to clench his teeth to hold back for just a second.

Dragging in a hard breath, he braced his feet against the shower floor and began driving full length inside her.

Her back bowed, a tremulous cry falling from her lips as her arms wrapped around his shoulders, her lips moving to his neck.

She marked him, as he had marked her neck each time he took her. He was so desperate to ensure nothing or no one was stupid enough to try to take her, that subconsciously, each time he fucked her, each time he kissed her, hell, the first time he kissed her, his lips had found her neck and left one of the darkened blemishes against her silken flesh.

And now, he would carry hers.

Something broke inside him at the thought.

Something so powerful and overwhelming that he didn't have the chance to fight against it.

"God, Skye, baby." His lips covered hers.

He'd sworn he wouldn't do it.

He'd told himself it was too soon, and by God it was. He knew it was.

Kissing her like a man starved for the taste of his woman, he kept his lips on hers until they were both desperate to breathe, desperate to do more than simply share a kiss.

Pounding into her, his thighs clenched, his dick rock hard and impaling her with all the rising hunger he couldn't contain, he was forced to jerk his lips back, to breathe.

"Logan, please." She strained against him, her legs

tight around his hips. "Yes. Please, yes," she moaned. "Love me." The words sounded torn from her, ripped from a heart that pushed them past lips that were unaware of what they were saying.

Drugged with passion, heavy lidded, her lashes were almost closed, her face flushed as she lifted and rose against him.

"I do, Skye," he whispered as he stared back at her, pausing for a second, then slamming inside her again. "I do baby. I love you, Skye."

Her lashes lifted in surprise, her lips parting in disbelief.

"Fuck, I love you," he repeated, refusing to release her gaze, refusing to allow either of them to hide from it. "Forever, Skye. I'll love you forever."

Her head tipped back as he felt her coming then. Felt her body jerk and shudder, her pussy clamping down on him tighter, milking his dick harder until it triggered his own release.

Spurting hard and deep inside the lush, gripping depths of her pussy, Logan gathered her closer, buried his lips against the crook of her shoulder and neck, and marked her again.

Marked her as his woman.

Marked her as his lover.

His life.

As the most precious gift a man could ever receive.

CHAPTER
TWENTY-TWO

Archer walked slowly into the restaurant of the Viceroy Ski Resort, paused just inside the entrance before catching sight of his targets and moving across the room.

The table was set in the corner, overlooking the lake, while the tables that would have sat around it had been moved and replaced to allow the ultimate privacy for the three men as they enjoyed their lunch.

They didn't seem to be enjoying it much, though.

Marshal Roberts, Saul Rafferty, and John Corbin were silent, their expressions dark as their food sat untouched before them. Only the wine in their glasses had been disturbed.

They were silent as Archer pulled a seat from a nearby table and pulled it close. Sitting down and stretching out his long, jeans-clad legs, he watched the three men with an arched brow.

Marshal Roberts sat closest on his right. Propping his elbows on the table and staring out at the water through the windows, he clasped his fingers before his lips before speaking.

"I heard Rafer was hurt. How bad was it?"

Archer nodded slowly. "Not sure how bad. Looked like a broke ankle or leg to me. What did you hear?"

"Leg. In two places," Marshal answered. "And Cami was shot."

His voice seemed to grow heavier.

"Yeah, in the shoulder."

"Rumor is one of her bodyguards tried to kill her?" Saul Rafferty asked.

Damn, Logan looked a lot like his granddad, Archer though. The same piercing green eyes and intent expression.

"That's what Rafer said," he agreed. "Word was, he received a text from someone claiming that the bodyguard contacted John here, offering to sell her location."

John Corbin lifted his brows in surprise, his blue eyes suddenly darkened and tightened in anger. Archer had a feeling this information was new to him.

"I never heard from anyone," John finally answered. "And I sure as hell wouldn't have taken the offer if I had, I can promise you that."

"Archer, something doesn't sound right here," Saul said then. "Even twelve years ago, none of this stuff happened with the exception of that summer when those poor girls were killed. Now, not only are more girls being killed but there's rumors some criminal just took Rafer and Cami off?"

"Those boys have made some unusual contacts over the years," Archer lied, because he didn't know what the hell was going on himself. "Rafer would do anything to protect, Cami, just as Logan would to protect Skye."

"They're dealing with criminals now?" Corbin tried to inject disgust into his tone, but Archer could have sworn he detected a measure of pride instead.

"It would appear so." Archer shrugged. "The man has a criminal sheet a mile long, John. I wouldn't want to run into him in a dark alley, or get on his bad side. I know he's been poking into what's going on, lately. I don't like that much, gentlemen."

"I can't say I blame you, Archer," John stated stiffly. "I wouldn't either."

Archer grimaced. "You might get to experience it," he sighed. "I could have sworn I heard him mention to Crowe and Logan that he would be checking into that text and its origins as well as any possible angle of danger to Skye. He wasn't a happy criminal at any rate."

All three men seemed to stiffen.

"Just what we need, one of their low-life friends poking into our business," John grunted. "Couldn't you arrest him or something?"

"Plenty of officials have already tried that route," Archer shrugged. "I can't do anything until I catch him doing more than threatening to break the law."

"Wonderful." John finished his wine in a single drink as the other two glanced at each other warily.

"You act as though it's more than an inconvenience," Archer stated.

"A hell of an inconvenience," John sighed.

"A little beyond that," Marshal retorted. "A criminal

looking into our affairs? How could those three hooligans possibly top that one?"

Mockery spilled from his lips, but if that wasn't amusement sparking in Marshal's gaze, then Archer didn't know what the hell it was.

What were these three up to and how did their grandsons play into their scheming? The fact that the Callahans came by their manipulating little games wasn't lost on Archer as he stared back at their grandsons.

"Is that why you're here?" John finally asked. "To inform us what the brats are up to?"

John shook his head slowly. "No, I'm actually here to figure out why Marietta Tyme had a receipt from the restaurant here. I wanted to talk to the maitre'd but," he looked around, "he hasn't shown up yet, it would seem."

"Monday's usually his day off," Saul stated. "He won't be back till morning."

"Ahh." Archer nodded. "I'll see if his assistant is here."

"Don't." It was John who stopped him as he moved to get up. "Don't speak to anyone about it, Archer."

The request had Archer sitting back in his chair slowly. "Why?"

The three men looked at each other before giving small, decisive nods and Saul leaned forward slowly, his fingers still knotted loosely before his lips. "Marietta met with us," he said softly.

Surprising. "Why?"

"The bar she works at in Denver belongs to me," Saul explained. "I knew he was going there and she was supposed to keep an eye on him for me. She called that morning and asked us to meet her, but she didn't

show up. We waited for several hours." Marshal glanced
at the other three who nodded in return.

"No hint what she wanted?" Archer asked.

"All she said was that she needed to meet because she
had some information for us," Saul stated. "She liked to
think of herself as his guardian angel." The hint of sadness in his gaze was enough to make Archer suspect that
Marietta might have cared for Logan more than he knew.

"This Skye girl, she's not exactly got an unblemished
record," Saul said then. "We had her checked out. Her
father was a diamond broker by day and no more than a
drug and flesh peddler at night. She's lucky he didn't use
her to buy his safety that night."

If there had been just the smallest degree of spite, just
a little malicious intent, then he could push more, Archer
thought. He would have reason to dig deeper and see if
one of them messed up.

But what he saw in each of their eyes instead was
concern. These were men who had never bothered to
hide what they had to say, or what they did. At least, not
as far as he could tell.

"We have a problem then," Archer sighed. "Because I
think Marietta did know something. And I think it may
be what got her killed."

John shook his head, his eyes suddenly warning, his
expression stilled, emotionless. "Information didn't get
her killed, Archer," he said quietly. "She was more than
a friend. Just as the other girls were. I don't know who and
I don't know why, but someone is damned determined
to make sure those boys have no one but themselves.
And no information possible could have stopped it."

"Unless she knew who it was," Archer said softly. "What if she knew who the Slasher was, gentlemen? And if she did, don't you think she would have found a way to hide the information?" He turned to Saul then. "Help me, Saul. Where would she have hidden the information?"

Saul shook his head. "I worked with her, Archer, I wasn't her best friend."

Archer nodded again. "Well, I better be going then." He smiled tightly as he stood to his feet. "Enjoy your lunch, gentlemen."

"Archer." John stopped him before he rose from his chair. "No one needs to know anything about this meeting other than the fact that you asked about that text," he warned quietly. "Not your impressions, no attitude you may have detected. As far as your concerned, we're cold, hard bastards."

What had John seen? Archer wondered, as he watched them.

"Anyone?" he asked. "Who would question it?"

"I'm sure it will go in a report," John said coolly. "And you want to be real careful what you say in that report, or to anyone else."

Archer leaned closer. "What do you know, John?"

"I know I don't want my grandson dead any more than Saul or Marshal does," he stated. "And I know I'd prefer to stay alive myself for a while longer. That would definitely help both ventures. Just as I said. We're stone-cold bastards that don't give a damn what happens to those boys. You got that?"

Archer almost sneered back at all of them. "Funny, John, I've rarely doubted otherwise."

He turned and left the restaurant, feeling their gazes on him as he left the dining room. Oh yeah, they knew something, he just wasn't certain what, and he wondered if they even knew for sure what they knew.

One thing was for damned certain though, he'd just caught that little warning. Someone close to his office could be a spy, leaking information.

Now, Archer just had to figure out who.

A lifetime had been wasted by those men. Three boys had grown to mature, deserving men any father or grandfather could be proud of. Instead, they had disowned them, filed suit after suit against them and their inheritances. They had done everything to destroy them, but Archer knew for a fact, sitting there staring at those three old bastards, he knew, they cared much more for their grandsons than they had let on.

Moving outside the resort, he was almost at the SUV when his cellphone rang.

Pulling it from the case at his side, he flipped it open and brought it to his ear. "Sheriff," he announced.

"Sheriff, it's Deputy Caine." Caine's tone was cold, hardened steel.

"Go ahead."

"We're at Riker's Ravine outside town," he stated. "You better get here. We just found another girl."

CHAPTER
TWENTY-THREE

Logan finished his coffee that night, watching as Skye emptied the dishwasher of dinner dishes and fed Bella a treat.

It had taken Logan himself hours to get the pup to take food from Skye. Finally, Bella had done so with a little puppy yip and a wag of her tail.

The little bit of nothing canine was growing fast. She'd almost doubled her size, but she was still, and always would be, far too tiny.

"Old Mrs. Jenkins thinks you and your cousins should invest in bodyguards," Skye stated as she stacked plates out of the dishwasher in the cabinet.

"Does she now?" he grunted as he rinsed his cup and watched as Bella collapsed on the floor with one of her favorite toys.

They were waiting, and the waiting was nerve-wracking. Crowe was on Crowe Mountain trying to track the code name King Arthur using his own computer, while Resnova had Cami on his estate and one of his bodyguards was preparing to drive Rafer back the next day.

So far, everything was quiet. Too damned quiet.

"Old Mrs. Jenkins just likes to make Mr. Jenkins jealous," Logan told Skye with a grunt. "Besides, we have enough damned excitement around here without giving the gossips something to watch as well as talk about."

"How do you think I got the majority of my information before I made it into your bed?" she informed him with a wink. "Mrs. Jenkins was my main source."

He shook his head with a grin as she leaned against the counter and crossed her arms over her breasts and as she watched him with a sassy smile.

Damn, he liked being here with her. He had liked having her go to bed with him in the afternoon and wake up with him in the evening.

Holding her, waking up with her in his arms, feeling her warmth, knowing her heat, was something he didn't want to lose.

It wasn't that he hadn't had a few relationships before. It was that those relationships had always remained short. If Skye walked out on him, walked out on what he was discovering with her, he wasn't certain how he would handle it.

The danger was there. The risk. He could feel it getting ready to move in, and it was making him damned nervous.

It was making her nervous as well.

Lifting his hand, he rubbed at the back of his neck

before pacing to the living room and staring into the shadowed expanse of it.

"You feel it too," she said softly.

"Yeah, I feel it."

Turning back to the kitchen, he rejoined her, a frown on his face as he watched her fold the dish towel before turning back to him.

"You should have gone with Resnova," he told her then. It was a thought he'd been considering since the bastard left. Hell, before he'd arrived. It had been Logan's intention to send Skye with the other man until Resnova had shown an interest in just that.

"No, I shouldn't have," she pointed out. "This is my fight too, Logan. I've told you that."

Because of Amy and now because of him.

Skye considered it her fight because her foster sister had died at the hands of a murderer, her battle because Logan was now her lover and the stalker was crashing even further into his life.

"It doesn't need to be your fight, or your risk," he told her as his gaze roved over her expression, only to have his gaze caught by the small love bite on her neck.

Where he'd marked her. Where he'd placed his stamp of ownership on her. Proof that she was his woman.

There was a primal thrill in that mark totally at odds with the fact that he knew keeping her with him was only endangering her.

"Don't start," she warned him as his lips parted again. Pointing a finger in his direction as she stood next to the center island, she all but wagged it at him in disapproval.

Every time he thought of her in this fight his gut

tightened in warning, and he'd learned to heed his instincts.

Tomorrow he'd call Resnova, he decided. Tomorrow he'd have to make her leave. No matter what it took.

For now.

He touched her.

As though he needed her touch.

As though to hold the claim he had made on her heart, he had to.

He didn't dare want anything as much as he wanted this woman.

As he had needed her more than six years ago when he'd seen her and realized who she was, and again six months ago when he'd seen her in his rental.

But he hadn't recognized her. The shy girl of six years before had been replaced by the confident, perhaps a bit innocent, woman she was now.

As he stared into her sultry, heated gaze Logan realized he'd wanted her since about the second glimpse he'd had of her. And he remembered where and when that had been. At Carter Jefferson's gubernatorial celebration party in D.C. six years before.

She would have been twenty-one.

And he'd known she was Carter's foster daughter, just as he'd known she'd been watching him just as closely as he was watching her.

He'd wanted her until he'd ached with it that night, but he'd left instead.

He wanted her with a need that made no sense and an overwhelming hunger that he couldn't seem to control now.

A hunger that shattered with the explosive, passion-destroying retort of bullet striking through glass to bury itself in the wall across from the center island.

Only inches from where it would have first struck his delicate, too-short, too-alive lover directly in the back of her head if he had been just a breath slower. Just a breath in the wrong direction as some internal alarm screamed through him a heartbeat before the glass shattered.

With the first crack of the window Logan was moving.

The obvious sniper rifle had discharged, shattering the window with the first impact of a bullet as Logan reacted.

Instinct. Survival. Twelve fucking years of training, of killing, tearing through his senses.

The assassin had to reload.

Logan had Skye to the floor, rolling his fingers, burying them in a quivering scruff as he jerked a terrorized Bella from her spot next to the center island and rolled, his larger body bracing over the two too-delicate forms as he fought to reach safety.

Discharge. The bullet struck flesh by the barest glance.

It drew first blood from Logan's shoulder as he rolled, bracing it against Skye's head to protect her, the pup now between them.

A few seconds to reload.

Logan all but threw Skye's delicate weight over the short step into the living area before following her, Bella held securely in the crook of his arm, silent and trembling.

Discharge.

The third bullet tore a hole in the wood. Once again, the exact position of Skye's head less than a heartbeat before.

With each shot Bella growled, a babyish little snarl of immature fury that matched each curse that spilled from Skye's lips.

Once the sniper no longer had line of vision, no longer had a target to draw on, Logan was on his feet, jerking Skye against him and all but carrying her and the furious Bella, as he ran.

The door to the garage slammed against the wall as he tore through it, Skye held tight to his side as she now gripped Bella in desperate arms.

"I can run!" Skye screamed, and Logan realized it wasn't the first time she had made that declaration.

He ignored her, just as he had the first time. Son of a bitch, she was his; he wasn't taking a chance with her or Bella. Or any child Skye might be carrying.

God help him. Had he been insane?

Wrenching open the driver's side door of the black four-wheel drive where he'd pulled it in, in reverse, he all but threw her in, pushed the growling, furious puppy into her, then followed. Twisting the key, he wrenched the stick into neutral, hit the clutch and then the gas, and tore through the garage door that hadn't had time to open more than a bare few feet after he hit the remote.

Wood and glass shattered around the vehicle as it shot into the street, drawing the shocked gazes of his neighbors, as they were drawn from their homes by the sound of gunfire.

Tires screamed, gripped asphalt, then like a black

bullet tore down the street as the puppy gave two excited little yips and turned an expression of pure puppy
excitement toward him. Bella seemed to suddenly be
infused with adrenaline. And she was loving the feel of
it surging through her little body, if her expression was
anything to go by.

Fuck! Son of a bitch. This had to stop. It had to fucking end before he lost the two most important parts of
his life. Before he lost his heart and soul.

"Oh my God, how many weapons do you have in here,
Logan?" Skye declared, her voice rising to be heard over
the sound of the motor, the scream of tires and the flight
out of town.

And what the hell did she have her gaze locked on?
What he assumed was a match to the very weapon that
had attempted to take her head off.

His sniper rifle.

The one loaded, locked, ready, and in its specially
designed mount across the front of the dash.

Along with it was a sawed-off shotgun so illegal he
swore Archer had paled when he'd caught sight of it a
few months before. That didn't count the Velcroed
Glock, the Beretta, and the six shot his grandfather J. R.
Callahan, had owned.

Skye had the Glock in her hand, twisting, turning, her
gaze constantly moving as she held the weapon with
both confidence as well as experience.

She was Logan's match. That didn't mean he wasn't
scared the fuck to death right now. Accidents happened.
As Skye had said, there were monsters in the dark.

Twisting the wheel, he took a side road as they shot

out of town. Pushing the truck as fast as he dared for the next mile, he then veered from the narrow road onto another and raced deeper into the mountains.

Jerking his emergency cell phone from the dash mount where he'd put it weeks before, he hit the speed dial for Crowe's number.

"Crowe." He answered the phone before the first ring ended.

"We have trouble," Logan snapped. "Where are you?"

"Home," Crowe answered quickly. "What happened?"

"Our fucking King Arthur," Logan snarled. "The fucker shot the house up, stayed about a quarter of an inch from a kill shot with each reload, and I have no idea if he's on my ass or not."

"Get up here," Crowe ordered, his voice cold now. "I'll contact Rafer and Resnova and we'll have to change plans."

"ETA thirty minutes," Logan told him.

"Ten if you keep this speed up," Skye stated as he took a curve nearly on two tires. "Or we'll see heaven first."

"I've taken it faster," Logan assured her as he kept the speed on, desperate now to get her as far away from those bullets as possible.

"You're a wild man, Logan." She laughed, amusement, warmth, love, so many emotions, sparkling in her voice, but with them concern and regret that it was danger she and Logan were facing rather than a life they were beginning.

Barely a quarter of a mile down the stretch of road, with a twist of the wheel and a flip of his thumb to throw the vehicle into four-wheel drive, he felt the tires tearing into grass and rock as he began to climb above the valley.

Crowe Mountain was partially in Corbin County and partially in Pitkin. It bordered the Callahan ranch as well as the Ramsey ranch. Once the plans for the resort they had in mind were completed, the three properties would be merged along with a smaller piece of land Logan still had possession of through the same individual listed on the house in town.

It was almost as though Logan's parents had known him too well. Or perhaps they had feared he would be too much like his mother, who had nearly given her trust back to her father when she'd received it.

If she had, would she have still been alive?

"This is crazy," Logan muttered as he started up a back road onto Crowe's property, lights off and the four-wheel traction tearing into the dirt of the incline. "God, Skye, if something happened to you—"

"Stop; don't borrow trouble," she warned him as she held Bella close now, rather than the gun. "We're in this together, and I wouldn't be anywhere else right now."

He could hear the truth in her voice, hear the determination and the love of life, the love of him, that echoed in the declaration.

But it didn't change what they were facing, and it didn't change the fact that without her, he doubted he'd even want to fight any longer.

She was the reason he hadn't taken the suicide assignments in the small unit he'd been a part of. She was the reason he'd fought, daily, to find a reason to fight for an inheritance that had brought nothing but blood and death. She was the reason he lived; it was that simple.

"We're heading into Crowe's now," Logan told her long minutes later as the truck bounced onto a smoother, though no less narrow path leading to the top of the mountain. "We cut these paths onto the mountain ourselves; to make sure we had access other than the main road."

Their lives were such a daily fight for survival in this county that they couldn't even trust using the main road to enter or leave one of their homes.

The thought of the lives they'd lived since they were no more than babies, before and after their parents' deaths, broke her heart.

Logan had had no one, and now she knew he was second-guessing the decision to allow her into his life. *Not that he'd had much choice,* she thought smugly.

But perhaps they'd both lost themselves to such an extent that they had made the same mistake his parents had.

She pressed her hand unobtrusively to her stomach, knowing the chances that she'd conceived were high. Neither of them had enough control once they touched to even think about protection or the danger their lives would bring to a child.

All Skye could think about when she thought about a baby was whether it would look more like Logan or her. A boy or a girl? And seeing Logan's joy in the pup Skye had seen forced into his life, she wondered how much more joy he would find in a baby.

The Callahans hadn't known a lot of happiness in their lives. It had been one battle after another, one fierce fight to survive after another. Adapting to a measure of peace would be a pleasant change for them.

"We're going to beat this." She turned to him as she glimpsed the lights of Crowe's house through the trees in the distance. "You watch, Logan. We'll beat this. And when it's over, we'll have all the things we've both lost out on in our lives."

He reached over, his hand gripping hers, before he turned and placed a gentle kiss against her palm. The warmth of his lips, the feel of them, sent a wave of heat that wasn't entirely sexual rushing through her.

"I'll hold you to that," he warned her.

"You do that." She smiled back at him despite the tightening in her stomach, the instinctive primal warning that it wasn't over yet. "You'll see. We're going to make it."

Pulling into Crowe's drive, Logan slammed the truck into park before turning to her. "Leave Bella in here until we see if that wolf bitch has made an appearance again. Crowe's been expecting her any day to return to have her pups. Bella would make a nice little snack."

The pup was silent, unusually so. Perhaps she could feel the presence of the wolf, probably just waiting and licking her chops at the thought of a nice little Bella treat, Skye thought in amusement.

Tucking a faded blanket Logan had folded and lain along the back of the seat against the pup, Skye opened the door and hurriedly jumped out.

She tucked the Glock in the back of her jeans, pulling her shirt out over it before meeting Logan at the front of the truck and moving quickly to the opened door.

They moved too quickly.

Perhaps if they had walked slower, if they'd paid more attention—

Regret slammed into Logan as he and Skye stepped inside and they both came to a resounding stop.

"Close the door, please." The voice was rough, guttural; was obviously disguising it, but it didn't matter. If the gun pointing at them was any indication, then they might not need to worry about his identity.

He wasn't very tall, barely six feet, if that tall. He was broad, though, a little on the heavy side. And there was something vaguely familiar about the set of his shoulders.

She couldn't see his eyes; a mask covered his face and dark sunglasses covered his eyes. *Most attackers with the intent to kill didn't bother hiding their identities,* she thought as she felt herself slipping automatically into the skin she'd been trained to use when facing danger.

At his feet, Crowe was sprawled, unconscious, his hands secured behind his back with heavy nylon restraints and again at his feet. The back of his head was wet, and blood had dripped to the floor.

For one horrified second Skye thanked God she and Logan had left Bella in the truck.

"Logan, don't make me shoot you." The gun suddenly snapped in Logan's direction as he moved to stand in front of her. "Now, we can do this easy, or we can do this the hard way. The hard way means all of you die. The easy way means you live."

"What do you want?" Logan's voice was pure death.

The rasp, the utterly controlled, even sound, of it sent a shiver down Skye's back.

"Just a few things." The gunman gestured to the computer still running at Crowe's desk. "I won't be much longer."

Reaching into the pocket of his jacket, he pulled more restraints free before tossing a pair at Skye's feet. "Put those on your boyfriend's wrists, Miss O'Brien. They should be fairly easy to figure out."

Thank God her cover in the bureau was buried so deep, because she knew how to put the restraints on and make them appear to be tightened correctly when they would actually be easier to work loose.

Skye picked up the restraints carefully.

"First." The gunman stopped her. "Logan, your weapons please."

Logan's face tightened savagely. "I didn't bring anything in. I wasn't expecting Crowe to be taken so easily, and there was no time to grab my holster or backup."

The gunman tilted his head to the side as though weighing the chances that Logan was lying. "Why did you leave in such a hurry?" he asked curiously.

"Because your shooter nearly took our fucking heads off," Logan snapped.

Skye thought she could see the movement of brows lifting in surprise beneath the black mask. "How interesting," the gunman mused. "But he's not my shooter. He's an inconvenience to me, if you want the truth."

"That makes two of us then, doesn't it?" Logan mocked.

The gunman chuckled. "You know, Logan, it's a shame, because I actually like you."

The tone of his voice, the familiarity, yes, he knew Logan, but Skye guessed she knew the gunman as well.

She was positive of it.

"Lift your shirt and turn around," he ordered. "Let's be certain you're not lying."

Lifting the shirt high enough to reveal the band of his jeans as well as the area under his arms, Logan turned slowly.

"Pant legs." The gun waved toward his ankles.

Logan bent, lifted each pant leg, and revealed only the white socks he wore.

"Very good." The gunman nodded then, smiling again before turning to Skye. "You can take care of it now."

Moving behind Logan, she had to draw in a hard, deep breath as she noticed the tension in his large body. He was like a volcano ready to blow. Because he sensed what she suspected as well, that this man wasn't at Crowe's just to play with his computer.

He was there for something more.

"You're not the shooter?" Logan asked as Skye slid the double-loop nylon restraints over his wrists and at the same time pulled the Glock from beneath her shirt and slid it in the waistband of his jeans, then tightened the notched closures of the restraints.

There were no locks, no keys, no way to get out of them without being completely obvious without the aid of a damned sharp knife or sturdy cutters.

Or so the gunman thought.

Her fingers gripped Logan's for a moment before she released him, then moved to return to where she had been standing.

"You're not done," the gunman told her before turning to Logan and pointing to the wood table chair behind him. "Have a seat."

Carefully, Logan sat down, always keeping his eyes on the gun and the man who held it.

"His ankles." The gunman nodded to Skye.

Skye slid the restraints around Logan's ankles, though she could almost guess the gunman wouldn't check them, at least not closely.

"Put a pair on yourself. I'll tighten them." He smiled.

There, the slightest overbite to his teeth, barely noticeable, as well as a nick in the right corner of his front tooth that looked fairly new.

Skye fought to notice as many distinguishable traits as possible, because if she and Logan managed to get out of this alive, then she was going to kill the gunman herself.

If Logan and Crowe didn't get to him first.

Sliding her hands into the first loop, she tucked the notched strap into position, then she stood still and silent as he moved to her.

Tucking his weapon behind his back, he gripped the strap closer and pulled it snugly before stepping back from her.

The smile that shaped his lips was terrifying.

Yes, there were definitely monsters in the dark.

"I knew the shooter would be there tonight, though," he said as he moved back to the computer desk, laid the gun on top of it, then crossed his arms over his chest and stared back at them.

Skye could feel her heart beginning to beat hard and sluggishly, instinct slamming in her head, warning her, urging her to run.

"You're his partner?" Logan asked, obviously trying to buy time and praying Crowe would wake up or something else would happen to give him the slightest advantage.

"No, I'm not his fucking partner," the gunman snapped, clearly sensitive to the subject of the shooter. "That bastard. Let's say our boss didn't like the fact that I couldn't find Cami or get to your little girlfriend here. He hired someone who could. Of course, if he had let me use a rifle, the job might have been done by now."

The thick beat of her heart was about to strangle her.

"Your boss?" Logan asked, his tone darker.

"The Slasher," the gunman answered. "Though he didn't know I'd be here tonight, so your pretty girlfriend won't have the pleasure of being raped by him." He smiled at her, a slow curve of his lips before he licked them wetly. "But she still has me. As much fun as Ms. Tyme was, she was rather a dead fuck after we drugged her. I'm betting your girlfriend here is livelier."

Skye felt the oxygen expand, then ooze from her chest, leaving nothing for her to breathe for precious seconds. The room seemed to dim, to darken, and for one horrifying second she thought she would scream.

"I'll kill you," Logan promised him. "I promise you, I'll find you and I'll kill you."

The gunman shook his head as he grinned again. "No, you won't. You haven't yet. And by the time you have it all figured out, it will be too late."

"We'll never leave this county if she's hurt," Logan snarled then. "Whatever you're after you'll never get it."

He laughed at that. "Of course you will. Once Rafer sees the tortured, dead body of your girlfriend, then he'll make certain Cami never returns. And he'll ensure nothing hurts her. Oh yes." He lifted a gloved finger and waved it at Logan. "Do tell Rafer to ensure she isn't knocked up until the conditions of the trust are completely broken. If there's an heir, I promise you, I don't have a problem killing a child as my partner did. And I'll actually enjoy it."

Skye stayed perfectly still. She didn't dare move, didn't dare react, or she knew she would shatter.

She twisted her wrists in the restraints, bending them, working at the only weakness she'd been able to provide herself in the discreet way she'd twisted them.

"I'll enjoy killing you either way," Logan swore as the other man began moving toward her. "Don't fucking touch her!"

He laughed as Skye began backing away, searching desperately now for a way out, for an escape route or anything before he touched her.

When he did, she stilled.

His hands gripped her shoulders, holding her still as she stared over his, forcing herself to weigh her options, to consider her line of attack.

"How pretty," he sighed as he brushed back a long

curl that had slid over her face. "I'm going to enjoy fucking you, Skye."

He was wearing cologne and deodorant, both scents distinctive. She had smelled them before.

"You know, I really like you too," he told her conversationally. "I think I'll just do it slow and easy, enjoy it. There's no one here to tell me to hurry so they can take another turn on you. At least, not yet. Right?"

She continued to stare over his shoulder, refusing to act or to react until she knew exactly what to do. Not until she figured it out.

One second she was trying to make sense of her own thoughts as well, then she saw a glimpse of movement in the computer monitor across the room.

"You going to be a good girl and suck my dick first?" His fingers tightened in her hair and jerked her head back to stare into her eyes. "Look at me, bitch," he sneered. "Ask nicely to suck my dick. It might keep you alive long enough for Logan to figure out he can't get free."

Her lips curled in a sneer. "I rather doubt you have a dick worth sucking."

A second later her head was exploding in pain. A surprised cry fell from her lips as she flew several feet across the room, hitting the floor with jarring force.

"You bastard!" Logan screamed, the thump of the chair indicating his fury and his attempt to free himself.

"Get on your knees, whore." Gripping her hair again he jerked her to her knees. "You can suck my dick if you want to live for a few minutes."

It wasn't going to happen.

He would have to kill her first.

But she had no intention of dying.

Lips tightly closed, she glared up at him.

She saw the blow coming, tried to throw herself to the side to deflect the blow, but the force of it still exploded through her and sent her crashing to the hard floor several feet away.

Still reeling from the blow, Skye lay still, trying to convince herself she was going to get through this. Eyes closed, afraid if she opened them she would pass out from the pain, she lay perfectly still, bent to protect her stomach and praying the blows went no lower.

"I said get up." Hard hands gripped her hair again, jerking her to her knees as she struggled against him.

Each time she lifted her hands to try to lessen the grip on her hair, another blow landed against her head, until she was swaying dizzily, held on her knees by the cruel force tearing at her hair.

"Now, I said suck my dick!"

She would kill him first.

She just had to find the right opening. She had to wait until she knew she could get in the right blow. Because she would only have one chance—

Logan was losing his mind. He could feel it.

The small, dangerously sharp knife he kept tucked in the hem of his sleeve jabbed into his wrist again, wetting it with yet more blood as he fought to saw his way through the hard nylon securing his arms.

Skye hadn't fully secured his ankles, but the ones at his wrists were taking too fucking long.

"Let her fucking go!" he screamed again, sawing at the nylon, the blade nicking his wrist again as another blow was delivered to her head after she was dragged to her knees.

Holding her hair with one hand, her attacker was releasing his pants with the other.

His expression was lust filled, his complete attention centered now on raping Skye rather than ensuring Logan couldn't get free.

He was almost there. Almost.

The bastard pulled his cock free, holding it securely in his hands as he moved closer to Skye's secured head.

As he neared her lips she suddenly moved, slamming her arms upward between his thighs and nearly putting his balls through his throat when he moved at the last minute.

Still, he howled in pain and stumbled to the floor, holding himself as he curled into a small ball for long seconds.

Just a little more, Logan prayed desperately. *Please, God, keep him there just a little while longer.*

Logan watched as Skye shook her head, still trying to process the feeling that her brain was completely rattled and trying to think through the pain.

She had to get Logan free. She had to find a way to stop this. God, if Logan had to see the gunman rape her, see him kill her . . . If her autopsy revealed what she suspected, that she was already pregnant, Logan would lose his mind.

She couldn't allow that.

Breathing heavily, she swung her head around,

searching for a weapon. She saw blood dripping to the floor by Logan's chair. He was ready to tip over, he was struggling against the restraints so hard.

He was screaming.

She could see him screaming, but her senses had narrowed to one thing and one thing only.

A weapon.

Then reality took the strangest twist.

As she swung around and slammed into another of her attacker's hard fists, she could have sworn she heard a dog howling.

Bella was much, much too little for that sound.

As stars exploded in Skye's mind, the sound of glass breaking seemed to come from a distance; then she was crashing to the floor again, her head bouncing against the wood.

The sound of snarls, growls, a man's terrified scream, and then—

She frowned, dazed, the world trying to recede.

She could swear she heard the sound of a gunshot.

CHAPTER
TWENTY-FOUR

It wasn't Bella howling. And it wasn't Bella who jumped through the window.

Struggling to sit up, Skye stared at Logan as he came out of the chair, lurching for her attacker as he faced down the wolf and fired again.

Before his finger tightened on the trigger, Logan jumped, throwing his off balance but not taking him down as the wolf jumped for him as well.

She couldn't have seen what she thought she did.

The wolf gave a sudden, bone-jarring stop before stumbling. The attacker, at first surprised, didn't pause in the small reprieve.

In a matter of seconds he had taken a running leap, jumping through the window the wolf had taken out as Logan grabbed the gun that had been dropped and began shooting.

Training was an amazing thing, though.

A lifetime of training was even more amazing.

She couldn't pull herself to her feet; instead, she had to drag herself to Logan.

A wolf, and that bitch was huge, too, stood over Crowe's unconscious form, her teeth bared, snarling at all of them.

Her gold eyes seemed to reflect a haze of red as spittle dripped from her glistening fangs.

She would lower her head, push at Crowe, lick his cheek, then snarl again as though the fact he wouldn't wake up would be taken out of their asses.

"Logan." She leaned her head against the coffee table as he rushed to her, his hands skimming her, quickly. "Did you see who he was?"

"No." His breathing was harsh, his voice filled with fury. "Fuck him!"

The wolf was snarling like the hounds of hell were nipping at her furry ass.

"Son of a bitch, Crowe, wake up!" she muttered. "Shut that bitch down."

She turned her gaze to Logan, desperate to make sure that he was safe. Blood marred his wrist, but the restraints were free and he was staring at her as though he couldn't believe she was alive.

Hell, she couldn't believe it herself.

Skye turned her head back to the wolf. She was lying close to Crowe now, staring at them as though daring them to come nearer.

She sighed heavily as Logan rose to his feet and moved into the kitchen. The wolf watched suspiciously.

Drawers banged, metal clanged. Seconds later, Logan

was back with a pair of wire cutters and snipped the restraints from her wrists.

"We need to call someone," she said wearily.

"I did. While we were standing there listening to his bullshit," Logan snarled. "I was able to hit Resnova's number, waited a minute, then disconnected and hit Archer's."

"Smart move." She laid her head on his shoulder as he pulled her into his arms, his hands holding her close, smoothing up her back.

"You're still not safe. You or Cami." Tortured and wracked with pain, the sound of his voice tore at her heart.

"I know," she said softly. "And the grandfathers will likely not help."

"I couldn't trust my own, and I know Rafer and Crowe won't trust theirs. We have to figure out how to find him, Skye. I can't lose you."

A moan from the other side of the room drew her gaze. Crowe moving.

The wolf bitch, still heavy with pups, was licking his cheek again, then lifting her head to growl back at them.

"That looks really weird, Logan," Skye sighed as the huge black and gray animal whined at Crowe before nudging him again.

"He raised her," Logan said softly. "Years ago. That's why she takes over the house while he's gone. We don't let anyone know she's anything but a wild wolf, that way our enemies don't target her. He found her, barely alive, her eyes not even open, when he first moved into the cabin. He kept her alive; hell, he even house-trained her. She's wilder than hell, but when she walks in that door, if Crowe's here, and conscious, she's tame as a puppy."

"Wish Crowe was conscious," Skye sighed as she laid her head back on Logan's chest. "We gotta problem."

"Yeah?" He kissed her forehead gently.

"Yeah."

"What is it?"

"I think I'm concussed."

His chuckle was rough. "Ya think, babe?"

"Yeah," she sighed. "I bet it's bad for the baby too."

That shut him the fuck up.

"It's not been long enough." He sounded strangled.

"A woman always knows." She burrowed deeper in his chest. "We always know."

"You can't be pregnant." His voice still sounded strangled. It also sounded about half panicked.

"Bet me."

The sound of sirens and an approaching helicopter could be heard. "And Ivan the Terrible is arriving. Bet he tries to boss me. Bet me."

"I don't bet against a sure thing." Yep, that was a strangled-sounding voice.

"Will you take up for me?"

"Not this time, baby," he sighed, holding her closer. "Not this time. I think we both need to go. Just to be sure."

"Just to be sure."

She could hear shouts. The wolf was snarling, snapping, about to go ape shit over Crowe until he tried to lift his hands and he whispered something. She bounded from the room, but she didn't run outside. Skye watched as the wolf went as fast up the stairs as her heavy body could go, disappeared through the rounded hall, and a few minutes later—hell, the sound of a door closing.

Crowe was struggling to sit up, his hands and feet bound, his gaze a little uncomprehending as he stared back at the scene spread out in his living room.

"I have a feeling this is going to be a hell of a story," he muttered.

Then nothing else could have been heard. Ivan's men were rushing the house, automatic weapons drawn as they began to secure the lower rooms, their eyes hard as Ivan swept into the room along with Rafer.

Skye watched as Ivan propped his hands on his hips, the scar on his face seeming to pulse, whiter than she'd ever seen it.

"Had to have all the fun yourself, did you, little girl?" He finally knelt beside her and Logan and gently, very, very gently, brushed back a mass of curls that had fallen over her shoulder.

"You know what, Ivan?" she said querulously when Logan didn't protest.

"What is that, my little Skye?"

"I need a big brother."

To that, Logan groaned as though in pain.

Ivan tipped his head to the side. "I was bargaining for husband, remember?"

"I would have shot you," she told him somberly.

To that, he nodded rather seriously. "I would have expected that."

Was Logan laughing at her? His shoulder was shaking a little, making her head worse.

"Make the 'brother' offer and I'll take it," she suggested.

He glanced at Logan, but whatever look they shared, she wasn't lifting her head to decipher it. Finally, Ivan turned his gaze back to her, the blue of his eyes incredibly gentle and really rather brotherly.

"I have need of a troublemaking, bossy, gun-toting, calculating, manipulating little sister," he stated with the utmost seriousness. "Would you like the position, Ms. O'Brien?"

"I believe I would, Mr. Resnova," she said, hearing her voice grow weaker. "Yes, I believe I would."

"And I will make an excellent uncle," he declared smugly.

"How do you know?" Her head felt as though it were reeling.

"It's too soon." There was that strangled sound again.

Ivan shook his head before looking at Logan, his gaze concerned now. "We need to get her out of here now, my friend. Her pulse is weak and thready, her eyes too dilated, and she's slurring."

She didn't hear anything after that. Logan shifted and she cried out in agony as pain exploded in her head again. She heard them cursing, Ivan was barking out orders, and then everything went blessedly black.

And she missed the single tear that ran down Ivan Resnova's face as he touched the blood that smeared her neck from her rapidly swelling nose and the gash down her cheek.

But Logan didn't miss it.

Just as he didn't miss the complete, truly brotherly love that filled Resnova's gaze.

It wasn't sex he'd wanted from Skye, Logan guessed as the other man beat him to threatening to kill the men strapping her down on the flat board to transport her to the hospital. It hadn't been a wife Ivan had needed. He had simply wanted to protect the delicate, too-caring, too-soft-for-her-job little FBI agent who had stolen Logan's heart.

No, not just his heart.

She had stolen his soul.

CHAPTER TWENTY-FIVE

The young woman a hunter had found in Riker's Ravine was Jenny Perew.

Two days after the attack on Crowe, Logan, and Skye, they were finally released from the hospital, but still carrying several of Resnova's shadows, whether they liked it or not, when Logan arrived at the sheriff's office to give him a statement concerning his involvement with her.

Skye stood beside him as he stared at the pictures, his gaze heavy, bleak, as he saw the damage to the young woman.

"One night," Logan stated harshly as Archer watched him sympathetically. "And it was months ago. I'm guessing six months. Has anyone checked on Ellen Mason?"

Skye and Logan both knew someone now had her in hiding so deep only God could find her. Resnova could be frighteningly efficient. Ellen had always wanted to

see Greece, and Ivan just happened to have several contacts there.

"We can't find her," Archer sighed heavily as he
shook his head. "I sent two deputies to her apartment,
but it had been cleaned out. Completely."

"Then she's on the run?" Logan looked up, as though
surprised.

"So it would appear." Archer nodded. "I'm sure
we'll find her, though," he sighed. "I just wish someone
had managed to convince Miss Perew how serious you
were of the danger when you called."

As had he.

Rising to his feet, Logan put his arm around Skye
and led her from the sheriff's department. "We're heading home." He spoke into the earbud he wore, so tiny it
was impossible to detect beneath the long cut of his
hair.

"House is secure," Resnova's man reported. "My
partner will remain inside until you arrive, then he'll
head to the basement."

Privacy wasn't going to be easy to maintain.

Returning to the house, Logan stepped inside with
Skye and stared around the rooms silently as she leaned
her head against his chest.

It wasn't over by any means, and they were no closer
to finding the Slasher now than he and his cousins had
been when they first returned.

At least, they had some help now.

"I have a few days I could spend out of town," he
told her as he led her to the upstairs bedroom he'd

arranged to have set up. "We could disappear for a while ourselves."

"What's a few days? And where would we go?"

He let his hand smooth over her rear as she moved ahead of him and he locked the door carefully behind him.

"Wherever you want to go, baby."

Carefully, with the utmost gentleness, he undressed her then.

She was bruised in multiple areas, though thankfully the attacker hadn't gone for her vulnerable stomach.

Where his baby lay.

Laying her back on the bed, Logan quickly tore his own clothes off, watching as her knee lifted and bent, her little foot resting comfortably on the mattress. The position gave him the briefest glimpse of her lush, already wet pussy. The folds glistened in temptation, flushed, swollen for him, awaiting his touch.

Coming over her, he couldn't help but kiss her first. Feeling her lips open to him, her tongue touch and taste his as he touched and tasted was much more erotic than it should have been.

It was perfect.

As his tongue penetrated those pretty lips, Logan settled between her thighs, felt her legs grip his hips, and the wet heat of her pussy as the folds parted for the thick, blunt head of his cock.

There would be few preliminaries.

The need flying through both of them was too hot, too hungry to allow them to go slow this time. Maybe later he'd be able to take her with all the time she deserved.

Maybe in fifty years or so his hunger for her would allow him a little control.

As he pressed inside her now, feeling the heated muscles of her pussy clamp on him, he knew he was lost.

Skye arched back, her eyes closing as pleasure slammed through her system and the stroking, hardened length of Logan's cock began to fill her, to stretch the tender depths.

Sensitive nerve endings blazed to life as her vagina stretched to accommodate the full length and width of the shaft burying inside her. Pleasure screamed through each one, then throbbed through the rest of her body and sent out an imperative demand for release.

It had been too long since he had touched her.

Forty-eight hours in a hospital bed under observation hadn't left much privacy for them. And Ivan had simply been an ass when it came to ensuring they had no privacy.

Now, as his lips slipped from hers and moved to the tender tips of her breasts, Skye cried out for him. Her arms wrapped around his shoulders as his hips began thrusting, sending his cock shuttling deep into the heated depths of her.

It was like having a warm, overly hard length of iron filling her. Stretching her. Pushing inside her with the slightest rasp and stroking her with so much hunger that within minutes she was crying out, arching, her release striking at her clit, her womb and rippling through her with destructive force.

Within seconds, Logan was following, his semen

spurting inside her as her spasming pussy milked around the hard flesh. Logan buried his face in the crook of her neck, groaning her name, whispering his love as the heated pleasure seemed to rock through them for long moments after their release swept through them.

"I love you, Skye," his voice, tortured, filled with the hopes and fears that loving her brought as he held her close, his body shuddering above her. "God help me, I love you."

Her lips pressed tenderly to his hard, muscular shoulder.

"I love you," she whispered. "Forever, Logan. No matter what. I'll always love you."

No matter what tomorrow might bring, no matter what the future held.

They loved. And they could only pray that when tomorrow came, that love would survive a murderer intent on destroying everything they held dear.